SPRING'S ARCANA

SPRING'S ARCANA

LILITH SAINTCROW

TOR

TOR PUBLISHING GROUP

NEW YORK

SPRING'S ARCANA

Map by Jon Lansberg

A Tor Book
Published by Tom Doherty Associates / Tor Publishing Group
120 Broadway
New York, NY 10271

www.tor-forge.com

Tor® is a registered trademark of Macmillan Publishing Group, LLC.

The Library of Congress Cataloging-in-Publication Data is available
upon request.

ISBN 978-1-250-79165-8 (trade paperback)
ISBN 978-1-250-79164-1 (hardcover)
ISBN 978-1-250-79166-5 (ebook)

Our books may be purchased in bulk for promotional, educational, or
business use. Please contact your local bookseller or the Macmillan Corporate
and Premium Sales Department at 1-800-221-7945, extension 5442,
or by email at MacmillanSpecialMarkets@macmillan.com.

First Edition: 2023

Printed in the United States of America

0 9 8 7 6 5 4 3 2 1

For Claire and Lucienne,
who believed more than enough

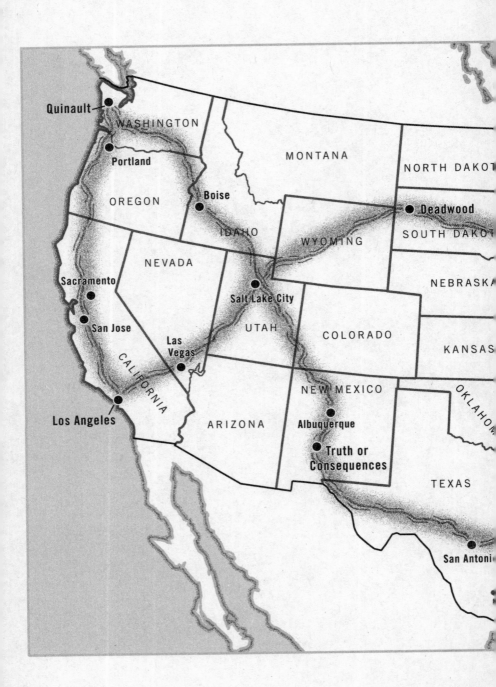

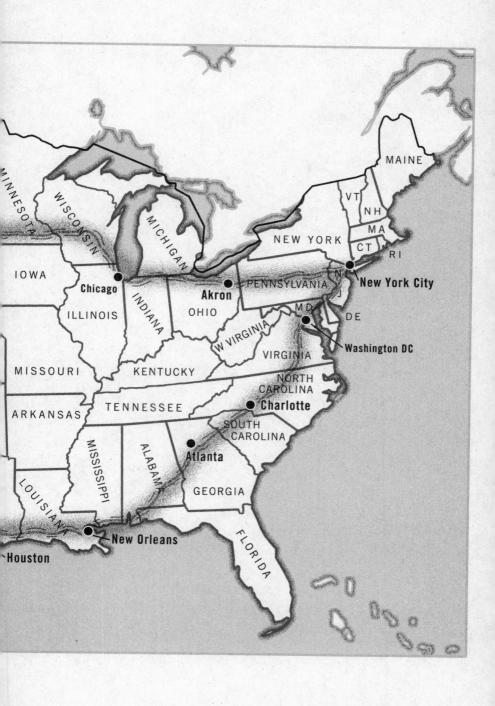

Now, here, you see, it takes all the running you can do,
to keep in the same place.

—Lewis Carroll

THE TOWER

OTHER THAN WINTER

The entire city was full of dirty ice-whipped slush after the first hard freeze; it had only reluctantly warmed enough for snow. A whistling, iron-cold wind poured down both the Hudson and East Rivers, slicing between feathery falling flakes. Thanksgiving was over for what it was worth, Christmas lights blooming everywhere, and it was hard to believe anything other than winter had ever existed.

The bus was a blue-and-white metal beast wallowing up the slight incline of Pastis Hill on a cloud of diesel smoke; the subway was warmer but wasn't worth the stairs involved for this part of the trip. Nat Drozdova's throat ached, her nose was full, and her eyes watered. She could claim it was the cold or the persistent creeping fingers of car exhaust slithering from street level to irritate tender membranes.

Crying on the 2:00 P.M. downtown special was what Mom would call *your silliness, Natchenka, now stop it.*

It was standing-room only; the vehicle swayed and she was almost thrown onto a thin, sour-faced businessman who had forgotten to bring his tie back over his shoulder after lunch. He'd also had more than one martini if the simmering alcohol fume was any indication, and his wingtips were going to be slush-soaked by the time he got back to the office.

Well, everyone had problems in this world, as Uncle Leo grimly intoned at the slightest provocation. Nat wiped her cheeks, a sting of woolen glove-fingers against already abraded skin, and set her chin. A baby fretted somewhere along the bus's flexing, swaying length; a crop of wet croupy coughs bloomed on either side. Nat hung on to the pole, trying not to bump the businessman again, and closed her eyes.

Just a moment, that's all she wanted. A single breath's worth of rest.

The darkness behind her lids was terrifying, so her eyes flew open again, filling her head with a regular Wednesday afternoon full of regular people. Except her surroundings lasted only a few seconds before melding into a familiar, pale pink hospice room holding softly beeping machines, the reek of disinfectant, and her mother's gaunt face, now-graying hair neatly braided and resting against a sanitized pillowcase.

It was the light, Nat decided. An echo of fluorescent hospital tubes ran down the bus's throat like streptococcal stripes, their pitiless glare showing every pockmark, every pimple, every stray hair, every scrape and scuff and loose thread.

Just like it showed Mom's veins, blue and branching, or the papery skin under her chin.

I'm too young to look this way, Mom had said mournfully during her last visit, and Nat had to agree. She had to keep blinking; everything blurred because her eyes were full of brimming hot water yet again.

The bus crested Pastis; skyscraper valleys swallowed a wheeled aluminum tube-pill. Snow whirled past the windows as she counted the streets: Nieman, the funny curve of Totzer, the park blocks between Crane and Gallus a stone's throw from Times Square full of wet green tinged with ice-pale lacework. If the contraption jerked again she'd be thrown onto two private-school boys with their shoulders and temples almost touching as they bent over a game, unaware of anything other than pixels on a handheld screen.

The stoplight went on with a soft chime, Nat was thankfully not tossed into the laps of strangers, and she began the laborious process of elbowing towards a door.

They were saying at least three inches of snow, but Nat rolled the air across her tongue the way Leo had taught her many winters ago and decided there was going to be more. Quite a bit more, in fact, and that was part of why she was downtown today, even though her shoes would fill with slushmelt and her calves would freeze almost solid.

It happened so fast, too. One moment she was sitting at her cubicle desk in Brooklyn, the phone jangling, coffee solidifying into syrup at the bottom of its pot, one of the salesmen whistling "Jingle Bells" and another in the depths of the office yelling about quarterly figures. Then she was outside, breathing deeply against the chill, the business card in her wallet weighing down her purse like a scoop of compressed matter dragging everything into the heart of a brand-new black hole.

Maybe they wouldn't even notice she was gone. Christ knew she felt pleasantly invisible most days, except when Bob—his new toupee was the *exact* color of brown shoe polish—had a new idea and someone had to wrangle him out of it. Middle managers inevitably rose to the level of their incompetence, and he was a shining example who might even make corporate one of these days.

The bus finished disgorging fellow travelers and heaved away; Nat turned up the collar of her navy wool peacoat and set off too, her office flats crunching scattered deicer pellets. Gallus and Third was the address on the card—heavy ivory stock, deeply pressed letters blacker than ink should be, the corners crisp no matter how long it sat in Nat's wallet, glaring at her each time she paid for coffee or groceries or anything else.

Did you see her yet? Do you have an appointment? The tremor in Mom's voice, the impatience disguised as helplessness—Nat tilted her head back while matching the speed of sidewalk traffic, more to get the tears to crawl back into their holes than to gaze at skyscrapers, their tops lost in billowing white as the sky scattered tiny, frozen pellets struggling to turn into snow.

When her chin came back down to save her fool ass from skidding off deicer and into the street, the building was *right there*. She stopped for a moment, ignoring both the hiss of a man in a dun-colored trench coat who had to do some fancy footwork to get around her and a cacophony of horns from Gallus Street, where the slush was busy snarling end-of-lunch traffic with a side of fender benders and screaming out windows that should have been rolled up to keep the heat trapped.

People would waste even precious resources to yell obscenities out a window. It was a fact of human nature.

Tiny iceflakes swirled on the back of a whipping wind, and maybe it was only the vagaries of air moving between man-made concrete cliffs turning the white curtain into a tornado before neatly flicking it wide-open as a sheet to hit the other side of Gallus Street and the Vogge Mutual Building, a high thrusting needle with a granite-sheathed base. The Vogge had blinking multicolored lights in deference to the season; there was even a tree in its foyer, a multicolored migraine gleam through bright windows.

The Morrer-Pessel Memorial Tower, on the other hand, was an unornamented black-mirrored building, its walls curving like the architect hated even the idea of a straight line. It seemed to squat even though it challenged its neighbors for height, and the concrete forum-park set before it was always curiously free of beggars and buskers.

Maybe it was the statues. Whoever did the art installation had some weird ideas about human anatomy, and the host of copper and stone figures in various attitudes dotted around Pessel Square—as the sign between two forlorn, winter-naked bushes proclaimed it, with more hopefulness than declarative thunder—were tinged with frost, beginning to grow shaggy white winter coats as the snow decided to quit fucking around and get its afternoon work started.

Did you see her yet? Mom kept asking. Not *hello*, and forget *how are you*.

"I don't want to," Nat muttered. It was one thing to endure Mom's disappointment each time, but if Nat got the brush-off here and trudged into Mom's hospice room during visiting hours tomorrow to report not just a lack of appointment but a complete failure to even get in the door, what would happen?

Mom had already gone so far downhill over the past couple months. It was silly to think Maria Drozdova's heart would finally break and the rest of her might not be far behind, wasn't it?

Your imagination, Natchenka. Tch, tch.

A wet, invisible fingertip touched her nape; her hair was up in its usual office-friendly twist. Letting it down would be fractionally warmer, but only until it was soaked through. She had no hat, her legs were already cold despite black wool tights, and her shoes were never going to be the same.

Digging out the card to check it once more would be a waste of time. Even *thinking* about it called up the spare, elegant words on the front, and the purple-ink writing on the back.

Y.A.G.A. Fine Arts and Antiques, Import-Export. Morrer-Pessel Memorial Tower. No phone number, no email, just that beautiful, chilling fountain-pen writing on the reverse.

Let her in.

Well, maybe they would. Or maybe she could stand out here and freeze to death, just another statue in a park not even the homeless liked despite its benches lacking the hard, hurtful metal studs designed to keep them from sleeping.

The entire world was unfair, and her own problems less than a speck of comparative dust. Nat Drozdova shook her head, couldn't hitch her purse strap higher on her shoulder because it was trapped under her coat for safekeeping, and took off across Pessel Square, threading between the statues.

She was very, very glad that despite her lifelong overactive imagination, none of them looked like they were about to move.

SOME WEATHER

The Morrer-Pessel foyer was just as cavernous and mirrorlike as the outside; Nat had time to wonder how they cleaned the place before the pair of shaved gorillas in three-piece suits at the security desk noticed her. She was a sight, certainly—almost wet clear through, shaking deicer pellets off her cheap flats, her hair starred with snow and her skirt crooked enough she wanted a few minutes peering into a restroom mirror before she attempted any human contact.

But this place certainly wouldn't open up its bathrooms to anyone off the street, so Nat unbuttoned her coat and dug in her purse, her head down as she shuffled for the desk, trying to appear businesslike and polite at once. Her wallet squirted through her damp fingers. She finally fished it out, and when she reached the security desk—a big, black, dull-gleaming curve, probably with monitors and screens all along its inside for the guards' delectation—she found one of the beefy men in matching dark suits had stepped back a bit, his fingertip to his ear where a tiny plastic bud nestled.

Just like in the movies.

She held up the card—its ink was exactly the same color as the desk—and tried a placating smile on the remaining goon, a slab of fair-haired muscle with the pink-rimmed blue eyes some blonds were cursed with. "Hi," she said, as brightly as possible. "Some weather, huh? I'm here for Mrs. de Winter."

You've got to be kidding, she'd said to Mom. *Tell me her first name's Rebecca.*

But her mother, usually so happy with literature in-jokes, had merely frowned. *Don't ask, my dumpling. Just go, and be polite, she'll know what you're there for. Please do this for me.*

"Dumpling" meant Mom was disposed to be kind and wanted her daughter to do something very badly indeed, and the thought that maybe Nat had put this off because the kindness was such a rare occurrence rose like bad gas in a mineshaft, was strangled, and went away quietly.

"Some weather," the blond agreed, cautiously. The dark-haired one behind him dropped his hand and studied Nat—at least, what he could see of her over the desk, which left her hips safely out of the equation. His gaze settled on her breasts, as fucking usual, and Nat bit back a cheeky *see something you like, sailor?*

He didn't look like he'd get the joke. So instead, she simply laid the card on the desk, her wet fingertips leaving a quickly vanishing streak.

The blond glanced at it, then at her. "Turn it over, please." There was no purchase on this cliff; his face was a wall just as straight and unyielding as the Vogge building's granite skirts.

"Okay." So she did, and he stepped back as soon as the purple letters came into view. "Mrs. de Winter's an old friend of my mother's, and—"

"Yes ma'am." He almost collided with the dark-haired fellow. They really looked astonishingly alike, except for their noses—the blond's was a big beak, the brunet's was mashed. "Through the stile, last elevator on the left, press the P key."

Well, that's simple enough. Nat took the card back, trying not to notice both of them staring at it like they expected the paper to grow scales and fangs, and also tried a small wave at the blond one. Maybe their imaginations were just as vivid as hers, which would be a welcome change. "Thanks. I appreciate it."

The duo stared mistrustfully at her, and Nat's smile faded. The trouble with social anxiety was that you couldn't tell what was someone having a bad day versus them trying to tell you they hated your guts personally and forever, so your brain picked the latter as default just to be safe.

The turnstile made a dry, bony click as she stepped through, and the faces of glossy black elevators multiplied the few people waiting for a mechanical box to carry them up on either side, ghosts standing in mirrored halls. Nobody was waiting for the last one on the left, and there was no summoning button to press because it was standing open, red carpet on its floor a welcome break from all the black.

Nat stepped in, pressed the round silver circle next to the P at the top, and waited for the doors to close.

They did, and even their inside was mirrored. She stared at a pale brownette—not blonde, not brown, somewhere in between—with a crooked skirt and a wet coat, damp curls coming loose from what had been a businesslike French twist and her cheekbones standing out alarmingly. Acceleration pressed along Nat's body while she did her best to repair the damage.

She was still tugging at her skirt's hem when the elevator slowed, dinged, thought about what it was chewing, and reluctantly opened its red-carpet mouth to deposit her before a wall of frosted glass broken only by double doors—also glass, with brass handles shaped like falling leaves. Whatever lay beyond glowed with snowy light, shadows of office workers hurrying back and forth like more trapped ghosts.

No holiday lights here. Maybe this de Winter lady felt the same way Mom did about Christmas.

An arc of gold-foil letters on the door smugly announced Y.A.G.A, with a small, tasteful IMPORT-EXPORT underneath, in case anyone accidentally arrived up here and didn't know where in the woods they'd landed.

Nat took a deep breath, stepped decisively to the door, and had to glance at the hinges. It opened in instead of out, which was probably against fire codes, but what did she know?

Chin up and her feet squishing, Nat stepped through.

OUTSIDE CAPABILITIES

The grande dame was in a mood today, standing behind her massive curved mahogany desk like Napoleon in a campaign tent. Her shape flickered between a round-hipped, unbent crone and a tall, stately middle-aged professional poured into a pantsuit, both forms with ivory hair piled high and coal-black eyes narrowed. It was probably the snow; whoever was on duty shaking out her bedding was working their little heart out.

You never wanted to be found underperforming when Baba was in charge. Look at what had happened to Dascha, after all.

Dmitri liked lounging on the apostrophe-shaped black leather couch, mostly because he knew it irritated the old woman. He liked stretching out his feet and admiring the bright caps on his boot-toes for the same reason, but the slicked-back hair and well-tailored suit—not black, a few shades off *true* darkness into indigo—were worn because they pleased him alone, like the inked lines crawling over his knuckles, up his arms, down his back, across his chest. Certain folk would see bright colors there, others just the deep bruise-blue of prison ink, and some would avert their gaze without knowing why, especially when he smiled.

At the moment, he was more occupied with watching the dame slip between her shapes than with his toes. When she was in this mood, it paid to be vigilant.

A mannerly tap at the heavy door was followed by sloe-eyed Daschenka in her trim green knee-length skirt and matching jacket, her blouse a froth of soft white ruffles upon her capacious chest. Her dark hair was an elaborate confection, looped and braided fit to trap-tangle a pixie to death for later consumption, and her green stiletto heels made crisp little sounds until she noticed the mood Baba was in and they turned silent as fawn hooves amid deep, dead grass. Dascha's lipstick, a perfect carmine, had just been reapplied— or she'd taken advantage of her lunch hour to have a quick snack.

The old lady at the window didn't turn. "Well?" she snapped, staring at the whirling flakes like she intended to count each one.

It wasn't outside her capabilities, but it sounded boring as fuck. Dmitri rested his head on the couch back, his eyelids dropping to half-mast. He wasn't quite hungry enough, he decided. Not yet.

Even if he was, what would it get? A mouthful of cold air and ashes, so why bestir himself?

Daschenka didn't look at him. "A girl with the card, Grand-mother." Of course her tone was soft and utterly respectful.

"A card?" The dame settled into her middle-aged professional form, the bust swelling slightly as she turned. Her pantsuit was dark with white pinstripes, the contrast sharp and distinct. "If it's another penny-ante piece of trash, get rid of it. I'm not in the mood."

Daschenka did not move, though she paled very slightly. "*The* card, ma'am."

"Horrible child. Why didn't you say so?" Grandmother pushed the desk chair aside with one ample hip, the curve hard as stone under her trousers. She bent, placed both hands flat on the desk's mirror-polished surface, and exhaled sharply.

Normally such an operation was followed by a tingling crackle and the old dame's short, corrosive laugh, or a heavy sigh as she gazed upon whoever was foolish enough to come to *her* office. To-day, though, the snow strengthened into soft damp flakes outside the eightieth floor, feathers and chunks riding errant wind-currents, and Dmitri watched Grandmother study the desk's face, a line en-graving itself between her iron-gray eyebrows—left untamed when she was in this form, and curling at the tips.

She was, for at least thirty long mortal seconds, deadly silent.

"I see," she whispered, and sucked on her top lip for a moment, a thoughtful, habitual motion. "Grown up, have we? Dascha, be a good girl, make some coffee."

"Shall I show her in first?" The girl didn't move when Grandmother looked up with a silent snarl.

"Of course, ninny. And remember, Dima likes his with a little sting. Hurry, hurry, and send her in." She watched Daschenka sashay away with an extra fillip to her green-clad hips, and *tch-tch*'d like a woman standing in a queue for hours when it finally moved an inch forward. "Well, well. I hope your calendar is clear, Dima."

"At your service." Dmitri tasted each word, let them fall like wounded birds. *That was, after all, our arrangement.*

She laughed, peeling her hands from the mirrored desktop, and that was the first intimation of something truly out of the ordinary, because Baba actually sounded *amused*. "We'll see about that, won't we? We'll . . . just . . . see." She straightened, touched her lower back as if it ached, and her lips were sheathed with neutral brownish gloss now. Her eyes were still hot coals, though, and her hair hadn't changed much either, parchment braided into a coronet.

The door opened again. "—sure?" Dascha, sweet as summer honey, but with an edge of disbelief.

"Thank you, but no," the visitor said. Soft voice, uncertain, and Dmitri Konets's mouth filled with heat.

It generally did, when prey came waltzing past.

The visitor was a girl with honey-tinted chestnut hair in a gloriously loose twist, wide dark eyes to rival Dascha's, and a woolen peacoat that had seen much better days. Melting slush clung to her cheap, sensible flats; her black tights were damp to the knee. Her nose was pinkened and her eyes red-rimmed, misery shimmering over her like heat above concrete in summer, and the unalloyed quality of that sadness was far too strong to be purely mortal.

A subtle, floral perfume touched the office's interior, tiptoed to his sensitive nose, and Dmitri did not stiffen. At least, most of him stayed relaxed, inert, without a single twitch or eyelid-flicker to warn her or Grandmother of his interest.

"I appreciate it," the girl added, unnecessarily, but Dascha had already shut the door, probably glad to be free of whatever problem this guest represented. So the girl glanced at him, visibly didn't like what she saw, and turned those limpid dark eyes to the dame at the desk. "Hello, ma'am. I'm very grateful you agreed to see me. I'm Maria Drozdova's daughter. She's in hospice care, and she sent me."

Daughter? Dima tensed, a viper coiling under a rock. *You have got to be fucking kidding me.*

Baba didn't even so much as glance at him.

TWINKLE TOES

I f she'd known it was going to be this weird, maybe Nat would
have just attempted a slight fib and endured her mother's sharp
annoyance. *No, Mom, I went but they didn't recognize the card, I
couldn't get in.*

Like every good lie, it would be believable. God knew every
"friend" who came to visit Mom in the little yellow house had vanished almost overnight once she got sick, and the Drozdovas had
no extended family unless it was Uncle Leo or back in what Maria
called, with a curl of her lip, "the old country." Now Mom was stuck
in hospice like a wildebeest in a drying water hole, her only visitors
dotty old Leo and a daughter working two jobs, one of which was
probably being offered to a new candidate right now because Nat
had technically walked off midshift.

Maybe she could file for unemployment. The thought filled Nat
with fresh, overwhelming weariness.

The lady behind the desk was definitely what Mom would call *a
power player* and Uncle Leo *a cast-iron bitch,* devotchka, *and I should
know.* Mrs. de Winter was tall and spare despite generous swellings
at hip and chest, and even those curves looked hard and unforgiv-
ing. Her eyes were a little like Mom's when she got angry—so dark
iris and pupil blended together instead of Maria's usual cornflower
blue, but still impossibly vital, a coal seam burning underground.
Her tarnished-ivory hair was swept into a braided coronet held
decoratively fast by two dull black pins that were probably iron to
match her presumed temperament; the whole 'do looked heavy as

hell. Her suit was designer if Nat was any judge; those pinstripes were amazing.

The office itself was empty as an unlocked warehouse, a dark wooden cabinet—also looking custom-made—along one curved wall holding all its mouth-drawers prissily tight. The floor was the same wood as the massive desk; the desk's top was empty though a sleek black computer was placed on a small additional cabinet to the right, and the chair was a very expensive ergonomic number.

Looked like things were good in the import-export business, all told, and a faint familiar swimming unease began at Nat's finger-tips, sliding up her arms. Her toes were cold, too, but that could just mean they were wet.

Don't start your "imagining" bullshit. Come on.

The only other piece of furniture was a kidney-shaped black leather couch, and the man taking up all of it despite his lean-ness was in a suit similar to de Winter's, but with no pinstripes. Bright silver caps decked his sharp-pointed boot-toes; his hair was slick-combed back from a ferocious widow's peak, and everything about him shouted *gangster*. Uncle Leo had even told young Nat what some of the bluish tattoos on a man's knuckles, chest, or back meant in the old country.

Oh, for God's sake. Mom's sent me to the Mob. Nat swallowed hard, holding Mrs. de Winter's gaze, and the silence turned ridiculous. The wall behind the woman was sheer glass from top to bottom, and the snow was whirling past. If Nat let herself, she could probably even see faces in the swirls and sheet-veils.

So inventive, Mom always said, indulgently, despite a sobbing child's insistence that it was *real*, that she wasn't lying, that she heard, she *saw*.

"Maria Drozdova," the hot-eyed woman finally said, a ghost of an accent fainter than Mom's riding each word. Her desk was bare of even a pen cup, and the surface was buffed to a high shine. The janitorial staff probably left it for last each evening, and cleaned it twice to make sure. "I see. And you are?"

"Nat, ma'am." She couldn't help it; she put one toe behind her and bobbed a little curtsy, like in kindergarten ballet. Office parties around here were probably a real hoot. "Her daughter."

"You said that, yes." De Winter's eyes narrowed, and her lips parted slightly. Strong white teeth peered out, and Nat's arms were completely numb now. Her legs were following suit. "Well, well. Little Marotchka had a daughter after all." Her fingers were tipped with bloodred nails, the polish impeccable and glowing gemlike; her left hand twitched, sending each varnished fingertip tapping against the desk in turn. "Come in, come in, sit down. Dima, fetch the chair, the poor thing has come through the snow to visit her old grandmother."

What the hell? Nat's jaw threatened to drop. "Ma'am—"

"Not old enough to be a *baba*," the man muttered, each word flat and uninterested except for a faint edge of amusement. His own accent was eerily like Leo's; her uncle never sounded this coldly amused, though. "Is that what I should say? Should I also bring bread and salt?"

"Nasty child." The businesswoman's lip curled a little further. Her lips were painted with pure business gloss, not matching the crimson nails at all. "Pay no attention to him, *vnuchka*. The hospital, you say? What could be wrong with my darling Marotchka?"

You don't know? You look like you've got enough money to find out whatever you want to. Nat bit back both the words and a welcome burn of irritation. It was her usual response to one of Mom's games, at least nowadays.

Now that she was an adult, thank you very much, with plenty of bad teenage decisions firmly in her past and the ability to check out self-help books at the library.

"Cancer," she said, perhaps a little more loudly than she needed to. "That's what the doctors think. And some dementia. She collapsed two months ago and—"

"Doctors, with their scary words. *Diagnosis*, they say. Most of it's lies; they guess as much as other mortals." Those red fingernails jabbed, not straight at Nat but slightly to the side, and the man from the couch glided into Nat's peripheral vision, carrying a straight-backed wooden chair that must have come from a hidden closet.

In fact, it looked an awful lot like the Penitence Chair in her elementary school principal's office. Nat suppressed a flinch as he settled it precisely in front of the desk, a little too close to be comfortable, and stepped smartly aside. Those silvery toes glittered— *twinkle toes,* she thought, and had to suppress a giggle that might have tasted like lunch if she'd been able to eat anything.

"Mom wanted me to come see you." Nat took care to make the words as brisk and business-adjacent as possible. "So I have. I don't know what happened between you two, but she's dying." Her chin set, a tiny defiant movement she could *feel* vibrating down her aching neck. "Maybe she just wanted you to know." Her right foot squelched as she shifted her weight, and it was probably the last moment she could have stamped out, taken the elevator, gone through that bone-clicking turnstile, and plunged into a winter afternoon with her duty done. "I'm sorry to have bothered—"

"Dima," Mrs. de Winter of Yaga Imports said, "put her in the chair, please."

One moment Nat was getting ready to exit in dramatic fashion, the next the gangster in the almost-black suit had her arm and was dragging her. His lips skinned back from his similarly pearly teeth; he thrust her into the chair and shook his hand like she'd burned him. "*Fuck,*" he snarled in Russian, just like Uncle Leo when he was working on a car engine. But *unlike* Leo, who really wasn't her uncle at all, this man didn't immediately raise his dark gaze to ceiling or sky and mutter to Christ for forgiveness.

"There it is." The businesswoman folded her arms, and those bleak, black eyes pinned Nat to hard wood. Just like being in school again, teachers watching your struggles with narrow-eyed pleasure.

Nobody cared, not in this world. The sooner you figured that out, the better.

"Now," the woman continued, "Marotchka sends her daughter here. How quaint. How very *droll.*"

The man, still shaking his hand ruefully, cast de Winter a sly sideways glance. "Not word I'd choose, but if it make you happy—"

"Shut up, Dima. Now, as for you . . ." She returned her coal-hot gaze to Nat and leaned over the desktop, flattening bony, ruby-tipped hands on its surface. The custodial staff would probably swear at all the smudges, Nat thought hazily, and tried to move.

No good. She was nailed to the chair, held invisibly fast, and hadn't the faintest idea how the hell *that* had happened.

"Tell me, *vnuchka moya.*" Now de Winter sounded almost kind, but she leaned avidly forward, lips slightly parted and those white teeth gleaming like the snow-filled window. "Would you like to make your mama all better?"

DRAMATIC EFFECT LOST

Y ou're insane." Nat strained against the chair. Her hands gripped the arms, her knuckles white with effort, and in a moment she'd get up and run for the door.

Just as soon as her body started obeying her again.

"*Conditions of absolute reality,*" the man muttered, and his eyebrows twitched when the old woman glared at him. "What? I'm not illiterate, you know. Just get it over with, *Baba.*"

"Since when do I take orders from you, *Dima*?" The businesswoman—de Winter *couldn't* be a real name—made a soft clicking noise with her tongue, again like Leo. Or like Mom sometimes, when she was exasperated but not quite angry. "I'm not insane, *vnuchka.* Your pretty mother, with her blue eyes and her golden hair, would be the first to tell you so. She lives in a yellow house, does she not? And there are flowers everywhere, even in the dead of winter."

Well, the Drozdova house was indeed yellow, because the paint was cheap. And hadn't this lady ever heard of houseplants before?

Or the woman knew exactly where Mom lived but hadn't bothered to visit even once. Nat found her voice. "So you've kept track of her. She told me all our family was dead in the old country." Was it hypnotism pinning her in the chair? Or something else?

The hard wooden seat groaned slightly. Nat found she wasn't completely trapped. She could, in fact, shift the merest fraction. A burst of relief went through her, so strong and hot the chair creaked again.

"Well, she's right, after a fashion." The businesswoman—there was no way she was Nat's grandmother, either, she didn't even *look* like Mom—gazed serenely at her. "But I'll ask you again, little Natchenka who the cats speak to, would you like to make your mama better?"

How does she know about the cats? Nat stared at de Winter, and the chair made another low, unhappy sound. Maybe it was going to fall apart like a cartoon prank and they'd laugh at her like everyone else did.

"Won't hold her for long," the man said softly and drifted away to Nat's right, heading for a slice of wall. It opened at his approach, panels sliding silently aside, and a wonderland of jewel-glowing bottles on glass shelves was revealed. Maybe there was a switch in the floor, and anytime someone walked past the liquor cabinet lit up?

God, that sounds useful. Must be nice to be rich.

"Long enough." The businesswoman didn't even glance in his direction. "Speak up, girl. I can't hear you."

That's because I didn't say anything. Nat swallowed a hot, sour wad of irritation verging on actual anger. "I don't . . ." An invisible hand over her mouth tried to muffle the words. ". . . *like* practical jokes," she managed. Her lips were clumsy—so was her tongue—but she spat the words like she might hiss at a mugger, or a frotteur on the bus.

The man paused, looking over his shoulder like the cats when Nat gave the peculiar little trilling noise that meant she wasn't averse to handing out some chin rubs. Feral creatures of any sort liked her; some people were just gifted with animals. It didn't *mean* anything; it could even be the overactive imagination of a lonely little girl, a sign of instability, or even schizophrenia.

Wondering if she was crazy and had finally flown far enough above the radar for it to be noticed was depressingly familiar territory.

Now more footsteps sounded, pert little heel-taps. The secretary in the bright grass-green blazer and skirt reappeared, her chest bobbing softly like a ship's prow as she set a fantastically carved silver tray on the desk's naked acreage. The cups were whisper-thin porcelain, the coffeepot bright silver to match the tray, and the secretary glanced incuriously at Nat before straightening with a slightly theatrical sigh. "Will there be anything else, ma'am?"

"Hm? Oh, in a few moments, certainly." Maybe *Mrs. de Winter* was one of Mom's little jokes, though the guys at the desk downstairs seemed to recognize the name. The businesswoman smiled thinly at the green-clad secretary. "As soon as we agree on some terms and conditions. Run along, Dascha."

The assistant made the same little movement Nat had, a mini-curtsy, but she swayed like a flower on her stilettos. "Yes ma'am." She headed for the door, completely ignoring Nat's pleading stare.

Nat strained. Her chapped lips parted again. "My . . . mother . . . had a cousin." It got easier to talk once she had a few words out, but she had no clue what she was actually saying. "Named *Dasha Lyetka,* and she wore green—"

The secretary's footsteps faltered, and the businesswoman frowned. "None of that," she snapped, and the tiny tapping quickened. "But good attempt, little Natchenka, little *matryoshka.* There's something in you after all."

"So many compliments." The man settled a hip on the desk, reaching for a single cup full of very dark, very thick coffee. Nat could smell it, java tainted with a nose-scouring alcoholic bite.

Leo drank his exactly the same way.

"It probably means she wants you to do something," he continued, and poured an additional stiff shot from a carefully selected crystalline bottle into the cup, filling it to the brim. "Now me, I'm much nicer. You always know where you stand with Dmitri Konets."

"Keep telling lies." De Winter eyed the tray as a door closed softly behind Nat. The secretary was gone. "I'll ask you one last time before throwing you out into the snows, granddaughter. Do you want to make your mother better?"

Oh, for God's sake. "Why else would I be here?" Nat's temper broke, the chair groaned, and she found she could move. She rocketed to her feet, but any dramatic effect was lost when her shoes squished. "Mom's been going on and on about it for so long, and I thought—"

"You thought you'd shut a dying woman up, was that it?" One curling, ferocious, iron-colored eyebrow lifted. Funny how her hair didn't look dyed, even though the eyebrows didn't match. De Winter stared at Nat, those dark eyes boring in. "Oh, I see . . . huh. Oh, Maschka, you slithering little thing."

That's it. "I can see why she never talked about you before." Nat's throat hurt, just barely containing a scream. So did the rest of her, as if she'd run several staircases instead of taking the elevator. Her hands vibrated like windblown branches, but she didn't want to stick them in her pockets. Instead, she sidled away from the chair. Coffee-smell, rich and familiar, filled her nose.

"No doubt you consider that a stinging reproof." The business-woman took the other cup from the tray, and shook her head. "It so happens I am very well disposed to help you and your dear mama. In fact, I think there's no reason we can't help each other, *neh*?"

What? "What?" Nat repeated, stupidly, caught right before a grand exit. Snow thickened outside the window, caught in an updraft, and for a moment it looked like a face, eyes and mouth wide in mock-surprise.

I just didn't have lunch, she told herself. It was harder to keep the world behaving like its usual self when she was hungry.

Child-Nat would have howled. *But it's real! I saw it, it's real!*

And Mom would say the same thing every time. *Then do it right in front of me, Natchenka, or go finish your chores.*

"You must have told Dascha you don't want coffee, which is your bad luck." The businesswoman didn't smirk, which might have driven Nat right out the door anyway. Instead, she looked faintly pained. "Now, you want to help your mother, hm? What would you say if I told you I could?"

"*I'd* say you should run away and hide, *zaika*." Dmitri-Dima grinned at her, but the expression was a mask. The idea that he could take it off, roll it up, and stick it in a pocket was unsettling, and wouldn't go away.

It was coming again, the silly stupid urge to believe there might be a way out for Mom. Since this woman—whatever her real name was—knew about the cats.

Or she guessed, in which case . . . Nat's brain tried to turn in a complete circle like a cold, exhausted dog settling in a too-small hiding spot.

My little Natischka, one day you'll know exactly what to say. Mom's shaking, too-thin hand on her daughter's hair, smoothing the brown that was such a disappointment . . .

. . . right before she collapsed and Nat called the paramedics that awful night two months ago.

She hadn't even had time to tell Mom, *I'm moving out.*

Nat's ears were full of a panicked rushing, and her mouth opened as if she was six on the playground again and about to tell Sister Roberta Grace Abiding about the aneurysm that would six months later drop her in the middle of chapel like a string-cut marionette. "I'd say I'll find it for you, Grandmother, but more I cannot promise."

Oh, shit. Nat blinked as the slipstream receded. The gangster's smile was gone as if it never existed and the businesswoman's cup halted on its way to her mouth; even the snowflakes in the window seeming to pause. *What did I just do?*

"You see, Dima?" Grandmother took a delicate sip, and smiled a feline, satisfied smile. "This is my granddaughter after all."

MUCH TO LEARN

Dusk came in midafternoon, which meant night arrived early under an orange-tinted sky accompanied by yet more falling snow, fast-clotting flakes shrinking as the temperature dropped.

"This isn't like you." Dmitri lifted the bottle, eyeing the amber liquid inside. It didn't look like nearly enough, but then again, it never did. Snow caked his dark hair, stacked itself on his surprisingly broad shoulders.

"You're too young to know." The old woman stopped before one of the statues, peering into its weeping copper eyes as she flicked a finger; the red-and-white Santa hat someone had perched upon this particular malefactor was whisked away on a cold, dissatisfied gust.

No snow clung to Baba, of course. She smiled, a sleepy, satisfied expression. A cricket-faint sound rose from carved, frozen lips before dying away as she made a soft patting motion with one vein-wrinkled hand on the statue's cheek.

Every once in a while, one of the more perceptive among mortals remarked, perhaps with an atavistic, ignored shudder, that parts of the art installation in Pessel Square were really very . . . lifelike.

Dmitri could maybe free one or two of these bumblers—some of them were, after all, thieves—but he granted his aid to the careful, the skilled, the desperate, and occasionally to the lucky. You could make the case that being caught meant they were none of the above, and besides, many of them had not *stolen*, they had merely betrayed the grande dame in some other fashion. "You honestly think she can get it?"

"Masha hid it, which means only Masha or her fledgling can retrieve it." Yaga—*de Winter* was her own private joke; the old country loved literature a little too well—said it as another might have said *the weather has changed* or *the traffic's bad today*. "I taught her well, the little flower."

"Too well." Dmitri took a hit off the bottle, relishing the sting.

"That's debatable." The dame was in a fine mood; even his graceless swilling could not disturb her. There was no point in drinking at all, sometimes. "Anyway, you'll go along and keep little Natchenka safe."

It would be stupid to ask *from what*. The girl was incarnating, and the trembling vulnerability of that state would call more than one predator. "What will stop me taking it from her the moment—"

"Maschka wouldn't lay it down without a protection or two." The dame gave him a sideways look, but didn't make the spitting sound she reserved for stupid questions. It was good to know he could sometimes not-quite-surprise her. "It's probably in a setting, and how do you think that will go if you put it in your chest, greedy boy?"

Unspoken, of course, was what could happen if someone else—oh, maybe even Friendly with his little pink nose, or Seamus the Bastard, or even that Cosa Nostra fellow with his cannolis and bad accent—got their filthy paws on the gem.

Maschka wasn't able to eat it, but she could very well *trade*. And where would Dima be then?

He knew exactly where. "Bitch." There was no heat to it; sometimes, only the politest of insults was necessary. Dmitri shook snow from his hair with a quick, flicking motion, a razor cleaning itself. "Fine. I'll watch over the little rabbit. Might even be fun."

"If anyone else finds out what you're after, it will be." The dame nodded thoughtfully, shuffling to another statue and examining its face closely. "Yes."

"I'm sure you'll undertake to tell a few people." No, he didn't feel like drinking much more tonight, he decided. There were clubs he could visit—the city was full of them—but he also didn't feel like watching naked flesh jiggle at the moment.

Which left the fights, or visiting a few of his favored ones to see if they had any offerings for their beloved uncle, the one who kept them from the notice of the authorities. He could be generous when properly propitiated.

Like the grand old dame herself.

"How suspicious you are, Dima." She gave the statue a final pat on its verdigris-veined cheek, then turned widdershins for the next one. A garden required work even in winter; sometimes pruning was best done when the world slept under an icy blanket. "Why on earth would an old woman do that?"

"For the same reason I'll get it out of the setting and repay the one who tried to keep it from me." Dmitri leered, sharp teeth whiter than the fresh snow. "I will fill my mouth with her blood."

"Is that a vow?" Her interest piqued, the old woman continued the counterclockwise turn and faced him instead, her expression bright, interested—and predatory. Now that she no longer needed the shell of seeming, her nose was a blade and the lines deeply graven on either side of her mouth were a caution. The coals of her eyes remained the same, full of hot, sharp good humor, but underneath it was the gaze of one who had seen the whole world's rotation more than once and found barely anything edifying or satisfactory about the spectacle.

"It could be," Dima allowed. "Of course, it would end badly for you."

One of her wildly curling eyebrows twitched, but did not fully lift. "Really?" The snow cringed from her vicinity, sensing a much deeper cold. "What brings you to that conclusion?"

"Your little Maschenka wouldn't have gotten her hands on it if you hadn't let her, Grandmother." Dmitri gave her a lazy salute, two fingers to his forehead, and carried the bottle with him into the darkness between shivering lamps. He blended with the night and was gone before he reached the edge of the paved area, snow collapsing inward around a suddenly vacated space.

He must be disturbed, to enter his thiefways so visibly. Or he was making a point—even lacking what he did, Dima Konets was still a divinity.

"Oh, little boy," the old woman said to the blowing, shuddering snow. "You have so much to learn." She turned against the sun once more, and a desperate quivering through the next statue on her internal list turned her smile sour. "And so do you. Ai, little thieves and big thieves, all jostling each other."

She patted cold copper, and the cricket-sound of screaming was whisked away on a rush of cold wind. When the curtain of falling flakes cleared half an hour later, Pessel Park was empty.

Except for the doomed, standing still as cold white continued to coat them.

FAMILY AGAIN

All things considered, Nat thought she was handling the entire day pretty well. She took the red-throated elevator, crossed the foyer at a dead run, plunged out of the Morrer-Pessel building without being grabbed by security, almost hit warp speed to catch the bus—the vehicle bore strap-on reindeer horns, half the people-movers in the city were all dressed up for the season—at the far end of the square, and overall managed to look like a girl in a hurry instead of one having a complete nervous breakdown.

At least, until she got home, sat at the plastic-covered kitchen table, and burst into tears.

Her shoes were a mess, her toes were numb, her shoulders ached. Her coat dripped, snowmelt spattering clean bright yellow linoleum faithfully mopped with yarrow water every Saturday.

Mom said yarrow brought good luck and made everything fresh, but Nat thought bleach would do just as well. All Mom's plants—crowding every window, or perched under bright lamps—were doing just fine without the rituals of daily songs and misting with different color-coded spray bottles. The laundry was still loyally addressed every Saturday though; the parlor was dusted "for company" too, every knickknack separately rubbed with a soft cloth, all the wood polished, all the upholstery cleaned.

Nat wasn't quite brave enough to halt that particular set of chores. The house looked like a stage set, a place where no actual living was done. Like de Winter's penthouse office, immaculate and dust-free, with a wooden chair for a penitent little girl to sit in.

Hypnotism. Maybe it was some kind of reality show bullshit. Whoever "de Winter" was, she was damn good at it. What kind of an acronym was Y.A.G.A., anyway?

Dmitri will pick you up tomorrow evening, vnuchka. *Be ready for a party.*

Her mother's kitchen was bright and cheery, the sunflower towels hung perfectly even across the bar on the white enamel oven door. All the cookware was scrubbed; the cabinets, hand-painted with geometric patterns, were dusted. The little yellow house felt a lot bigger inside than it looked from without; the brownstones up and down the street frowned at this gaily colored intruder in their midst all year round.

Most days, it didn't bother Nat. Today she'd fled their judgmental stares as well as the tinsel and blinking multicolored lights, slipping and scrambling through snow and the slick paths of rock salt or deicer in front of a few porches. She ran as if the neighborhood boys were chasing her home from middle school again; serve her right if she slipped and cracked her head open, but she was home, whole, and safe from . . .

From whatever *that* was. Maybe drugs? The Mob, of whatever stripe, was big into intoxicants. All the news stories said so.

You fucking know what it was, Nat.

Nat Drozdova buried her face in her cold, chapped hands and tried to muffle the sobbing as if her mother was home. Mom would take one look at her daughter and flick a little cold water from her fingertips as she attended to something in the sink, rolling her big blue eyes.

Oh, stop your blubbering, Natchenka. It could always be worse. Why, in the old country—

"*Fuck* the old country," Nat moaned into her hot, slick palms, and a laugh hiccupped through the wrenching jolts. Didn't this just take the cake? The cake and the whole fucking bakery too?

To make it worse, she couldn't quite figure out what she'd agreed to. Just that the man with the silver boot-toes would pick her up tomorrow evening at seven sharp; de Winter wanted Nat to fetch something, and when the lady had it, she'd help Mom.

You will call me Baba. *We are family, after all.*

The whole thing was ridiculous. If it was a practical joke, it was a long, involved, complex one even for Maria Drozdova. It was even bigger than the No Easter Candy Debacle when Nat was eight years old.

The sobs quieted, but not by much. She had time before her uncle returned from—

"You're home early," Leo said from the arched doorway to the dining room, wiping his hands with a thin red shop rag. She'd forgotten today was Garage Day instead of Pretend to Play Chess Day at the coffee shop up on Larkins Street or, in good weather, outside at Princo Park like every other old man in this slice of Brooklyn. He hurried to the wide double sink, salt-and-pepper head bobbing almost birdlike because of his limp. "How was my Natchenka's day? I found problem in engine; it will be all right soon."

Oh, God. Nat found one lone paper napkin left in the wire holder on the table and blew her nose with a honk that would have done an ancient Siberian train proud.

"Eh? What's this?" Her uncle swung around, his broad-knuckled hands turning into knots. "Something happen to my little girl?"

"I'm f-fine," she managed. "I just . . ." The entire afternoon balled up in her chest like a rat king made of licorice whips.

Now *there* was a vivid, ugly mental image. Mom loved the salted black stuff; it was the only candy she'd eat. Why anyone bothered when there were Snickers bars around was beyond Nat.

Leo studied his niece—although by the time she was ten Nat had figured out that "uncle" was really a figurative instead of truly descriptive term—and his expression was a usual one, pained affection mixed with deeper anxiety. "I make you coffee." He dug in his pockets, one after another, vainly searching for another rag and coming up empty. "You visit your mama?"

Well, that was a fair guess. Sobbing in the kitchen was, after all, what Nat usually did after daily hospice visits. She'd missed today and would have to call instead; Mom was going to be wondering about that. Or maybe Maria Drozdova was drifting on palliative morphine.

Was it wrong Nat was hoping for the latter? Drugged to deal with the pain, her mother was sometimes even affectionate.

She could have lied, she supposed, but she was dismal at it and besides, she never had to hide from him. Even if he didn't believe her, he'd at least listen. He never told her she was too imaginative, or too frightened, or—Mom's favorite—*too dreamy*. "No," Nat said, finally, and unloaded her nose into the napkin again.

It was holding up well, one of the pretty ones with flowers dyed in the corners; Leo must have splurged at the store. Mom always got the cheap ones unless Company Was Coming, in which case the folded linen, each edge crisp and re-ironed before arrival, made an appearance.

There hadn't been company for years, now that Nat thought about it. Not since she was in middle school and Mom started losing weight each winter, her face thinner and thinner until spring returned and pasta-bingeing came back into fashion.

"I went to Manhattan," she added. "Took a powder from work, actually." Goodbye to the accounting office; Nat wasn't even going to bother checking her email for the severance notice.

The only thing worse than low-tier jobs was the depressing ease with which they were acquired. You could tell how bad a place was by the turnover rate alone.

"Manhattan?" Leo washed his hands carefully, as usual, but not with the peach soap. His grease-stripper was harsher, and he carried the tube in an overall pocket because Mom didn't want it sitting next to any of the inside sinks. "I am an old man, tell me slowly."

But not too slowly, or I might die before you finish. He hadn't said that last bit in years; Nat tried to summon a forlorn smile. "I visited *her*. The woman in the Morrer-Pessel building. She was just where Mom said."

The water, warming reluctantly even though the hot tap was turned all the way, made a musical, secretive noise in the sink. Uncle Leo's hands hung, soapy and suspended, a few inches from the stream. He stared out the window like he was seeing raccoons along the back fence instead of just a snowed-under postage-stamp yard Mom kept trimmed, weeded, and neat until the snow came and obliterated all trace of green each year.

There was more salt than pepper in his hair now, and his small potbelly was no longer the hard gut of a gentleman worker but the sag of an elderly retiree. His shop shoes were battered and daubed with successive splatters of paint so ancient they had lost color, and his suspenders were darned along the left strap with Mom's careful stitchery. His ears stuck out from his head as aggressively as ever, and his shoulders were still wider than Nat's or her mother's.

But her beloved, basso-voiced, beery-smelling Leo had somehow gotten old when she wasn't looking.

"Manhattan," he repeated, harshly. He must have been smoking in the garage, as usual; he coughed immediately afterward and bent back to washing his hands. "Grandmother Winter."

"That's what Mom calls her." *I have my doubts.* It was a good thought, something she might have said to a best friend if she was in a sitcom. There was no laugh track riding in to save her, though, and she hadn't had a "best friend" since sixth grade. Or maybe before. "Anyway, I went like she wanted me to. It's done."

He muttered something, shook his head.

"What?" Nat smooshed the sodden napkin in her cold fist. "She wanted me to, Leo. She wouldn't stop about it." It was an effort to say *stop* instead of *shut up*.

You thought you'd shut a dying woman up? Well, that was one thing "Grandmother" had in common with Mom; both of them could say terrible things without batting an eye.

If it was a genetic trait, it had missed Nat entirely.

"May Christ forgive her," he said, softly, reaching for the sunflower towels before remembering and opening the cabinet for one of the floursacks. Nat rarely heard him utter that phrase unless he considered someone truly beyond *human* forgiveness, and now she was wondering just what her dear old uncle had against the woman in the penthouse.

It didn't look like the iron-haired lady was interested in making friends.

"Is she really my grandmother? I don't see the resemblance." *And*

Mom won't say. Just "go see her, go see de Winter, have you gone yet?" The glow from kitchen fixtures stung her eyes; the more light the better, Mom always said. Or maybe it was the tears again, prickling at her lids.

Stop sniveling, Mom hissed once, exasperated at Nat's stubborn insistence that she wouldn't pass the haunted house at the south end of the block, even if it was the shorter way to school. *I will march you into that place at midnight, if I have to.*

Swallowing your tears and finding a way around the pronouncements of an uncaring authority was a skill, too, and one Nat Drozdova was depressingly familiar with.

"Grandmother?" Her uncle laughed, a short humorless bark. "Oh, *da, da.* She is *the* Grandmother, little *zaika* bunny-girl, and don't you forget." He moved to the coffee machine and began his ritual; according to Leo, there was nothing caffeine with a slight dusting of vodka—or vice versa—couldn't fix.

The silver samovar crouched on the stove turned everything upside down on its bright belly. His reflection swelled, hiding behind sudden mist. Nat blinked furiously, even though it made her eyes leak more.

Letting her imagination run away with her yet again today was the absolute last straw—but it hadn't quite *run away* with her, had it? She knew what she saw, even if Mom and the rest of the world didn't care. "She wants me to find something for her."

Uncle Leo stopped again. He took a deep breath, and for a moment Nat was entirely, dismally sure this time his temper would snap. He'd never lost it once during her life, but Mom told stories of things he'd done before.

Some of the stories were fanciful, like juggling red-hot horseshoes or outrunning a steam train, but others were just plausible enough to terrify child-Nat. Sometimes, when Leo picked her up and spun her over his head, she would shriek with joy—but every once in a while she'd stiffen and cry.

Poor Leo always looked sad when she did. *I left my temper in the old country,* he said each time, and would take her for ice cream if they could get out the door without Mom sighing about the cost of double cones or about some home maintenance needing doing instead of catering to a little girl's whims.

"So I need to go ask Mom a few questions tomorrow; she has something this de Winter woman wants," Nat continued carefully. Her coat dripped yet more melted snow, but at least her fingers were waking up with painful tingles. "And then, de Winter said she'd help."

"Help with what?" Leo coughed again, as if he wanted to curse but knew Mom would overhear. "Help your mama die, eh?"

He'd never said it quite so directly before. Neither, for that matter, had Nat. It was always *when she gets better, when things calm down.*

"Maybe help with hospital bills, so we're not homeless when it happens." Nat dropped her gaze to the clear plastic covering the table's intricate lace cloth. She didn't know what the tax situation with the house was, but it couldn't be good. Her uncle was too old to work, and Nat . . . well.

You don't need college, Natchenka. Don't worry about it. Most mothers were the exact opposite; they shoved their kids school-ward with single-minded intensity.

Of course, most mothers also didn't live in tiny yellow houses with listing picket fences and bright rioting gardens, or make an uncle drive them around like a chauffeur in an old black movie-grade Léon-Bollée, or boil strange stinking concoctions on the stove late at night and take them to the flagstone patio, pouring steaming liquid while muttering in a language she didn't want Nat to learn. *Leave the old country alone.*

Most mothers came to parent-teacher conferences regularly, not just when they wanted to prove a point, and they didn't show up in long bright skirts, scarves, tons of gold jewelry, and a thick, partly fake accent either. They didn't date your eighth-grade History teacher one whole uncomfortable summer, while strange sounds came from the biggest bedroom and your uncle stayed out of the house as much as possible.

Leo had played a lot of chess in Princo Park that year, and took second place in the unofficial fall tournament. Mr. Harrison had vanished in September; rumors that he'd been fired ran around the school for a while but died like tomatoes after a hard frost.

Mom had been in a good mood that winter, though, and Leo came back from wherever he was sleeping—probably in the park too, worrying Nat almost to distraction. For a while it was almost like being a family again.

Almost.

"As long as I live, you are not *homeless*," Uncle Leo said, loyally. The coffeemaker began to burble, and he shuffled for the big white enamel fridge with the funny chrome decal on its front, every curve and edge more like an ancient, gas-guzzling motor vehicle than a mini Antarctica. The freezer swung open, and he retrieved a bottle only lightly traced with frost.

"That's a nice thought," Nat heard herself say, dully. If she un-screwed some of the bulbs, the kitchen might not be lit up like a surgical theater. She could always remember to tighten them before Mom came home, right? "Maybe this Grandmother de Winter will send me to college. So I can take care of you."

He seemed to find that funny. At least, Leo laughed, and when he poured the coffee his liver-spotted hands—once able to cover the scalp of a tangle-haired, scab-kneed, imaginative little girl with a single warm palm—shook a little more than usual.

It wasn't hypnosis, Nat. And not drugs, or you'd be feeling the hang-over. She shuddered, her chair squeaking, and her uncle turned from the counter, holding the bottle loosely by the neck. His mouth was drawn terribly tight.

Sometimes there just wasn't anything to say.

He stared at her, the lovely dark smell of coffee filling the kitchen with a promise of warmth and maybe even understanding married to a slight buzz of caffeine and bitterness. Her uncle's bloodshot, faded dark eyes shone; he rubbed at his ferocious gray stubble with damp, callus-scratchy fingers. He brought two cups to the table, neither very full, and poured a glug of vodka into hers, topping off his own with a much healthier measure.

Mom would be mad. Still, it was Nat who brought the bottles home from the corner shop when he needed them; ever since she was eleven Mrs. Lang had quietly winked at her delivery service. A lot of kids probably did that for their uncles, though maybe not with hard liquor. It was natural, if not normal.

But there was absolutely no ordinary, rational explanation for the de Winter woman, or the secretary in green. There was none for the gangster with his wide white smile and bright boot-toes, or for Mom's muttering over bubbling pots at two in the morning, or the cancer raving and gobbling its way through Maria Drozdova's fever-struck body. There was *especially* no natural explanation for being stuck to a chair until anger pried you free, or a business card that was pristine even after a month in a grubby, carried-daily purse.

But if this strangeness had a chance of saving Mom, then it was settled. She'd do it.

Nat reached for the condensation-sweating vodka bottle. She poured until her cup was just as heavy as his. "I haven't even thought about dinner." She'd brought home a supermarket Thanksgiving last week, she and Leo eating processed "turkey," grainy instant potatoes, and canned cranberry sauce Mom would never in a million years allow.

She and Leo had agreed maybe Mom had the right idea, but they'd finished the meal *and* leftovers the next day. It was one thing to sneak some turkey in; it was quite another to waste food in the little yellow house.

"I make grilled cheese," her uncle said, and her eyes turned hot and full again.

"Do we have bread?" Her shoulders hunched. *Should have thought of that.*

"Go clean up." Leo didn't bother to stir his coffee, just slurped from the top.

"Okay." But she didn't move. Her eyes watered fiercely, she was sniffing like Mrs. Mancy's old bulldog half a block down, and her coat was heavy and sodden, prickling at cuffs and collar. After a few sips the vodka began to uncurl behind her breastbone, a delicate heat-vine, and the two of them sat, silent conspirators, until their drinks were finished.

AND THIEVES

The nurse's desk at the hospice said Mom was sleeping and they'd tell her about the call, so Nat hung up the old, cheerful yellow landline with a guilty sigh of relief. Kitchen trash didn't need to be taken out but she did it anyway after dinner, restraining a childish urge to swing the half-empty bag while she shuffled in her uncle's old motorcycle boots. She needed at least two pairs of thick socks before they wouldn't slip off her feet midstride, but they were the footwear conveniently near the back door.

And comforting, too.

The temperature had dropped, hard snow-pellets instead of fluffy flakes hissing as it rode a knife-sharp norther. The plows would work through the night but her street was far down on the list, a white wasteland, the sky a low orange lid clapped over a frozen entrée. The alley was a deserted black throat where the weak glow of a few lamps didn't reach; those who decorated for the holidays didn't bother with back windows or fences.

Nat shivered, wrapping Leo's old, bulky striped cardigan closer. It was no use, none of them would be out tonight. It figured; normally she couldn't get them to shut up, but the moment she actually *needed* help—

A small voice, soft and restful but with a shadow of rumbling behind every word, vanished into the wind. "Well, what do *you* want?"

Nat looked around wildly, snow shaking from her sloppy ponytail.

"Down." The cat hunched in the lee of a gray plastic trash bin, tabby stripes blending into shadow and her gold eyes lambent. "Look down. It's amazing how you monkeys never think of that."

If I was looking down, you'd be up somewhere high. Nat suppressed a sigh and the urge to roll her eyes like a teenager again. "Good evening." If anyone came down the alley behind the brownstones, they might assume she was talking to herself, or a crazy cat lady.

Stop lying, Natchenka, cats don't speak in this country. Mom's voice, harsh and hurried. Of course she had no time for anything other than keeping the house running, right? *Go wash your hands before you set the table, you're filthy.*

"Can the formalities." Whiskers twitched, and a fluid shiver passed down the tabby's spine. "It's cold."

"I know." Nat crouched awkwardly and held out a hand. The cat deigned to sniff, a mannerly inspection of fingertips, eyes half-lidded and whiskers twitching in rhythm. "I can carry you to the porch."

The tabby's tail lashed once, thinking the matter over. "I won't stay."

"Of course not." Feline etiquette meant never admitting hunger or submission; Nat wished a little of it would rub off on her the way their scent did. If she was crazy, at least the insanity was specific and consistent, and she was very deliberately not thinking about why Mom would send her to the parchment-haired de Winter and yet not believe her own daughter's insistence on similarly strange things. "But we can at least keep your paws dry."

"Very well."

Nat gathered the small furry body carefully; the cat didn't struggle, but also didn't help. Trudging through the back gate, Nat restrained the urge to rub her chin on a small snow-starred head. "Normally I wouldn't," the cat said as she passed one of the garden boxes, dormant shrubs stretching skeletal arms in strange patterns. "But *she* is gone. This is your house, now."

It was a day for uncomfortable truths, it looked like. Nat sniffed, not to express her opinion but because she was leaking again. Maybe Mom didn't believe her daughter because she'd seen the strangeness too and, like any reasonably sane person, didn't want to admit it. "I met my grandmother today."

It always surprised her how easy it was to talk to them. People ran right over you verbally, but cats gave you *space*. If they didn't know something, they admitted it—indirectly, of course, but still. And they never told her she was lying when she wasn't.

All in all, she vastly preferred them—and dogs, and birds, not to mention squirrels—to human beings. Mom claimed an allergy to animal dander, but sometimes Nat saw a buried gleam in her mother's blue gaze and thought the Great Pet Ban in the yellow house had a deeper reason.

She just hadn't figured it out yet.

"*The* Grandmother." The tabby shifted uneasily in her arms, growing heavier for a moment. Claws touched Leo's cardigan, and even though his old boots were waterproof Nat's feet were numb. "Well, it had to happen. Sometimes even Baba is merciful."

"Baba." She couldn't imagine calling the parchment-haired woman *Granny*. And *Yaga*, what a sardonic little laugh that was, now that Nat wasn't nerving herself up to visit the Morrer-Pessel or too tired and heartsore from two jobs and the hospice visits to think. "They're true, aren't they. Those stories." Either the old tales were true or the Mafia believed them more than child-Nat ever had; the difference was probably academic. "But Mom always . . ."

"Monkeys." The tabby stretched to sniff Nat's jawbone, shifting like a tired child. "You believe what you tell each other. How very strange."

"I guess." Going up the three porch stairs without slipping and falling on her ass was a little harder than Nat liked, between Leo's boots and the second helping of vodka with dinner. "So what does she want me to find?"

Because *that* had been left out of the directions too. Baba had simply laughed. *Go ask your mother,* vnuchka. *She knows what I'll take for a miracle or two.*

"A jewel of great price." The cat's laugh was a high chirruping *miao*, much nicer than de Winter's. "Set amid iron vines only Spring may loosen. Oh, there are other things to gain first, but *that* is the prize. Reach in and your arm will wither, but knock, and you shall be answered." The tabby sneezed, delicately. "Set me down there."

Nat bent. The world swayed a little; she managed to settle the cat on a thickly folded pad of ancient, fake-grass carpet. Before Mom started getting so tired, she never would have allowed something so tacky even on the porch. Leo's great idea for Astroturf paths through the garden had died an ignominious death at the dinner table one night, but he'd already "organized" a roll of the stuff. No refunds, of course, and he wouldn't hear of just getting rid of it.

The old country taught both him and Mom to be thrifty. When you were annoyed, you could call it *cheap* or *hoarding*. Still, Nat supposed, when you had to leave everything behind, accumulating enough weight in the new country so you didn't blow away again like dandelion seeds was a reasonable strategy.

The dish of dry kibble tucked under the wooden swinging bench was full, and Nat tested the other plain pottery dish. Maybe the house was leaking warmth; the water never froze if she placed it in the right spot and asked it politely not to.

"That sounds like a riddle," she observed, straightening. Mom's generously curved shadow wasn't going to fill the back door, haloed with incandescent light and irritation. *Stop feeding those fleabitten things. Come inside, it's cold.*

"I'm a cat." In other words, what else did Nat expect? The tabby sneezed again. "What would you trade for your mother's life?"

Everything. Nat opened her mouth to say as much, but the cat hissed, ears suddenly flattened. It stood bolt upright—fur stiffening along its spine, tail straight skyward and fluffy as a brush—staring at the back fence where a sinuous shadow moved. There was a twinkle of silver, a flash of pointed ivory; Nat stepped back and almost fell onto the bench when her uncle's boots tangled together.

The wind swept across the yard, a curtain of tiny rattling snow-flakes.

"Who's there?" Nat called, stupidly, as if there would be an answer. At least her uncle didn't throw the back door open, and Mom wasn't here to see her making a fool of herself.

The tabby's tail lashed, still puffy. Nat cast around for some kind of weapon, and a faint nasty baritone laugh pierced the snowy quiet before shredding into the distance.

She thought she knew that voice, and all the vodka in her veins couldn't stop the cold.

Finally, the tabby craned its neck, peering over its shoulder. The golden eyes narrowed, and the cat considered her speculatively. "Beware," it said, very softly, under the whispering wind. "Beware of shadows, child, beware of light promises. But most of all, beware of thieves." A tail-tip flicked, and the tabby turned toward the fence again, its fur sleeking down once more.

But slowly. And it watched like it expected something to appear.

"Shadows, promises, and thieves." *Sure.* Of course, nothing would make sense until after the absolute worst had happened; cats were worse than birds for speaking in metaphor.

At least felines—and canines—had longer attention spans. Most avians couldn't keep their mind on business for more than a few seconds. And sometimes the cats said something unequivocal, though Nat knew better than to tell anyone else about it.

She wasn't very bright, God knew, but eventually, she learned. Long ago she'd given up wondering if other kids heard what she did but didn't want to be different, and so trained themselves out of it. Other parents might not do things Mom's way, but they still agreed, without exception, that imaginary friends and talking animals weren't real.

Nat thought maybe they should visit a certain floor of the Morrer-Pessel building and find out differently, but so many callers might make that particular grandmother a little cranky.

De Winter. What a laugh.

"It's all real," she murmured, staring at the back fence. The marks along the top were just smears of knocked-free snow, but she thought the alley might show prints of sharp-toed boots before falling white filled them in. Shivers, only barely controlled by a warm vodka-fueled buzz, made her teeth ache. "All this time."

"Go inside." The cat's tail lashed again. "We will keep the shadows away, as we always have. Nothing will disturb your dreams tonight, daughter of the Drozdova."

The Drozdova. Like *the* Grandmother. Everyone was putting stress on definite articles today.

Ever since she'd walked out of her job at the Humboldt Insurance office that afternoon, impelled towards a downtown skyscraper by the faint fading dream of helping her mother stave off death, the world had been just a degree or two off-kilter. Something told her it wouldn't right itself anytime soon. Nat felt behind her for the doorknob. "Are you sure you want to be outside tonight?"

"I won't stay," the cat repeated, and its tail twitched again. "Go."

Inside the mudroom, Nat slumped against the back door, fumbling for the deadbolt. It threw with a tiny click and she was glad Leo had already shuffled off to his small bedroom, where a white plastic television perched atop his dresser was already muttering some infomercial or another. He loved shopping shows promising cheap new products, the American dream hanging tantalizingly just out of reach, hucksters enthusing through perpetual grimaces of agonized good cheer.

It took a long while before she could step out of her uncle's boots, peel off the outer layer of thick hand-knitted socks, and slip her feet into her old, familiar embroidered slippers. She kept peeking through the door's beveled windows, her breath causing a faint mist. The snow kept whirling down, and the piled freeze knocked off the fence-top looked entirely natural now.

She couldn't see the tabby, but tomorrow morning the kibble dish would be empty and she'd miss another day of work—at both jobs this time, an insurance office and the big box store on 158th would both need a new cog to shove into their corporate wheel.

Nat would be on an errand for a Mob grandmother with a very literary name who could stick someone to a wooden chair with just a harsh glare. If that was a skill, it was one Nat Drozdova could use, if she could just figure it out.

The feeling that she'd stepped off the side of the world and into whirling, dizzy-sick space just wouldn't go away. She scrubbed at her chapped cheek with cold fingertips, seriously debating the advisability of stopping in the kitchen for another hit off the bottle in the freezer.

An internal vote was taken, and passed with a minimum of fuss. Maybe she'd wake up and find the past day a particularly vivid nightmare like she used to get in high school.

It would mean she'd also wake up with Mom still dying, the business card still pristine in her purse, and the constant querulous questions following her all through the day. *Have you visited her? Did you go? What did she say?*

God and Christ both help her, as Leo would mutter, Nat couldn't help hoping she'd wake up and find out the world really was magic, instead.

It would mean she had a shot at making her mother better.

A WILLING EAR

Laurelgrove Hospice near Fort Greene Park used to be a Gilded Age mansion, and a few graceful touches remained—wall sconces, the pressed tin ceiling in the entryway, and heavy wooden wainscoting painted so many times its grain and carvings both blurred. There was a plastic tree in the lobby, blinking with strings of lights; empty, brightly wrapped "presents" huddled at its base. It was trying to be cheerful, Nat guessed, which was about all you could do this time of year.

Signing in, showing ID, filling out the questionnaire—if you had symptoms of anything you couldn't visit, because of the immunocompromised—it was all familiar by now, and Nat knew exactly when to smile, how to make the right self-deprecating joke, which staircase to head for. She knew the nurses on the third floor and passed all the same rooms as usual, each with a handmade sign on the door's left proudly announcing trapped occupants' names to the world.

Did prisons have those signs too? Her mother's sign bore bright yellow crayon stars and the room also had a window, which effectively doubled the price. Nat didn't even want to think about the bills.

Stop worrying about it, Mom kept saying, *did you visit her, did you go? We won't have to worry if you go.*

Maybe de Winter would be taking over the payments. That would be a relief. Nat knocked at the door, her usual two brief taps, and stepped inside.

The top half of Mom's bed was up, and Maria Drozdova was awake. The IV pole near the bed held a bag of clear fluid, and

Mom's big blue eyes were bloodshot. Her cheekbones stood out alarmingly and her hands, motionless for once, lay on a fuzzy beige hospital blanket. She wasn't wearing her three gold rings; they were safe at home, in the little gilt jewelry box atop the cedar vanity in the big bedroom. Nor did she wear the big gold hoop earrings; those were tucked away as well. At least she had a glossy black kerchief with bright red roses covering her strawlike, thinning hair, and her mouth wasn't pulled tight with pain.

Instead, Mom looked almost cheerful. Pale, snowy sunlight poured over a small bench with pink vinyl cushions under the window; the suite's bathroom, with enough space for a wheelchair if the person helping the patient was a contortionist, reeked of damp disinfectant smeared on gleaming tiles.

Maybe other rooms had a tinsel decoration, or cut flowers. Mom didn't even want one of her beloved houseplants here. *It will shrivel in the window, bad light.*

"There she is, my daughter." Maria Drozdova's voice was a throaty whisper. A clear plastic tube dipped across her face, loops secured behind her ears, its top arc passing just under her high-prowed nose which was, Nat could now see, very like Baba de Winter's; the oxygen machine tucked behind the IV pole made a soft whispering sound. "You're early today."

I'm about to be a very busy girl, Mama. Working for the Mob or trying to find another low-end secretarial-slash-retail job accessible to a girl with a bare high school diploma—what a choice. "Hi, Mom." She leaned over the bed to press her lips gently to a papery cheek. "How are you feeling?"

"I ate today." A slight click of distaste, tongue against teeth; Mom deplored hospital food. *No proper black bread and not a spot of good soup, no wonder people die here,* she liked to grumble; under Lysol and the brassy smell of pain a ghost of her perfume lingered like dried flowers. "Did you sing to the begonias this morning? They need *two* full choruses if I'm not going to be there."

"Your begonias are fine, Mom." Every plant in the house was, though the way her mother talked they would all droop and turn brown overnight without her rituals. Nat skirted the bed, set her canvas visiting bag on the bench. "Uncle Leo got those crackers you like, so—"

"Sweet man." Mom waved the subject of Nat's uncle aside with an irritable motion of one thin, clawlike hand. Her crimson nail polish—another similarity to de Winter—was chipped and cracked. "But listen, Natchenka—"

"Yes, Mama. I went and saw her yesterday. That's why I wasn't here after work." Nat busied herself with digging in the bag.

The silence was full of footsteps in the hallway, soft humming machinery noises, the low indistinct hum of conversation. Someone was coughing in another room, dry croupy explosions.

"They'll bring you milk; you can dip these." Nat drew out the package of plain saltines, the specific kind Mom liked—not brand, not generic, somewhere in between and of course difficult to find in bodega or supermarket. "I can bring some broth too. We can figure out how to heat it up."

"Come over here, sit down." The words had all their accustomed bite, a short-term flush of strength filling Mom's blue eyes with new fire, spotting her pale cheeks with bright carmine coins. Her bed jacket, a cheerful black-and-red quilted number sewn on the ancient Singer during a morning full of leaves and mist when Nat was eleven, was saggy-loose and creased instead of properly ironed. "*Now*, Natchenka."

"Is she really your mother?" Nat obeyed, settling a cautious hip on the bed past the railing, near her mother's knees. "She doesn't look like either of us." *Except the nose—and she sure as hell acts like you.*

"In a manner of speaking, she's everyone's grandmother." Mom reached out, two frail, birdlike hands with their red-streaked nails. "Come closer."

"I can't, the railing's up." Nat clutched the saltines box. She longed to put her head down on her mother's shrunken chest and listen to her heart, but there was no way to do that without hurting her. And besides, once Nat was old enough to walk to school alone, her mother had decided she was old enough to be self-sufficient. Other parents coddled, but not the queen of the little yellow house.

"She had some tattooed guy with her. You sent me to the Mob, Mom."

Maria Drozdova stared at her daughter for a moment. A sly gleam filled her faded blue eyes, and for a moment she was radiant again through a thin mask of illness. Her gauntness turned ethereal instead of skeletal, and she stiffened, lifting herself from the pillows. "What did she say? What did Baba say?"

Shouldn't you address her as my lady de Winter? "She wants me to find something for her. Said you'd know what." Nat's throat was dry, and the coffee she'd managed to take down—free of vodka this morning, though Uncle Leo's had smelled suspiciously doctored— gurgled in her stomach. "Mama, why did you always tell me cats don't talk?"

She sounded eight years old again, Nat realized, and the box's cardboard was slippery against her sweating fingers. *Stop lying to me. Or tell me you knew I was special, but you kept saying those things because . . . because why?*

"Because they don't in this country, Natchenka. Not yet." Mom sagged against pillows, that transitory beauty gone. Only its ghost remained in her bone structure, the ruins of a white-columned temple on a sunny, forgotten hillside. "I told you she'd know why I sent you. Clever bitch, that one."

In this country? They don't talk yet? It was a sudden about-face from every other answer Nat had received on the question, and the change made her even dizzier. "Mama—"

"Shhh." Her mother made a distracted, peremptory movement, no less sharp for being slight and weak. "She probably has a mouse in the room. All her spies, the damn rodents." Mom's eyes half-lidded, and she visibly considered the situation much as she had the question of school shopping trips every September—a necessary evil when she would much rather be thinking about other things, a painful expenditure of cash that could be used elsewhere. "Very well. You didn't promise her anything, did you? Tell me you did what I said, tell me you didn't promise her anything."

Oh, for God's sake. Nat strangled her own impatience, something she did so frequently it was almost reflexive by now. Uncle Leo had been so proud of finding the crackers, and here she was putting creases in the box. "I told her I'd find it, but I wouldn't promise more." *Because I was glued in a chair and hypnotized. And I think that guy with the tattoos was on our back fence last night. Watching me.* "What else was I supposed to do? And the man with her—"

"Oh, don't you worry about *him*. Dima's easily led." Her mother's hands fell to her lap, dry fingertips rubbing at each other. The rest of her under the sheet and blanket was two long barrows and tiny foot-hillocks, nothing solid remaining. A strong wind might blow her away. "It's Baba you keep an eye on. You mind me now, Natchi."

"Yes, Mama." The same old dismal feeling—of being a parent with an adult-sized toddler—returned.

Since the Easter Nat turned eight, it had been a quasi-constant companion.

Her mother knew this "Dmitri" too. Well, growing up meant finding out about your parents' unfinished business; maybe Mom and Leo had been trafficked into the States? It made some kind of sense to think about it that way, but not enough.

Not *nearly* enough.

"Still . . ." Mama examined her, and Nat was aware of her own muddy complexion since she didn't use the rosewater her mother did, aware of her brownish hair slipping free of its twist, of her peacoat still damp from yesterday and reeking of wet wool. There was probably shed hair on her shoulder from the tabby, too, and this morning a tuxedo cat on the stoop had chirped *Good day, Drozdova* before turning sideways and vanishing as Nat locked the front door.

There were, in fact, feline footprints in the snow all through the back garden, circles and loops, lines and the odd blank space where one had leapt instead of striding or trotting. Maybe they'd held a whole damn convention there last night, like that old story about the King of Cats.

"Still, I suppose it's not bad," Maria Drozdova continued. "You will hurry and fetch a few things, then Baba will make me all better." Mom laced her skeletal fingers together, the knuckles turning white. It was the only sign of anxiety she permitted herself, even now. "But listen, you must bring everything to me. Not to *her*, you bring everything to *me first,* you understand? You must think of your Mama."

"Yes, Mama." Nat worried at the top of the cardboard box, working stiffened paper free of industrial glue. She had her mother's tapering fingers and cupped palms, and sometimes Uncle Leo studied her hand with a strange expression, rubbing her knuckles with his thumb. *Dancer's hands, just like your Mama.* "Sure you don't want some of these?"

"I'm not hungry, Nat." There was a flare of her mother's patented temper, still terrifying even when she was knocked horizontal and full of metastasizing cells in failing organs.

Nat swallowed, hard. "All right." *Why did you accuse me of lying all those years? You had to know.* But asking would only make Mom sullen, so Nat turned—as always—to what would please the queen of the little yellow house instead. "So I bring you this thing, whatever it is, and she makes you better? That's it?"

"That's it. And then it's home to see dear Leo." Mom's eyes darkened, half-lidded, her eyelashes gray instead of rich chestnut with gold at the tips as they had been until two months ago. "He didn't come this time, either."

Considering how you act when he does, I'm not surprised. But keeping the peace was Nat's job, so she suppressed a weary sigh. "It's hard on him, Mama."

"Hard on *him.*" Mom closed her eyes, her kerchief rustling against the pillow as she shook her head. "I'm the one dying."

Don't say that. But honestly, Nat hadn't expected anything less from her mother. When you grew up with someone, you learned more than you ever wanted to know about them; weren't all children supposed to keep secrets and bear up under the weight? "How exactly is Mrs. de Winter going to help you?"

"She has her ways." A faint glimmer showed under Mom's lashes. Was it tears? "Now, you might want to write this down, Natchenka. You know how your head is."

"I think I'll remember." *I'm not twelve anymore, for God's sake.* And she'd just managed to save up enough for first, last, and deposit on a shitty little sublet in Bed-Stuy just before her mother's collapse. So, so close to escape, scrimping hard because, of course, most of what she brought home had to go into the yellow house's hungry mouth.

Cradling her mother's bony form on the kitchen floor, waiting for the ambulance, and Nat thinking *just when I was about to get out of here too*—the memory filled her with unsteady loathing each time she thought about it.

"Very well, but if you forget . . ." All trace of excitement or strength was gone. In its place was Maria's old familiar weariness, a creature enduring because submission was not even close to an acceptable option. "You should take care too. Not even a scarf on your head, you'll catch cold. Then where will I be?"

"I guess you'll have to make do with the nurses if that happens." *And good luck bullying them around instead.* But that was a terrible thing to think; if Nat was lying in a hospital bed all day feeling her body die by inches, she'd be a little cranky too. "So what's this thing I have to get?"

"Many things, and one very important." Mama made another irritable little motion. Even her feet twitched. "Come here so I may whisper, Natchenka. Baba has her ears everywhere."

Oh, for God's sake. Nat hauled herself up again, stowed the crackers, and moved to put the railing down.

After all, what was the harm? Mom couldn't grab Nat by both shoulders and terrify her with hissed imprecations anymore. If she wanted to whisper like girls at a slumber party, fine.

KNOCK THRICE

It hurt to breathe, it hurt to move. It hurt to look at the wistfully pretty young woman with her honey-tinted hair and her dark eyes. But she did, because she was Maria Drozdova, the original instead of the copy, and she'd trained the girl to be obedient.

To be a good child, to do as she was told.

It had been difficult, yes. First, of course, there was wringing the parasite free of your own body, and she could have swallowed it then—but that wasn't the best solution, was it?

No, if you wanted something better, something more permanent, there was another path. Drozdova thought she'd had more time; the flower had stubbornly refused to open after a steady diet of Catholic school and American television, the penitential poison and that hateful glass teat dripping its toxin everywhere, siphoning off good energy that could be used for other things.

Still, it was sometimes pleasant waiting in the little yellow house. There was Leo, and there were other lovers—though none with his usefulness, and even he started to fade as she did. There were also the stray sips and swallows she could gather around the edges, while a tear-streaked face was lifted to hers and a little maggot sniveled *"But I heard it, I did, I'm not imagining!"*

Though you could encourage, it didn't do to outright hurry a flower; delicate processes respond poorly to brute force. So time passed and this inimical country scraped every inch of the Drozdova, a relentless abrasion.

Sometimes it was little prickle cat-claws, hair-fine needles doing almost no damage. Most often, though, it was the roughest possible sandpaper stripping away her power, her grace. And every bit of scouring was cumulative.

Her daughter was taller now. She waxed while Maria waned, and forcing the child to visit Baba had been unexpectedly difficult. The layers of obfuscation, of careful misdirection, that allowed Maschka to crouch in the little yellow house had turned in her hand, like a sharp garden tool biting its user. Soon not even the house's carefully painted camouflage would keep the angular shadows at bay, and once Maria's daughter was eaten the shadows would come for her.

Which would be ironic, and infuriating as the deep, grinding cancerous ache burning in her belly.

So the Drozdova lay in her hospice bed, enduring the shouting nurses and poking, prodding doctors, waiting for the culmination of careful work she'd done for nearly two decades. Not very long; an eyeblink, really, for one of her kind.

Time had crawled at a mortal pace, these past two months. And the little honey-haired bitch might be enjoying her new status, unaware of what all that fresh, warm strength meant. She'd always been stupid, dreamy—a thoroughly American child.

It didn't matter. Finally, the tiny spaniel had trotted to Baba's, probably shaking and shivering with fear the whole way. Now she was even asking about the *cats*, Christ forgive her as Leo would mutter, though the man knew how she felt about that pale bastard stealing one of her most treasured festivals.

All the pragmatism Maria had tried so hard to inculcate was going to peel away from the little maggot-child in layers, another irony. If the Drozdova could gather the strength to rise from the bed, she'd be able to browbeat the girl more effectively. Everything depended upon the thing that had swollen in Maria's womb next to that deep, constant angular ache, upon the last twenty mortal years of careful training and pruning forcing a sapling into the proper shape.

If all went well, the little parasite would do as she had been taught.

Of course the Baba would leap at the chance to reclaim a glittering, coruscating gem with its own secret pulse; Dima might even cooperate, with this tempting morsel dangling before him. After all, much of the world—mortal or divine—could be seduced by wide eyes and carefully watered naïveté.

The Drozdova caught more than one bit of prey that way, after all. Even here in America.

Maria's trembling hands brushed the shoulders of Leo's old coat. The old man's useless, doddering affection clung to the thick fabric, robbing her skeletal fingers of strength needed to catch, to hold fast. It was useless to wish she hadn't scattered the items quite so widely after all.

What else could she have done? It was a huge continent, and re-serving what she had stolen against this stage in the game required extraordinary measures. Maria shouldn't have waited so long; she'd done her work too well and now the girl believed nothing at all.

It didn't matter. Greedy Baba would force the parasite to do what it should, Konets would make sure of it, and Maria's plans would come to fruition. Now she had to rest, conserve her strength.

Maria Drozdova drew in a rattling breath, the tearing pain in her middle so familiar she barely felt it anymore. Next to the child's waiting ear, she whispered the riddle, hoping the leech was only intelligent enough to unravel its fringes. Giving just enough training while still keeping it weakened enough for her purposes was a balancing act, and much would depend on how well Maria had performed the circus feat for two short, stupid, endless mor-tal decades.

"Listen," she breathed, hating the rattle in her throat. "Listen to me, little dumpling."

The girl went still; the Drozdova gathered all the power deep-buried rage could summon, and if she could just concentrate enough, it would be not a riddle but a proper geas.

Now, when it counted, she was weak—but when your prey was even weaker, it didn't matter so much.

"*This, then, is the way to the Black God's Heart,*" she croak-whispered. "*The path starts with the Knife; the path to the Knife starts with the man who believes in the future. Then find the rest—the Cup is in the well to the West where the iron horse leads, the Key rests in the*

greenest place at the very edge of the world. After all the treasures are
gathered, find the salt-black tree with the snake at its roots. Knock thrice,
my daughter, and what you seek shall be given you."

Maria fell against the pillows, spent and drained, the deep dry
pain in her belly mounting though the relief of a secret shared and
a burden shifted filled her hollowing bones.

She only hoped it wasn't too late.

⋊⋉

If there was a mouse in the room, it heard nothing but cloth moving and a hot susurration, breath brushing a willing ear. Masha
Drozdova, her body failing, whispered the riddle in her daughter's
ear before collapsing into the pillows once more, her eyes fluttering
closed and her failing strength retreating to deep hollows, clinging
to life.

Her daughter simply stared at the window, perplexed.

ONLY TARNISHED

The snow kept threatening to leave but never quite managing, like a bored and highly demanding lover who hasn't found your replacement yet. That was fine with Dmitri; he liked the infinite sky overhead and a few flakes spattering here and there while people hurried along sidewalks strewn with chemical pellets. There was a bumper crop of fender benders, always a good time—except it was too cold for tempers to flare very badly. Still, overworked cops called out to minor traffic accidents weren't causing problems elsewhere.

Which made his in-laws *very* happy. Well, some of them. Others cursed and shivered, feeling bad luck upon the wind. Any man with a big family knows it isn't possible to please everyone at once. It is, however, very possible to please nobody at all, which Dima rather liked doing.

Still, they were good people, his in-laws. Devious, yes. Corrupt, certainly. Violent? Ah, exquisitely. But they had no other gods before him, displaying the necessary skill of knowing very well what they could not afford, and he was content to have it so.

For now.

One of his very favorite local nephews met him inside Holy Saint Agata Cathedral near Claremont Park, in fact, sliding into the pew while Dmitri leaned back, his fingers laced behind his head, staring at the high, shadowy ceiling. Many of his in-laws had helped pay for construction, others tossed no few blood- or coke-dotted bills in the offering plate while they prayed not to Rome *or* Moscow *or*

Constantinople but to the one who kept their fingers light, their prey unsuspecting, and their lungs clear of blood.

Such prayers pleased their loving uncle-in-law mightily. Especially during the holiday season.

Sergei Serafimovitch Kezagov—not his original name, to be sure—settled his heavy buttocks firmly upon hard wood polished by many a more penitent set of asses. His graying hair slicked back and his mustache magnificently waxed, he wore sober charcoal wool, a tie of gaudy maroon silk, well-polished wingtips, and the heft of a very successful businessman as well as a plain gold wedding ring.

Stolen, of course. *Technically* an in-law couldn't have a wife; human ties were inevitably used against you. A lover was one thing, a sacrament quite another—but rules were meant to be flouted by the lucky or the skilled, so most of the time Dima winked, well pleased.

Besides, the ties were not only useful to enemies. They could be useful to an uncle, as well.

"You're late," Dmitri said, and continued his perusal of the ceiling. In the old country there would be ikons gazing from every direction, gazing into varnished eternity. Here, it was only dust and plain paint, but that didn't mean he disliked the simplicity.

Quite the opposite.

"Traffic is very bad." Sergei sounded very correct, as always—propitiatory, but not fawning. He proffered the paper cup; Dmitri sniffed, slowly slithered to sit upright, and accepted the offering.

Strong, harsh black coffee—several shots of espresso, with a dash of drip over the top to keep it warm. A bite of something other than vodka, a hint of caramel . . . and the rusty, coppery tang of a traitor's emptied veins. Dima sniffed again, his nose twitching, and took much of the near-boiling eighteen liquid ounces down in several long swallows, his throat working and every candle in the church blessed with a pinprick of flame wavering for a moment as a cold breath filled the nave.

Maybe the effort of bringing a gift—and standing in line at the coffee shop—made up for a few minutes' worth of waiting. Dima hadn't quite decided yet, but the traitor's agony was real, raw, and excruciating.

In other words, delicious. He lowered the cup, exhaling. "Did he go well?"

"Well enough, for a two-faced bastard." Sergei's tone was hushed, whether out of deference to the setting or his companion was an open question. Not too long ago—well within a mortal lifetime—Dima had withdrawn protection from an in-law who made the mistake of spitting at the bishop during a parade.

You could wink at formality, but only so far.

Movement brushed the edges of sacred hush. Someone was polishing with beeswax in the vicinity of the choir loft, a few old black-wrapped babushkas dotted pews nearer the altar, their kerchief-wrapped heads bent. Yet more invisible activity was tapers being replaced, a priest chanting softly—practicing for a greater mass—while riffling thick, antique pages in a very large book.

You might almost think some true power resided here. If it did, Dmitri had never been troubled by it.

"I heard a rumor this morning." Sergei stared at the altar.

Well, that was quick. "I heard one as well." He wasn't quite lying, Dima heard rumors all the damn time. They filled the air like radioactive particles after a power plant explosion, like small denominations at a strip club, like batons and groans in a "police action."

Sergei forged ahead. "Mine is strange, uncle. I heard the way to a heart has been found."

"A what, now?" Baba had wasted no time whispering the news into unfriendly ears, or the very air itself carried tales. Either was equally likely. "Heart, eh? Such a little thing." Dima studied the altar and the cross above, a massive gold-leaf glowing thing. Its extra bar was a broken appendage, maybe a nice branch for a pale milksop to rest his feet while the nails were found and a hammer arranged. "What good is it?"

"I'm sure *I* don't know," Sergei agreed, loyally. "What should I do?"

If it had been a normal day, Dmitri would have ordered the rumormongers brought to him, either for a lesson or their secrets to be fully plumbed. Yet this bright morning he stretched, languidly, and admired his boot-toes. They were much better than the cross. What could two lathes lashed together give you that stamping on a man's face wouldn't?

Not a whole lot, he thought, as he did every other time. Still, even sheep needed divinities; the wolves ate better when a shepherd prepared the meal.

"Find whoever is whispering of such a thing." His tone had turned quiet, and a faint thread of ice ran underneath the words. "Collect their names."

Of course, he might be out of town soon if Maruschka's little daughter managed to get the location out of her dear mama. Maybe the blonde bitch had hid it in this very city—unlikely, but if it were so, Dmitri wouldn't have to travel very far.

And then he would feast.

"Yes, uncle." Sergei hesitated, in case his superior had another task to give him.

Fortunately, Dmitri did. "There's a yellow house on South Aurora, in Brooklyn." *A place that was hidden until a little girl came to visit grandmother. Maschka, you beautiful liar.* He gave the address, knowing his faithful little nephew would memorize what was written on air. "I want a watch kept. Everyone who goes in or out—and my eyes must do it *quietly,* little one, for above all else I wish to know who else is watching."

If Maschka had help other than Baba's, it would be good to know.

"Yes, uncle."

He waved Sergei away and took another gulp of copper-laced coffee as the old man slid from the pew, crossed himself, bobbed a bow, and paced off carrying his overcoat over one arm. The caffeine was a pleasant burn, and new strength washed through him. Offerings were good; so was faith.

But what Dima liked best was the *fear.* There was never any shortage of turncoats; someone should get a benefit, no matter how small, from the treasonous. Friendly wasn't going to like that one of his moles had been pried free of the tunnels.

Brooklyn. All this time, she was hiding right here.

He could even find it amusing. Oh, he hadn't expected anything other than eventual betrayal from grasping, starving Maschka Drozdova. He'd even enjoyed himself for a while. Knowing how the story would end meant you could appreciate the ride.

Dmitri listened as Sergei reached the front door, his tingling ears alert for a sigh or any chance that his nephew disliked the task he'd been set.

There was none. An old wolf knew very well whence his next meal arrived. And a heart was such a little thing indeed. It could be argued that lacking one was a distinct advantage here in shining, roomy America.

Dima could almost taste the *zaika*'s blood, once he had her charmed into finding the gem and taking away whatever setting Maschenka put it in. Baba was right, it wouldn't be like Maria Drozdova to simply steal the thing and hide it in a sock.

She wouldn't have been so entrancing if she were that uncomplicated. But now Dima wondered just how lovely she was anymore.

It might be time to visit her. But as soon as he thought it, he realized he didn't want to. Let her lie abed and wait, knowing her precious daughter was in Dmitri Konets's hands and soon, soon, soon indeed what was his would be returned.

He eyed the pews, the babushkas in the front, the altar. Someone in the assembling choir—whispers and ruffles of paper, children gathering to sing to a pale, distracted masochist during a celebration far older than the divinity it claimed to honor—had a guilty conscience, and the tiny wickedness was a sharp counterpoint to the incense-soaked air and the whispering candles. Even the priests in the building were only tarnished, not truly soiled.

Nobody here had the courage to do something worth forgiving.

Dmitri finished his drink, leisurely sips as it bubbled. When the cup was drained, he chewed the lid, swallowing chunks of masticated plastic with a gulp, and set his strong sharp white teeth to the waxed paper.

That way, he didn't lose a single delicious drop.

When he was done, he rose, crossed himself, kissed his fingers to the altar, and left with a spring in his silver-toed step.

There was much to be done.

DESTINY ON TIME

De Winter said *be ready at seven thirty*. So Nat was, with ID and cash tucked into her peacoat pocket and her gloves pulled securely over each finger, her favorite green knitted hat over her tightly braided hair, and her secondhand combat boots bought over on Stroy Avenue securely laced.

The old woman had also said *a party*, but Nat knew better than to get dressed up or even pack a Santa hat. She could be the one person who showed up to whatever this was in real clothes, it wouldn't do her any harm. At least now that she wasn't going to work she wouldn't have to wear business casual, either. If you were in a damn office where the customers only heard you over the phone, why not wear jeans? It was ridiculous.

Everything was absurd. The world was a giant April Fool's, grinning and saying *just joking* when you knew damn well it wasn't funny. And Mom, with her morphine-addled riddle—Baba was going to have to tell Nat precisely where this fucking thing she wanted was, but at least Maria knew her daughter was doing what she'd demanded.

Maybe the best that could be hoped for was de Winter agreeing to cover the hospice care. Nat lingered by the big front picture window, watching the snowy street while Uncle Leo muttered in the kitchen. He didn't like this at all, but what uncle would?

At least he didn't say he disbelieved her. He never really had, even when Mom rolled her eyes at Nat's "imagination."

Thinking about that was unpleasant, because it led to her mother in the adjustable bed, the rasping breath and the pauses between each lungful, and how thin Maria Drozdova was, her wrists like sticks and her chest sunken. Every time Nat visited it seemed impossible her mother was still holding on, still awake and alert.

But then, Mom was a force of nature. You couldn't keep her down for long, and she wouldn't die until she was good and ready. Or so Nat thought, picking nervously at the peacoat's cuff. Little wool balls, just right for worrying at until you realized you'd worn a hole right through.

The plows had been at work all night and all day too; even though the sky was a featureless gray lid promising more snow the roads were reasonably clear. It was amazing how human beings clustered around solving a problem, like white blood cells swarming an intruder.

Which just made her think of Mom again, a frail body eating itself in tiny cellular bites. The Black Forest cuckoo clock in the front room chimed the half hour, a pleasant little carillon as familiar as Nat's own breath.

The mobster was officially late.

Instead of relief, a mounting anxiety bubbled under Nat's diaphragm. Maybe it was all a vicious little prank, and they were laughing at her right now just like the kids in school until Sister Roberta Grace Abiding went down on the playground. One moment blowing her whistle, the next she was an empty doll in a dislodged wimple, lying on the bark chips under the swings.

The other kids left Nat alone after that, except for the taunting while she was walking home. *Witch-girl*, they would hiss. *Freak.* Or, like the nuns, *Devil's child.*

Mom brushed off child-Nat's tears. *They're fools*, she said, briskly. *Now go polish my figurines.*

It was Leo who comforted her, who taught her to make a fist—*thumb outside, little doll, otherwise you break it, see?*—and who sometimes shuffled to the corner to accompany her the last block home, a baleful glare and the fact of his adulthood keeping the worst at bay.

Nat's eyes prickled. Living in the past was no good. How long until Leo was in a hospice bed too? Then she would be utterly, completely alone.

It was terrifying to contemplate that kind of freedom. All paper-work for the house and everything else lived in a locked file cabinet, deep in Mama's bedroom closet. Getting it open would require a crowbar, or at the very least, the key from Leo.

Her uncle had taken over the monthly paperwork, and at least he didn't sigh over each bill and stare balefully at Nat. Instead he wrote checks with a distracted expression and spidery, precise pen-manship, handing each envelope to Nat to be sealed and stamped.

They hadn't done the ritual yet this month. She was afraid to ask how much was left in Mom's accounts. Afraid to admit she'd been about to move out, afraid to ask Leo if maybe he thought an apartment would be better for the two of them.

What if he said no, or worse, told Mom?

Headlights cut a cone through winter night, bouncing aggres-sively off plow-piled but still sparkling snow. They were bright as halogens, or brighter, and Nat wiped at her cheeks. Tears were to be expected when your mother was dying by inches and childhood stories were coming to life, but she still hated them. The little yel-low house was silent except for a faint clinking—dinner dishes, grilled cheese again, though neither she nor her uncle had eaten much.

The car was a giant black SUV, no clumps of filthy ice daring to cling to its gleaming sides or pristine mudguards. It paused on the other side of the sidewalk near the garden gate, white puffs idling from its hindquarters though its lower half vanished under a tiny mountain range of packed white freeze. The neighbors' Christmas lights reflected tiny multicolored gleams off its paint.

It looked a little bit like a rhinestone-bedazzled, cigar-chomping dragon smoking from the wrong end; Leo said they used to try to treat drowned people with nicotine-smoke enemas.

A jagged sideways laugh tried to crawl out of Nat's chest. She swallowed it, felt the weird internal bubble that meant she'd given herself hiccups.

Great.

The SUV sat there, but Nat didn't move. The cuckoo clock ticked back and forth. One second she was sure it was all a coincidence, misunderstanding, and a giant practical joke, the next she was sure the big black car would heave away from the curb as soon as she opened the front door. If the gangster wanted her, he'd have to come up the walk.

If he didn't, would Mom die? And was Nat a monster for considering the prospect so calmly, with such a shameful hot feeling of relief?

Finally, a wad of muscle in a suit and a trench coat that matched the car's black gleam slunk out of the front passenger side, closing the door with crisp authority instead of a slam. He looked vaguely military, his gleaming bullet head bearing a high-and-tight waxed to within an inch of its life, and despite the hour he wore mirrored sunglasses.

Apparently for mobsters, cool didn't stop when the sun went down. Those shoulders were amazing, but he looked for all the world like a bear forced into a suit and black coat, standing on its hind legs and faintly discomfited by the pose.

He opened the back passenger door, bowing slightly like an old-timey coachman, and Dmitri flowed from the car like oil. The gangster's boot-toes glistened, his dark hair gleamed, and he wore a knee-length wool coat that had the same vaguely military air as the bear's but was obviously of much higher quality. The gangster immediately ruined the coat's lines by plunging his hands deep in his trouser pockets, and he stepped across the ice-rimed sidewalk with finicky care.

Nat realized she was holding her breath, her pulse pounding in her temples, and let out a sigh.

The garden gate swung inward by itself, like it sometimes did when Mom didn't have a hand free to push it; Dmitri glided up the flagstone walk Leo had shoveled with frequent breaks for schnapps-spiked hot cocoa that short afternoon. Even sprinkled with just the right amount of rock salt—Mom would rather someone fall and break a hip than have too much sodium in her garden, naturally—it was bound to be slippery; the thought of Twinkle Toes landing on his ass cheered Nat up immensely.

She turned sharply from the window, strode across the living room, reached the front door just in time, and jerked it open just as his knuckles were descending for the first knock.

They regarded each other over the threshold. Cold air poured in and Dmitri grinned, his teeth only a shade off from new snow. He looked impossibly vital, impossibly *alive,* just like Baba de Winter.

Just like Mom used to.

Nat's throat was slick and dry as a windshield baking on a dusty summer day. She coughed, hoped she wouldn't hiccup again in the middle of the sentence, and managed to say, "You're late."

"Destiny is always on time, *zaika.*" Under the woolen coat a charcoal suit lurked, tailored to within an inch of its life. The shirt was black silk, and his trouser hems broke beautifully over those boots. A chunky gold watch gleamed on his left wrist, but his hands—fingers oddly delicate, yet strong enough to strangle—were bare of any ring.

He really needs a diamond on that pinkie. "I expected Mrs. de Winter to come too."

"Oh, you wouldn't want her here, at charming little house. I am much nicer." He took her in from hat to toes, and his eyebrows arched. His accent was indeed very much like Leo's. "That? Is what you're wearing?"

"Of course." Nat pushed down a deep flare of annoyance. "I didn't know what to—"

"Does nothing for you. Well, come on." A peremptory beckoning motion with one of those buffed, manicured hands. Even his tie was expensive, a faint purple tinge to its deep black. At least he wasn't tanning-bed orange or leathery; all in all, this guy was handsome as could be expected for a criminal. "We have time. The party doesn't get started until midnight."

Midnight? "Party?" In other words, she wanted more details before she stepped outside, and Nat folded her arms. The heat pump kicked on, soughing warm air through all the vents, and Leo stopped rustling and splashing in the kitchen.

Suddenly, Nat didn't want her uncle anywhere near this man. She made a little shooing motion of her own. "Move. I'm coming out."

"Might want to stay in there, *zaika*." His smile didn't alter one whit. "Let things happen how they should, huh? Only natural, after all."

You mean let my mother die. "Move," she repeated. "I told Mrs. de Winter I'd get this thing she wants, and I'm going to." Maybe she'd end up a drug mule working for a literary gangster queen.

It had to pay better than any job she'd had since she was thirteen, stocking shelves at the Dolla Emporium two streets over because the proprietor knew Mom and didn't bother with things like child labor laws.

"Your funeral." Dmitri took a half-step sideways, the narrow strip of the front porch creaking sharply once under his boots. "Come out and play, little girl."

"My name is Nat." She wasn't hiccupping anymore, but it felt like she had a live coal lodged somewhere under her breastbone. No amount of water—or milk with radishes, which Leo swore by— would make it go away; she would just have to find a quiet corner, close her eyes, and try to summon a burp.

"Is it Natasha or Natalya? You can tell Dmitri." Was he actually trying to sound cajoling?

Dream on, dude. Everyone wanted to know her full name, and all of them could go piss up a rope. "Just Nat."

"You should be nicer to me." His tone turned caressing, as oily as the gleam on the big black car's paint. "I would be very good to you."

"Oh, yeah. And there's a bridge you'd like to sell me, I bet. Goes right over the Hudson, only slightly used." Nat stepped decisively over the threshold, pulling the door closed. Her house key—the only one she carried, with a plain silver ring and a leather tab bearing Leo's careful stamping—was in her peacoat pocket, and she took her time throwing the lock.

Just to be sure.

The gangster loomed disturbingly close, and the edge of his body heat was far warmer than it should have been. Nat didn't want her back to him, and almost whapped him with her elbow as she turned. There wasn't a lot of room on the porch, and he was taking up most of it.

He smelled of tobacco and faint lemony aftershave, but under it was an edge of burning not quite like cigarettes. A metallic tang of snow, as if he'd been outside a lot longer than the walk to her front door, and she wondered if he'd been around the corner or across the street watching until the SUV showed up.

The mental image of him lurking in a doorway, grinning with that sharp good humor while passers-by shivered and turned up their collars, was unexpectedly vivid. Still, she indicated the front steps. "Well, lead the way."

"Lady goes first."

Now I definitely don't want my back to you. Nat took refuge in stubborn silence, as if Mom was trying to get her to drink beet juice again.

It is good for you, Natchenka. Come, for Mama.

Not even that blandishment could force her to down beet-blood. It reeked of iron, and there was always fine gritty dirt that lodged between your teeth no matter how well-washed the bulbs grubbed up from the garden were.

That was the final component to the gangster's scent, Nat decided. Cold earth, opened up.

Like a grave.

She shuddered, tried to quell the movement with little success. His smile widened. Apparently Dmitri was having a grand old time.

"Cautious little girl. Very well." He flowed down the stairs; they didn't screamsqueak under him like they would for a salesman.

Mom hated door-to-door, even the kids working their way through college.

Nat followed Dmitri's broad back down the flagstone path, her boots crunching on salt, and her stomach turned over, hard. The gate was still open, and when she was clear it gave a groan and swung to, latching with a snap like tiny bones.

Oh, God. A flash of pain bit behind her heart, and Nat had to take another cold, cold breath.

She had a deep, unsettling feeling she might never see the yellow house—or Leo—again. Maybe she was wrong.

But it was the same pressure behind her eyes and breastbone that made her blurt out a warning to Sister Roberta Grace Abiding; the urge to turn around, plow through the gate, flee into the house, and lock every door and window shook her like the cold.

Just think about making Mom better, or at least making the hospice bills de Winter's problem. Focus on that.

The bear held the door for her, a pair of tiny Nats shivering on his mirrored lenses. She climbed into warmth and the smell of leather, and the molten bubble behind her breastbone vanished.

There was no turning back.

SO VIOLENT, SO FAIR

The SUV must've had expensive shocks, because it barely rocked on the worst parts of South Aurora before heading northwest. The leather interior was almost tropical, too, and the driver—another bear, only slightly smaller than the one in the passenger seat but without mirrored lenses covering his eyes, for which Nat was unendingly grateful—took them over the bridge onto the island. Nat stared out the window, uncomfortably warm in her peacoat, sweater, and hat; it would have taken her forever to ride the bus or, God forbid, walk this far.

Blocks flashed by, lights turning green almost as soon as they approached, and they didn't even get stuck behind any lumbering plows or salters. Brooklyn Bridge should have been a solid stream of brake lights reflecting off ice, wet slush, and damp automobiles, but apparently it was one of those odd traffic moments—cars behaving more like particles in a cloud than self-respecting automobiles with places to be—that only happened in movies or when nobody was around to take advantage of them. Manhattan glittered, the skyline beautiful if you didn't know what lived underneath its jeweled crust. A helicopter veered sharply overhead, police or news impossible to tell, and the SUV aimed farther north as if they were heading to Soho.

Finally, Tamlin Street swallowed them, and Nat's unease hit cosmic levels. Getting home from here was easy, but she didn't like the subway at this hour. Nor did she like this particular slice of town; the streets alternated between tony gentrification and dire *you don't want to be here after dusk*, sometimes changing in the middle of the block. It reminded her of bubbling yeast right after the ancient starter in the earthenware kitchen crock was fed.

Tamlin was one of the gentrified avenues, and the big black vehicle slid to a soft stop before a row of tiny, hideously expensive boutiques, their windows glowing with the hungry golden light of *you can't afford this*. Baba de Winter's mobster glanced at her, his eyebrows twitching once. He grinned like he was having a good time, reaching for the door on his side.

Nat didn't wait for anyone to grab hers, sliding across the seat, spilling into freezing air, and landing on ice her boots were thankfully well equipped to handle before skirting the back of the SUV and hopping the mound of plowed snow, landing on pavement with a jolt. The cold was a relief from the car's close confines, and Dmitri shook his sleek dark head.

"Don't you know how to treat a gentleman, *zaika*?"

If you were one, I'd've waited. Nat restrained the urge to say it *or* cross her arms defensively. Instead, she just studied him; even in the tailored suit and expensive coat he still bore a heavy five o'clock scruff. The effect wasn't bad, she supposed, but the way his eyes gleamed would warn anyone with half an ounce of sense that he wasn't a manicured, cellophane-wrapped trust-fund broker or banker wandering around unsupervised.

All she got for her restraint was a shrug, and the turning of his black-clad back as he stepped through a fortuitously placed break in the knee-high mountain range of shoveled-aside snow already solidifying into glacial immobility. The bear with the mirrored lenses slammed the rear passenger door, giving Nat what she could swear was a reproachful look, and she hurried after Dmitri.

The small hand-painted signs in the shop window said *Atelier '39* and *Closed* in antique, ornate curlicues, but Dmitri turned the crystal knob-handle and walked right in, a tiny golden bell overhead giving a soft sweet forlorn tinkle. It certainly didn't look like a party.

In fact, it looked just like what it said on the package: a designer boutique, recessed spotlights shining down like the movie versions of alien abductions highlighting faceless black mannequins draped in glittering outfits. Nat had to blink several times, her eyes watering; the clothes fluttered lazily on warm drafts, edges and seams twist-fraying like clay under fast water. The floor was mellow hardwood polished to a satin shine, and there was no sign of a cash register—if you were worried about what anything cost, you clearly shouldn't be shopping here. A few black velvet love seats lurked where rich women could sit and be fawned on while they decided what to hang on their expensively dieted stick-skinniness, and there was a crystalline glass case against the back wall full of sharp hurtful spears of jewelry refraction.

Nat made sure the door was closed, wondering if she should dig for her phone and surreptitiously check the closest rideshares. She heard a soft rushing like a subway's arrival without the screeching of brakes, and when she turned back there was a slim graceful shadow standing before Dmitri.

Tall, arms crossed, and completely sheathed in black—a scoop-neck cashmere sweater and tailored wool slacks breaking over sharp-toed stiletto heels that were four inches if they were a millimeter—the woman eyed Dmitri from behind a pair of black cat's-eye glasses with a single rhinestone on each flaring tip. Maybe the sparkles were diamonds; the rest of her certainly looked like she could afford it. Her nails were crimson talons much like Baba's or Mom's a few years ago, kohl rimmed her pale, oddly colorless eyes, and her platinum updo was either natural or so expensively dyed it made no difference.

"Sign says closed, Dima." Her voice was a pleasant burr, sliding between lips as candy-apple as her nails but far more matte. "I know you can read something other than Cyrillic. Besides, you're late."

"I can tell Baba you refused, Gabi." Dmitri tilted his head in Nat's direction. "And take this little girl somewhere else for a rag."

That strange colorless gaze swung to Nat.

The woman pushed past him, her hands dropping to her sides. "Oh." She took three steps, halted, and flat-out stared. "Oh, Dima. I forgive, I forgive you *everything*." A faint hint of an accent touched the words, but not like his. This was softer, throatier, the *r*'s burred and the words losing their endings. "Look at that. The bones, the coloring . . . oh, she looks like—"

"Now will you be helpful?" Dmitri turned on his heel, looking past the woman with a wolfish grin. "Says her name's *just Nat,* won't answer any questions."

"Then she's wiser than most. Answering a man's questions is boring." The woman's hands fluttered at her sides, clawlike nails gleaming. "Come in, *enfante,* come in. Just look at you. We must get you out of those rags, *n'est-ce pas?*"

Nat dug deep into her store of high school French, her wet boots squeaking as she stepped forward and offered her hand the way Mom did when she genuinely liked someone. "*Enchanté, madame. Merci.*"

"And so polite, too!" The woman clapped her hands. "It is Coco to you, my darling, and Dima, go fetch us some champagne. Where are you taking her, Jay's?"

"Of course. Baba's request."

The woman in black absorbed this, nodding as her gaze continued devouring of Nat inch by inch. "And she's . . ."

"The daughter." Dmitri's lip didn't curl, and Nat had the sudden woozy certainty that *this* woman knew her mother, too.

What other secrets was Maria Drozdova hiding? Maybe, just maybe, she hadn't been cruelly flattening her daughter's imagination, or even lying. Maybe Mom had been trying, strange as it sounded, to actually protect Nat from this?

It was, she supposed, just barely possible. It sounded like some bullshit from a Victorian book about orphans or secret gardens, but Mom had sent her to a woman named *de Winter,* after all.

"Ah, now I see." Coco clasped Nat's hand, a cool, tender touch. "Such skin. Oh, we will make you *très belle, enfante,* you'll be the toast of the party. Such a shame about your mother."

Oh, God, you probably think she's already dead. "Yes," Nat said numbly. There was a strange humming in the other woman's touch, the blurring buzz of a power transformer sleeping on a dusty summer afternoon, deadly voltage dream-humming under a metal carapace. "Do you know her?"

"I knew *of* her, of course; I'm just old, not dead. Come, come." She tugged at Nat's coat, pulling her past Dmitri. "Dima, I told you to go fetch champagne; it's boring to repeat myself."

"Champagne." He rolled his eyes, that sharklike smile widening, and headed for the door. "Don't take all night, Coco."

"Evil man," Coco said, *sotto voce* but not very. "He'll bring us something nice, though. Not like that terrible Corleone, with his filthy fingernails."

"*Don't* mention him." A snarl rode under Dmitri's tone. "I'll be back in time to see you undress, *zaika*."

"Pay no attention." Coco claimed Nat's arm and all but dragged her past the glass case. A heavy maroon velvet curtain next to it rippled enticingly; she pushed it aside as the bell over the door jangled again. "Men, all beasts and children, and he's no different. Take that coat off, *chère*, and let us see what we have."

I am not nearly skinny enough for this. "I, uh, don't have any—"

"Don't insult Coco by mentioning money, *enfante*, it's so boring. Green, I think, like your mother . . . or was that her cousin? But a different green. They were so violent, and you are so fair."

The atelier's back room was as cheerfully crowded as the front was bare simplicity. Bolts of fabric all but leapt from cubbyholes, sewing machines—some antique, others brand new—hummed as they worked, and Nat's breath left her in a rush.

There was nobody at the machines. Fabric gathered, bunched, and was stabbed with bright needles; heavy wooden tables past the rows of humming activity stood stolid, cloth under gleaming metal shears cut into strange shapes and whisked away as soon as the last thread was snipped. Scraps fluttered on warm breezes, flocking together by size, and either vanished into a small, deadly black hole in the wall or were whisked to progressively smaller cubbies receding into infinity, snuggling home like dogs into warm kennels.

This place must take up the whole block, Nat thought, and the swimming unreality of seeing something impossible wasn't the problem.

No, the problem was how familiar it felt. *You and your imagination, Natchenka,* her mother would say, wearily. Why? *Why* would she keep lying, over and over, to her own daughter?

Whatever else this was, it was also *real*. And terrifying.

"It's beautiful," Nat breathed. "It's . . . magic?" *Please don't laugh at me. Please don't let it be a practical joke.*

"Of course it is, *chère*." Coco laughed, a bright trilling sound with the rhythm of a flashing needle underneath. "Even better, it is *fashion*, and you will be *élégante*. I can tell already; it is in the bones. Come, the private dressing room. We must try one or two before we find the right color. Don't worry about Dima, I won't let him peek."

If magic was real, a peeking gangster was, Nat suspected, suddenly the absolute least of her worries. She began to clumsily unbutton the peacoat, and Coco hurried her through another door.

A GIVING MOOD

The rehoboam of Veuve Clicquot was his own special little joke, and Dima could barely wait to bite it open and make the *zaika* shriek with pleasant fear. Coco's shop enfolded him in its humming bath of power—quite acceptable in its own way, even if it was merely woman's magic. Still, all his many nephews liked to dress well, and it did a man good to have an appropriately feathered *devotchka* on his arm.

This girl was a little whey-faced and sickly, though who wouldn't be under Mashenka's thumb? Far more intriguing was the fact that she seemed utterly and boringly naïve, but that was all to the good so far as his plans were concerned.

The unwary were easier prey.

Coco didn't have the girl in the front dressing rooms, so he passed through the workroom with only a single glance at the dancing shears, the rattling machines—one of which popped bright colorless sparks from its interior when it noticed his gaze; he showed his teeth in return. The silver needles would be uncomfortable if they hit anything vital, but only the belief in them could truly wound.

Even a child might poke a hole in divinity, given a sharp enough blade.

The fashionista had taken the girl through the low door, down a short hall with an ebony floor—oh, a mortal might think it merely grimy or old, but Dima knew quality when he saw it, a thief's instinct for the best—and between two pillars made of the same stuff. The threshold was a strip of worn stone, but its reflection at the top glowed golden—either a tear in the illusion, or more likely, one of Coco's little jokes.

Women. They were all in league, and this one gilded the trap for others.

Dmitri stepped through, the silver caps on his toes giving one vicious twinkle, and a ripple passed through him. The marks on his back, his arms, his chest, his knees—ink forced under the skin with handmade implements, everything done the old way in a dank malodorous prison cell or the hush of a tavern's back room, bamboo biting or electricity buzzing—ran like little mice, and his muscles twinged for a bare moment.

"Lift your arms," a cooing alto said in the dimness, and Dima hefted the bottle, smiling broadly, prepared for a cry or two when he rounded the corner to see some *déshabillé*.

Instead, he stepped into bright golden glare and stopped, his toes placed catlike-precise and his mouth open to deliver a slightly sarcastic remark.

Coco stepped back, one half of her bright crimson mouth starred with silver pins, and nodded sharply. "Yes," the other half said. "Oh, yes, *chère enfante*. Just a little longer."

The *zaika* was in three-quarter profile, gazing at her twin in a limpid, shining full-length mirror. Her hair hung in honeyed waves to the middle of her back, ripples remembering the braid it had been twisted into, and the cloud looked very soft. Seen from this angle she was a statue in a neoclassical garden, wide dark eyes and proud nose over a flower-mouth, a vision suddenly uncovered by an ambling visitor.

The dress was green, but not just any green. It held none of the pale gold of cold early spring, or the bright cheerfulness of fir tips after the first soft rains and less-than-icy nights. Instead, shade after shade of tender new growth crowded against valleys of old, rippling forested hillsides teeming as they clung to the girl's curves, now free of the shapeless peacoat and jeans that did nothing for her.

Her spread arms, innocent of any tan, were nevertheless dusted with the faintest hint of gold and smoothly muscled; she held them in a ballet frame like a good little girl, though her remote expression suggested the pose was uncomfortable. The dress was a Directoire revival of a classical peplos, and the sway of heavy silken drape managed to show and reveal at the same time. No dainty sandals—if there had been, he might have liked it a little more. Instead, low Cuban heels the color of pines baking on a bright slope peered from under the hem.

"What I wouldn't give for some absinthe grosgrain," Coco continued in her singsong, tapping the sweet curve of the *zaika*'s hip. "But here, gold . . . no, not that shade."

The ribbon uncurling from her crimson fingertips obediently shifted color, wrapping serpentine over the hillock; Dima suddenly envied a scrap of cloth with quite uncharacteristic intensity. Even the girl's fingers were a little different—Coco had applied the faintest blush to buffed, smoothed nails, pink pussywillows just dying to be stroked.

His own fingers twitched, and the rehoboam almost slipped free. Dmitri closed his mouth with a snap, leaned against the doorway's left pillar, and watched.

"We'll curl your hair, but leave most of it down." Coco coaxed the ribbon into a knot. "Such a nice color too. Just like sun through a jar of buckwheat honey. Oh, your mother was never this beautiful, *chère*, I can tell you for a fact."

"I've seen pictures." The *zaika*'s voice was hushed, a husky toe-curling purr. "I think I got the nose from my dad, though."

There was an interesting question. Who had Masha selected for that duty? Dmitri set the thought aside for further brooding. It was always best to enjoy what was in front of you.

For a little while, at least.

Coco's laugh was a brush of warm fur. "Lucky, lucky man."

"I wouldn't know." Did she sound sad, the little girl? "She doesn't talk about him."

Well, that was to be expected. Dima considered lighting a cigarette, but neither woman seemed aware of him. It was probably a pose on Coco's part, but the idea of watching this fresh new divinity while she was unaware was unexpectedly . . . appetizing.

"Of course not." Coco nodded, one of the pins shifting in her mouth and the crimson on her lips deepening just a fraction. "You're all she could have wanted, and more. I would scold her, if she . . . well, this would be easier if she'd brought you before."

"I can't imagine her getting anything designer." Was it a faint touch of sadness? "She's all about saving money. Thrifty, you know."

"Pfft. As if that's a problem for *us*." Coco straightened, a line appearing between her manicured eyebrows. "Arms down. Very good. Now the hair. Stand very still, *chère bébé*."

"I'm trying." The girl hadn't sounded this relaxed or amused with Baba, or with him, and Dmitri's envy took on a darker edge. It was ridiculous—she was just a silly little *zaika* for the pot, so who cared? He certainly shouldn't be measuring every other word he'd heard from her against this soft levity. "What do you mean, for us?"

"I wonder your *Maman* didn't . . . ah, interfering is boring." Crimson-tipped nails plunged into the girl's honeyed mane. "Coco's job is the soap bubble, the luxury, the little things that make life worth living. Just like Dima's job is to be a greedy little boy."

Well, *that* couldn't be borne. "The greedy little boy can hear you." His own tone dripped boredom. "Perhaps you don't want what I brought, then?"

The girl stiffened, Coco tongue-clicked in disapproval. "Stay *still*, or I will pull."

"She means it," Dima added. "The *zaika* looks nice, Madame. Not to my taste, but at least not embarrassing. We need glasses, unless you want to drink straight from the bottle."

"*Not embarrassing*, he says." Coco's eyes narrowed, and she freed one slender hand enough to snap, a sharp whipcrack of sound. The girl flinched, the champagne cork popped free to sail across the room like a bullet, and flying alcoholic froth just barely missed Dima's suit because he arched away like a surprised cat. "Pour for the ladies, *mon petit voleur*. Try to display a *little* class."

"Just a little, since you ask so nice." Dima's fingers tingled. It was so easy, especially with more than one of their kind in a confined space. The air itself hummed with readiness, like a well-paid lover. Three champagne flutes built themselves from wishes and longing, crystal ringing high thin notes as it settled into the perfect shape, and he was mildly irked that Masha's daughter didn't bother to watch the miracle being worked.

Instead, she held very still while Coco's claws plunged into her hair again, and a faint sheen of gem-bright sweat showed on the slim column of her throat.

For now, it was enough. Coco hummed, accepting a filled glass of Cliquot with queenly indifference, but the girl tried to shake her head.

Dima grabbed her wrist, expecting that same spike of pain jolting up his arm. But maybe she was too stunned to resist, because it was a mere warning rattle, an unpleasant buzz as he pressed her warm fingers around cold crystal.

He'd even chilled the flutes, because he was in a giving mood. "Don't waste it." Each word edged with just a little bit of disdain. "See? I'm much nicer than Baba. You should remember that."

"I remember everything." A glare from under those long dark lashes.

Dima retreated to the door. He didn't swill from the bottle—he was in a good mood, wasn't he? Especially when Coco bustled off muttering about a wrap, her glass refilling with bubbling alcohol and ribbon trimmings floating snakelike in her wake.

He dangled the large bottle by its neck, taking a long hit off his own glass and enjoying the subtle sound of its refill, the trails of bubbles lining up the insides, the delicacy required to translate liquid from one space to another. The girl touched her bottom lip—now just barely reddened, a subtle stain—to her own glass, but didn't drink.

"You think I poison you?" Dima throttled the urge to slurp. Playing the crude buffoon was only fun when you *didn't* feel like one.

"I know better than to drink in fairy tales," she replied, darkly.

Maybe she wasn't joking, either. Because while he wheezed with laughter, his vision blurring with hot water as his nose tingled with the champagne's breath, she simply regarded him with those great dark solemn eyes.

THE
KNIFE

GUTS FOR SHOELACES

A magical dress and a gangster's car; maybe both would vanish at midnight, leaving her stranded in Long Island. But what really unsettled her was the even, endless inevitability of the ride—maybe all traffic jams were caused by cars like this punching through holes between other vehicles, pulling the road's fabric into bunching behind them.

It wasn't quite snowing, but the headlights made a bright cone full of tiny speckles before the high-backed, gliding car. The SUV crossed the Queensboro Bridge in full defiance of evening rush hour, turned north and east, and wallowed through plenty of curves and turns. Here, the streetlamps were well maintained even though far apart. At certain intervals a wall would rear on one side of the road or the other, generally flaring into an oversized wrought-iron or heavy wooden gate set just far enough from the road to mutter *don't press the button unless you have business here*, each guarded by a stubby intercom post set inconveniently far from a driver's window.

Some gates had blinking multicolored lights or even weatherproof tinsel. One particularly large, vulgar specimen had what looked like custom reindeer antlers fastened to its top curve, which gave Nat a shudder.

Dmitri lounged in the back passenger seat, thankfully not drinking anymore. The big-ass bottle of champagne was left with Coco, who had gravely kissed Nat on both cheeks and trilled *très belle, très belle, remember who dressed you tonight, darling* before shooing them out, Nat terrified the pretty green heels were going to slip on snow and ice.

But they didn't. They grabbed just like boots, and the only thing she had to worry about was minor calf pain. The heels were only an inch high, sure, but that was enough to grant any wearer a backache. Even the wrap was perfect, heavy green watered silk a few shades darker than the dress, startlingly warm and very soft, covering her bare arms and ingeniously buttoned down the left side.

She hadn't realized that her actual clothes—including her beloved combat boots—were gone until the car was halfway down the block. They, and her backpack, were left behind a sable curtain while Coco chivvied her into whisper-light silken underthings probably sewed by invisible hands. The tiny jeweled emerald-green clutch Coco had produced held Nat's ID, her prepaid cell with a few minutes still left for the month, her house key, and the twenty for emergency cab fare—but out here, could she get a signal? And a twenty wasn't going to cut it. Even a rideshare would cost a small fortune, assuming someone would take the job.

Here she was, at night, in a car with three strange men, dressed like . . . she couldn't even say what it was like. And not even Leo knew where she was.

Stories beginning this way always ended badly.

Nat snuck a glance at Dmitri. The gangster was watching her in return, his wide toothy smile full of sharp, cheerful implications. "Don't worry." The grin faded, degree by degree, as hilly fields behind a split-rail fence undulated outside his window. "I promised Baba. You are safe as little baby chick under hen."

Oh, I doubt that. "Is she your grandmother too?"

"What?" A swift snarl crossed his face, peeling back the handsomeness for a second, and Nat's breath caught in her throat. "*Nyet, zaika,* and anyone else say that, I take their guts for shoelaces."

I thought it was guts for garters. But even years of soaking in English couldn't ferret out the ghost of a mother tongue underneath. Leo and Mom both had a few sayings that were just a shade off-center, though perfectly appropriate. "I just wondered."

"Stupid. But you're pretty, so it doesn't matter." His fingers flickered on his knee, then he stirred, digging in a breast pocket.

For a moment Nat was mortally sure he was going to pull out a weapon.

Instead, he produced a battered white pack of cigarettes with red-and-black Cyrillic splashed across dingy cardboard, the letters crumpling when she tried to read them. He tapped up a black-wrapped cylinder with a gold band, offered it in her general direction.

"No thanks." *And it's rude to smoke in a car with someone else.* She refrained from adding as much with an almost physical effort.

Were his tailored jacket or well-hemmed trousers made by invisible fingers, too?

He shrugged, stuck the filtered end in his mouth, and the smokes disappeared into their dark little home. "Baba's old, *da*." The snarl vanished, and his sensitive fingers flicked again. A red-hot spot dilated on the end of the cigarette and he inhaled, deeply. "She is Winter, and a grandmother to many. But I tell you something."

Nat braced herself for acrid smoke and started looking for the window controls. Instead, a heavy, almost spicy scent filled the air when Dmitri inhaled, and the white vapor from burning tip and exhalation vanished almost immediately. It didn't sting her eyes, and she didn't immediately feel like an asthma attack followed by lung cancer was inevitable.

"She endures, and they all fear a northern winter," Dmitri continued, each word accompanied with a faint smoky puff. The heavy accent changed, became almost lilting. "But me? I was born the first moment some bastard took what they shouldn't. And that was long, long before the monkeys walked upright."

Uh, okay. Nat punched the window button and privacy-tinted glass rolled down. Cold air poured in; the SUV slowed. A blank concrete wall loomed on her side, veined with cables of ancient ivy, leaves glittering in icy filigree. The brakes grabbed, and when she looked back, there was a concrete wall carefully shaped to resemble masonry out Dmitri's window too. He examined her, the mocking smile in place and the red tip of the cigarette bobbing.

"You're all nuts," she muttered. But what could you expect from fairy tales and magic? The normal world Mama was so insistent on had weighed anchor and sailed away; Nat was stranded . . . here, wherever *here* was.

The worst thing was the feeling of complete familiarity. But why would her mother keep saying, all those years—

The car slowed further, banking to the left like a small plane. Nat leaned forward, peering at their destination.

A pair of giant metal gates stood invitingly wide, sparkling like the icy ivy. Giant ornate initials—*J G*—were tangled in the bars, but the lower right chunk of the *G* had been chipped away. The wound looked fresh, which was the only reason you could tell it wasn't another letter, an *O* or a *C*. There was a slight bump, and the faint vibration of packed, ridged ice under the tires turned smooth as glass. A wide black driveway cut between snow-crusted bushes clipped into fantastical shapes, recessed floodlights dyeing them brilliant colors. The effect was a candy-shaded wonderland, blue and green and pink and yellow, splashes of vivid red at intervals just frequent enough to be not quite random.

The driveway seemed to go on forever, and no snow clung to its ruler-crisp edges. Finally, it broadened into a swooping circle around a vast, glittering pile of confectionary sugar and lacy metal—a frozen fountain, or the skeleton of one that had been misted with a hose and left to shiver into lacework. More colored light played over its dry arms, throbbed in its heart, and the glow strangely didn't look like floodlights.

Maybe it was waterproof LEDs, caught in the ice like tiny sugared fireflies.

The house was three stories and lit like the trees hauled yearly into Times Square, every window golden-aglow. The architect—assuming there was one and not just a collection of coked-up Hollywood producers whipping set designers into a frenzy—clearly couldn't decide between French château, rococo revival, Seven Gables, or Italianate whatever. Still, the structure managed to retain a coherent message, and it was one Leo would have translated as *more money than sense*, with some swear words thrown in between syllables to really get the point across.

Shadows moved against the gold. The massive double front doors were wide open too, a glittering throng crowding up red-carpeted stairs—actual *red carpet* on a short but very wide swoop of granite steps. Between every massive ground floor window, ice-frosted topiaries jeweled with those confectionary lights reared in whimsical shapes, some animal, others geometric. Starbursts of white flashbulb came from somewhere, a seizure-inducing imitation of paparazzi.

"Shiny, eh?" More white vapor curled through Dmitri's nose, a dragon contemplating a treasure pile. The cigarette didn't seem to ash, though it shrank and the baleful red gleam at its end moved closer to his mouth when he inhaled. He pursed his lips and a perfect smoke ring bloomed, right before his words distorted it. "You like?"

"My God," she managed. "It's obscene."

Dmitri found that funny. At least he laughed, producing far more of that incense-scented smoke than he could have possibly drawn lungward, and the SUV joined the end of a slowly moving line—cars of every description, a stretch limousine the exact color of the strawberry stripe in Neapolitan ice cream, a carriage that looked like a silver pumpkin drawn by four champing, stamping white horses who shouldn't have been out on a night like this, an actual honest-to-gosh *sleigh,* its runners resting against the black driveway in absolute defiance of rationality. She couldn't quite see what was pulling it, and part of Nat was very, very glad about that when she glimpsed the mass of heaped furs it carried, a somber triangular white face with a coal-black, burning-vivid gaze swiveling atop a scrawny pale neck.

Nat sank back into the seat and shut her own aching, smarting eyes. *It's all true,* she thought again, deliriously. *All of it. Everything I ever saw.*

It was a relief to find out she wasn't crazy. What was *not* a relief was wondering why her mother had lied all Nat's life. And what, exactly, Baba de Winter was sending her to fetch.

Dmitri's laughter trailed off in fits and starts. The SUV crept forward, but Nat kept her eyes shut until the steady motion stopped and the smell of his strange cigarette was cut off between one moment and the next.

"Time to play, *zaika*." Maybe he sounded kind, or merely, savagely indifferent. "Come meet the family."

COMPLIMENTARY

Athrob-driving tune she couldn't quite place poured through the foyer. The immediate effect was dangerous lunacy—a crush of riotous color atop black and white marble squares, a haze of sweet-smelling smoke with only the faintest acridity of burning tobacco or skunk-edged weed, stairs leading up, a giant grandfather clock complete with ponderous, polished pendulum crouched at the far end, any tick, tock, or chime lost in the babble.

The long-legged woman who took Nat's wrap was tall, blonde, and dressed in what looked like a black swimsuit and stringy fishnets, black four-inch stilettos like Coco's, and was also wearing the best set of soft brownish costume rabbit ears Nat had ever seen. Or they were *real*, because they twitched as she handed Nat a small brass tab with a strange symbol etched on its burnished face. Even the inside of the ears—bright pink, with tiny dark veins—looked absolutely solid, detailed, and legitimate.

A swimming sense of must-be-dreaming threatened to tip Nat off her own shoes and onto the tessellated floor.

"Thank you, ma'am," the bunny-girl chirped with a twitch of her pert little freckled nose, and took off into the crowd. Perfectly perched on the swell of her buttocks was a fluffy cotton tail, just where you'd expect.

Several more bunny-girls circulated through the crush of fantastical costumes, but they were a minority compared to the ones wearing soft triangular cat ears in couth shades just a bit off their hair colors, long lithe tails twitching as they stalked on heels sharp enough to qualify as weapons.

Dmitri shrugged out of his long coat and gave it, plus a meaningful look, to a cadaverous gray-haired man in a butler's funereal suit. "Jeeves. You're looking well."

"Thank you, sir." The butler's snow-white shirt covered a concave chest. It looked like the front half of his ribs had been removed, and his white-gloved hands had more than the usual number of fingers. The phalanges were too long and thin, an extra knuckle in each, and Nat looked hurriedly away.

Invisible seamstresses were easier. You could call it a bad special effect, or something with wires. But this . . .

There were more butlers circulating through the crowd as well, half-chested, bland faces set as if they smelled something awful, gliding softly on polished wingtips and occasionally bending like clockwork toys to pick up a fallen or discarded article. The guests—if the word applied—magnanimously ignored the staff, except for the cadaverous black-suited waiters bearing silver trays loaded with what had to be alcoholic liquid in chiming crystal glasses of every shape and size.

There was a *lot* of drinking going on. A pair of massive staircases swooped upward, music pouring from the golden arch where they met; on either side of the foyer's keyhole-shaped floor, dimly lit hallways receded with rustling whispers and half-seen shapes in glittering dresses or natty evening suits.

"Don't go down there," Dmitri said, his hand closing around her left arm. "That's for the unformed."

"Unformed?" She sounded like an idiot, but who wouldn't, faced with this?

"Need a little more time in the oven," he muttered. Then, a little louder, "Where's Baba, *dvoretskiy?*"

The butler's blank eyes—pale blue, but otherwise startlingly reminiscent of poached eggs—blinked blearily at him. "Up there, sir." He indicated the crowded stairs. Not many people were moving, she realized; most were standing and taking hits off whatever tumbler or glass they held, chattering brightly at each other while they peered upward or smoked.

It was too much booze for just standing around. Dmitri nodded and set off, which meant she had to as well or be ignominiously dragged. He headed straight up the middle of the left-hand staircase, paying no attention to the shining throng on either side; they parted like a river around a stubborn rock. A few whispered behind their hands, like a woman with a black asymmetrical bob bearing a striking resemblance to an action-movie actress Uncle Leo particularly liked or the squat, toad-like, pasty man who smiled broadly when he caught Nat's gaze, his eyes dancing with golden twinkles and his suit matching, the exact shade of fresh deep wheat. His teeth were blackened stumps behind pale rubbery lips, and he bowed deeply in Dmitri's direction.

The gangster didn't even appear to notice, but his hand tightened on Nat's arm. "Don't encourage them," he muttered. "If they think you can help, you'll never get rid of bastards. Eyes up, *zaika*."

He sounded just like Mama telling young Nat not to give spare change to beggars. *They'll take everything you have. Don't even look.*

How could you not, though? Suffering demanded empathy, no matter how hard-boiled you pretended to be. "Whose house is this?" She had to almost yell over the rapidly swelling music; Coco's heels clung to the steps here, too, instead of slipping.

At least the stairs weren't made out of glass, and there weren't twelve princesses with worn-out shoes.

"Does it matter?" Dmitri snagged a champagne flute off a passing butler's tray, turning almost sideways as he continued rapidly up the stairs. "Here. Drink. Good for you." He all but shoved it into her hand, rescued a squat amber-glass tumbler from yet another passing butler—where on earth did they all *come* from, and what was wrong with their ribs?

The questions kept walloping her. Nat would think she was adjusting, but another strangeness would appear and *wham,* all the breath left her metaphorical lungs and she was left gasp-blinking and perplexed.

The golden arch at the top of the stairs was flanked by two identical bruisers in black turtlenecks, hip-length jackets tailored over shoulder holsters, and black trousers as well as those funny little earpieces she'd only seen in movies. Instead of eyes or sunglasses,

mirrored lenses grew out of their cheekbones—blank, slightly con-
vex, fitting perfectly into the socket—and vanished into their eyebrows, the transition so gradual and natural-looking Nat's knees
turned even gooshier. The light green liquid in her flute sloshed, her
stomach cramped, and Dmitri smiled, bright white teeth gleaming.

"Well, nephews," he barked, "this is the *devotchka*'s first time,
eh? Show some respect."

"Mr. Konets." The one on the right bowed, and Nat was too un-
nerved to be happy about the fact that she wasn't being towed along
anymore. A rippling mutter went down the fantastic costumes on
the stairs, an almost-hungry buzz. "And . . ." The mirrored gaze
came to rest on Nat.

The one on the left had bent too, a perfectly choreographed
movement. ". . . Drozdova," he finished, and Nat realized the eye-
mirrors weren't showing what was in front of them. There was no
tiny Dmitri or pale Nat in green clutching a glass of useless, similarly green liquor. No, some other scene was reflected on those
silver oblongs, chips of white confetti falling and lights flashing, a
corpse lying broken on a tar-black road leading to infinity. "Honored to have you, ma'am. Won't you please . . ."

". . . come in?" the one on the right said as he straightened. There
shouldn't have been room for the crowd, these two huge men,
Dmitri, and Nat on this landing, but somehow it happened.

The left spoke up again. "Everything here is . . ."

". . . complimentary," the right finished. "Enjoy the party."

Tweedledee and Tweedledum, only with guns. Nat could find absolutely nothing to say out of all the words she had accumulated since
childhood.

Dmitri laughed and started forward. Nat was swept through the
arch into a flood of bright jazz, golden light somehow managing
to retain the intimacy of candleflames, and steady motion. She
snapped a glance over her shoulder, and it was impossible—from
this side, the door wasn't an arch but another keyhole, the foyer's
shape echoed vertically. There was a strange dropping sensation
right where her diaphragm should be; her lungs and legs struggled

to catch up, like stepping over the unexpected variance between an old house's rooms because the foundation had shifted.

Dmitri slung the cargo of his tumbler far back into his throat, exhaled sharply, and tossed the glass down, hard. It shattered with a high tinkle, melding with a stinging hi-hat and a horn holding a long note trembling on the edge of a screech; the dancers on ballroom floors spreading like petals from the central landing and keyhole door didn't condescend to notice. Feathers exploded, glitter swirling through the air, and Nat's eyelids fluttered too, chopping the moving throng into bullet-sized pieces.

She was beginning to think all of this was a mistake when a deep, soft tenor laugh wrapped around her.

"Daisy!" a man called, and a pair of large, warm, very expensively manicured hands grabbed her shoulders.

DEEPEST WELL OF ALL

He'd never brought arm candy to one of Jay's parties before, and Dmitri found he liked the attention. Of course Coco wouldn't have let the girl out her boutique door without doing the absolute best she could; when Fashion had quality raw material to work with, the result was a stunner.

Still, even Dima Konets wasn't quite prepared for the dapper, well-tanned Pasha of West Egg—in a pale linen summer suit, of course—to descend upon his companion, air-kissing over both her downy cheeks, subtracting the flute from her pretty hand, and whisking her away. Her arm was freed from Dmitri's grasp like a sapling bending on a passing semitruck's slipstream, and as his face congested, a dark spot among the dancing throng whirled to a stop, her weathered cheeks apple-red with exertion and her high-piled now-gray hair twisted with twigs dipped in black iron. Baba's black eyes gleamed too, and her tight-set mouth was painted fresh crimson.

She had laid aside the business suit; instead, a long black dress clung to near-skeletal thinness. Its cuffs frayed over her hands, bone-white fingers peeping through, and the plunging neckline showed décolletage too plump and firm for the rest of her bony frame.

It was, after all, her time of the year. For a moment Dmitri held the old woman's gaze, wondering if she would open her arms for a dance. Perhaps the black hand would descend, maybe on his shoulder, maybe on his nape, and that would be that.

Or maybe it wouldn't, because he was still strong. Stronger than a good many on the dance floor, from *the* Marilynn Harlowe simpering in her white backless dress, her features blurring in approximation of the highest box-office grosser of the month around the famous mole on her upper lip, to the hipster ExperiMental lifting what was definitely not a cigarette to their chiseled lips and remarking offhandedly to a coterie of adoring bubbleheads that they'd done the remix on the number Jay's captive bandmaster was playing upon a giant gleaming pipe organ fastened to the western wall. More wide, brim-stuffed ballrooms stretched in either direction, mirrors reflecting each other, all crowded with fantastical shapes.

The Producer was holding court in a corner behind red ropes, several velvet chaise longues groaning under glittering, translucent figures nodding along with his declamations; by the way his suit was swelling, it looked like a couple of unformed *celebritii* were trying to hive-hatch off soon. Cashe was at one of the bars, surrounded by wasp-waisted goldflies, both warriors and drones pursing their honeyed lips as a hexagonal silver coin spun over bony knuckles; s/he darted a venomous look at Dmitri and motioned for another drink. Nothing would ever take down *that* old horse, and while s/he was around, Dmitri's own position was all but assured.

The crowd stilled in a tiny bubble around him, watching avidly to see if the black hand would show tonight. But Baba merely smiled, sharp white teeth peeking through her crimson lips. "You took her to Coco."

"She was going to wear *jeans*." He beckoned a passing Jeeves and subtracted another whiskey from the proffered tray. "Eating well tonight, Grandmother?"

"None of your business." Her fingers twitched through masses of fraying black thread at her cuffs. Those tiny snakes could bite deep in less than a heartbeat. "Your friend Koschei's in town, Dima. You'd best keep an eye on my granddaughter."

As if it wasn't her idea to bring Maruschka's daughter to be ogled, and start the game. He hadn't known of the sorcerer's return, though, and that soured the evening just a bit.

"A pleasure." Dima showed his own teeth. Which must have

satisfied the crone, for she melded back into the whirl of dancing glitter.

A rotund man in a dusty black suit and top hat, his red suspenders peeking out as he cavorted past, was followed by a string of greenbacks, the cadaverous Mother of Accountants following with a disapproving glare, her pencil skirt hitting just at mid-knee as she hurried to make sure the debits matched the credits pouring off old Moneybags, Cashe's pampered grandson. Kelebritas Proper was at the bar, flickering between shapes like the mutable butterfly they were; purple-haired Hygeia hovered anxiously near a sweeping staircase leading to the mezzanine, her white dress flowing like the *zaika*'s and her blind gaze searching the crowd for distress.

"Didn't think I'd see *you* here," a tiny piping voice said, and he glanced down to find Noelle in red and green, her fair round face wrinkling and tiny plump paws holding a flask of bubbling mulled wine, a gout of pale fume off the liquid falling in curdled billows like dry-ice smoke and vanishing before it hit the floor. Of course, it was her time of the year too. "Don't you have a convenience store to rob or something?"

"Don't you have a little child to lie to?" He tossed more whiskey far back, enjoying the sting. "And a big fat *Ded Moroz* to suck off?"

"I'm not a capitalist." Noelle took a hit off her own flask in response; her bright blue gaze gleamed with predatory glee. "That's your gig. But I could give you a present, if you like."

"Save it." The skin roughened up Dmitri's back. "And if I find you anywhere near my little girl in green, I will end you."

"Good luck trying." The child smiled, and a shadow of ancient knowledge moved in her blue eyes. "In green, huh? I thought Dascha wasn't allowed out of the building." Long ago, they would sacrifice upon smoking altars in Noelle's honor to bring back the sun after deep-frozen solstices; nowadays, only money was immolated in useless trinkets each year. Her consort had turned into a corpulent man in ermine-trimmed red wool, and even if she disliked the change, there was nothing to be done about it.

Some marriages were like that.

"Not Dascha. Matchenka's girl; the old one is dying." He didn't mind giving away that particular bit of information. "Guess the New World doesn't agree with her after all."

Noelle's soft mouth opened slightly; she outright gaped at him. He sauntered away, satisfied that he'd just dropped a bucket of bloody chum into a knot of swimming sharks. Of course when Noelle laid eyes on the *zaika* she'd probably go running to fucking Koschei with the news, but that couldn't be helped.

Sooner or later, the thing they called *Deathless* would have found out there was an open avenue to a very valuable item anyway, and the chance to at once do Dmitri a disservice and perhaps force a greater creature to his bidding would be irresistible.

Once the sorcerer bit, Dmitri Konets would have *his* chance to do a little disservicing. It wasn't the prize he was after in the long run, but it would be satisfying if he could cause the Deathless some major damage.

Noelle vanished into a cavalcade of brightly clad TeeVees, their outlines pixilating as they drank and their forms shimmering between stereotype and obverse. He was about to follow them, but a heavy hand landed on his shoulder and Dmitri reached up without thought, locking the wrist and half-turning, preparatory to tearing the limb that dared to touch him without permission free of its host.

"Konets." The big man in blue with the wide leather belt smiled at him, tipping his hat brim up with one blunt finger. The service revolver at his hip was big and shiny-bold, and his jackboots were polished to mirrorgleam. "You looked like you were contemplating breaking the Law, my friend."

"Don't you have a civilian to shoot?" Dmitri could have broken the *politruk* fucker's wrist, but he let go after a token hard twist, tendons groaning. Tonight wasn't for such games, not least because the *zaika* was borne past in Jay's arms, doing a good job of keeping up with the waltz and listening to a constant stream of whatever was coming out of his mouth. It wasn't like him to dance for more than a few moments . . .

. . . but she was wearing green, of course. Coco knew her business; Jay wouldn't be the only one enamored tonight.

"Business before pleasure." Friendly's smile widened. His kind had once been black-jacketed kommissars; he was a homegrown version of those ideological sociopaths. His nose, very broad and pink, twitched once; there was a shadow-suggestion of two bumps swelling on either side of his sweat-shiny forehead and dark half-moons showed under his armpits, salty exertion soaking into a uniform. His kind was the same in every country, even if Dmitri's varied due to local conditions. "And I could help you on either count. Mason's over at the bar, he'd love a case to work on."

There was a word for a thief who worked with Friendly and Columbo Mason's type, and it wasn't a pleasant one. "When I want your services, *politseyski*, I'll pay for them. Like always. Go make yourself useful near the punch bowl."

Friendly's right hand dropped casually to the big black baton at his side. It was a showy blunt weapon, and if he was in a bad mood tonight—or if Dima looked weak—he'd go for it.

That would mean Dmitri's straight razors, pearl-handled or black and nestled in their small leather homes, would leap free to drink before Jay could arrive to insist on mannerly behavior. He didn't really want to kill tonight, but if this *mykop* insisted, well, a man did what he must.

Always.

"Dmitri!" A woman with a cloud of graying, frizzy hair separated from the crowd, yellow pencils stuck in the mass and her dark eyes blinking behind steel-rimmed glasses, shouldering Friendly aside. His expression turned sour. "Haven't seen you in *ages*. Care to comment on the new visitor?"

"Ah, Lois. Beautiful as ever." Because he liked pissing Friendly off, Dmitri took her long capable ink-stained hand, calluses scratching at her fingertips where they struck typewriter keys, and bowed over it. Her grubby mackintosh was nobody's idea of party attire even if a string of Christmas lights blinked merrily under the lapels, but her sister Mitford would be dressed in another of Coco's finest gowns and swanning among the upper crust—or what passed for it, here—while ferreting out information, useful or not, to hoard. Or to sell. "You hear about Friendly? He wants to work for me."

"I thought he already *did*." Lois's eyes gleamed behind the spectacle lenses. "It's a hero crowd tonight, by the way. I just saw that caped dumbass over by the biggest canapé table."

"Stuffing his face, no doubt." Dmitri grinned at the lady's knuckles. The brightly clad "hero" kept chasing Lois, and she kept giving him short shrift. "Just like a few other pigs."

Friendly's cheeks pinkened, well on their way to brick red. It wouldn't be difficult to provoke the god of property protection tonight.

Still . . . Jay took a very dim view of serious altercations on the second floor. Drunken fisticuffs outside were one thing, the unformed on the first floor were hungry enough to disregard any of their host's strictures, and so few were invited to the third floor there was often nobody there to cross swords with, let alone fists or other weapons. But when the Pasha of West Egg opened his doors for the amusement and culling of his fellow divinities, powers, principalities, and other forces he was very clear about the etiquette on the *second* floor, world and literature without end, amen.

Dmitri had only seen the result of Jay's pique once. The man had descended upon combatants with the high, screaming roar of an old-fashioned dive bomber, knocking both supine while he bellowed *It's just not cricket, old sport.*

And when the altercation had continued after that warning, Jay had become truly irate. Crimson ichor dribbling down his chin as bright white triangular teeth broke the hard crust of one of his own kind—*that* was how the Pasha of West Egg had survived so long, maybe.

A place in the literary canon wasn't a guarantee unless you tapped into something deeper, and Jay's longing was drawn from the deepest well of all.

"Someday," Friendly said, very softly. "All it takes is one wrong step, Konets."

"I can quote you on that." Lois's dark eyes danced with corpselight sparks as Dmitri straightened and dropped her hand. "*Neighborhood Officer Threatens Citizen at West Egg Shindig.*"

Friendly glared at her, executed a military about-face, and marched towards the bar, his buttocks working independently under blue serge like the haunches of two different beasts forced into unwilling tandem.

"That was unexpectedly satisfying," Lois continued, subtracting a tall narrow glass full of sticky red fluid from a passing Jeeves. "So, do a girl a favor. Maschenka Drozdova's dying at last; she's been in town all this time?"

"What would you pay to know?" Dima's grin didn't alter a whit, though a faint tendril of relief uncurled inside his ribcage.

One day he'd kill the blue-coated bastard. Just not tonight.

"Looks like Jay likes the new incarnation." Lois dropped him a cheeky wink—a journalist had to try, after all—and stepped back, vanishing into the dancers as the music changed, wild beat slowing and golden glow dimming just a fraction.

"There you are, old sport!" Jay appeared again, stepping smartly out of the flow; the *zaika* in his arms was pale. He brought her to a stop right in front of Dmitri, dropping her hand but keeping his grasp on her waist. "Isn't she beautiful? All in green, too. For a moment I could've sworn . . . listen, *listen*, old sport, have you seen Daisy?"

"Not yet tonight." It wasn't a lie; still, the words tasted bitter and metallic, so Dima finished his whiskey and tossed the glass again. It shattered, and the *zaika* flinched. Her dark eyes were huge, a doe caught in headlights. "Mind if I cut in?"

"Oh . . ." Jay beamed mistily at him. "I suppose I should look for Daisy. Well, it's been a pleasure, Miss Drozdova. Did I tell you I've been to Russia?"

"No," the girl said, faintly. "You didn't. I hear it's nice."

"Capital!" Jay crowed, handing her over to Dmitri and turning, craning his neck to look over the party. Dima wasted no time, sweeping her back onto the floor as West Egg's resident genius—in the old sense, although "monomania" might qualify as the newer definition if fueled by enough cognitive horsepower—sauntered

away, almost immediately clustered by several other guests probably fishing to know who the new girl was.

Nat was light as a sparrow in Dima's arms, and he whirled them
into the heart of the dance.

STUPID QUESTIONS

It would have been fascinating and pretty, Nat supposed, if she could have found a quiet corner and just watched. But first the guy in the linen suit—and now Dmitri—dragged her through complicated steps she barely remembered practicing with Leo after Mama stopped sending her to ballet classes. *You'll never be Pavlova, Natchenka. Give me the shoes, they're still worth something.*

That was a bad memory. She stiffened, the whirling variegated crowd pressing too close. Everyone was *looking* at her.

"Eh, *zaika*." Dmitri's hand at her waist was sure and implacable, and his fingers were warm. He held her hand like he was cradle-caging an egg. "Gonna throw up?"

Oh, for God's sake. "No." Or at least, if she did, she would aim it where it did the most good. Like right in his self-satisfied, smirking face.

She swallowed an acidic burp. Nat thumped back into her body with a sound she was surprised didn't crash through the music. Someone was actually playing the massive, brass-shining pipe organ fastened halfway up the far wall, banging out a rocked-up rendition of "Ain't Misbehavin'" or something close to it.

"It's natural the first time." He kept trying to draw her closer while their feet moved, breaking the frame; Nat kept trying to lean away. "Relax, will you? I'm helping."

Nat didn't bother laughing at an obvious lie. "That doesn't seem your style."

"You'd be surprised. You like Jay?"

"Is that his name? I couldn't hear half of what he said." Her stomach settled abruptly, probably because she wasn't being swirled at high speed through a crowd of funhouse-distorted laughter and wavering forms. Dmitri had slowed down, and aimed them past a knot of giggling, cadaverous women in fluttering white with red crosses on their headbands, their pale cheeks striped with bright crimson.

"Least he didn't make you Charleston." His grip changed as if he was going to let her swing free, but at the last moment he changed his mind, and their feet moved through a complicated turn as if Coco's heels knew the dance and were just carrying her along for the ride. "So, how you like the party?"

"It's . . ." The skin on her back roughened into gooseflesh. *Terrifying* was the word, but a strange excitement also bloomed right behind her heartbeat, her skin tingling and every hair on her body attempting to stand up. *It's a hopped-up holiday hootenanny from hell, thanks.* "I don't know."

"Good." His dark eyes twinkled merrily. There wasn't much difference between iris and pupil, but this close she could see the division, a single thread ringing the hole light struck his brain through. "You're honest, at least."

"More than you." Irritation was good fuel; it got her through eight to five at an office every day and dealing with hordes of harried, unhappy customers during evening shifts. Maybe life was merely a series of irritating things to be endured, even if cats *did* talk and there were places where strange creatures gathered to drink and dance. "You're a gangster, right?"

"Am part of American dream, *zaika*." The grin left and he turned somber, which she liked better; at the same time, a chill ran down her spine as he tried to draw her in again. "We're everywhere."

"I thought you were Russian." The tingling sense of danger ran cold fingers over her nape and slid away when he gazed over her shoulder, apparently intent on steering them. At least he was looking where they were going, which was more than she expected from a guy like him.

This can't be real. She'd wake up at home, clutching her pillow, sweat-soaked and unsure whether she'd just suffered a nightmare . . . or something else.

Something worse.

"Everyone here from elsewhere, even the first rubes." His lips barely moved, almost too quiet to be heard over the music. "And they all killed what they found."

"Yeah, well." She'd discovered as much in history classes, though Mama had always sniffed and remarked that true *history* was hidden and all teachers talked about was merely *events*. "That's America."

Maybe she'd said the right thing for once, because his smile softened. "I love America." The grin was still predatory, but the sharp tips of his canines dimpled his lower lip, pressing just on the edge of cutting. "America is great if you have money. The money is easy if you don't mind the screams. And best of all is when you make the strong scream and take what is theirs." He kept staring over her shoulder, turning them left, right, left, dipping and wheeling like a hawk over a rolling field. "The weak are no challenge, after all."

That sounds like a life philosophy. She hadn't dared drink anything, but her head felt full of fumes anyway. "What are all these people?" Nat hated the quaver in her own voice, the last word almost breaking in half. She was doing really well at treating all of this like it was normal.

But it wasn't. Not by a long shot.

Dmitri paused. It wasn't quite a stumble, and he smoothly recovered, steering them through a high arch into another smaller ballroom, just as crowded but somehow a little quieter. "What your mama tell you about asking stupid questions, *zaika*?"

You son of a bitch. Nat dug her heels in. To her surprise, they stuck fast. Dmitri pushed, but for once Nat Drozdova pushed *back*, or maybe she simply refused to move any farther. She tried to tug her hand away; his fingers bit down cruelly.

So she simply stood, immovable, an iron rod in a draped green dress. "It would be a stupid question if I knew the answer already."

For the first time, the gangster seemed a little less than completely self-possessed. He examined her face, something flaring deep in tar-black pupils. "You don't know what you—"

A shiver ran through the crowd. Music halted, the last notes draining away with a gurgle like soapy water down a half-clogged drain. For a moment Nat was sure she'd committed an unforgivable sin and the entire party was going to vanish into snowdrifts, ash, and sticks, leaving her shivering in an empty field, dressed only in cobweb scraps like in all the old stories, when someone shouted *God help me* during a fairy revel to break the spell.

Maybe that's why Mama sent me to Catholic school. Nat's breath came hard and fast, her chin tilted, and she waited for all the magic to drain out of the world.

A crystalline chiming broke the airless silence. It was Westminster Quarters, that favorite of cuckoo and grandfather clocks everywhere, and when it finished the timepiece—maybe the one at the back of the foyer, with its syrup-slow pendulum—began to count off the hours. One, two, three, four, five, all the way to twelve, and the goosebumps were hard, swelling eggs under her skin.

Midnight.

Wait. How is that possible? We were at Coco's just—

"It's time," Dmitri said, and that spark in his pupils was gone as if it had never existed. "You're gonna like this, *zaika*. Come on." A smart half-turn, her arm tucked through his, and he hustled her at high speed for the central ballroom, where a rising mutter sounded like an excited crowd at a football game. The crowd parted before them.

Over the carnivorous surf-mutter came a piercing cry.

"Daiiiiiiisyyyyyyy!"

WANT TO CHARLESTON

Ahalf-dozen of the butlers with their concave chests dragged the linen-suited man into the middle of the ballroom, their noses lengthening and twitching as he twisted and screamed. Nat froze, her arm trapped in Dmitri's and every face around her bright and avid, from the little girl in the flapper costume with a long black cigarette holder in her pudgy right hand to the man in a spotless white robe, his brown hair just brushing his shoulders, his goatee neatly clipped, and his bare feet pierced with round, red wet-gleaming holes. The latter glided forward when it looked like the butlers were having trouble, beaming a soporific smile and lifting mutilated hands—two more terrible hole-wounds were cradled in his palms.

Suddenly, Nat knew who he was supposed to be. The thought that this was just a crazy sort of holiday costume ball and nobody had told her might have been comforting if the deep, weeping wounds in his hands hadn't looked so utterly *real*. "Oh, God," she whispered, and attempted to surge forward, but Dmitri grabbed her trapped arm with his free hand as well, hot fingers sinking into her bare flesh.

"Don't," he said, his profile sharp as a Roman statue's. "Happens every time, *zaika*. Just watch."

Somehow, an X of raw lumber had appeared on the polished wooden dance floor. A ripple went through the crowd, fantastical shapes blurring and shivering at their edges. The butlers held Jay grimly as the white-robed man arrived, a soft reddish glow beginning behind the fabric at his chest as if someone had turned on a night-light inside his ribcage.

"Quiet," the white-robed, goateed man said sharply. "Doesn't hurt that bad, and I should know."

"Y'all can just be quiet too. Ain't even got the holes through your wrists proper, you Protestant bastid." This was a barefoot tow-headed girl in denim bib overalls, one strap frayed through and dangling as she melted out of the crowd on the other side. "He's got a right, and don't you forget it."

"*You* should be seen, not heard." The white-robed man scowled at her, forgetting his pacific expression.

Jay moaned weakly.

"And you're supposed to be a rabbi," a woman in a grubby tan mackintosh and steel-rimmed glasses sniffed. "Leave Scout alone." Next to her was a big, dark-haired man, red-and-blue spandex hugging his rippling muscles, a long crimson cape hanging from his broad shoulders.

Nat could barely believe her eyes.

"Children, children." A large rawboned man in a funeral director's dusty black suit under a stovepipe hat raised his big lobsterlike hands. Nat began to feel distinctly faint; she knew that craggy profile from history class and copper pennies. "We do this every night. Let's just get it done."

"Wait, let me get a picture." A man with an ancient camera, a silvery round flash atop it, pushed forward. He was in a tan coat like the woman with glasses, and his fedora was at a jaunty angle. He was elbowed aside by a big, heavy man in a blue serge uniform, a glossy black nightstick dangling from a black leather belt and his forehead oddly swollen.

"Oh, fa cry-eye." The man in blue looked like every cartoon illustration of an Irish cop ever made, right to the gin blossoms on his twitching pink nose and the stiff reddish bristles of his stubble. "Back away, jackal."

A deep, rich, resonant baritone broke the rising mutters. "You're one to talk."

The owner of that voice was a copper-skinned man with a battered top hat at a jaunty angle, silver conchas starring its band. Beaded necklaces of turquoise and crimson melded with a tattered, variegated scarf at his neck. Jeans clasped his long legs, ending in run-down boots with strangely soft soles and bright beadwork glittering almost like Dmitri's toe caps, but far more pleasantly. The sleeve-fringes on his leather jacket swung idly as he moved, and he carried an old-fashioned peace pipe that definitely didn't look like a carnival prize.

The white-robed man sized him up. "Well, isn't this an honor."

Hard on the heels of that statement, the blue-uniformed cop barked a question. "Why the hell are *you* here?"

"I am where you least expect me." But the baritone's dark gaze darted over the crowd, and a zing like biting on tinfoil jolted up Nat's spine.

Other voices began, swirling at the edges of the onlookers, chattering over each other, an expectant crowd who had paid the door fee and wanted its money's worth now.

"We have a new one tonight."

"Daisy," Jay moaned. "Oh, please, *Daisy*."

"Can we just finish this?"

"It happens in its own time." A familiar, iron-colored voice intervened. "Like everything else."

Baba de Winter stepped out of the crowd. She was just as thin and angular as she'd been in her office, but her hair was now a high-piled rat's nest of gray and black instead of tarnished ivory, a tower pinned with iron knitting needles. Her dress was a vaporous, moving cloud, torn black lace wrapped several times around a stick-thin figure with a hard, aggressive chest-prow, the cloth starred with silver safety pins and her cuffs masses of fraying thread. Her lips were no longer crimson but chocolate-cherry, red so tarnished it was almost black.

"I should make you do this," she said in Dmitri's general direction, the gesture heavy because her bone-white fist was weighted with an old-fashioned claw hammer, a bit of electrical tape fluttering on its wooden handle.

"Pay me and I will, Baba." The gangster grinned, but his grasp didn't loosen at all.

Baba de Winter turned away with a very teenage roll of her dark eyes, and bent to her work. Other hands held the nails steady, and the hammering started.

Nat pulled at Dmitri's grasp. "Stop it," she managed, breathlessly. "Please ohgod *stop* it—"

"He chose this, *zaika*." Dmitri didn't let go. There were bruises beginning under his grasp, she could *feel* them. "Be quiet."

"*Daisy! Daisy! Daisy!*" Jay screamed in time with each hit, but Baba knew her work. Three swift, ear-shattering blows at each wrist, and the crunching as the heavy iron railroad spikes went through made bile whip the back of Nat's throat. The guests surged forward, hiding what de Winter did to Jay's feet, and Nat almost lost what little champagne she'd had at Coco's all over the floor.

When the X was lifted Jay sagged, and the screaming drained to a low cricket-whisper buzz, his lips vibrating. Nat shuddered, limp in Dmitri's grasp. "You sick fucks," she whispered. "Oh, my *God*."

"Look at that," someone said. "Somebody's first time."

"You always remember your first," someone else intoned, and there was a high glassy giggle. Baba appeared again, pushing between a pair of wasp-waisted, gold-dipped bipedal forms who chittered gently as they fawned on a tiny round man who looked exactly like the guy on the Monopoly boxes.

"No explanations, I see." The old woman fixed Dmitri with a dark glare. The hammer was gone, but her right hand was still loosely curled.

As if it still felt the handle, and liked the sensation.

"More fun that way." Dmitri sounded like he was at a garden party, instead of watching a man get murdered.

Nat tugged hopelessly at his hand on her arm. There was a deep thrumming sound; Jay's belly swelled as he slumped against raw-splintered lumber. Next came a queer, awful *stretching* noise, his linen suit creak-bulging, and the little girl in overalls appeared near the bottom of the torture device, puffing serenely on an honest-to-gosh corncob pipe.

"Beautiful little fools, both of ya," she said in her high, clear, piping drawl. "Even my daddy would say so."

Fabric ripped, flesh tore; there was a spray of bright red tinted at its edges with golden coruscation. Jay threw his head back and screamed, his throat vibrating, and a venomous green glitter poured from his split belly. It hit the dance floor with a double click, staggering on low heels very much like Nat's. The shapeless mass stretched, becoming ever more bipedal, strings of bright verdant glass beads dripping from a boy-slim but definitely not male figure. She stretched, her arms streaked with that gold-laced blood, and Nat choked, gagging.

It was *impossible*. Especially when the woman—delicate and slim, wide blue eyes very much like Jay's, a snub nose, a smattering of golden freckles, and a bright headband sporting a viridian-dyed ostrich feather plumping and fluffing as it dried—stretched, spread her rapidly lengthening fingers, and turned to regard the ruined, deflating body on the X.

"What's that thing?" she asked, in a bright contralto very much like Jay's voice. "Has anyone seen Jay?"

"Every damn time," Dmitri muttered. "See, *zaika*? It's not so—"

But Nat had torn free, her arm giving a livid flare of pain as his fingernails dug furrows in bare skin. She bolted past the cop in blue who made a halfhearted grab for her, but she was quick enough to evade that big knob-knuckled hand and spilled through a knot of costumed motherfuckers straight off a bad '70s album cover, complete with bell-bottoms and furry chests under shirts unbuttoned to the waist; Nat pelted for the keyhole doorway.

"Don't let her—" Baba de Winter began, and Dmitri's curse rode a swelling wave of bright laughter.

"Oh dear," the newborn woman said, stretching lithely as Jay's body deflated still further, shrinking on itself like any spent cocoon. She brushed at her bare arms, stamped her dainty green-clad feet; her wrists cracked as she rotated them. "Where's the music? I want to *Charleston*."

A few throbbing notes began, and the assembly cheered the nightly marvel. Daisy accepted her accolade, a disbelieving smile

spread over her fair, innocent, hungry little face, and a passing butler handed her a tall slim glass of amber champagne.

The cocoon kept shrinking, the crowd surged forward, and the
crowd began to dance once more as unpainted, splintering lumber crumbled into creosote-smelling ash. Eventually the particles,
working themselves smaller and smaller, would vanish entirely.

Nat was, however, out the front door, her heels clattering and
her hair streaming free of Coco's magisterial efforts.

Running flat out, she almost reached the end of the driveway
before a large dirty-white van with a red racing stripe skidded to
a stop right next to her, black shapes with strange heft and quite
unshadowlike solidity springing from its side door, and she was
bundled into darkness.

A TASTY REASON

The van heaved left as it cleared the gate, its taillights laughing little ruby mouths.

Dmitri dug his heels in, leaving long smoking furrows in the slick black driveway. Behind him, Baba drifted to a stop, a tall gray glass tumbler in her skeletal, sticklike right hand steaming against the chill. "Oh," she said, softly, a singsong of sarcasm. "How surprising. How very, very surprising."

He rounded on her. "*Bring her to Jay's,* you said. I should carve your face off and eat it."

"Did you expect him not to find out? The girl has to be taught what she is." She shrugged, her pointed shoulders lifting and dropping with clockwork jerks. "Besides, I'd like to see you try."

"One of these days, *Grandmother.*" His face contorted. "Just when it was getting interesting, too."

"Well?" She took a long draft of whatever was in the tumbler and exhaled with deep satisfaction at the end, her black eyes closed, her lips smeared with cherry-red. "He can't really hurt her, but he might strike a bargain. What are you going to do about it?"

"Bitch." He turned sharply away, his breath pluming on chilly, sharp, very clear air. Snow-silence hung over the hills and fields; the music spilling from golden-lit windows didn't reach this far. "She took it well, though. Girl has some guts." Another language trembled behind the words, struggling for freedom, but he denied it, snapping his teeth together like any wolf with the hunt before him and the night fading fast.

"She survived Maschka." Baba sounded thoughtful. "She'll be all right."

"Your precious Maria didn't tell her what she is."

"I guessed as much." Baba took another long drink. "I suspect she had a very tasty reason for refraining."

It had been a long time since he felt anything approaching loathing, but Dmitri Konets felt it now. "It's amazing." He coiled himself. "Maschka's just like you after all." There was a soft sound, a cough like an owl's wings as it exploded into hunting flight, and Baba blinked slowly as a puff of stinging-fine snow was thrown into the air.

"So are you," she said softly, and stepped aside. Headlights swelled behind her. An old Cadillac roadster, coal-black, its tires somehow making a herd-galloping racket, whooshed past on a wind that was, for a moment, redolent of rotting cypress and desert spice-sand all at once.

Baba de Winter's empty gray glass hovered in midair for a moment, then fell into a snowdrift as a black bird lifted from the field, winging hard for a bright confusion of spilled gems upon the skyline, a nighttime city studying its own reflection in the black mirror of the sound.

The Cadillac yipped once, fire blooming behind its front grille, and barked as it turned hard right, fishtailing before the back end bit and propelled it forward.

Someone else had decided to leave the party, too.

REALLY REAL

Inside a dark, rocking, confined space, Nat sprawled on cheap harsh nylon carpeting, the end of a scream trailing between her teeth. The van swung into a wallowing turn and she tumbled, fetching up against a wheel-well with another barking, breathless little cry.

At least the magical new dress stayed largely where it was supposed to.

The van's interior reeked of the chemical soup they called *new car smell*, with a definite note of burning diesel. She thrashed, trying to brace herself against the metal bulge of the well so she could sit up, but the vehicle immediately turned again and there was a soft feathery bump underneath, as if it had veered to hit a small animal or bounced over a slight hillock.

Nat finally gained hands-and-knees. The first shock was the entire back of the van turning out to be empty, a cold carpeted cavern. The second was the two bucket seats—driver and passenger, a huge console between glowing with multicolored blinking lights in a rancid, stomach-churning pattern—correspondingly empty too. The steering wheel drifted from side to side with merry disregard for any law of physics or normalcy, seemingly unconnected to the rest of the car's lunging through space. The speedometer's orange needle was all the way to the right, hovering well past 120; spectral glow from the dash picked out the nap of flecked velour covering the seats.

I've been kidnapped by the seventies. Nat choked back a braying laugh. The van bounced again, and when she pulled herself semiupright, clinging to the back of the passenger seat, she almost wished she hadn't.

The windshield was a cataract eye milky at the edges, the city approaching at high speed. That wasn't the problem—it was actually a beautiful sight, electric gold glittering through ice-choked windows, bright flashes of holiday lights, concrete spires rising like gem-crusted teeth from snowy streets.

No, the problem was the white-fringed, choppy waves under the van, which kept bouncing just enough to make her seasick. Bouncing, in fact, on a cushion of empty air.

The van was *flying*. Over Long Island Sound. Deep, dark, cold water, just waiting to swallow whatever dropped into its embrace.

Ohshit, don't tell me we're going to Yonkers. Nat's knees gave out. She curled up behind the passenger seat, clapped her hands over her ears, and realized she was making a soft keening noise, like Jay hanging on a lumber X or Leo trying to sob quietly in the shower upstairs the night after Mom's collapse and the ambulance, the hospital and diagnosis.

Mom. Think about her, think about helping her.

She tried. The van lunged upward, more like a helicopter than a car that needed good solid pavement corralled by painted stripes, and Nat gagged, retching once again as her stomach struggled to escape.

Oh, it'd seemed exciting, like she might finally be able to do something right, something Mama would appreciate. Imagining her mother restored to health, finally smiling and saying *well maybe there's something to all your wild stories, Natchenka,* was all very well, but this goddamn van was flying over the ocean and she'd just seen . . .

What *had* she seen?

Jay. Jay and Daisy. Oh, the problem wasn't recognizing the names. That wasn't it at *all*.

The problem was admitting the implications. No practical joke could be this elaborate, no hallucinogenic trip this seamless and durable.

"It's insane," she found herself moaning, rocking back and forth as the van veered to the left and continued climbing. Two raisins short of a fruitcake, a few sheets short of a wind, bats in the belfry, *crazy Nattie freakgirl* like they called her in school.

The van leveled out. The other eerie thing was the sudden quiet, the engine more a vibration than a sound. Some wild part of Nat wanted to crawl to the frost-starred back windows and look out, but the thought that they might swing open and some kind of depressurization launch her into space held her rigid-frozen.

Just like Jay, nailed to what she now realized were railroad ties.

The van shifted, banking like Jimmy Sparlick's motorcycle the one time she'd gone riding with him. He'd ended up stranding her at Canarsie Park; the whole affair had been a particularly cruel prank, but she'd liked the sensation of speed and wind roaring past.

She'd never even been on a plane since Mama didn't travel. Did this count? Her arm throbbed; Dmitri's nails had scratched long angry red furrows.

Oddly, the thought of the gangster and his stupid shiny boot-toes made her angry enough to take a deep breath, forcing her hands away from her ears. She still couldn't bring herself to go near a window, but she hugged her knees and concentrated on her lungs, the air slipping through her constricted throat, her throbbing arm, her aching calves, her iron-stiff neck and the buzzing in her head from the engine.

I'm here, she repeated, like she would in her closet at night after she'd cried all she was going to over the taunts of her classmates and Mom's eternal impatience. *I'm alive, I'm here. I'm me.*

As usual, there was the sense that there were two Nats, badly superimposed on each other, the true core where they overlapped solid and real but the rest hazy and indistinct, pulled in different taffy-stretching directions by the impersonal gazes of everyone who saw a kid with too-wild dark hair and crazy ideas she didn't have the sense to keep quiet about. It was easier to move into the solid overlap now that she was older, and the constriction around her lungs eased.

"Really real," she found herself repeating. "I'm here, I'm me, and I'm real. I'm *really* real."

Mom loved that song. *Rosie Real knows a thing or two*, she would always say, and turn up the ancient yellow Bakelite radio in the kitchen that always had such a clear, warm sound.

There was a bounce, a change in the engine hum, a jolt that lifted her off the carpet and bumped her down again. Her ass was going to bruise, and that was the final, utterly *last* straw.

Nat Drozdova began to cuss.

HATE WHAT IT HOLDS

She was still producing blue words under her breath at a good clip when the brakes grabbed and the van came to a jolting halt. Nat scrambled for the driver's side—it was, after all, as far as she could get from the biggest door, and what came next after a driverless van kidnapped you?

The big passenger-side door would open, of course, and she'd find out who had sent the whole contraption. It could have been a rescue attempt, but she wasn't betting on that. Not after being held to a chair by a grandmother's dark gaze, not after a shop full of invisible seamstresses, and definitely not after seeing a man nailed to raw creosote-soaked lumber split open and a . . . a *thing* come out.

The talking cats of Brooklyn had nothing on this.

Her brain shivered. She *felt* the movement inside her skull, despite knowing it was an absolute impossibility; you could crack open someone's head-case and poke around without a lot of anesthetic because the gray matter didn't send pain signals.

She was shaking her head, too, tiny little tosses like one of the cats with whiskers burnt by misadventure, or like a best friend in sixth grade when Nat led her to the dry spot under the skirts of the holly tree on the playground at Mother Mary Elementary and the tiny mushrooms growing there, singing in their bird-piping voices.

What was that little strawberry-blonde girl's name? She'd run away and never talked to Nat afterward; the childish heartbreak still wrung at Nat's heart.

Jenny Tisdale. That was her name. Her family moved away. "Sonofabitching mother*fuck*," Nat whispered, and followed it up with a few choice terms Uncle Leo muttered while working on engines, when he thought Nat couldn't hear.

"And good evening to you." A rich, dry, but somehow fruity baritone reverberated outside the van. The door rolled open and cold air rushed through; she glimpsed concrete, the orange edge of city-night glow against low smooth clouds ready to dump more snow at a moment's provocation. Where in the fucking city was she now? "You sound like your mother, you know."

All the spit in Nat's mouth dried. She hugged her knees, wishing she had refused the green dress. The heels still clasped her feet and the skirts still covered everything they should, but her hair was a mess of curls falling in her face and the rest of her felt wildly disheveled.

Nothing was visible out the door except a concrete half-wall, a slice of something that looked like an HVAC hood, and painted lines like a basketball court. A thin scrim of ice in faint ruffled patterns turned the ground into a slick glitter, and a dark shape in the near distance was the familiar bulk of the Morrer-Pessel Tower.

From the angle, she was on a rooftop in Soho. Pretty high, too. Who needed the subway when you had a flying van?

The dimness near the door turned sharp, and as she watched, a shadow detached. It swelled, like a paper doll unfolding and acquiring terribly real weight, and the woozy terror came back.

She could pinch herself, she supposed; when it got bad in middle school she'd worn long sleeves to cover the bruises, each one a savage little bite as if she could train herself not to see what was clear as day.

What other people *didn't* see. Or maybe they did and pretended not to, and she'd never acquired the trick or was incapable of learning, like she was apparently incapable of getting the kitchen clean enough or finding a job that would earn enough for escape or—

"Don't worry. It's only a helpful shadow, not the other kind." The baritone swelled into a gentle laugh, but the sound spread goose bumps up her arms. "I apologize for the impoliteness, and for the bumpy ride. But I felt it necessary to move before someone could convince you to do something rash, my dear Drozdova."

The paper cutout vanished, folding back into the deep gloom in the back of the van. Nat stayed where she was, trying to keep the door, the back, and the passenger seat in view all at once. The thought that she was in a few shadows herself wasn't comforting at all. "Who the hell are you?" She meant to channel some of Mom's *you'd better have a good answer to this question, buster* tone, but instead, what came out was a breathless squeak.

"Oh, yes. How rude of me, naturally we haven't been introduced." A flowing laugh, like a tide of desert sand creeping over desiccated bones. "But names—we all have so many. For example, you are Drozdova, the Lady of Black Earth, Granddaughter of bleak Winter, and the rising sap in the bough. But you are also . . ."

The urge to say *it's just Nat* warred with a second, much deeper imperative to give her other name, the *real* one—not the one on her birth certificate, because Mom said that was just Nat, too.

But the cats said otherwise, and Nat was glad she'd listened to them at least that once. She bit her lower lip, sinking her teeth in so she didn't give anything away.

Fairy tales and the cats were both very clear on *that* point, thank you very much.

"Wise little girl." He laughed again. How could a voice sound so dry? Even her cheeks felt tight, as if she'd opened the oven and bent into the first blast from its mouth. "Wiser than her years, which isn't surprising. I am called Kolya, and the Reader, and He Who Hides. But I am also called Koschei the Dollmaker, and I welcome you to my domain. You may enter freely. None of my servants will harm you if it can be avoided, and neither will I." Each word was given equal weight, a clock's dry ironic recital of seconds passing. "There is much profit to be had in our alliance, Miss Drozdova. You are the means of finding something Dmitri Konets wants very badly, but if he does reacquire it he will tear you into small bits and probably consume quite a few of them."

It wasn't so much what he said as the tone—placid, amused, with the ring of complete sincerity—that convinced her. After all, she'd seen Dmitri's teeth, and even with his funny shiny boot-toes the man was terrifying.

But it didn't answer the question of whether this guy, whoever he was, would end up being worse. Not to mention Baba wasn't the only one wanting her to pick something up at the corner store, so to speak. She was betting this guy didn't just hanker for a bottle of vodka. "And what do *you* want?"

"I want you to find the gem, of course. It's in an iron setting like dead twigs, and your mother stole it from Baba Yaga upon a moonless night. I don't suppose the old witch told you that."

"She . . ." Nat gulped in a mouthful of frigid air. Were there flickers of movement in the oppressive shadows, or was it just her imagination? "She just told me that if I found something for her, I could save my mother. And Mom . . ." Her mother's voice, soft as a cricket-whisper. *Don't tell anyone the riddle, Natchenka. Everything in it is a signpost, and you don't want anyone else to guess. Go along with what Baba says until you get to the Key, but hurry. I can't hold on much longer.*

That was what was so terrible about this guy, Nat realized. He sounded like Mom, like death. Or dying.

"I possess the power to show you where the Knife is, Miss Drozdova. That's the first piece you need to find, isn't it?"

Her mother's voice, riding tepid breath into Nat's ear. *The path starts with the Knife.*

Nat scrambled for the door, nylon carpet burning her palms and rasping her skirt. She tumbled out onto a rooftop, Coco's heels grabbing a rippled sheet of ice as surely as cleats, and found herself blinking against a stinging cold wind—her hair doing its best to blind her by lifting in a cloud—and facing a cadaverous man in a matte black suit, his bolo tie pulled very tight against a scrawny neck. The bolo's slide was a dark oval gem with a secretive vertical gleam in its heart, very like a cat's-eye, and his wrists protruded from his cuffs, dangling large, soft hands with long expressive fingers. For all their delicacy, the phalanges looked very strong, kelp waiting to wrap around an unwary swimmer's legs, dragging down to cold lung-crushing depths.

His trousers were hemmed a little too high as well, and his wingtips were ferociously polished. He had a sharp high bony nose, bladed cheekbones, a head slightly too big for the rest of his wispy body, and the skin drawn tight over his scalp only boasted the most anemic of gleaming comb-overs, three or four black strands plastered down in defiance of even a hurricane. If not for the obscene, vivid life in his deep-set eyes, he could have been a grinning skull set atop a stick-made scarecrow. But those eyes—black as tar, black as pitch—burned like the coal in Leo's barbecue before it gathered a coat of protective ash, and that hot, hungry gaze was terrifying.

Like Baba's, in fact. Or like Dmitri's.

Fortunately, Nat had already been scared out of her wits over and over again since showing the business card to a pair of security guards in a building she'd thought about for weeks before gathering enough courage to step inside. Maybe she was just running out of fear-juice.

And here she thought she'd had a lifetime supply. "I know where it is." Technically it might even be true. Except Mom had only said, *with the man who believes in the future.*

Was there anyone around who didn't? The future kept happening, whether you wanted it to or not.

"Oh, you do, Miss Drozdova?" The man's fingers twitched. "My, it's breezy. Come inside, and we'll discuss it."

"You know where I was." She made it a flat statement of fact. "You know what happened."

"Oh, yes. Jay throws a party, the divine dance and drink. Come midnight, nature takes its course." His sharp-starved shoulders lifted, dropped; the shrug said it was no big deal to watch a man's wrists or feet hammered through with railroad spikes. "And the carrion crow performs her ancient function. What's dead must be eaten, so it may be transformed."

Well, that was ecology in a nutshell, wasn't it. "Energy can neither be created or destroyed," she hazarded. It was just like talking to a drunken college student who didn't want to pay their tab just yet, let alone give a tip. "Right?"

"Is that what they're saying nowadays? I prefer the older proverbs, myself." His head gleamed, the black tendril comb-over almost shaping a letter she couldn't quite remember. "But come, you're cold. A cup of coffee and answers await you, Miss Drozdova. Ideally, I'd like to be inside before Konets comes along."

"You don't like him?" *Imagine that.*

"My dear, nobody likes him, and that's the way he likes it. But he reserves a special place in his cold, missing little heart for me."

"You guys are enemies?" If they were, maybe it meant she was halfway safe.

But Nat wasn't betting on it.

"Does a mirror hate what it holds?" He twitched again, that tiny movement that could have been another shrug or a settling of moistureless bones inside a sack. Then he turned on one worn wingtip heel and set off across the rooftop, heading for what looked like a glass pyramid, glowing golden with bright electric light.

Wait a minute. That wasn't there before. Or had it been? There was even a pulsing eight-pointed star at its apex, a helluva tree-topper. The star's stuttering made her uneasy.

Nat glanced nervously at the van. The side door was closing, silently oozing along its tracks. It didn't look so much like a door as a slowly healing scab, really. Nat shivered and set off after the scarecrow-thin man, trying not to notice the way his shadow didn't quite follow the rest of him.

The shadow's edges were heavy, and moved a few fractions of a second after he did. The lag was enough to give you a headache, and she had all she could handle in her skullcase right now. So she set her chin and hurried, grateful that the heels kept up their grabby-soles magic and didn't dump her on the ice. Being terrified into near-incoherence was one thing, but pratfalls were just *undignified*.

It was a good thought, a sane thought, and she clung to it as the wind keened along the skyscraper's edges and tugged at her hair, almost as if trying to warn her. A few hard ice-pellets rattled across the roof.

It would start to snow again soon.

OBJECT LESSON

The trouble with Koschei's home—or den, or haunt, whatever you preferred to call the bastard's lair—was that it moved like Baba's chicken-legged personal domicile. Not only that, but the man, if you could call him that nowadays, was so fond of obfuscation and camouflage even a wet pink nose like Friendly's would have difficulty catching a whiff of a trail.

Fortunately all Dima had to do was sniff his fingertips. He'd clawed the *zaika*'s arm, trying to keep her from hurting herself, and every time he held his hand near his nose he got another shot of that heady green fragrance with its floral edge, jasmine and spice over rising sap and crushed grass.

Maschka had been heavy black earth under the strong sunshine of the old country, mud firming and the slight astringency of sunflowers beginning a long stretch towards an endless sky. Her daughter held no carrion reek of rotting bodies pressed into dirt gone semi-liquid from the thaw, no edge of ice from streams roaring with melt.

Perhaps she was gentler. But she would learn.

Sooner or later, they all did.

Dmitri crouched on the half-wall skirting the First Mutual building's roof, his hair shaken down over his forehead and his eyes alight with bloody gleams. His suit was spattered with slush and melt; the falling snowflakes vanished before they touched him, cringing into water when they encountered a simmering haze of anger. Most of the time his rage was black ice waiting for an unwary foot; tonight, however, it was the red glow of a just-fired artillery shell.

He sniffed at his fingers again, his eyelids fluttering, and felt the unphysical tug all the way down to his guts. Not only did he have the *zaika*'s flesh under his nails, but Koschei appeared to have forgotten he was merely a jumped-up tick, hanging bloodfat on the skin of the world's ear.

Dmitri was otherwise. He was the patron of thieves, and the Deathless—oh, he called himself that, and Dima longed to truly put it to the test—had *stolen* something Dmitri Konets was not finished with yet.

There. That way. Dmitri straightened, a frigid wind pushing at his back, and leaned forward. His boot-toes twinkled, there was a hard *snap* like wet washing in a laundress's calloused hands, and he was on the street fifty stories below, streaking along, little flashes of wickedness curling across his path but nothing interesting enough to slow for. Tonight he wouldn't wander among muggers or slip into a gaming hall, pass unseen between pickpockets at an airport lounge or meld into the shadows of a businessman's bedroom while the fucker dreamed of leverage and buyout. Tonight, though he was invoked, propitiated, and sometimes demanded, he was out of the office.

Besides, it did not do to answer every cry. Humanity tended to take the reliable for granted.

Squeezed between two piles of concrete and glass, a wedge-shaped anomaly leered and throbbed. It was a brownstone excrescence, mortared with fudge-like growths gleaming damply despite the ice, and pulsing at its crown was a confection of spun steel and glass, the pyramid collecting and focusing numinous force. The crowning star glowed more fiercely as it sensed his attention but he was already on the steps, his boots a fast light tattoo. The front door shattered as he drove through, his left fingertips just below his nose and the smell a bright highway instead of a thread or even an obedient ribbon in Coco's crimson claws.

This cavernous space was far too large for the brownstone's outer appearance. It was the bottom level of a parking garage, echoes bouncing from concrete and lines of chipped paint glowing with radioactive hatred. Movement boiled in the shadows, and Dmitri's right hand flicked down.

The gun—dull matte black, automatic, its blunt muzzle swelling at the end with a silencer when he needed quiet but now innocent of any addition—spoke, and the shot whined off a thick, striped concrete pillar. One of the things hiding in the shadows squealed, and now that he was inside he could hear the heartbeats far above.

So Koschei had her in his foul nest already.

Don't worry, Drozdova. I'm coming.

His left hand dropped, and a warm handle of blackened ivory filled his palm. The straight razor's blade was a bright star in the dark, and if his heart had been entirely his, it would have been pounding in fierce anticipation.

As it was, he smiled, his teeth gleaming like the razor's flanks. "*Housekeeping!*" he caroled, and danced forward while the misshapen things lumbered from parking spaces, their sides painted with chrome stripes and their eyes headlight-bright. They were slow, easily dodged so long as Dmitri kept moving.

Oh, he did like a waltz or two, and had he simply happened across Koschei's habitation one chilly night he might have left it at that. But the Deathless—and how Dima hated that name, as well as the fucker who claimed it—had done the unforgivable.

Someone had stolen from Dmitri Konets, from the lord of thieves himself. And that could not be borne.

Dima straightened like a matador as the first abomination bolted for him, groaning in its mechanical voice and slavering foaming oil. Its teeth champed right where Dmitri had been standing a moment before, it howled as his boots touched its broad, low-domed head, and he shot straight down, severing the nexus of unholy power granting it a semblance of sentience.

The monster made a grinding, terrifying screech; the rest of its siblings echoed the cry. The sound bounced through several floors, cold concrete connected with spiraling ramps suddenly full of stealthy movement, bright white gleams, waking motors, the reek of exhaust. He could have bypassed them easily enough, but each one he killed was an object lesson to the fucking sorcerer.

Singing a dirge from the old country, interspersed with snatches of a country song currently popular among the gangs on this city's

Lower East Side, Dima leapt from his first victim, landing with a pleasant jolt. He killed again, and again, and again as metal screeched with pain and safety glass shivered into pieces.

The world was full of things mortals barely dreamed of, and he enjoyed murdering any number of them.

NATURE'S COURSE

A strange camera-shutter door flowered in the side of the golden glass pyramid, and just before Nat stepped out of the stinging, biting wind and into sudden deep sweating warmth she realized she wasn't that cold at all. Maybe it was Coco's dress, insulating her though her arms were bare; maybe it was just plain old adrenaline.

The glass triangles made a dry rasping sound as they closed behind her. Instantly it was quiet, and the rich smell of coffee and warm earth drifted up a wrought-iron spiral staircase. Polished wooden parquet glowed through the holes in the metal. She held grimly to the banister as she descended, because the stairs quivered as if the whole thing wasn't quite fully bolted together.

A long, broad space at the stairs' foot could be a ballroom; she almost shuddered at what kind of parties *this* guy would throw. All the same, it was a lot more cheerful than Jay's mansion, because there was greenery everywhere. Household stalwarts like airplane plants and philodendrons hung in baskets, monsteras with giant fronds swayed happily. A tangle of orchids crawled over a black iron stand packed with moss and other strange vines, a riot of colorful alien blossoms. There were even low, shallow tubs full of tulips in gemlike shades, but she caught sight of other vegetation tucked here and there, familiar from the part of Mom's garden child-Nat was never allowed in.

Things like aconite, and foxglove, and glowing nightshade berries thickly clustered on woody stems. Like horehound, and poison oak so fat and virulent it was coated with gleaming reddish ichor, and morning glory vines holding long thin seedpods. A giant castor nodded, two different colors of jimsonweed flanking it. Opium poppies spread bright papery petals amid fat swelling pods almost bursting with milky sap, and there were a few cannabis plants in the mix as well.

Maybe this guy was a supernatural dealer, and all the other greenery cover for magical drug smuggling?

Silvery rue lingered at the edge of the poison garden, and there was mugwort in giant square pots as well as mallow and a water installation thickly crowded with giant lily pads a frog prince would find acceptable, glowing lotus flowers floating serene and pale above a bottom that had to be mucky. The plants exhaled humidity, rustling as she threaded between pots, stands, and shelves.

The scarecrow-man glided through the labyrinth and broke into a vast savannah of more polished parquet, ambling unhurried towards a bonfire trapped in a massive stone hearth. Well-seasoned wood scratch-popped and crackled like an old vinyl record as it was consumed. A long table draped with snowy white damask held a bright silver epergne and dome-covered silver dishes polished to a high gloss; an ornate iron chandelier high above, on a chain festooned with barb-wire claws, shed far too much light for the candles trapped in its towering tiers.

An antique silver samovar bubbled on a curlicue-legged, tiled table to the left of the huge fireplace; a matching table on the right held a wonderland of alembics, Bunsen burners with steady blue flames, glass piping, and a whole host of other crap that looked like a mad scientist's equipage in an old '50s black-and-white horror movie.

"It's not much to greet Spring with," the scarecrow said, that rich, dry voice momentarily swallowing the fire's ambient noise and the damp, rustling greeting of greenery. "But, as they say, it's home. You have so many questions, don't you."

Oh, God, that's the understatement of the year. "I like the chandelier." Compliments were the best strategy in awkward situations, right? Her fingertips trailed the vine of a purple inch plant—Mom called them *wandering Jews,* but that didn't seem quite polite. The vine stretched like a cat on a sunny windowsill accepting a favored human's scratching, and she glanced guiltily at the man to see if he noticed. "It's very bright."

His back was to her. "Should be, considering what it runs on. What a polite child you are after all; I'm sure that tickled Yaga's heart." He laughed, a mellow sound that spread goosebumps down her bare arms. "Are you familiar with dachshunds, Miss Drozdova?"

"They're dogs?" Somehow she doubted *wiener dogs* was an appropriately mannerly term too. She put her hands behind her back, but the plants had noticed her. None of them were making the high distressed noise that meant they needed water or more space. Whoever this guy was, he cared for his garden—or he had an army of people to do so for him.

Maybe an army of plump heavy shadows carrying watering cans. A shudder made Nat's skirt sway.

"Yes." The skeletal man began fiddling with the samovar, his reflection swelling and shrinking against its fat, polished belly. "Bred to go after rats. Have you ever been down a rathole?"

"Uh, no." The little yellow house never had a problem with mice, though sometimes Leo muttered darkly about poison for the shed during particularly damp springs. And though rodents sometimes spoke to her, Nat never quite liked their piping little voices as much as the cats' purring. "They're too small."

"You'd be surprised." But he laughed, as if she'd made an excellent joke at a dinner party. "Anyway, a rat in a confined space is quite an excellent combatant. The dogs were bred in job lots, and trained to be vicious as well."

It was a good thing she hadn't eaten. Nat's stomach was decidedly uneasy. "Oh."

He whirled on one heel, his head cocked, and examined her from green-clad toe to tangled top. Those terrible, devouring black eyes moved slow and unhurried, measuring her like a talent scout at a beauty pageant. Still, he didn't seem angry, just mildly amused. "In this particular situation, Miss Drozdova, you are the dog. Yaga has sent you down a hole."

Does that make you the rat? Maybe earlier in the evening Nat would have asked, but all her bravado was gone. A holiday-party crucifixion and a flying van could do that to you, she supposed. Not to mention magical seamstresses and a gangster whose fingernail marks on her arm still smarted. The only thing to do was pretend she was in the headmistress's office yet again, her own fingertips aligned with her side seams and her chin perfectly level, using the rushing noise in her ears to drown out whatever an uncaring authority was attempting to shame her with this time.

Except she couldn't afford to let the slipstream fill her skull and anesthetize her at the moment. Still, she could give a good impression, and stare into those black eyes like she didn't give a single fuck in the world, like she was Mom eyeing a belligerent neighbor. The plants were murmuring behind her, and that was comforting.

"How very interesting," he finally remarked. "You don't seem surprised, though your command of resources is clumsy at best. Would you like some coffee?"

I think I'd like to go home, change into pyjamas, and crawl into my closet, thanks. "That would be lovely." Her Mom imitation was pretty good. Or at least, it was good enough that the man's lips curved even further. His grin had absolutely no warmth to it at all, a skull's reflexive grimace.

He did another military turn back to the samovar, and liquid splashed. The warmth in here was all but tropical; she wondered about his power bill.

Maybe people like this didn't pay bills. Nat crossed her arms defensively. She didn't want to leave the edge of the green zone. Striking out across the parquet suddenly seemed a very bad idea.

"Good, good. Come in, my dear. I'm not in the business of harming fragile flowers, as you can no doubt see."

What would her mother say? Nat wished she had the trick of lifting one eyebrow; she'd practiced in the bathroom mirror during her teenage years, never quite managing. "I suppose it would be impolite to ask just what kind of business you *are* in."

"I grant wishes."

Of course you do. Why wasn't she more surprised? "No kidding."

"Most sorcerers do, you know. If paid properly for it."

"Okay." *C'mon, lemme see ya saucer!* Bugs Bunny's voice caroled through her head; Leo loved Looney Tunes. "You're a sorcerer." It even made a mad kind of sense.

All of this did. The most unsettling thing was the familiarity, a song on the radio she couldn't quite place until the lyrics began.

"I am *the* sorcerer, my lady, as you are *the* Drozdova. Or you will be, if the process continues. New growth is so invigorating to witness, isn't it." An edge crept into the non-question. Maybe he was getting bored.

"The" sorcerer. Well, at least this guy has some healthy self-esteem. "Isn't my mother *the* Drozdova?"

"And yet this land is killing her." One tiny, bony shrug, as if it didn't matter one way or the other. "She is an alien here, but you— well, nature takes its course; she knows that better than anyone."

This land is killing her. Well, Mom wasn't too big on the old country either. Nat couldn't blame her or Leo; sometimes after dinner the two of them mentioned terrible things that had happened back there. "The doctors say she has cancer."

"Human doctors." Koschei's laugh was a rasp against sunburned skin. "They believe in other things than you or I, my dear, or even your poor Mama."

A galvanic thrill ran through Nat, from the heels to the ends of her curls. "You're implying my mother isn't human." *Which would explain a helluva lot. And nothing at all, at the same time.*

"Human enough. As such things go." He turned away from the samovar. He carried dainty porcelain cups on equally thin, expensive-looking saucers like a man who had never waited tables, so Nat had to step away from the plants to be polite and accept one with unwilling good manners drilled into her since childhood.

The greenery rustled, rustled. Someone else might think it was a breeze from overhead fans, but the air was still, dead, and humid. One of the cups chattered against its accompanying plate, because Nat's hand was shaking as she accepted it.

"How curious," the sorcerer said, gazing down at her. This close, he smelled strange. Not unpleasant—slightly spicy, with a mineral edge. But there was no hint of flesh or the oiliness of an adult male mammal, lingering even after aftershave or the drench of "manly" body spray high school boys liked so much.

No, he smelled very much like she imagined a mummy might. One left in its tomb even after the robbers had come through.

"You must be possessed of great courage, to tread among us thinking you're human." His grin hadn't altered, and at this short distance it was even more of a rictus. "Or maybe deep down, little Drozdova, you have suspected something you dare not admit even to yourself."

I don't think I like this guy. At the moment, Nat might've preferred Dmitri, even if he was a gangster. Her scratched arm throbbed. "All I know is that my mother is dying. She sent me to de Winter, and Baba's sending me to get something Dmitri will kill me for if he can. All I've got is a bunch of riddles. So, maybe we could stop with all the cryptic theater and get to business."

"Theater? And why not?" His laugh this time was a soughing wheeze, probably because it was more genuine than the smooth radio-announcer voice, and his eyes danced merrily. "It's good magic, my girl, possibly the best. Oh, I wish we had more time together."

I can't say I agree. Nat glanced down. It was almost a letdown to find the cup full of prosaic brown coffee, a lighter brown lump of sugar tucked between its porcelain belly and the saucer painted with blue forget-me-nots. Nostalgia seized her—Mom had a set just like this in the huge hutch in the dining room. She never used it, never let anyone else use it either. It just sat there, lovingly dusted every two weeks while Leo polished the already-shining silver from the big cypress box with its carving of running stags.

The rushing filled her ears. Nat's stomach gave a sudden sickening sideways lurch, and the pretty cup with its fluted sides leapt free. It fell, somersaulting lazily, and she would have dived to rescue it but she couldn't move. Her hair lifted on a hot dry draft, and her feet hit something so hard the shock jolted in her hips and shoulders. She staggered, a tinkling crash echoing against hard surfaces, bouncing back and forth, and a wilderness of green-clad figures sprouted around her.

What the fucking hell?

Nat screamed.

SHOW ME

It was only mirrors. Nat's yell petered away as soon as she realized as much, but the fact that she was suddenly standing on dull black floor, trapped between two sheets of reflective glass, wasn't comforting at all.

I fell. I definitely fell. Trapdoor? But she hadn't landed asprawl, and there was no sign of the pretty porcelain cup, or the parquet, or the plants. Or the fireplace.

Or the sorcerer.

The mirrors marched away facing each other, and in the near distance her own reflection stood, staring with wild white-ringed eyes. She was wringing her hands, and for a moment she looked a little like her mother. The likeness was a swift punch to her gut and she bent over, retching violently.

"*Oh, I had me a giiiiiirl . . .*" The voice, desiccated but deep and resonant, echoed down the glass-walled hall. "*In a tiiiiiiiny jeweled box . . .*"

Nat reached blindly for the left-hand wall, trying to steady herself. Pain flowered up her arm and she let out another miserable little cry tinged with bile, staggering away.

"*Careful,*" the sorcerer's voice crooned. "*I won't harm you, Drozdova, and they'll show you what you want to know. But mirrors are hungry, hungry things.*"

Her fingers were bleeding, tiny razor cuts. Nat cradled her hand against her chest and straightened, slowly. If she had her boots she could kick one of these fucking glass sheets, but Coco's heels might not stand up to that sort of treatment and if the goddamn things were magic what was to say they wouldn't ignore clothing and bite the skin it protected?

She stood for what felt like a very long while, her breath coming in great shuddering gasps. Every so often she heard distant popping, or creaking. Maybe it was the wind—but she had a sudden, uncomfortable mental image of mirrors moving on invisible, well-oiled grooves, reflecting indistinct bluish light from somewhere above, sheets of silvered glass sinking and rising to re-form in a different pattern.

She'd read a book about a priestess in a labyrinth once, the heroine navigating by memorizing turnings. But that only worked if you had an eidetic memory and someone willing to teach you.

Nat was, as usual, completely on her own.

Finally, she hopped forward, nervously, her unwounded hand doing its best to keep her skirt away from the smooth wall. The faint noises were unsettling. Was the passageway shrinking behind her? She couldn't even see the source of the light because the ceiling was mirrored too, and seeing herself repeated into infinity was disorienting, to say the least.

What would happen if the soft blue glow failed?

Sometimes, Nat, your imagination just works too well.

Most times, in fact. She watched her reflection draw nearer. Mirror-Nat was wearing a bitter little smile, probably what she looked like while Mom was lecturing her about *"those crazy ideas"* and *"be a big girl, Natchenka."*

But if Mom wasn't human, and Mom *knew,* why had she said those things? If she was protecting her daughter, maybe she could have given Nat something other than disbelief for armor.

Maybe once she'd found the thing that would fix Mom's illness, she could ask all the questions. Maybe then Maria Drozdova, the undisputed queen of the little yellow house, would even answer.

Maybe then Nat could start her own life, even if it was in a shitty apartment shared with six other people also working dead-end jobs.

It was a lot of *maybes,* but as good a goal as any she'd ever had. So Nat closed her eyes, breathing hard, and tried to remember that long-ago fictional priestess.

Arha. That was her name, only it wasn't. Of course, she'd lost her labyrinth once a man came along. That was how it always went.

But assuming Nat was in the right place to find the Knife, she had a chance.

When she opened her eyes again the light had dimmed a little, from that frost-stinging blue-white to a warmer glow. The mirrors on either side had gone dark, and maybe the dry mummy-skeleton dude was behind one of them watching her.

Nat stepped forward. It felt like the right thing to do, and her reflection gave an encouraging smile. She had to hand it to Coco, the dress made Nat look like she halfway knew what she was doing, and even with her hair a mess it wasn't that bad. Mom might not tell her to *straighten up, Natchenka, you're not a serf, for God's sake.*

Once or twice Nat's tongue had burned with a reply she didn't dare even *think* too loudly. Her reflection grew somber as she stepped closer and found she was in a T-junction, mirrored hallways stretching to either side.

Leo said people lost in the woods just went in circles, thinking they were choosing randomly but really just following their dominant hand. She would have turned left, except the mirror at the end of the opposite passage turned hazy. It was like watching a TV screen resolve its focus, and Nat let out a harsh, cawing breath.

The picture firmed. Her mother was ambling down a snowy street, beautiful dancer's hands in the pockets of a long dark furry coat. Next to her a man paced, bending close and obviously attempting to make her smile. Mama turned her head, her profile sharp-serene, and gazed up at him. He leaned in for a kiss, and something about the set of his shoulders was familiar.

What the hell? Nat set off down the hall. The picture turned clearer and clearer as she approached, as if she could step through and gingerly cross the slick frozen wooden sidewalk innocent of any deicer. The streetlamps were all wrong, too—they were old-fashioned, and tiny flames burned in their bulbous heads.

Gaslamps. Even the buildings were subtly, crucially *wrong*, and there wasn't a car in sight. A sleigh with a high prow jingled past, drawn by a set of matched bays, and Nat could see every stitch in the driver's black knitted muffler.

"Mama?" she whispered like a three-year-old, but her mother didn't hear. The picture vanished, and Nat let out a small, hurt sound, glancing wildly to either side.

More passages, each with a glowing sheet of glass at the end. Nat's ribs heaved. "Mama," she whispered again. *Oh, come on. Show me something else. That was her in the old country, I'll bet anything.*

The thought that maybe she *had* bet everything by going to see de Winter, and was furthermore about to lose the wager horribly, drifted through her aching head. She hadn't even had a chance to drink the damn coffee, although that was probably a mercy.

Who knew what that guy had put into it? *The* sorcerer. Like Baba was *the* Grandmother, and Mom was *the* Drozdova.

All right. If this was a story, Nat would know what to do. So she licked her dry lips and tried to think. "Show me my mother."

The mirrors shivered in their seatings, tinkling prettily. She carefully avoided touching them, edging towards the one which brightened most.

There was her mother, lying on her back in a green sunny field. Nat could almost smell the crushed grass. Mama's belly was high and proud, probably with baby Nat, and Maria Drozdova stroked the curve lovingly as her lips moved. Daisies nodded in ankle-high grass, turning their faces towards the plaid blanket Mama reclined on.

Next to her, a dark-haired man with his face turned away was propped on his elbow, reaching for a dandelion. The stem broke silently, and Mama's expression soured between one moment and the next. There was no sound, but Nat could very well imagine the cutting remark slipping between her mother's pink-glossed lips.

The screen darkened and Nat was off again, walking towards the next brightening. Her skirt brushed the glass to her left and a thin fragment of green cloth whispered free, but she didn't notice.

Mama, creeping down a dark hall Nat recognized because she'd been there yesterday; it led to Baba de Winter's office. Her mother was pregnant, but not nearly as heavily—just rounded a bit, like

Leo's midlife potbelly. On her it looked natural, beautiful, and *right*. The baby bump pulled up the skirt of her yellow flowered dress, and her bare feet had pink-polished toenails.

Nat watched, spellbound, as her mother crept into de Winter's office. The only light was from the huge windows, bathing the room in the dusky, dusty orange of a moonless summer night in the city. Mom obviously knew where she was going; she headed to the left instead of the huge bar on the right Dmitri had revealed just yesterday.

It felt like a million years ago.

Soft and stealthy, Nat's mother pressed on the gleaming black wall, her fingers moving in a tortuous pattern. A slice of the wall pulled back; Mom stiffened, glancing over her shoulder.

The picture faded just as Mom was reaching into the wall cabinet. Nat's heart pounded so hard her head felt hollow and swollen. It was work to turn away, looking for the next screen.

A baby-blue, 60s-adjacent Mustang zoomed down a two-lane highway, rolling grass on every side. Mountains were a purple smudge on the horizon, and the only other landscape feature was a giant, twisted tree in the middle distance, roots diving into a pile of bright yellow sand, tangled branches loaded with pink blossom.

Wait a minute. I know that car. Mom talked about it all the time, but the Mustang was lost and only the ancient black Léon-Bollée remained. Nat reached for the mirror, yanked her hand back just in time. Her fingers stung anyway, and she gasped. *Hey, no fair! I didn't even touch it!*

Now both her hands were bleeding and the injustice filled her throat, hot and acid as bile. She once more considered kicking the goddamn glass, swallowed her rage with habitual speed but without the usual ease, and looked for the next glowing picture.

Nothing. Three avenues branched away, and all three were dark.

"That's all I'll give for free." The sorcerer's voice filled the passageway, tugged at her hair and skirt with a dry hot breeze. *"Now you must ask, Drozdova. Choose wisely, choose well—and hurry."*

Ask? Ask *what?*

The popping noises were getting louder. Mirrors creaked, like skyscraper windows on windy days. The vibration met her shoes and ran up through her bones, settling in her teeth.

Whatever Mom had stolen was in parts. Was this the man who believed in the future, who was supposed to give her directions to the first piece? If not, why had he scooped her up from the party?

Except he wasn't really living up to his end of the deal, if that even *was* the deal. A good daughter would figure out how to negotiate, how to hold him to his bargain. But he was a fucking *sorcerer*, he had her trapped in a mirrored labyrinth, and had anyone thought to warn her? Of course not.

Nat's hands were fists. Hot blood slipped between her fingers. She tried to glare down each hall at once. "This is bullshit," she muttered. Then, because she couldn't help herself, she inhaled hard and screamed. "*This is fucking BULLSHIT!*"

Cracks spiderwebbed along the darkened glass on either side. The floor rumbled, groaning, and Nat swayed, terror igniting behind her breastbone.

The scary thing wasn't the thought that she had somehow caused it. No, the absolutely terrifying thing was that she *knew* she had.

And it felt good.

More popping, cracking sounds. She realized what they were just as a mirror exploded behind her, glass smashing across the hallway to pepper its opposite twin. Nat flinched, and the screen to her left flickered.

She knew what she was going to ask—the one question she could never, ever voice, the one her mother would never forgive. It slipped between her teeth, bolting like a runaway horse. "My father," she said, desperately. "Where's my father?"

Between the popping, the groaning, the creaking, and the shattering, the sorcerer's laugh tiptoed. *Are you sure you want to know?* that chuckle said, and Nat's right fist jumped up, pistoned out.

The mirror to her right shattered. It hurt, but the pain was a sweet clean jolt. Her other fist leapt free too, and left a bloody print in the center of a star of breakage. "You'll show me everything," she said, and it was Mama's *you do not know who you are fucking with, sir* voice, filling her throat and streaming free like a spring storm tearing through tossing branches weighted with new growth. "Or so help me, I will *end* you."

The mirror down the leftmost passageway lit, blazing with pitiless white. Nat looked, her eyes growing rounder, and she recognized that table, the chairs, the thick white china mug of hot chocolate with the chipped rim—

A terrific crack speared the picture, shivering it from top to bottom. Glass fell, crashing musically, and Nat let out a miserable little cry. Her bloody fists leapt up as she ducked, bare arms over her head a pathetic shield against flying shards. Little razors kissed her bare skin, almost painless as the sting waited to creep up catfoot, and she had wasted her one question asking something she did, after all, know the answer to deep down, in the most secret places of her aching, pounding heart.

MISBORN THINGS

Each of the creatures in the garage turned into hideous, bubbling scrap by the hatred wedded to Dima's bullets was a stab to Koschei's prestige; energy the Deathless poured into his dolls could not be renewed, only laboriously gathered afresh. Dmitri worked his way up, floor by floor—the stairwells were hidden and more often than not turned into greased slides, but his boots gripped well and he found each camouflaged door.

Nothing better than a thief for that particular task. Everything hidden, everything of value gloated over by a miser late at night, everything treasured, was all within his purview. Or, at least, the finding was, and what did you do once you had found it?

Only what was natural. Only what you were meant to, what you had been made for.

He ascended from parking garage to anonymous building-layers masquerading as offices, glass doors shattering and cubicles exploding with particleboard, paper, shards from tiny crouching mimic-goblins, sparks from electrical snakes hidden in the walls. The straight razor flickered, the gun roared, and Dima sang, hopping over a trap disguised as a secretary's desk and shooting a skittering gremlin chirping about rates of return. A large rectangular taupe plastic thing masquerading as a printer waddled towards him, rumbling a deep chthonic curse he stepped mincingly aside to avoid; he kicked it and his silvered boot-toes did as much damage as the countercurse he spat in a language from the banks of a dying river under a smoke-choked sky, a former incarnation's knowledge rising from the buried past.

The only really troubling parts were the pseudo-bathrooms. It just wasn't right for urinals to make that noise.

Past the office floors the terrain changed. Now it was apartments, blank doors on either side of indifferently lit halls with cheap nylon carpeting that turned to mush dragging at his soles, the smell of fatty food burned on hot plates rising choke-thick, the doors taffy-stretching until the straight razor slashed and they screeched, flapping open and cringing. Behind each one was a different stage set, some with the deadly quiet of carnivorous traps and others with howling violence lurking behind lumpen furniture.

This was mere foreplay. Above, it would become much more interesting. Koschei's mightier clockworks were kept closer to the nest, and now the poking, prying little bastard knew he had a guest. He would be hurrying to do whatever he could to the Drozdova, but she was a tough little nut, resistant to cracking.

Dima could admit as much, even as it irritated him enough that he missed a single strike at a lumbering beast built to look like an ancient Frigidaire. Which meant he had to shoot it twice; as he did so a lamp-shaped thing with a conical cream plastic shade wrapped its cord around his ankle and bit, burning his calf through Italian wool.

He *liked* this suit. Dmitri roared a curse and kicked the thing, sending it skittering into a corner with a shower of venomous green sparks. Bad enough that Koschei aped his betters, but the man had no creativity.

Dmitri found the escape from this particular floor and raced up concrete steps lit by angrily buzzing fluorescents, bursting out into a long gallery of glass rectangles arranged in rows. Each case held a wrapped cocoon, varying shapes and sizes swelling or deflating as the things inside accreted towards birth or failure. The former Koschei would probably keep.

The latter were simply released to hunt wherever his domicile happened to be perched, bringing home prey to add to the sorcerer's numinous force. Dima showed his teeth in a wolf's grin, though wolves—unlike humanity—did not destroy merely for the joy of it. The gun barked in his hand, his boots flickered, and he leapt from case to case, spreading fractals under his stamping heels. Falling glass shivered, and he heard a high tinkling echo from above.

Now what do you suppose that is?

The linen-husked things screamed as their safe little hutches were broken and the inimical outside flooded in. It was to be expected; only the strong survived in this world.

"*Bastard*," a lipless voice thundered through the long wood-floored room. "*What the fuck are you doing, Konets?*"

It spoke in the language of the old country, and Dima's hatred turned bright as the straight razor in his left hand, still innocent of any stain. It took practice and skill to carve without smirching yourself.

He shattered the last case, pausing to concentrate. The gun accepted its silencer; from here, the work would be quiet. He used the moment to listen to the painful piping cries of the misborn things; maybe Koschei could salvage a few once Dmitri had what he wanted.

But maybe not.

The entrance to the next level was cut into the popcorn ceiling, and it throbbed with sorcery. Koschei's voice rose in a chant far above, and that shiver-tinkling sound of breakage kept going though Dima had demolished every case on this floor.

He pursed his lips, whistling a high drilling note, and coiled himself to leap.

SEE SOME THINGS

Broken glass glittered everywhere. White surgical light foamed over Nat in a stinging wave. There was a clattering, a low male grunt of effort, and two short pops.

"Oh, really?" the low, dry, smooth voice of the sorcerer said, and his tone was so prosaically aggrieved she almost opened her eyes again. "Shooting me, Konets? Have you no—"

Next came a swish and a terrible throaty gurgle. Nat let out a small helpless sound, her stinging arms still clasped over her head. A hot droplet touched her cheek.

Like a child awake after a nightmare, she was afraid to look in case it was real.

Soft footsteps, glass grinding finer and finer. The steps circled her, and she drew in huge, shuddering breaths. Knowing who it was didn't help.

"Oh, *zaika*," Dmitri said, and under the fresh scratches on her left arm the older ones from his hurtful grasp throbbed. "What you do to yourself?" There was a click, and Nat peeked between her bare, bleeding arms to see Dmitri, his suit rumpled and covered with strange burns and spatters, scratching at his forehead with the muzzle of a big, dull black gun. The weapon had a strange elongated snout she recognized from movies as a silencer.

His other hand, dangling at his side, held a bright cutthroat razor, its worn black handle almost slipping from his fingertips. Despite the precarity of its position, it still held a bright, evil gleam, and something told her his loose grip wasn't ornamental or thoughtless.

"Oh," she said, blankly. "It's you." *State the fucking obvious, Nat.*

"Or was it him?" Dima made a swift movement, gesturing with the gun as if it was welded to his palm, though by some curious circumstance it never pointed at her.

The scarecrow-thin sorcerer lay amid whorls of broken glass, but not nearly enough for the labyrinth Nat had been caught in. The wreckage amounted to only a couple medium-sized windows; the shards spread outwards, an exploding flower with reflective petals. Two smoking holes in the scarecrow's chest matched a tidy one in the very middle of his forehead, and under his chin his throat gaped in a great smiling slice that showed the raw edge of meat and a chip of white bone, but no blood.

In fact, he wasn't bleeding at all, though Nat's arms were covered with oozing, shallow slices. The sorcerer's fingers twitched, and a horrid dusty wheeze rattled from his collapsing lungs through the clean cut in his throat.

"I hurt him again," Dmitri announced, turning on his heel. His boot-toes twinkled just as much as ever, but they were suddenly much less funny when the razor answered. And the bright metal on the shoe-caps looked just as sharp as the blade itself.

He stalked to the sorcerer, who kept making that wheezing noise. The scarecrow's long fingers twitched, and his thin dry lips were moving. Of course there wasn't any breath to make his vocal folds resonate, but Nat could decipher one or two of the words.

Looked like he was cussing Dmitri out.

Shaking went through Nat in waves, muscles quivering between the urge to run and the absolute knowledge it was impossible, that if she attracted the direct attention of the murderous gangster stalking the undead sorcerer-thing on the floor something even worse might happen.

"Eh, old man." Dmitri bent over the sorcerer. "You're a mess. How you gonna fix this one?"

Koschei's lips twitched with renewed speed. Incredibly, his hands were moving, smoothing his pullover, exploring the twin holes in his chest. He glared at Dmitri, those terrible, vital dark eyes all but shooting invisible hate-rays.

"What's that?" Dmitri grinned, the wide white smile of an utter lunatic. "I can't *hear* you," he chanted, and the gun spoke again and again, making soft little coughing noises as the scarecrow's body jerked.

Nat cried out, unable to stop herself, and Dmitri glanced at her. His snarl smoothed so swiftly she might have doubted ever seeing it, and he administered a final kick to Koschei's midsection. His boot-toe sank in with a sound like an axe biting well-seasoned wood, and Nat's stomach revolved again.

"You worried about him?" The razor flickered once, twice, before snapping closed and disappearing, whether into sleeve or pocket she couldn't tell. "It would take more than that, *zaika*, though I do admit, sometimes I'm tempted to keep going. Just to see." He strolled toward her, and she couldn't help staring at the gun. He carried it like a mechanic would a tool when called to answer some kind of customer question, like Leo wandering into the kitchen with a ratchet on a bright summer day wanting lemonade, his fingers black with engine grease and Mama muttering about the marks he'd never dare leave on the yarrow-washed floor.

The thought of Leo made her flinch again. Dmitri's free hand flashed out; his fingers, warm and hard, circled her right wrist. "Easy," he said, much more softly. "Let's see what we got, eh?" His dark head cocked, and he inhaled, shuddering slightly. "All's well. Dima's here."

"M-my mother." Nat's lips felt at once too large and too small for the words. "The m-mirrors."

"See some things, did you? Come, we take care of this."

Even if she was capable of objecting, she might not have. Because he made another quick movement, the gun disappearing, and bent to pick her up like an overtired toddler at a late party. He was wiry but strong, and his footsteps made no more noise against the scattered, crunching glass than they had before.

"You're lucky," he said over his shoulder, a diagonal cord of muscle on his neck standing out. "Next time I see you, Koschei, we find out how long it takes the parts of you to crawl back together when I'm done scattering them."

There was a deep groaning wheeze. Nat wished she could bury her face in the convenient black-clad shoulder, but the stains there were fresh and smelled truly awful. Besides, Dmitri's hands were a little too tight, as if he expected her to start struggling and screaming at any moment—and would clamp down without a second thought.

So she just closed her eyes and tried to breathe.

"*Drozzzzzzdovaaaaaaa*." A thick, rasping chuckle. The image of Koschei cradling his own head in his bloodless hands, pressing the edges of his sliced throat together, were sick-making, and she almost choked on bile. "*You know where the Kniiiiiife iiiiis*."

Dmitri halted, and his eyelids dropped halfway. He had turned to stone.

"Let's just go," she whispered, with no real hope he'd agree.

But he started moving again. Nat finally sagged against him, trying not to look at anything but his dark-stubbled chin. Whispering laughter, brittle as old caramel dried to a crackglaze, filled the shattered room behind them. There were no plants, no fireplace, no glass pyramid. Just a corpse, some broken glass, and the high dusty cavern of a warehouse with its walls running like smoky oil on dark water through veils of visual static.

"Don't look," Dmitri said. "Give you a headache, *zaika*. Close your eyes."

So, like the good little girl she once was, Nat did.

MAMA'S IN

There were weirder things in the city than some guy carrying a bleeding woman in a green dress down a sidewalk growing increasingly icy as the temperature dropped. Nat had even seen one or two of them tonight, but she still flinched every time a car rolled slowly by, feeling strangers' gazes burn over them. Dmitri refused to set her down.

"You might run off again, *zaika*. And it's been a nice evening."

So she gave up and let herself be borne along, trying to ignore how the cold didn't touch her, how her skirt was sliced cleanly in a few places, and how blood was slowly clotting on her arms and fingertips. She also tried to ignore how the pavement was doing funny things underfoot, or how the buildings seemed to change places when she wasn't looking. They were no longer in Manhattan, but that was *impossible*.

Just like everything else tonight. This was probably Baba de Winter's idea of a good time, and definitely Dmitri's. At least, he was whistling as he carted her along, a wandering tune that wove in and out of something she vaguely remembered hearing on the radio lately.

"Put me down," she repeated.

His whistling broke off. "You're shaking."

No shit. "I'll manage."

"No." And that, his tone clearly said, was that.

"You're hurt." She didn't know if he was or not, but it stood to reason with the way his suit looked he'd been in a fight with *something*. Probably not to rescue her, though—he seemed to hate the scarecrow more than he liked her, which was about par for the course. "You shouldn't be carrying me."

"Ah, she cares." His chiseled lip lifted a little, mockingly. "So sweet. But no, *zaika*, Dima is not hurt. That which does not kill me had better tell Hell who sent them."

"That's not the saying." Nat peered over his shoulder and wished she hadn't, because the streetlights looked warped. He stepped sideways, then the opposite direction, and each time her vantage point showed a different avenue. One looked like Flushing, and the other a little like Jersey for all she could tell, and both moved like building blocks in a child's nightmare.

"Close enough. Stop peeking, you'll get sick."

"What are you *doing*?"

"Traveling, *zaika*. A thief has ways of moving. You'll have your own, once you stop fighting what you are." His heels dug in, scratching a long furrow through a sheet of ice, and they jolted to a stop before a high narrow brick building squeezed between two dingy, closed-down storefronts. "Hello, girls."

A bright crimson neon cross burned on the roof, the only part of a much bigger billboard still functioning. A blonde woman and a brunette, both extremely underdressed for the temperature, stood on the front steps, smoking thin joints tucked into improbably long holders.

The blonde stared at Dmitri like he was something scraped off the soles of her white pleather go-go boots. Red garter straps vanished under her impossibly short skirt, sinking cruelly into tender skin, and her bright red mouth pursed. The brunette, in a shimmering yellow minidress and sunny, strappy platform wedges, exhaled a cloud of skunk-smelling smoke that was *definitely* not tobacco. "Mama's in," she said, in a pleasant but neutral contralto.

"She better be." Dmitri finally set Nat on her feet.

She swayed, hoping Coco's shoes would continue to hold up and she wouldn't fall on her ass. They did, gripping sparkling ice, and she realized the street in front of this place was unplowed, an unbroken sheet of white with thick clear ice-frosting.

The gangster patted at her shoulders, tugging at various parts of her dress with an impersonal, critical expression, like a kid with a doll. "Good enough," he muttered, finally. "Just tell her it was Koschei, and it'll be fine." Then he offered her his arm, just as he had at Jay's mansion.

Nat suppressed a shudder, but she took the support anyway, with something approaching gratitude. Her knees weren't quite steady.

After all, she'd seen two men murdered tonight. Or was it murder if neither of them were dead? "Jay," she said, refusing to move when Dima leaned as if to step forward. "Is he . . ."

"Oh, hell no." Dima snorted, the sound turning into a genuine laugh at the end. "Come high noon he'll be fine, right as rain and searching the entire house for his missing flower. Inside, little girl. You'll like this lady."

"Is she like de Winter?" She couldn't make herself say *grandmother* right now, even in another language.

He threw his head back and laughed afresh while he set off for the stairs, and once more she had to follow or be dragged.

The blonde examined them critically, then met the brunette's gaze and shrugged. *I just work here*, that shrug said, and the brunette giggled. It was a hard, bright sound, and echoed all the way down the street.

The front door was a beautiful Art Deco survivor of wood and beveled glass, a gem in a prosaic alloy setting. It opened with a cheerful jingle, a cascade of small brass bells hanging from tangled red yarn wrapped around the inside knob; Nat and Dima plunged into dim crimson warmth and the smell of nag champa.

Curls of perfumed smoke floated down the staircase to the left; the house was built narrow and squeezed mercilessly from either side. A low doorway to the right held swaying strings of pink heart-shaped plastic beads; an antiseptic glow near the end of the long hall parallel to the stairs glittered off black-and-white linoleum, making Nat think *kitchen*.

She missed the little yellow house with uncharacteristic fierceness. She'd scrub every floor, sing every song to every plant, and perform every useless, fiddly task Mom had ever devised if she could just crawl into her own closet once she was done and forget all of this.

"Who is it?" A velvety voice drifted down the stairs. "I smell a man, you'd better have a good reason for—oh. It's Dima. What have you . . . Oh, honey, what happened?"

Clip-clopping footsteps hurried down the stairs and the gangster pushed Nat forward a little, almost like a shield.

The first surprise was that the woman was dressed like an old fifties cheesecake pinup of a nurse, complete with deep-plunging cleavage exposing two-thirds of plump coppery breasts that looked both free of any silicone adjustment *and* gravity-defying, right to the perky little nubbins of her slightly asymmetrical nipples pressing against thick snowy cloth. A little starched cap with a red cross to match the neon one outside perched in her cloud of dark curls, and her wide chocolate eyes sparkled with kindness. Her nails were moderately short, but painted just as neon-crimson as the cross or hat, and her legs, innocent of any pantyhose, were gloriously long, muscled like a pole dancer's, and ended in white platform brogues that gave a good impression of being the heavy-duty shoes of a woman who worked on her feet for twelve hours at a time.

She had a cute button nose, and her lips were just a few shades darker than her nails—maybe Coco had done her makeup. "Oh, honey," she repeated, and swept down the rest of the stairs in a rush. "You come right on in, now, and let's take a look at that. We'll make it all better."

"Hello, Candy." The gangster actually sounded respectful, for once.

"Speak when you're spoken to," she snapped. "This is not your house, dark one."

His shrug also served to shake his arm free of Nat's; he surrendered her to this new strangeness without demur.

That was how the young Drozdova met Nurse Candy.

BLOOD-TOUCHED DIAMOND

Half the kitchen was a regular 60s-era throwback complete with avocado-colored toaster, matching ancient Frigidaire, and bulky, vile-orange stove; the other half was painted white and looked like a surgical suite. Candy motioned her towards a high, three-legged wooden stool instead of the two examining tables or the dentist's chair with a dead, shrouded light fixture hovering over it like a scorpion's tail. This place, despite its narrowness, was much bigger on the inside, like Coco's boutique or Jay's palatial home—but then again, wasn't everything in fairyland?

Nat couldn't stop shaking, though she wasn't cold. Candy glared at Dmitri when he stepped over the invisible line demarcating the medical side from the kitchen. Both were floored in those spotless white and black linoleum squares, and Nat wondered who cleaned all this.

Magic? Or people who didn't know what they were scrubbing? What if it was people who *did* know, and how young had they been when they learned to keep their mouths shut like she had?

"You make her nervous," the nurse snapped. "Go outside. And you leave my girls alone if any come along, they're off tonight."

"Weather like this hurts business." Dima tipped Nat a lazy, two-finger salute. "I wait outside, *zaika*. From now on, I keep both eyes on you." He backed halfway down the hall, his gaze holding hers, before turning with a flourish and stalking out the front door. He didn't slam, though, just closed it gently as if leaving a sickroom.

"Fucking men." The nurse shook her head. "Well, hi there. I'm Candy, honey. And you're the Drozdova."

"N-Nat." Her throat was a pinhole. "How. Do you. Do."

"I haven't heard that one in a long while. It's a nice change from *Hey baby*." Candy smiled, and touched Nat's wrist. "I'm just gonna take a look at this, all right, honey? Where you been tonight to get hurt like this?" The slight feather of urgency in the last question was almost nice, really.

Nat could pretend someone cared. "J-Jay's." Of course her teeth would pick now to chatter. "Then a van. Then K-K-K-Koes—"

"Koschei? I heard he was in town, with that flying sleigh of his." Candy touched the inside of Nat's elbow with a gentle fingertip. "Which explains why Dima's bothering. Let me just take a peek at how bad it is. . . ." A quick, narrow glance at Nat's stunned expression, and Candy's tone turned excessively casual once more. "So, do you have the Heart? Can I see it?"

"The what?" Nat shook her head. "I don't have anything, and my mom's going to die."

The woman looked up from examining Nat's right arm, her eyebrows peaking with surprise. "Maria Drozdova is still alive?"

"I h-hope so." Nat's lower lip quivered; she tried to firm her expression. "She sent me to Baba de Winter to find something she wants, and de Winter will cure her, but I was supposed to ask the right q-question and I didn't." *I sound five years old again.* But Nat couldn't help it, the woman's eyes were kind, and she listened like nothing else in the world mattered.

It was a warm balm; nobody ever paid attention like this. Even Leo.

"*Cure* her?" Candy dropped Nat's arm and took a step back, her platform shoes squeaking slightly. ". . . Oh. I see." She half-turned, and one of her hands jumped to her mouth. The bright lighting—it didn't buzz like fluorescents or make Candy look sickly, though it was probably not doing Nat any favors—dimmed for a few heartbeats.

She should have been terrified all over again, but Nat was simply too tired. She examined the cuts on her arms and fingers instead. Hair-thin, none of them very deep—it was a good thing, she could have bled out in that terrible place.

So the sorcerer probably hadn't been trying to kill or really injure, just terrify? He'd done an A-plus job of that.

Nat's fingers were too slick with tacky-wet blood to grab at the sides of the seat, so she couldn't shut her eyes—she'd probably fall right off, with the way the shakes were going through her. It didn't matter much. She focused on the bright orange stove in the kitchen half, wondering how they got the burner shields so spotless. Her mother would be interested in that little housekeeping trick. A macramé holder in the darkened window held what looked like an aloe vera with huge drooping arms, but no aloe she'd ever seen had thorns like that.

"I'm sorry, honey." Candy turned back again, now with a bright smile. "I just needed a moment. Let me guess. Your mother let you grow up thinking you were normal, didn't she. It makes a certain amount of . . . oh, the bitch. The grasping little *bitch*."

Normally, Nat would have leapt to Mom's defense. After tonight, though, it didn't really seem important. She just stared at Candy, wondering what the woman wanted. Leo was right, there was no trusting anyone.

That thought hurt. She sucked in a tiny breath, as if she'd been punched.

"Oh, honey." Candy was suddenly very close, and wrapped her arms around Nat, blood and all. She had to bend to do it, and the cleavage pressed against Nat's cheek was definitely all natural. But the funny thing was . . .

Well, she smelled wonderful. Like flowers and black earth and fresh air after Nat's mother spent an afternoon in the garden, one of the fine summer days—not too hot—when Maria was in a good mood and things were growing as she liked them. A day when the lemonade had the right amount of sugar and Nat had performed her chores as soon as she got up, a day when Leo hadn't irritated Mrs. Drozdova too much and her daughter hadn't needed anything.

In short, Candy smelled exactly like her mother on a good day, and Nat's face crumpled. There was even the faint edge of talcum, and a breath of roses from the water Mama dabbed under her eyes each night *to keep them fresh, Natchenka, now run along to bed*.

"You poor little thing. I've got a mind to go find your mother and give her a bit of advice. Thinks herself so much better than the rest of us. Well, there's things *I* won't stoop to, not even for money, honey, and that's saying something. Why Baba let that . . . oh, well, I know why, because she's old and it doesn't matter one way or another, not to her. But sending you out with Dmitri? That's just too much. He's a bleak creature now, but what do you expect? Takes pure will to keep going the way he does."

It would be nice to have a noun, lady. All Nat wanted was to go home and go to sleep in her closet, hoping that in the morning she'd wake up to a world just as pale and cold and dull as everyone had always insisted. A world where her mother would just be some crazy old woman dying by inches and Leo just a . . .

"Oh, God," Nat whispered, her stomach twitching like a fish drowning in air. "Help me. Please."

"Honey, you are in the right place. I'm always here to help, and we should start at the beginning." The woman took a deep breath. Candy's arms slithered away, and she stepped back, eyeing Nat critically. "We're gonna need something that doesn't sting, but none of them are deep enough to need sutures. So it's butterflies and my special iodine, and I'm going to tell you a thing or two, little girl. You'd better listen to Mama, now."

Nat suppressed a guilty flinch. Candy's eyes widened slightly, and her jaw set. A small silver trolley trundled into view, obeying her impatient beckoning like a fat old sheepdog knowing it would get there in its own sweet time. On its broad back a shining steel medical tray made soft busy noises, a glass bottle of disinfectant clinking against a container of cotton balls as the wheels turned.

"Like a pinch on a bruise, is it? Sorry. Mostly everyone listens to their mama, sometimes it just comes out. And I've got my girls to keep me in the habit, we're everywhere the wind blows, mostly. They do their best by me and I reciprocate. That's what it's all about. 'Course I might not go where there's no people but *you*, you'll go everywhere. That's the nature of the thing." She glanced at Nat's expression, nodding slightly as if it confirmed a guess. "I call us *divinities*, though there's other words. It's as good a name as any."

Divinities. All right. "Okay." There was nothing else to say. Nat let her hands be lifted and examined under the steady bright light. Candy's bent profile looked very young, a trick of shadows or maybe really good makeup. Her lashes were too thick to be natural, but even this close Nat couldn't see the glued-on line, and skin that beautiful couldn't be real either.

But somehow, impossibly, it was.

"See, most of the time we just sort of coalesce when there's a need. But sometimes we move when our followers do. Your mama moved here, but she needed some way to stay. I suppose it wouldn't occur to her to just get out of the way and let a younger woman take over. It's terrible, but embedded patriarchy always is." Candy dabbed a little of the brown liquid on Nat's forearm, where the deepest pattern of slices still wept. Amazingly, it didn't sting; Nat's flesh just went numb, like Novocain was supposed to work.

Of course Nat had never been to the dentist's. She knew about the chairs from horror stories and movies; Mama had never taken her to the doctor except for shots—but now that Nat thought about it, she never went in for a booster, and just assumed Mama had taken her in when she was too young to remember. Nat had never really been sick—oh, a few colds or tummyaches, but no ear infections, no tonsillitis, never a broken bone.

"Anyway, she could always go back and see if she transforms," Candy continued, matter-of-factly. "It's painful, but it happens. Better than what she *obviously* decided. And sending you after the Heart to pay the toll, that's a fine how-do-you-do."

"Excuse me." Nat tried not to sound prim. "But . . . okay, you know what I'm supposed to get?"

"Nobody told you? Time was when Dima wouldn't pass up the chance to tell a girl with eyes like yours every little thing that crosses his mind. Well, I suppose you've passed the point of mortal skepticism after the night you've had. Maybe that was even Baba's plan; the old lady hates answering questions." Candy pursed her lips, painting another few shallow slices. The iodine smelled medicinal but also fresh, like clean laundry hung outside—maybe it was juice from that huge tentacled monster hanging in its macramé hammock. Mom would know; she knew *all* the plants. "There we are. Now, honey, you want something to drink. I'll make you some hot chocolate, but we've gotta be quick. You ain't my only client tonight, as the saying goes."

Candy kept painting the slices with a numbing, soothing touch, talking in a low confidential tone, and Nat's body turned cold, then hot, then cold again hearing it all spelled out so matter-of-fact. The light over the stove flicked on, a battered tin saucepan settling on a cherry-glowing electric ring, and milk was poured from a thick heavy glass bottle with no visible means of support.

Why not? Her dress had been made by invisible hands, too. Nat watched as the tiny cuts on her arms healed under sticky stuff that was definitely not iodine, no matter what Candy called it. The dress itself tugged and twitched, threads spinning across shallow razor-slices.

The cloth was healing itself.

If the sorcerer had wanted to really hurt her, he could have. Was he saving that for later, if Nat could be induced to give him directions to the jewel? It was, Candy told her, about the size of a man's fist, and scintillating.

"It's a gem, yeah," Candy said, examining a long slice on the back of Nat's forearm. "But it's also a Heart. One of *ours,* you understand? He gave it to pay for passage, is what I heard." She glanced at the hallway as if she expected someone to be lurking in the gloom, listening. "And listen to me, little girl. You better never, *ever* let Dmitri Konets get his hands on it. He'll kill you just for holding it, let alone being Maria's daughter. Do you understand?"

Nat nodded. She had no problem believing Dmitri could put a bullet or two in her just as easily as he had in the sorcerer. She was a means to an end, nothing more and as usual. "It's a . . . heart, but also a gem?"

"Like a big ol' blood-touched diamond. I imagine Maria has it in some kind of setting, to keep it from flying back to its owner."

"The owner . . ." *Oh, wow.*

"Oh, we can live without little things like hearts, honey. Just so long as they suspect, or even better, *believe.* Lovely little mortals.

Sometimes I wish they weren't so blind, but you know . . ." Candy shook her head, her earrings swaying. "Then I get angry, seeing what they do to my girls. Those are hungry nights."

"You're saying my mother is a . . ." *A divinity.*

"Well, she was. Now it's you."

"What's happening to her?" It was a stupid question, Nat realized. She'd been staring at what was going to happen to Mama for a while now. It had started well before the night with the ambulance, her mother losing weight and complaining of fatigue, staring at Nat with bright blue bloodshot eyes.

"Well, the younger supplants the elder in certain cases. Because sometimes, *where* you're born is important too." Candy skimmed her palm over Nat's forearm, almost cross-eyed concentration turning her face into a schoolgirl's again. A trick of light could make her look younger or weathered; her curls bobbed as she blew lightly across damp disinfectant. "Anyway, she should just accept it."

That's my mother you're talking about. Acceptance wasn't really in Maria Drozdova's dictionary, and Nat's heart gave a slight traitorous twinge. "So the Heart can make her not . . . not die?" Was that how it worked? That was probably why Mama wanted her to bring everything to the hospice first.

Simple enough, Nat supposed. She hadn't said *when* she'd deliver the item to Baba, and could even argue de Winter hadn't even said precisely what she wanted Nat to fetch.

It felt dirty to think that way, but she was trying to save her mother, wasn't she? That was worth a little filth.

Candy paused, studying Nat's face. Her pretty painted lips moved slightly before she shook her head, obviously choosing her words carefully. "Baba might be able to use it for that, I wouldn't know. Did she *say* she'd cure your mother?"

"I . . ." Now Nat couldn't remember just what the old woman had promised.

"Well, think about it. The old chicken-legged lady doesn't lie, but she doesn't tell all she knows either." Candy painted another long thin slice, the thick goop spreading welcome warm numbness.

"I just know Dmitri will kill whoever keeps it from him. He said so, and he meant it."

Yeah, I've got that part, thanks. "But my mom stole it?"

"From Baba herself." Candy let out a soft whistle, almost admiring. "Gotta hand it to your mama, she always finds a way. I can tell you will, too." A series of fast light taps on the front door made Candy straighten. "That's Dima. He won't want to leave you with me for long; he can't stand conversations he can't eavesdrop on. You just sit at the table over there with your hot cocoa—you look like the unicorn type—and drink like a good girl while Mama discusses things with her brother."

"He's your brother?" Nat wasn't sure she could slither off the stool, much less make her legs carry her to the tiny chrome-legged table with its two orange-and-green flowered vinyl chairs.

"Kind of. Every one of my girls is a sister to his nephews, you know. Even if they sometimes don't act very familial." Candy shook her head again, capping the jar of "special iodine" with a savage twist of her wrist. "Welcome to the most fucked-up family possible, honey. Excuse me."

Nat watched her sway down the hall, her skirt far too tight for her long, no-nonsense strides. *I wouldn't want to be in her way,* she thought, very clearly, and a wave of nausea passed through her, hard and bright as a polished silver spear. The door closed, and Nat looked at the table.

The saucepan was dangling in midair over a huge white mug. No—the cup's handle was a gilt unicorn's head, and its white china sides were painted with the body of that golden, fantastical beast.

Nat knew that cup. She'd bought it with chore money at the thrift store one winter, and refused to drink from anything else until it broke in the sink while she was at school one day.

Or at least, that's what Mama said had happened. Maybe Koschei's mirrors would have told Nat otherwise.

What did it matter? You learned not to make a big fuss, because after all, there were plenty of nice matching cups in the cabinets. You learned to get along, to make do, to keep your mouth shut. To find a job, and another job, to work until you were almost free and then to find a hospice for your collapsed and steadily ailing mother, to find a certain skyscraper downtown and a woman with winter-colored hair inside.

Nat was a champion at keeping quiet and finding things. The trouble was, she'd ignored what was right in front of her, and she had the sinking suspicion she wasn't going to be able to stay quiet anymore.

She might not be a good little girl at all, either.

Not now.

ESSENTIAL TRUTH

I don't like you very much right now." Candy stood on the top step, her arms crossed, and stared down at him.

"I was *good* to her!" Dmitri didn't like the urge to explain himself. "I took her to Coco, brought her champagne, took her dancing."

"You and Baba dangled her out at Jay's party hoping one of Maria's little helpers would bite, and one did. Probably wanted to tenderize her for the banquet, too." Candy's lip lifted, not quite a snarl but certainly a warning. "Even for you this is something, Konets. Time was, you wouldn't steal from the innocent."

"I steal from who I fuckin' please, Candy, and are we going to argue about this right here on the fuckin' street?" He glanced at the two camouflaged Amazons flanking their goddess.

Some of them remembered when she was Astarte, and further back to a land where male children were sold to neighboring peoples at the border markets and a star-shaped shield was alive with a divinity's consciousness. Even for the gods made of basic natural forces devotees meant more power, and as long as mortal men were raving idiots pulled around by their tiny heads Candy wouldn't lack for followers.

Mortal, or otherwise. And good luck bribing any true Amazon. All Candy's incarnations—not to mention her followers, conscious or not—were amenable to cold hard cash, but only on their terms.

The brunette goddess of those who healed with the body glared at him. "You know my rules."

Of course, every one of their kind had little rules. The world was full of those hedges and restrictions, no refunds, terms and conditions applied. "Which one of them am I breaking, eh?"

"You're going to let Maria eat her own." The accusation, flatly delivered, almost stung.

It was certainly what Maschenka *intended*, yes, but many was the slip 'twixt liquor and lip. In any case, nobody and nothing would touch the girl until she'd led Dima to his missing property, and the fact that he would have to turn around and surrender it to Baba again if he meant to continue as he wished to was beside the point.

It was the principle of the thing, or so Dima would have said if he gave a shit what Candy thought. He folded his own arms, hating the defensive motion as well. "Why should that bother anyone? Saves me bite or two." The night was growing old, and he had one or two things to think about while roaming the city alone.

Or standing guard.

Not that he minded having to make this stop, really. After a night spent dancing, fighting, and singing, a little female companionship was a good thing. He had hoped Candy might be in one of her rare charitable moods—or that one or two of her highly skilled priestesses might be in the mood to earn a little of what he had to give.

"Maria eats her, you eat Maria and take your Heart, then what? You go back to the old country to see if you'll transform?" A singularly inelegant snort at the thought, and Candy's glare was underlit by the small red sparks in her pupils. "You're being stupid, Dima, and it's not like you."

"I meant what I said, *holy one*." If this kept going the night, so far very pleasant indeed, would be ruined. His private arrangement with the beldam had been exposed to gossip, and for that alone he owed Maria Drozdova a world of pain. He would fill his mouth with the blood of one of their kind, and he was entirely within his rights. "She sewed up?"

"I've half a mind to send her out with a few guards." Candy glowered at him down her very fine button nose, suddenly looking much older in the reddish neon overpowering the anemic porch light. Once, and only once, he had glimpsed her true age.

The only thing more terrifying than her antiquity was the ravaging beauty of that final form.

"You got some to lose, then?" Sometimes, he had to remind even this divinity of just who she was dealing with, and in this particular matter he wasn't going to listen to any quarterbacking, on a Monday or any other damn mortal day.

Dmitri had handed something precious over for his own reasons, well and good—but Baba had let that little bitch steal not just from her but from *him*. From the thief of thieves.

It didn't matter that he'd suffer what Maschka was enduring right now if he put it back in his chest instead of returning it to the old lady's cabinet, it didn't matter that it would suckle his strength and leave him no better than the mortal toys they played with while a new form of Dmitri, native to this fascinating country, discovered the joy of traveling his thiefways and was propitiated by his uncles and nephews.

Of *course* Dima wanted to survive, and his agreement with Baba was still durable. But more important was the simple, essential truth: Maschka had stolen, from Baba but also from Dmitri Konets himself.

The insult, like many others, simply could not be borne. A thief avenged such slights, in the old country or in this one. Otherwise, he was no more than stupid carrion.

"I wonder what it would be like if we didn't have an agreement." Candy turned back to the door. "I tell you, Dima, I stand a lot but I ain't about to stand this. If you let Maria eat her own, you and your kind will no longer be welcome in my domains."

That was a surprise. "Like to see you try to keep me out."

"Oh, honey." Candy raised her left middle finger over her shoulder, with a contemptuous little dart of bloody light flicking off the nail at the end. "Mine were once temples. And they will be again."

"Temples over sewers," he muttered, but not very loudly.

She was, after all, Cybele's other face. Her guards, in disguise as a partly laughing concession to mortal conventions, might not be able to kill him.

But they could certainly make him suffer, and there was only so much of that a man actually pursued.

A BUSY NIGHT

It was the same black SUV, the same mountainous bearlike door-opener with mirrored sunglasses, and the same pillowy, gliding ride on what had to be expensive shocks, but Nat huddled as close to the door on her side as she could. Dmitri stared out the window, his index finger twitch-tapping the knee of his flayed, scorched, and stained trousers. At least he didn't smell bad.

And at least neither did she. The stuff-that-wasn't-iodine smelled vaguely spicy as it dried, with a medicinal tang. Slowly, the streets became plowed again—the route made no sense, but she was almost used to that now—and by the time things started looking familiar it had warmed before dawn. Thick feathery snowflakes drifted earthward.

It probably wouldn't hurt to be polite, especially since the tiny green clutch holding her wallet, key, emergency twenty dollars, and phone had shown up, nice and conspicuous, in the middle of the seat when she clambered into the vehicle.

Everything in her backpack was probably gone or sitting in Coco's dressing room, though.

Nat cleared her throat as the car wallowed through a right turn, and Brooklyn, the dozing familiar beast, swallowed them both. "Thank you." Her voice was a gravelly whisper. "For getting me out of there."

Maybe he deliberately misunderstood. "You left by yourself, *zaika*. Little rabbit running." He didn't turn, just kept staring out the window. "And Candy filled you up with news, didn't she. Just remember, women like that lie sometimes."

Women like that? You misogynist. "Everyone lies," Nat corrected, too tired to think that perhaps, just perhaps, she shouldn't rile up a man she'd seen shoot a sorcerer.

Sorcerers. Divinities. Hearts like big bloody gems. Belief. And Mom, brushing aside Nat's breathless explanations, Nat's lifelong attempts to make someone, *anyone,* listen or understand.

Well, I've always felt like an alien. This just makes it official.

"*Da,* everyone lies." Dima turned away from the window. He studied her, from tumbled hair to painted arms, and nodded. "So she has some sense after all, this little girl."

If he used that quiet, thoughtful tone instead of the grating, obscene glee, more people might listen to him.

Nat's fingers ached, clasped bloodless-tight in her green-gowned lap. "I meant, thank you for getting me away from the sorcerer." Amazingly, she didn't stutter. "And yes, I do have some sense. I'm believing all this, aren't I?"

"You can see it plain as day, though. Takes belief out of equation, but not by much." He shrugged, and settled more deeply against the leather seat.

It was a night for terror and cryptic, lunatic conversations, but maybe she'd be home soon. "Did you ever not believe?"

"Lesson for you, *zaika.* Don't ever ask one of us that." His teeth gleamed, lips peeling back in a non-smile. "It's not polite."

You're rude too. But Nat just dropped her gaze, studying the slightly sticky crusts on her arms. The slashes were gone, all that remained were Candy's careful, ladderlike brushstrokes. It could be abstract art, she decided. Body painting. The pinup nurse could probably win an avant-garde airbrush competition or two.

Almost home. Nat longed to get out and run, even if the sidewalk was a solid sheet of ice. Cracking her head on pavement seemed a fair risk at this point.

Why hadn't Mom *told* her? Nat would have set off to find this thing as soon as Maria started getting sick. She could have brought it back and made everything better by now.

"Little Drozdova." Dmitri made it a singsong. "Don't sound like your mama's got much time left."

"Then I guess we'll just have to hurry." *Leave me alone, asshole.* And there, like a gift, was a bright bodega window painted with a cheery holiday snowman at Falada and Fifty-fifth; they were two blocks from her slice of South Aurora. "You can let me out here."

"Ah, no, no, little girl." He waved one finger, its tip bearing a scorch-smudge. "I said you were under both my eyes, and I mean it. Until you find the Dead God's Heart, you have my entire attention."

Dead god's heart. If only someone would have said that without all the theatrics—but would she have believed it?

"Great." She didn't mean to sound sarcastic. Or maybe she did; Mom would call it *your nasty side, Natchenka, and don't you show it to me.*

It didn't matter. He was a liar like all the rest, only with Dima it was right up front. Almost a twisted sense of honesty in its own way, or maybe she was just punch-drunk after pulling an all-nighter. There was definite graying along the eastern horizon, or what you could see of it through the buildings, and she hadn't seen another car creeping through the city's iced-over concrete veins since they crossed from wherever-the-hell Candy lived into Brooklyn without so much as a glimpse of the water, let alone a bridge.

It should have bothered her, but after tonight she doubted she'd ever be bothered again.

"They say when you have a god's heart, you can make a wish on it." The gangster alternated between sneering and quiet thoughtfulness so quickly he was going to give himself whiplash. "What you gonna wish for?"

For Mama to be all right again. It was the sort of thing a five-year-old might believe, but then again, so were talking cats and flying vans. "Who says that?"

"Oh, you know. *They* do." His eyebrows twitched; he was laughing at her.

"Can you even tell the truth anymore? Or is it impossible?" Nat fumbled with her seat belt, grabbed the clutch, and reached for the door handle. "Just stop right here. I'll walk." She leaned forward, shaking free of the belt. "Do you hear me? Stop."

"My nephews don't take orders from you." Dmitri drummed his

fingers on his knee, and his non-smile widened. "I am gentleman, *zaika*. I take you to your door."

As long as you're not wanting a goodnight kiss. Still, Nat tugged on the handle. It didn't budge even though the door was unlocked, the little orange bar on a plastic tab only underlining her helplessness. "Let me *out*," she hissed, and the handle stretched like warm taffy against her fingers.

"You keep that up, Dima's gonna carry you. Again." His upper lip lifted even more, and it wasn't the snarl he had aimed at Koschei. The expression was somehow more chilling, because it utterly lacked the veneer of anarchic glee. "Be a good girl now. I've had a busy night."

Oh, you've *had a night?* Nat didn't let go of the door handle. It was all useless, but she didn't have to give in completely.

Did she?

The little yellow house slid into view, and she let out an inarticulate sound of relief. The SUV glided to a stop, the handle suddenly yielding as it should, and she slithered out, not waiting for one of the Sunglass Twins to open her door. Coco's heels clattered on ice as she lunged for the back of the car, made it around, and slipped through a fortuitous break in the high-piled, immovable mass of plowed and refrozen snow. The gate was already opening; a burst of white flakes trailed her as she ran up the flagstone walk, rock salt crunching underfoot and the bright golden light in the living room window a beacon guiding her to the porch.

Settled on the top step, her backpack was a plump shivering child punished by a few minutes in the cold, its top slightly open and her neatly folded jeans peeking out. She grabbed it as she crested the stairs, and the light in the living room told her one thing.

Leo, as usual, was waiting up for her. Nat Drozdova plunged through her own front door, slammed it shut, leaning against it with a heavy backpack dangling against her green-and-gold skirt, and knew the night wasn't quite over.

Not yet.

NO DIFFERENCE

He was at the kitchen table, an old man rolling vile-smelling *makhorka* in cheap papers. A whole pack's worth of hand-rolled cigarettes were lined up in front of him, and two shoeboxes along the right-hand side of the table were full of them too. Other than that, there was an ancient, freezer-burned bottle of vodka with a ring of condensation around its base—Mama would sigh before she snapped *get a coaster*—next to a single clean, dry glass tumbler, and another box.

The last item was wooden, handmade from the look of it, and about ten inches long. It was very narrow, like Candy's house, and the top held burned-in scrollwork that was unquestionably Leo's.

Nat dropped her backpack just inside the hall archway. It made a soft sound against the wall, hit the linoleum with a thump, and Uncle Leo didn't look at her. Instead, he finished rolling the cigarette, methodically, and fished in the breast pocket of his flannel button-up for his old battered silver lighter—not a Zippo, a foreign cylindrical model.

You can't smoke in here. Mom will go nuts. But Nat said nothing, leaning against the door frame in her borrowed dress.

How on earth was she supposed to return it? Or the tiny bedazzled clutch?

Flame caressed a twisted-shut cigarette tip. Leo inhaled deeply, then acrid tobacco smoke fumed through his nostrils. He didn't smoke like Dmitri; no, he was blessedly, comfortingly familiar.

Human.

All the signs were there, right in front of her. The shape of his front teeth, the dimple in his right cheek, chin with its slightly off-center point, the detached earlobes—Mama's were attached, and unpierced; her gold hoops were clip-ons. Leo had taken Nat to the mall to get earrings, and both of them had been in dutch for weeks afterward.

But what was done couldn't be undone, as Leo said, and Nat could wear hoops or dangles, though Mama said it was sluttish.

Leo's chair creaked. He finally turned the few increments that would let him see her at the door. He blinked several times, peering through tobacco vapor.

"Pretty as a picture." He nodded, rolled the burning ciga-rette between his fingertips. The smell was nasty and comforting, though it didn't belong in the kitchen. It belonged in the tiny ga-rage, along with the sawdust and the warmth and the comfort of knowing she wouldn't be scolded if she knocked something over or, God forbid, broke it as clumsy children always did. "Pretty as your mama."

"You waited up for me." Her throat swelled with a scream; it died away, shriveling to a harsh whisper. "You should have gone to bed."

He shook his head, blinking furiously. *Smoke in my eyes,* he would say sometimes, when child-Nat would whisper that she wished she had a dad like other kids. "I was up anyway."

He probably meant the lie to be kind, but Nat's hands ached. Normally he would have asked about the brown stains on her arms, where she got the dress, how her evening had been.

She'd never stayed out overnight before. "Leo? Is there some-thing you want to tell me?"

"Been waiting a long time for you to ask."

Why was that my job? "How could I not know?"

He gave her an agonized sideways look. Said nothing, so Nat took an experimental step into the room. She tacked unevenly across painfully clean flooring—still much more comfortable than the crisp black-and-white lino at Candy's—and her heels made soft sounds, like Mama had dressed up to go out and was moving in a cloud of warm perfume and high excitement while Leo and Nat watched her grace, both sorry she was leaving but also, perhaps, just the tiniest bit relieved.

"Leo." Nat settled into her usual chair, setting the clutch aside with finicky care. She should have been aching all over, but warmth stole through her. Pulling an all-nighter was supposed to make you crash eventually; the window was full of strengthening, depthless snowlight. "Please. You've got to tell me. Just say it."

"Hardesty," he said. "And talk to the Cowboy."

What the hell? Nat stared at him.

The orange glow of the cigarette tip danced, but not from draft or breeze—it was eerily glassy-still inside the house, even the Black Forest clock in the parlor hushing his stentorian tick-tock. Leo smoked while she waited, tapping ash into the dry tumbler. He crushed the cigarette out against its inside, dropped the tiny stub on the clean half for later picking. "It's a town, right where South Dakota starts thinking it's Wyoming, but it's not, not just yet. There's a bar. You'll know it when you see it. The moment you go in, Natchenka, he'll find you."

Disappointment crashed through Nat's ribcage. Was he ashamed of her, the way Mama always seemed to be? Maybe that was the answer.

Why, Mama? Why wouldn't you even tell me this? "The man who has the Cup," Nat said carefully, trying to be a good student anyway. The Cup was the second part; maybe she'd been supposed to get the Knife from Jay?

Or Koschei? That was the trouble with riddles; they were only clear in retrospect, like all life's worst moments.

"The man who knows where the Cup is. *Da.*" Leo's mouth contorted, worked for a moment as he peered at his night's work, carefully rolled and waiting in neat anchovy-packed rows. "I'd tell you, Natchenka. I would. But there is dirt in my mouth."

That wasn't a saying she'd heard before. "What does that even mean?" If she was five, or even twelve, she might have started howling at the injustice.

But Nat was old enough to drink, she had almost, *almost* enough saved for an apartment of her own, and she was on a wild magical goose chase. So she kept the howl to herself, locking it in her chest along with a tearing, familiar pain.

"In the old country, if you wish to keep a man quiet, you bake a handful of dirt from his own grave into his bread. And then he cannot tell what you do not wish him to." Leo's cheeks were damp, and his gnarled, strong, liver-spotted hands trembled even worse now. He flicked the lighter again, testing it, killed the flame with a snap of his wrist. "Love makes you weak, my Natchenka. I hope you never find that out."

Me too. Nat might have been shaking too, but not after tonight.

"You know . . ." Leo coughed, then selected another hand-rolled and clicked the lighter into brief life. His hand's quivering made the tiny orange flame dance. He inhaled deeply, sucking at the smoke. "In the old days—the *very* old days—they would burn him alive in the wooden statue, or cut his throat over the bonfire. Eventually, after all was said and done. But before then he was carried around the town, given the best of every dish, and *she* held him in her arms all night. I think every single one of them thought it was worth it until the fire started, or the knife came out."

"Is it?" She sounded like a completely different person, Nat discovered. Like a stranger talking to a dotty old man. But the stranger's throat was full, and her eyes were hot too.

She couldn't shake, but she might very well cry here at the table. It would be a relief, after . . . everything.

Wouldn't it?

"Sometimes, a man wishes to say what he knows, but he cannot." Leo nodded, but he wouldn't quite look at her. "You're strong, Nat. Like her. You cannot imagine the weak."

Funny, I thought I was doing great just seeing it in the mirror. "You're strong too, Leo." The name was bitter in her mouth, but she laid her hand on the table, palm cupped upward.

"I am a fool who believed too much." He finished smoking, again, and crushed the cigarette out. "The car is no good," he added, through the haze. "I can use the bus to visit your mother."

"I think I've got a ride." She left her hand there, as if it was just a leftover piece of some project she had to finish for school. "Leo—"

"Here." He touched the wooden box with a nicotine-stained fingertip, pushing it towards her. "You're old enough, after all. Every day I kept thinking, *this will be the last one*, but there was one more, and one more." His throat worked, and he coughed again, a flush rising to his stubbled cheeks. "Each was a gift. Do you hear me, little Natchenka? A *gift*."

Nat's fingers ached. Was he not going to hold her hand because Candy's "special iodine" was all over it?

Maybe he just didn't want to. It was a free country, after all. They were both adults now, and Mama wasn't upstairs in her bedroom or at the stove, in the living room dusting or the mudroom softly hissing imprecations at the amount of laundry three people in a tiny house made. They were absolutely alone in a brightly lit kitchen at the end of an impossible night.

And he couldn't say it. Because there was dirt in his mouth, or because he was ashamed of her too. Which one was more likely?

"I know you love Mom," she managed around the lump in her dry throat. "That's a good thing."

He stared at her like she was speaking a foreign language, not the one she could pick out phrases in, not the one he and Mama erupted into whenever he thought one of Nat's punishments was too severe. Then he pushed away from the table with surprising strength, rising to his full but still slightly stooped height, and leaned down a little to shove the wooden box across the tacked-on plastic protecting the floral tablecloth. Were those the only cigarettes he'd smoked? The ends lay, lonely and crumpled, in the tumbler.

Mama would have a fit. But she wasn't here.

Nat's hand lay empty. Leo turned and shuffled away. "Good night," he said in the doorway, a pair of harsh, strangled syllables.

Nat reached for the bottle. He didn't want to hold hands since she wasn't a little girl anymore. That was fine. It was just another change, like puberty or industrialization. A natural progression.

She didn't want to open the box, but dawn was almost here. It was beautiful work, the lid matching the sides with barely a demarcating line.

He was magic with wood, old Uncle Leo.

Inside, on a bed of worn-down black velvet salvaged from something else, was a straight, double-bladed knife. The hilt was plain and functional, and despite the blade's dark matte finish—like Dmitri's gun, she thought, and almost shuddered—the edges looked very, very sharp indeed.

It wasn't metal. It was grainy stone so dark gray it was almost black, knapped to a razor edge.

So. It had been here all along. Did Leo believe in the future? He had to, as long as he was alive, right?

Until the knife came out.

Nat slammed the lid back on, listening to Leo climb the stairs, one at a time. He went into his room and shut the door. There was no immediate burst of television noise, or even the staticky unsound of an appliance turned on and muted.

Deathly quiet returned to the little yellow house, broken only by small mouselike sobs tiptoeing past the painted fingers Nat jammed against her mouth.

The sun, indifferent, continued to rise. The snow was coming down hard.

FREEZE THE DEAD

All things had their time, and a thief judged them by instinct and the tingling in fingertips. In some it was a physical ache; they could tell by the intensity if luck was with them, or if it was a whispered warning from their protector instead. Very simple—all Dima had to do was think about the little yellow house and the precious dark-eyed thing he wanted to subtract from its demesne, and the tingle would say *not yet, not yet*.

Until about noon, that was, when the snow paused for a moment and the sky over the city darkened to a depthless iron sheet. From his vantage point atop a row of brownstones, snow clinging to his shoulders and making a tiny pyramidal drift on his hair, he saw the front door of the little yellow house twitch, a mouse whisker testing the air outside its hole.

Shadows around the house were sharp-edged even though snow-light was soft. Others had noticed the little Drozdova gathering strength.

Hungry others. Maschka's weaving of camouflage and misdirection was gone. The outer rings of *not here, not there* woven by passing cats were still strong, but wouldn't hold against a determined assault. Where did the feline loyalty lie, Dima wondered—with the dying divinity, or the new incarnation?

The sensation in his fingers wasn't incipient frostbite or the desperation of hunger driving many of his followers into calling upon their loving uncle. It was the painful pricking of an amputated limb married to the ache of unconsummated desire, and he snarled as he shook snow away in one supple, violent motion, rising from his perch. Leaning forward, his boots tapping the roof's edge, then he plummeted and as usual it reminded him of the violent wrenching when he had made his fool's bargain.

Who was the true fool, though? If Maschka had stopped to consider just what her plan of buying off Baba entailed . . . still, even divinities who sneered at mortals weren't immune to fearing dissolution. Fear was unavoidable, like the sea-tide or the cyclic subsuming of old gods into newer, more vigorous forms.

He hit the icy sidewalk hard, not quite caring if any mortal saw. They would forget as soon as the amazement faded; anything truly supernal was to be avoided, propitiated, or chased from waking consciousness as soon as it occurred. Of course, anyone living on this street had probably seen their share of strange things, between the ailing Drozdova's house set between two much higher buildings and the daughter tripping blithely along breathing small miracles into the air.

Maria Drozdova's illness was accelerating; now that her daughter had been presented at Jay's and found other divinities the process would gather strength and speed like a train pointed downhill. It was the most dangerous time for a certain honey-haired girl.

If Mama Dearest died and the daughter was taken by the starving ones, a certain heart-gem might never be found.

Which was unacceptable. Let Candy think he meant to let Maschka eat carrion in a fouled nest; let any-fucking-one in the world think what they liked. He answered to none of them, even the Cold Lady.

After all, he was still here, wasn't he? He had paid an honest price for something that truly mattered. A thief, even the thief of thieves, could choose to do so once in a while.

If it pleased him.

Dmitri's boots were soundless as he ambled along, falling snow melting into nonexistence as it approached him, the banked fire of his rage breathed upon and gathering strength. And yes, his instincts were sharp as the straight razors in their dark, comfortable homes; he heard the squeak of the front door as a mouse edged out, the faint rustle of a brown paper bag, grit under a light dancing step adding sandpaper rasp to a waltz.

She watched the flagstone path scattered with not nearly enough rock salt, that honey-highlight hair tucked under yesterday's green knit cap and yesterday's woolen coat blurring her outline. Despite that, her legs were lovingly cased by a pair of worn jeans, the thinness over the knees proclaiming them a favorite pair. The backpack was hitched to her shoulder—Coco must have sent it back, no doubt curious about where the girl had been hiding all this time— and she had the look of a woman about to set out on a journey.

Not without him, though. If the young Drozdova thought she could slip away from Dmitri Konets, she was about to be surprised.

Nat didn't swing the paper grocery bag. She carried it carefully, keeping well away from sticks of winter-sleeping plants. Now what, Dmitri wondered, could she have in there? A snack? A weapon? A spare pair of panties?

The last prospect pulled his lips back into a grin, and his teeth were just as cold-white as the drifts, though significantly cleaner. He halted at the garden gate, expecting it to open as it had yesterday.

It remained stubbornly closed, however, and the girl looked up. Her nose was pink, and so were the tender rims of her eyelids. Her eyelashes weren't matted because she'd splashed her face with cold water, and if a certain long-dead émigré novelist had been able to see her, Dmitri thought he might well change the name of the barely teenage character who had made him famous. It was all there—the faintly blurred beauty, the beautiful skin, the wide, slightly dazed eyes, and the volatile, eternal burning of youth and renewal.

Even Maschka had never looked like this, and Dmitri's smile widened, became a little more natural. It wouldn't do to scare her again.

Not yet, anyway.

Her breath was a white cloud. So was his, and the two faded without touching. She examined him, her cupid's-bow mouth tight and grave, and he wondered, belatedly, what had made her cry. It wasn't a usual reaction to seeing under the skin of the world.

What would it be like to grow up thinking you were one of *them*, the rubes, the worshipers? Dmitri tried to imagine the confusion, but the rage was back, burning in his marrow, raising thin traceries of steam from his damp shoulders. "Good morning, little Drozdova."

"Good morning, Mr. Konets." Polite and distant, clutching the rolled top of the grocery bag with whitened knuckles.

Cold silence built a wall between them. He searched for something to say, to demolish those invisible bricks. "You think you get away from me, huh?"

"I was pretty sure you'd show up." She lifted the bag a little. "Can we take this back to Coco? I don't want to . . . Well, anyway, it's probably on the way."

"And just where we going, *zaika*?"

"West." Her shoulders hunched. Could she tell there was a pale face in an upper window, gazing longingly at the front yard? Looked like an old man, and for a moment Dima considered kicking the gate in, then the front door, and demanding to know who the hell *that* was.

It wasn't an uncharacteristic urge, but he wasn't used to it in this sort of situation. So he cocked his head, listening for the internal shell-song that would tell him if something truly valuable was locked away inside the yellow house. Wouldn't that be amusing, the old Drozdova keeping her stolen thing close and the daughter leading him a merry chase?

But there was nothing but warm subliminal static. Only sentimental value, then. "Who's that?" He pointed, a quick, accusing jab of one finger, and there was a sharp crackling sound as the yellow house woke fully for one baleful instant and gazed at him.

"Nobody you need to talk to." For the first time, the *zaika* actually sounded . . . sharp. Protective, even. "Are we walking?"

"You didn't like the ride last time." But he tugged on the strings under the skin of the world, just because. After all, there was no reason to use shoe leather if you could drive.

"Fine." She took a step towards the gate, a little matador tempting a large angry beast. Shoulders proudly back, her expression just slightly disdainful. "Do you want to stop by your place and get changed?"

What the hell for? Dima looked down at last night's suit, still bearing evidence of battle. Visible reminders of once again serving Koschei a dose of medicine the sorcerer liked least; it pleased Dmitri to remember how the glass cases had shattered and the formless mummy-things howled. "Ashamed to be seen with me, *zaika*?"

"I thought you'd be cold," she informed him, lifting her chin a little more. Curls fountained from under the green knit cap, stirring slightly as the icy breeze veered. It was going to clear and freeze hard; the city would lose what little secret warmth it possessed once she left.

West, she said. If it was a dodge, she'd find out he was better at those games. So Dima stepped back from the gate and tried a more charming smile instead of mere teeth-baring. "Can't freeze the dead."

"Are you?" She didn't smile in return, just stared at him with those somber dark eyes. The old man behind the upstairs windows was saying something, his mouth moving around three tiny words while he spread a hand against clear glass, staring not at Dima but at the girl whose back, slim and supple under the big wool coat, was straight as a sword. "Dead, I mean?"

"Not just yet." The smile soured, and Dima beckoned. An engine purred a block away; unchained tires bit the packed, ice-corrugated road. Even this unsleeping Babylon could be forced to hibernate when winter decided she wanted her bony fists around its throat. "Come, then. We go west."

"Can we stop by Coco's?" Not giving an inch. Oh, it wasn't fair for a girl to be so solemn, with the high blush in her cheeks that wasn't awareness of him or her own power but instead a completely natural reaction to the frost. "Other than that, I'm ready."

"No luggage?"

"I'm not the type."

"What type are you, then?" It was mere conversation, Dima told himself. Polite, even—women liked it when you expressed some interest.

"Like you care." Quick as a rapier, her pert little reply.

"You're right." All trace of smile faded; Dmitri's face turned into a mask. "Better not leave anything behind, little girl. I drive fast."

Her eyebrows lifted. Even they were tipped with gold, though her lashes were sinfully dark. "We aren't walking?"

The low-slung black muscle car purred to a stop behind him, partially hidden by a small mountain of plowed snow. Soon the latter would freeze into an iceberg that could rip the bottom out of a ship, if one was so foolish as to come rollicking by on dry land. "You always this sarcastic?"

"No," she said. "But for you, I'll make an exception."

"I make exception for you too, then," he said, and knew it was a promise as soon as the words hit frigid air. It irked him, and he scowled. "Come out and play, Drozdova. I've been waiting."

"I should make you wait more." But she moved, taking a single step, and the man behind the upstairs window shook his head.

Maybe the mortal knew the danger she was in. Or maybe it was something else. Dima didn't care; he was too busy stepping through the break in the plow-mountains to reach for the passenger door.

Today, at least, he could be a gentleman.

IDEAS

Coco's atelier was closed and locked, but Dmitri said she could leave the paper bag on the front step. "Should just keep it," he grumbled, sinking himself a little deeper in the leather seat. The car's steering wheel was more of a yoke, like in small planes or race cars; the engine's purr was faintly menacing. It had the curves of an old, beautiful Chevelle, and the hood ornament was the silver snarling head of a fanged creature somewhere between wolf and bear. "Be careful, *zaika*."

"I can't keep it. That would be rude." Nat reached for the chrome handle. For a moment she was afraid it wouldn't let her out like the SUV last night, but the door swung wide and she just had to worry about slipping and falling on her ass.

Fortunately the ice cringed away from the boutique's doorstep in scalloped patterns, delicate seashell traceries revealing an invisible border. If Nat let her gaze unfocus just a little she could see a shimmer, just like whatever unseen thing—or series of things—did Coco's sewing.

I hope it's a union shop. She settled the paper bag snug against the bottom of the glass door and straightened, suddenly aware she'd left the car's side hanging open and there were eyes on her. The sensation of being watched was unmistakable and a little frightening.

No, a *lot* frightening.

"Thank you," Nat said softly. "It was beautiful. I felt like a princess." *Until they nailed a man to railroad ties and his body split open. That was a real corker, as Sister Eunice Grace would say.*

Why had Mom sent her to Catholic school? She'd insisted on it, despite Leo muttering *nothing good ever came from priests, I should know, Maria, and so should you.*

My daughter, Maria Drozdova said, *will obey me.* And that was that.

Wouldn't the sisters just have a ball with this? Imagining Dmitri among the black-and-white statues with their habits billowing on cold breezes was only moderately funny, in the way just barely escaping a terrible accident could make you laugh while sitting on a grassy verge and waiting for the fire trucks to arrive.

All this time she'd thought Mama sent her to the nuns because it was better than public school, or some holdover from the old country. Would anyone ever tell her the real reason? Maybe Baba would know.

Good luck scraping together the courage to ask *her*, though.

The sense of being watched sharpened, and she stepped gingerly away from the door. Getting back to the car was no trouble. Yet Nat paused, looking down the deserted, frozen sidewalk. Nothing about this was normal, but the sudden isolation was super-*duper* not ordinary, and the mad thought that she could take off, her fists pumping and her ribs heaving, and somehow, some way, outpace the big black car—

"Eh, *zaika*." Dmitri leaned over the center armrest, peering into the failing light. "Don't get any ideas, now." A storm was on the way; Nat's scalp tingled and her fingers ached a little.

The feeling wasn't fear, though. Or it was, but underneath was a deeper, darker swelling.

Anticipation.

I have plenty of ideas, she realized. She walked back to the car like a child returning to school, mutinous but unable to resist.

Yet.

She dropped into leather-cradling warmth, closing the door a little harder than she had to. Her backpack was on the narrow shelf masquerading as a backseat, and she wondered if he'd try to paw through it.

He seemed like the type.

Dmitri waited, his hands on the wheel-yoke. The engine settled into a low silken groaning.

"Well?" he said, finally.

"West." A lump had settled in Nat's throat. Leo hadn't even come down for coffee; the morning's stinging-hot shower had washed away the last of Nat's tears. She was almost light-headed, a strange clarity probably the result of pulling an all-nighter.

"Be more specific, *zaika*."

I don't think I will. "West," she repeated, stubbornly, and reached for her seatbelt. There was no reason to tell him the name of the town for a while, especially since she'd looked up routes and alternates this morning on her ancient, duct-taped laptop.

Paid good money and still works, Natchenka. You don't get new one if old still works.

Dmitri shrugged, dropped the car into gear, and pulled away from the curb. The unchained tires had no problem with slipping; they chewed up the freeze, reaching greedily for concrete underneath. "Keep your secrets," he muttered, and adjusted the rearview mirror, probably unnecessarily.

Nat intended to. She stared out the window, watching the frozen city sink deeper into winter's grip, and was shaken with the sudden certainty that she would never see Leo again.

Well, he didn't want her. There wasn't anything left in him, Mama had it all. Even the few small crumbs Nat had assumed were a child's natural feast were gone too, because she was all grown up now.

Yes, she had a plethora of ideas. None of them were comforting, so she wiped angrily at her dry cheeks and settled herself to endure this trip the way she'd endured everything else in her life.

THE
DRIVE

THOSE WHO EAT

Outracing the storm on a ribbon of pavement, the car gulping at sanded miles and taking shallow curves with graceful authority, wasn't a bad way to travel. She would have liked it better if she was the one driving, but at least Dmitri didn't bother pretending he liked her.

It was almost refreshing, certainly better than thinking you had an ally and finding out differently when it counted. Nat watched the scenery change, white-jacketed hills bobbing like waiter-ducks at a busy, watery restaurant. Some were wooded, but most bore a crop of houses and streets on their backs. Even the modesty strips left at the sides of freeways couldn't truly hide the nakedness of the land behind. Concrete arteries brought prosperity, like the historical iron horses galloping from coast to coast over the graves of the indigenous, but they were also digestive pathways, and a whole lot of shit ran off them.

Was everything she imagined real, or only some things? Once you started believing in crucified literary figures, pinup nurses with "special iodine," divinities, and miracles, who was to say where it ended? Did the roads have a divinity? The gravel shoulders, the signs, the trees crying out soundlessly when the chainsaw bit?

Once they were free of the city's broad sprawling arms and grasping suburban fingers, Dmitri pushed the accelerator steadily floorward and rolled his window down a bit. He dug in an inside pocket of his splattered suit jacket, fishing out a crumpled red-and-white pack of cigarettes, not last night's Cyrillic-lettered one. They didn't look American; it was no brand Nat had ever seen in bodegas or tobacco shops.

It was enough to make her want to laugh. Of *course* he would have a car and cigarettes she'd never seen before. Maybe they were divine cancer-sticks.

He tapped one out and stuck it between his lips, gave her a crafty sideways glance. "Like what you see?"

Do you not have any other clothes? She returned her gaze to the silver hood ornament's snarling as it clove empty air. "I was just thinking it's rude to smoke in the car when you know someone else doesn't."

"I am very polite." He kept two fingers on the wheel-yoke, flicked the middle finger of his other hand at the cigarette in his mouth, and inhaled deeply as the tip turned bright red. "I open the window. Also, I offer you one. Want a smoke, *zaika*?"

"God, no." She watched, but he didn't flinch. Was it blasphemous to think he might disappear if she started reciting in Latin? "Are there demons too?"

"Matter of definition." The words rode a long scree of perfumed smoke. These cigarettes smelled vaguely like incense with an undertone of grilled meat, not like tobacco at all. Maybe it was some kind of divine drug, and he'd get them into an accident before crossing the state line. "There are destroyers and things which eat, sure. But you and me, *zaika*, we're eternal. The hungry things flee us. Mostly."

Good to know. "You and me?"

"Oh, yeah. See, there are what little rubes make when they believe." He held the accelerator down, still steering with two fingers as the car swung into the left lane to pass a wallowing Trailways bus. "Those clot up after time, and attention keeps them fresh. They eat too, just not like the carrion. Then there are the *real* powers. Like us, like Baba. Like Candy, too. She took a shine to you, little girl. Threatened me to be nice."

"I'm sure it made an impression." Nat wrinkled her nose and cracked her own window a sliver. The slipstream was oddly muted, as if they weren't going very fast at all, but a cold fresh breeze tiptoed into the car. "You don't seem like the kind of guy to take advice."

"You don't know. I am reasonable fellow, *zaika*." He grinned, staring at the road like he saw dinner there. "You could just tell me where your mama hid it, I go get my property, and we are all happy."

Oh, sure. Nat decided she was better off not talking to him and turned slightly, staring out the window. She'd been too stunned to ask Candy much in the way of real questions; Leo had kept his door closed this morning. It was fine, though. Really it was. Everything went better when she just worked things out for herself.

But Dmitri liked having a captive audience, or he wasn't getting the memo about her ignoring him.

"The belief is good," he continued. "Tasty. But without it, real powers still exist, just in different shapes. Wolf chases away vulture and takes a bite, there I am. The flowers come and the dirt no more frozen, there you are. Two insects fuck in midair, there's Candy. And when black ice comes round to crack trees in depths of winter, there is old bitch Baba."

"You're saying we're not human." *I kind of figured that, thanks.*

"You bleed when you skin your knee hard enough. You cry when someone tells you no, bad *zaika*." He shrugged, took another long drag off the cigarette. Twin streams of smoke slid from his high-prowed nose. "I see something good, I take it. I see nice girl, I am nice to her. Human enough."

That's pretty reductionist, but okay. "But even if you're . . . a power, you can't travel? Go to different countries?"

"Oh, go anywhere we like, us real ones. But the rubes, they believe in borders. That makes it . . . complicated."

"Did your father—"

"Listen to her!" He caw-croaked a laugh, smoke chuffing between his teeth. "*Father.* Fuck no. I arrived whole, *zaika*."

So the "power" thing isn't handed down? But why did Mom have me, then? "Confusing," she muttered. If she acted unimpressed, sooner or later he'd continue talking just like any other crank on a city bus given a moment of eye contact. At least the heater worked in this black beast. The sky to the west was the gray infinity of snow; behind them a slumberous darkness swallowed New York.

She'd never been this far from the city before.

Dmitri was silent for a few miles. "Eh. Your mama, she never told you? Not any of this?"

"No." Nat blinked furiously. Her eyes were scratchy, even though she had no tears left. "There were always strange things, growing up. The cats, and . . . But she thought I was lying, making them up." *No. She just pretended to think that.*

Why would a mother, *any* mother, do that? If she'd meant to protect Nat, she would have . . . what?

What, precisely, would Mom have done?

Dmitri went quiet again.

Way to kill the conversation, Nat. Great. Nat snuck a glance and found him with both hands on the wheel, knuckles white, staring out the windshield with his chin slightly tucked and his eyebrows drawn together. His hair, no longer slicked back but disarranged from last night's fight and the morning's damp snowfall, fell over his eyes. The cigarette was burning down, and he puffed a short breath of smoke from the other side of a clamped-tight mouth.

He looked furious. Nat hurriedly shifted, returning her gaze to the window with her left arm prickling. This was way too confined a space. It paid to remember that he was goddamn dangerous.

Finally, he was finished smoking and tossed the butt through the window's hungry, parted lips. "We drive for a few hours, then we stop for snack." No trace of the murderous rage remained; he was back to a drip-dried gangster in a filthy, spattered suit.

The thought that maybe he was just hiding the anger was more terrifying than his lack of impulse control *or* the gun she knew perfectly well he was carrying. "Okay," Nat said, and wished she had her backpack in the front with her.

Hugging something, anything, would feel like a defense.

POP, SODA

Pennsylvania galloped alongside the car for a while, Dmitri following the road which felt right even if the *zaika* was keeping their destination locked up inside her pretty head. Maybe she was even sleeping?

No. Her tension radiated through the entire vehicle.

He liked driving, especially if there was cargo in the trunk to make it worthwhile. It was sometimes pleasant having someone in the passenger seat, even if true speed would make the mortality lingering on the girl rise in rebellion. Dima could smell her shampoo, and an almost-harsh tang of cheap fabric softener. Why the Drozdova would skimp on that he had no idea; what could one of their ilk not afford?

But maybe Maschka had been hoarding for a while. It made sense; the older the *zaika* got the more her native country would align to her moods, her wants. Growing into your power wasn't only a human phenomenon, though generally the transfer happened with the young divinity practicing, flinging around and testing things as kids always did, breaking toys and finding limits.

It boggled the mind that the *zaika* didn't know. How oblivious did you have to be? Then again, she was a good little girl, and what did good little American girls do but listen to their mommies and daddies?

Maschka hadn't felt like giving the girl a single weapon to keep herself safe with, and would trade a certain bloody gem to Baba in exchange for the beldam looking the other way during consumption. It made a chilling sort of sense, even.

His kind of sense.

Had Candy told the girl? Probably not. How did you inform a shivering child that . . . the very thought filled him with deep hot loathing again. He wasn't used to the feeling; filth was just a condition, after all.

He sometimes even enjoyed the sludge.

The black car ate miles steadily despite the ice on the road, not nearly as fast as Dima *could* travel and certainly not in the thiefways. Still, they would comfortably outpace the sharp black shadows of *those who eat* if he kept them moving. Snow swirled in their wake, the very fringe of the storm nipping at their heels, and Baba's claw-tip touch was in every flake.

So. The old bitch was keeping track. She thought he might eat the girl whole, or prepare her for Maschka's teeth before his own meal. Between Grandmother and Candy, he was beginning to feel distinctly underappreciated. It wasn't like either of them forewent any feasts, especially when an enemy crossed their path.

The *zaika* stirred. Dima waited, but she said nothing, just cast him a few sneaking glances. Maybe her plan to escape hadn't worked as well as she hoped, and she was waiting for a momentary inattention.

Suppose Maschka had wanted the girl as strong as possible before the renewal. Suppose, just suppose—how would you go about that? He could contemplate it calmly, of course; it could even be argued he had a natural bent for, or rulership over, such an operation.

Such a *theft*.

Well, Maschka would want the girl to give it up willingly. And what girl wouldn't want to cure her dear mama?

But what if the *zaika* didn't? Perhaps . . . Dima reached for another cigarette; smoke helped you think. If the waning-weakness had struck suddenly, if Maschka had let things go on too long, perhaps she would need other hands to finish the work.

Long, strong, cruelly boned hands that gripped like ice. The operation couldn't happen without Baba's blessing; the old dame stood at the doorway.

So to speak.

He had it all clear in his mind for a moment, but the *zaika* stirred again, reaching into the back for her bag. Dima quelled a twitch and an ill-tempered snarl; there was no way she could know she'd just interrupted a profitable line of thought.

"You, uh . . ." Nat trailed off uncertainly, watching his profile, then unzipped the backpack. "You want some gum?"

Do I look like I play baseball, little girl? "No." An anemic twinge somewhere inside his ribcage made his knuckles whiten again on the wheel.

Sitting next to her made his mouth water. The vulnerability was almost as attractive as the freshness; oh, he remembered what Maschka had been like, with that hard glint to her cherry-red lips and the depths to her pupils like sucking mud in the old country during the season of rain and melt.

What man didn't want to sink? Letting go was exquisite, the release of tension craved.

"My uncle always said it was good for driving. Means you don't get hungry and have to stop." She popped a cheap stick of spearmint in her mouth, neatly folding the foil wrapper with grave attention.

Don't do it, Dima. "You go on vacation much?"

"Me? Oh no." Her laugh wasn't sarcastic this time, but genuinely amused. Ice on the windshield melted, and the tires took a firmer grip. "This is the furthest out of the city I've ever been."

Now that's a damn shame. "You mean you've never . . ."

"We went to a Renaissance Faire in Jersey once. That's about it." She sobered, creasing and folding the wrapper again. When a girl was nervous, she played with things like that.

"Well then, *zaika*." He checked the signs, sniffed deeply, and clicked his teeth together twice. Yes, there was a prospect nearby, and a nice one. "Suppose we better do it right, huh?"

"What does doing it right entail?" Her attention was a thin sheet of sunshine resting against his right side.

Dima rolled the window down a little more—she wore no perfume, but an edge of jasmine colored her scent as she relaxed. His mouth watered afresh.

"Wait and see." His smile broadened. Yes, it was definitely a prospect; his fingertips were tingling. "You want to tell me exactly where we go?"

Maybe she was beginning to like him, because her mouth softened slightly. "Wait and see."

⋊⋉

The exit he wanted tried to sneak past but Dima swerved, the *zaika* yelped, and the car's tires dug through a thin scrim of fresh snow before he snapped the brakes on, producing a satisfying smoke-rubber squeal. At the summit of a long shallow overpass hill a Pilot station's big red-and-yellow sign glowed, a beacon in the gray almost-lunchtime while a winter storm settled brooding over timbered and slash-covered hills.

She'd grabbed at the dash; he chuckled and the black car banked again, bumping gently over mismatched concrete edges into a parking lot. Gas pumps sat wearily under their inadequate shelter. The black car rocked as it came to a halt, its nose pointed at the corner of the brick building. From this angle he could see a rust-eaten blue Chevy idling in front of the sliding glass door painted with a cheery *Happy Holidays*, headlights blear-blinking as the engine shivered on its mounts.

The reek of desperate, delicious wickedness lingered on the car, and Dmitri's grin widened still further. Right on time.

Pop. Pop. Two muffled sounds, just barely reaching through his window to land on his cheek like kisses. "What you want? Pepsi? Coke? Chips? Candy?"

Nat shook her head; her door swung wide. Looked like the little girl didn't trust the big bad wolf. He could have stayed in the driver's seat and let her figure out for herself, but she might get hysterical and run, and that would lead to a chase.

Which he didn't want. Not yet.

She hitched her backpack on her shoulder, striding through fat feathery flakes of bright new snow, and glanced at the Chevy as she went past, the quick look of a woman scanning only for a certain type of danger. Dima unbuckled his seatbelt just as a kid in a ski mask burst through the door, clipping it with his shoulder as his sneakers almost went out from under him. He almost bowled the girl over, too, and Dima snarled, suddenly outside the car and skidding to a stop at the end of two long lines scraped free of ice where his boots had cut.

"Stupid," Dima hissed, and his finger-flick moved the kid's snub-nosed, very illegal revolver's muzzle a few critical degrees so the bullet zinged between him and Nat. The weapon was stolen too; it obeyed without any hesitation at all.

"Wha*fuck*?" Ski Mask gurgled. His camo jacket flapped, and he fell into the driver's seat more by luck than design.

It was pleasing enough. The desperation, the high edge of adrenaline and greasy fear-sweat, the breaking of a thin moral barrier—oh, it was the boy's first time, and Dima liked welcoming a chosen few personally. Ski Mask was in the right place at the right time, and the divinity he had just pleased tapped the driver's door, pushing it closed with a bang.

The new thief howled, his knee barked by heavy metal, and fumbled with the wheel. A plastic bag stuffed with the take—pathetic, but at least the kid had some moxie—spilled over the passenger seat, and the Chevy's engine decided it was going to crap out at that moment.

"OhGod," Nat breathed, and hurried into the station. Dima shook his head, lifting an admonishing finger to his newest cousin.

The boy wouldn't be a real nephew without some hard work, but he was off to a promising start.

"One time," he said, softly, and exhaled. Snow flashed into ice, tinkling down in bright shards, and the blue Chevy coughed defiantly before roaring into fresh life. "But you bring Uncle Dima something good, little cousin, or I find you later."

Wide, terrified hazel eyes stared at him. Dmitri made a little shooing motion, and the Chevy dropped into gear. *Well, go on. I don't have all day.*

"Dmitri!"

For a moment he wasn't sure who had called him. Then he realized it was the *zaika*.

She sounded frightened. No, she sounded flat-out petrified, and she was calling for him.

Dima tipped the kid an old-fashioned salute and ambled past the painted glass door. The new thief had popped it right out of its track, a safety feature you hardly ever saw used these days. Bright fluorescent light poured out, and Dima stepped onto worn, faded linoleum.

"Dmitri!" she yelled again. "Goddammit! *Dmitri!*"

"I'm right here." He strolled past a spinning tower of sunglasses, absently pocketing a tortoiseshell pair that would look nice on her. "What?"

She was nowhere to be seen until he went on tiptoe to peer over the counter. The *zaika* had wormed her way behind and had her hands clapped to a bleeding hole in a uniformed clerk's chest. Her fingers, with a lingering ghost of summer tan, were still very pale next to that bright red.

There was nothing to be done, so Dima clicked his tongue and shook his head. Very sad, but that was how it went. "He gone, *zaika*. You want some Pringles?"

Her big dark eyes were afire with indignation, fear, and something else. "What? Get on the phone, he needs an ambulance."

"Phone won't fix it. *I* like Pringles. We get some cheese curls too."

"Dmitri." Cold weight on the syllables—if he hadn't known Maschka raised her, the tone would have told him. Did she know she sounded like her mother, only softer, almost pleading? "Help me. Please."

He shrugged. "What you pay me, *zaika*? Tell me where it is, I steal this man from—"

"You don't want to finish that sentence," a new voice intruded. "Ah, the Drozdova. I heard he'd been seen with you. How very interesting."

Dima spun on his bootheel, snarling silently.

STARVE THE WOLF

A mass of teased, dyed-black hair drinking in the light, a livid mouth pulled into a straight line, a black tank top and skinny-muscled greenish-tinted shoulders, the woman halted at the section of counter Nat had flipped up to get to the victim. The new arrival's dark eyes burned in the shadow of that hair. She wore hip-hugging black jeans, a wide black leather belt with a big silver buckle—an ankh lying on its side—and no shoes. Her bare feet were just as greenish as her shoulders and wasted, corded arms, and her chin came to a sharp point.

"Do you have a phone?" Nat kept her hand clamped over the hot, pumping wound. The clerk—just a kid, really, he still had acne on both cheeks and a wispy little goatee—made an inarticulate sound, staring over her shoulder at this new strangeness. "He's bleeding pretty bad, I can't—"

"No," the woman said. Even her voice was colorless, though it was far more sonorous than her narrow ribcage should have been able to produce. "You can't. Step aside, please."

What the fuck? Nat tried again. "We can get an ambulance. The cops—"

"You're in the way." The woman drifted closer, somehow fitting in the cramped space behind the counter. The shelves underneath were jammed with ephemera—binders with tattered plastic covers, a cardboard box labeled LOST & FOUND in shaky Sharpie, cartons of cigarettes, a pair of wet galoshes tucked in the footwell under the violated, hanging-open register. "Jake? Jake, look at me, honey."

The clerk's body jerked. His lips bubbled with blood and saliva. "M-m-m-mo—"

"That's right." The thin greenish woman sank gracefully, shouldering Nat aside. Her bare skin was icy; Nat cringed away, an instinctive motion. The chill reached right through her peacoat, a freezing spike turning her entire arm numb. "I'm here for you, Jake. Look at me."

"M-m-momma . . ."

Nat flinched again. The strength ran out of her legs; she tilted sideways, collapsing against a locked metal cabinet. Getting as far away as possible from that . . . that *cold*, was absolutely necessary.

"Yes," the woman said, and a faint curve touched her thin, livid mouth. "Did you have fun on the swings, honey?"

The clerk smiled, a dopey, dizzy, beautiful grin. His entire body relaxed, and a sharp powerful stink filled the tiny space behind the orange counter and the open register. Nat let out a soft inarticulate sound. Small replies whispered in the store aisles—crackle of plastic, a baritone humming, a soft slithering step as Dima selected snacks.

"There." The woman turned her head slightly, that fever-stricken gaze resting lightly on Nat. "It wouldn't have changed anything, you know. It was his time."

"You." Nat's mouth was desert-dry. Her arms and legs were quivering water. "You're . . ."

"Yep." She straightened, looking down at the body. "It wasn't a bad life. He loved his mother."

"Wait." The words tangled in Nat's throat. "Wait. You can't just—"

"You want to know about your own mother, don't you? Sorry, baby. Even another power can't unloose my lips, though night and day my doors stand open." The smile remained, terrible in its infinite kindness married to utter indifference. "For what it's worth, though, we're all watching very closely." She turned and stepped over Nat's legs, a high, balletic motion; her bare foot landed with soft authority and she halted, looking back over her shoulder.

"You keep sending me gifts," she continued. Her head twitched for a moment on her long, supple neck, and the shiver ran all the

way through, down to her soft bare toes. "You know I haven't returned a single one, dearest."

Then she was gone, gliding through the burst-open door into the
snow. Nat, her fingers tingling-numb, stared after her in disbelief.

"Nice lady." Dmitri stepped into view, his arms full of brightly
packaged junk food. "You wanna get me a bag? Lot of stuff here."

Oh, my God. "How can you?" she whispered. The stink was
awful, titanic, it was like an open toilet in Grand Central after
the drunks had come through—and she knew, without knowing
quite *how* she did, that it was normal. All the sphincters relaxed
when . . . when you . . .

That's going to happen to my Mama. Bile burned the back of her
throat. Of course Mom wanted to live.

Everyone did. If Nat could bring back something that would fix
her beautiful, demanding mother she might be able to make up for
the crime of being born, of costing cash every time she outgrew her
clothes, of intruding on an important life.

And maybe, just maybe, Nat could move out on her own, find
out what the hell this divinity bullshit was all about, and go to college. It sounded good.

It sounded *great*. But her hands were full of blood.

"It was quick." Dmitri regarded her solemnly. "Boy was lucky.
He got to look at you while he was going, too. Think that happens
a lot? Now be a good little *zaika* and hand me a bag, will you?"

She made it outside before she vomited, a thin stream of yellowish
leftover coffee that burned on the way out. It splashed accumulating snow, and Nat went to her knees, the fluffy white warm as a tropical beach after the terrible, devouring cold the black-clad barefoot
woman carried with her.

⚹

Back in the car, the engine purring and her mouth sour, Nat
scrubbed her palms against her damp jeans. There was no trace of
blood; Dmitri had simply glanced at her hands, *tut-tutted* like Leo
when she came home with her school uniform torn, and the streaks
of clotting, darkening crimson fled into invisibility.

Maybe he simply liked being in last night's dirty suit, the way Nat had used a big boxy sage-colored cardigan all through middle school. She'd worn that sweater almost to pieces, rain or shine.

Sometimes, you just needed some armor.

The gangster cracked a bottle of radioactive-green Mountain Dew and took a long hit as the black car reached the freeway again. "Needs vodka," he commented, and merged without checking his blind spot or using his blinker. The snarling hood ornament probably warned all other traffic out of the way.

There wasn't enough air in the car. Nat rolled her window halfway down, ignoring the rushing wind and staring at whirling snow. The tires reached through fresh flakes and old ice, chewing hard, and she wondered vaguely what others must think of a low-slung sports car without chains slithering through gaps left by more cautious drivers.

Did they even see this vehicle? The fringe of the storm had caught up with them, but it didn't seem to matter.

Nothing did.

"I got all good stuff." Dmitri tucked the soda bottle securely in his lap and rustled the plastic bag on the armrest between them, its sides bulging with junk food. "Corn chips, cheese curls, potato chips, Red Hots, Red Vines, Snickers, circus peanuts, Mike-Ikes, grape gum, Milk Duds—"

Her mouth moved slightly. She couldn't force the words out.

"What? Can't hear you. Roll up the window, *zaika*."

Fuck you. Nat forced her ribs to expand, took a deep breath. "You could have stopped him," she managed, a thin thread of sound over rushing, snow-freighted wind. "You could have."

"What?"

Oh, you asshole. She turned away as far as she could, staring at the ashen-bleached landscape as plastic ruffled and he made happy little crunching noises.

The window twitched, rolled up without her touching the old-fashioned handle. The interstate swoop-curved under glossy black tires. Nat's head ached, and she couldn't stop rubbing her palms on her jeans, trying to scrub away remembered warm slipperiness.

You keep sending me gifts, the woman said. And the smile on the boy's face.

The roar of the wind closed away. A faint tang of perfumed smoke mixed with Dmitri's smoky aftershave, her shampoo, and a faint edge of fried potato from the Pringles he was merrily munching.

She could break the fucking window and dump all his snacks on the road. That would be satisfying, but could she afford to make him angry? The cowardice of that consideration made her writhe. She wished she did have some real power, or that Mama had at least told her something, so she could have . . .

What could she have done? Anything but what she *did* do, which was absolutely nothing.

As fucking usual.

"It was his time, little Natchka-*zaika*." For once, Dmitri didn't sound sarcastic or murderously gleeful. "You gonna have a lot of heartbreak, you get attached to rubes. They are not *us*. Sooner you accept that, better it'll be for you."

I'm not us either. "You could have done something," she repeated. The words fell into warm air soughing through the vents, the heater working overtime.

They hadn't stopped for gas. What did this thing run on? Belief, like Candy said? Or something else, something darker?

"Like what?" Now he sounded genuinely curious.

"You knew this would happen. You could have stopped it."

"Why? They gonna shoot each other, stab each other, take from each other. Been that way since one of them had a shiny rock the other wanted. I'm not disease, *zaika*, I am symptom. Some days I wonder . . ." He exhaled sharply. "You got it easy. Everyone likes the Drozdova, she make the flowers bloom and the little deer frolic, *da*. But those green things got roots in the dirt and the rot, and for each little deer there a hunter, or a wolf with an empty belly. Gonna starve the wolf because the deer have big cute eyes? Been tried before. Never ends well."

In other words, everything had an ecology. Even "divinities."

But Nat's heart hurt. She kept scrubbing her fingers against her jeans, even though the blood was gone. "How . . ." *Forget it. I don't want to know.* Pennsylvania hills rolled along outside the window, the snow coming down hard now but the black car moving at the same even, gliding pace—too swiftly to be normal.

Nothing was ever going to be normal again, she suspected.

"You want to know how long we live. I tell you." He took another pull from the plastic bottle, nestled it back between his legs, and smacked his lips. "Long as we can, just like them." Dmitri twisted the cap back on, and thumped on his chest with a loose fist. At least he didn't belch. "One thing we got in common with the rubes, at least."

When he lit another incense-smelling cigarette he rolled his window down most of the way, while Nat stared at whirling white still warmer than the barefoot woman's devouring chill.

WEAR MINE PROUD

Even though the black car didn't need gas or chains, even though it streaked through whatever traffic it found like a heated knife through a block of butter, it was still a long while to the Ohio border. They didn't stop for lunch, and she didn't want any of the overprocessed crap Dmitri was chowing down on. Every mile under the tires was the farthest from home she'd ever been, and Nat expected to be . . . well, more afraid than she actually was.

She didn't want to stop at another gas station. Mom always said they were filthy and the restrooms full of diseased needles, but she hadn't mentioned anything about dying clerks, gangsters who wouldn't call an ambulance, or barefoot greenish women who carried a mantle of bone-chilling ice.

The image of that lady—oh, might as well call her what she was, the *goddess*—bending over Mom's hospice bed made Nat's entire body shrink against itself. She'd thought "flesh crawling" was hyperbole until now.

An early winter dusk swallowed the countryside. Dinnertime came, circled warily, and was left behind. Tired brakelight rubies slithered to the right, bleary diamonds in the opposite lanes. Dmitri steered with two fingers, still happily munching on junk food, and she was almost used to the way the car wriggled into holes in traffic, bumped over ridged ice, and growled when the flow of vehicles clotted on city peripheries.

"So," he finally said, as the sun died behind the horizon and the snow turned to small pellets of ice stacked at the very edge of the windshield wipers' arcs. "You ever been to nice hotel, *zaika*?"

Mom hates hotels. Nat rubbed her hands together. It wasn't fair that she was sitting here breathing, her heart beating, her bladder increasingly uncomfortable, while some poor kid's body was on a dirty linoleum floor behind a counter stacked with cigarette cartons, sunglass racks, and other bullshit. "I'm fine. I can drive." Had anyone found a nasty surprise inside a gas station with its seasonally decorated windows yet?

"Not this beast." Dmitri shook his head, and the engine gave a deep mechanical chuckle. "He picky. So, you ever been in hotel at all?"

You're just going to insult me if I say I haven't. Nat's fingers ached, her hands tightly clasped. "I thought cars were *she*. Like boats."

"Where you hear that?" He shook his head, giving her a dark, considering sideways glance. A fresh bloom of stubble had appeared on his planed cheeks and strong chin. Did he use those cutthroat razors for shaving?

She wouldn't put it past him.

"I just did." Of course he wouldn't get the joke. Nat was rubbing her palms on her jeans again; she stopped with an effort.

"Well, it's wrong. They just like us, *zaika*. Some boys, some girls. You like Motel 6 instead?"

I wouldn't know, I've never been. "It's fine."

He probably expected her to pay for her own room, too. Coco said money wasn't a problem for *our type*; now Nat wondered. Mom and Leo pinched pennies, but Nat always thought that was because of the old country.

"Uncle" Leo. What other bedrock assumptions were going to vanish before this was over?

Assuming, of course, that it would ever end.

Dmitri finished his fourth bottle of sticky green pop laden with corn syrup. His own bladder, not to mention pancreas, must be iron for him to take down that much without stopping for a restroom. "How far west we goin'?"

"South Dakota." *Where it starts thinking it's Wyoming but it's not, not yet.* Could you love someone so much there was no room left over for your own child? Nat had always known herself a burden, a clinging vine on her mother's pretty gracefulness, but every mother loved her kids, right?

Or did some of them just . . . not?

The question was more terrifying than magic, than flying vans or deathless sorcerers, than divinities or "things who eat."

"Not much out there." Dima wanted more information, and she supposed she couldn't blame him.

"You asked." Nat forced her hands to lay quietly in her lap. The heat blowing through the vents fought deep piercing cold outside, and the result was a perfect temperature. Maybe it was just good engineering instead of magic. Advanced technology was synonymous with sorcery, hadn't someone said that? "That's where we're going."

"That where it is?" He snuck a darting little glance at the passenger side; did his chest ache all day? How, exactly, did he live with his heart gone? How was any of this *possible*?

"I don't know, Dmitri." Now she sounded like Mom, impatient with child-Nat's questions. How long would Nat herself live, hearing her mother's voice when she got irritated or even just brusque? "I have pieces of a puzzle, all right? Once I get to one, it'll lead me to another. That's what Mom said." *Scavenger hunt. Except the other scavengers have big teeth, and bad tempers.*

"Your mama tell you why she stole it?"

"I didn't know she stole anything." Nat studied his profile. "I'm sorry. You must want it back really badly."

His lip lifted, a snarl exposing those teeth that put the falling snow to shame. "Don't need your fuckin' pity."

It's not. But she decided he didn't want to know, and gazed out the windshield again. Ice pellets tapslithered over glass; even a magical car's heater couldn't completely erase the fact of winter.

She could easily imagine his very white teeth closing on flesh, slicing through. He had a gun, but he hadn't done anything to stop the robber. The blue car had been gone when she staggered outside to heave uselessly into a discolored snowdrift.

A nice clean getaway. Had Dmitri arranged it?

"So Candy's a divinity." She hadn't meant to say it aloud, but she might as well. Silence was dangerous. "And de Winter is too. And . . . my mother. And you. And that guy—Koschei—"

"Not him." The gangster's lip lifted, strong white teeth peeking out. "Filthy little sorcerer, that's all."

He said he was "the" sorcerer. Well, if she could believe in walking gods and hearts like blood-tinged diamonds, not to mention mirrors that showed the past, she could believe in sorcerers too. "So what are you a divinity of?" *The Mob? Or all criminals? How does it work? Do you have family too?*

"Asking the obvious. Should ask how to keep me from tearing you to pieces when we get where we're going, *zaika.*"

I'll figure it out. Or she wouldn't and the whole thing would be academic. "My name is Nat."

"That's not all your name. But you're a wise little girl, keeping it hidden. Never can tell what someone's going to do with a name."

There was no way to explain that the cats told her to choose a name and keep it close; child-Nat had liked having the secret. It was a warm glow on nights when Mama sent her to bed without supper, or when Maria and Leo shouted at each other in the old country's rolling tongue. "Is yours hidden too?"

"Hiding something just an invitation for someone come along to lift it, *zaika.* I wear mine proud. Maybe you should too."

Yeah, I'll take advice from the guy who shoots sorcerers and threatens women. Spiffy. She pressed her knees together, hoping they'd stop soon, and said nothing.

Maybe he took pity on her, or maybe all the Mountain Dew was putting the pressure on below his belt buckle, because the gangster eased off the gas and worked them to the far right lane. "I take you to a nice place. Okay?"

I can't afford a nice place. But maybe it didn't matter. "Fine," Nat agreed, and leaned to her right, resting her head on the cold, throbbing window while ice whispered along the car's metal and glass skin.

STAYING SEPARATELY

Downtown Akron, held under snowy siege, had no shortage of places to sleep overnight. Nat supposed she should be grateful she wasn't on a lumbering continental bus, although a train ride might have been nice. Flying would be better, but good luck affording that.

It wasn't a Motel 6 or a Holiday Inn; it wasn't a Marriott or Hilton or Four Seasons. It wasn't even a tiny, practically nameless mom-and-pop cash-by-the-hour. Instead, the black car growled through ice-rimed streets and whipped aside into a paved alley turning into cobblestones under wide gleaming tires, and Nat didn't let out a terrified shriek this time because she was getting almost used to his driving.

Either that, or she was too busy keeping her own bladder locked up, considering she was halfway to renal failure. It was an open question.

The cobbles rattled the entire car; Dmitri let out a sharp yelp of laughter as he snapped on the brakes, bringing them to a thump-banging stop in front of a long red awning before a frowning brick façade. Old-fashioned gaslamps—and they were actual *gas* lamps, trapped flames flickering merrily in each glass cage—cast roseate circles through intensifying snow. The icy pellets were swelling into honest-to-gosh snowflakes, and when the engine stopped its rumble Nat was suddenly very aware of being in a confined space with a man who probably wanted her dead.

A trio of uniformed males—valet, bellboy, and what she could only assume was security—looked blankly at the car, wearing identical customer-service expressions; all three had lantern-jawed faces and blank, pale eyes despite the variances in skin tone. Crimson serge on the valet and bellboy gave them a faintly military air, and their pillbox hats were both tilted at exactly the same jaunty angle. Behind them, the bruiser looming in a black suit and no coat despite the freezing temperature touched his ear, the raw slash of his mouth moving with little bullet-words.

Oh, boy. "Is this a divinity hotel?" *Hilton for the God Squad?* There was even a dim sort of amusement in thinking about one or two of the more ruler-happy nuns getting a load of this, as the kids in high school used to say.

"Said I'd take you somewhere nice." Dmitri tossed an empty pop bottle into the backseat; every time he did that, she flinched. A quick glance showed nothing but a few scattered, unopened containers back there; of course he'd have a magical litterbag. "Lot of trouble for one little *zaika*, I hope you realize."

"I could just go on my own." She reached for the door handle; his fingers covered her shoulder and bit into heavy wool.

"You think you get away from me?" He gave a quick yank; her fingers fell away from the handle. "Sit still. I open door, I am gentleman."

"Yeah. Sure." But her words were lost; he was already out on his side, tossing a small glittering keychain to the valet. Nat scrambled to grab her backpack from the rear seat, knocking over a bag of Doritos—ugh, how could he eat that crap? He probably wouldn't want dinner after stuffing himself all day.

That was fine with her. Nat's stomach was a walnut-sized ball of anxiety; she couldn't imagine it relaxing enough to down one of the protein bars tucked in her faithful old schoolbag.

The gangster opened her door and extended a hand as if collecting her from a limousine, but Nat slid free of the car on her own, suppressing a groan. This was going to be an awful trip.

"—time since your last visit, sir." The security guy's voice was a flat, colorless rumble.

"Hope they kept the bar open for me." Dmitri even offered Nat his arm, but she stood very still, clutching her backpack and eyeing the large glass revolving door. It moved lazily, like a combine thresher or steamboat's paddle wheel, and the idea that the building was a giant monster looking to slowly digest whatever was so foolish as to step inside didn't seem outlandish at all. "Eh, *zaika*. Come on, you gonna get a cold."

I might almost prefer it.

"Drozdova." The security guy actually bowed, indicating the revolving door with a massive, beefy hand gloved in black leather. "The Elysium is honored by your presence. Please, enter in peace, and rest with us."

She shot a distrustful glance at Dmitri, but he was no help, just standing there like he expected her to take his arm and know what to say. "Thank you," she managed. "It's my first time, I hope I don't mess anything up."

"Impossible." A thin, creaking smile infected the security man's craggy face, and the bellboy hovered anxiously, obviously expecting there to be more luggage. "The Elysium is most accommodating, ma'am."

"Long as you don't break the *peace*." Dmitri snorted a laugh, making a brisk movement with his elbow, but she ignored him. "Truce inside the walls, and all that. Come on, *zaika*."

Nat, despite her misgivings, hitched her backpack onto her shoulder, and the revolving door behaved just like any other she'd ever been forced to go through. The foyer was a vast expanse of white marble, tables with brass vases holding sprays of fresh flowers. A gas insert fireplace the size of a Buick crackled merrily; a wall of smoked glass along one side imperfectly occluded a long bar crowded with half-seen forms, candlelight, and a mutter of conversation. Red carpet thick enough to lose a quarter in ran along likely lines of travel, and there were two concierge desks holding trios of uniformed staff in natty black and white, all examining the new arrivals with interest.

Nat felt distinctly underdressed, but then again, she had ever since walking into de Winter's office. Maybe she should have kept Coco's green confection.

The front desk was a massive mahogany affair, its face carved like a reed-choked river; Nat could swear she saw the plants move with the wood's grain, sharp edges whispering. A tall, cavernous, copper-skinned man, his shaved head gleaming, adjusted bright silver pince-nez on a high proud nose; his suit was so dark it was almost purple and a subtle sheen lingered in the fabric. "Mr. Konets," he intoned as they came into range, a wall of wooden cubbyholes behind him and his reflection moving on the glass-polished counter. "Welcome back. And Mademoiselle Drozdova, welcome to the Elysium—it is still mademoiselle, is it not?"

Oh, Christ have mercy. Nat managed a nod. Her throat had gone dry. They knew her name. Of course the gangster could have called ahead, or de Winter could have.

But . . . divinities. And magic.

"Eh, *zaika*, this Mr. Priest." For once, the gangster didn't sound mocking, just amused. "Little girl don't even know her own strength. You want to tell her the rules, or should I?"

"I believe that is my prerogative." The man's expression didn't change, but his tone grew thinner, if that were possible. "The Elysium is open to all divinities, principalities, powers, and demigods; we request that any feuds or nonconsensual violence be left outside. The basement is where you will find the Ring, the subbasement is for conveyance storage, the bar is open at any hour, and the exercise facilities are upon the third floor. We have a wide range of amenities; you will find a booklet upon the nightstand in your room. I assume you are staying separately?"

"No," Dmitri said, a "Yes," bolted from Nat's mouth at the same moment, and Mr. Priest—the name had to be a joke, but he didn't look like a man who had much of a sense of humor—simply regarded them both, eyebrows slightly raised and nose fractionally wrinkled like he smelled something just a tad objectionable but was too well-mannered to give any further indication of the fact.

"Yes," the gangster finally said, after observing Nat carefully in his peripheral vision. "But I warn you, *zaika*, you try to run—"

"Will you stop threatening me?" All Nat's social training tried to make her feel guilty for what Mom would call *causing a scene*, but for God's sake—and how bleakly funny was that particular phrase right now—she was fucking tired of a lot of things, and Dima's

nastiness was one of them. "I promised, didn't I? But okay. Whatever he says, Mr. Priest. I'm sorry I don't know the right etiquette,
but it's been a really long day." She attempted a gracious smile, but
it felt masklike and strange.

The awkward silence was full of the fire's soft breath and murmuring conversation from the glassed-in bar. Were there "divinities" in there with their noses pressed against the glass, looking at
the new girl in town? Principalities, powers, demigods—she was
going to get a whole new vocabulary, and quickly too.

"Separate." Dmitri's jaw hardened, and the word was a razor's
sharp gleam. "But adjoining," he added. "For safety."

Mr. Priest, however, watched Nat as if she could somehow over-
rule the gangster. Maybe she could, but at any moment she was
sure she was going to wet herself like an overexcited cocker spaniel.
"Fine," she said, and dropped her gaze to the carving on the desk-
front. The river wasn't helpful, but she had to have something to
look at. *Just let me near a bathroom. Please.*

"If I may commence? Welcome to the Elysium." It was impossible for the bald man to look prouder, or more forbidding. "This is
a place of rest. All feuds or battles are left outside the doors; while
inside these walls all are welcome, and all are held to the same standard. Nonconsensual violence towards another guest or an employee
is strictly forbidden and will result in banishment; all formal Ring
matches are, of course, exempt. All amenities are included in your
stay; whatever is required will be found. The bar is open to all; we do
ask for some slight moderation in imbibing, though we understand
it might not be possible in all cases." He stared at Dmitri during
that last sentence, and if Nat hadn't been about ready to explode she
might have had to suppress a laugh. "Meals are served in the restaurant at usual times or in the Ring; if you wish privacy while consum-
ing, simply pick up the phone in your room and we shall be happy to
deliver. The boutiques upon the second floor are also ready to assist
any guest; the pools are open at all hours though we do ask that strict
silence be observed in the sauna. The rooftop garden is closed for
the season, unless Mademoiselle . . ." Here he looked at her, and Nat
wondered what the hell she was supposed to say.

Apparently, nothing was an acceptable answer. "Very good, then." Mr. Priest made a beckoning motion; footsteps behind Nat turned into another bellboy with the same prominent jaw—were they all Habsburgs, she wondered, biting back another weary laugh—and oddly colorless irises, in the same bright crimson uniform and pillbox hat. "Samuel, please show Mademoiselle Drozdova and Mr. Konets to their rooms. Sixth floor, I should think. Mademoiselle, should you need anything at all, please do let us know. We are honored by your presence."

Yeah, thanks, I just want a toilet. "Thank you very much." She sounded prim even to herself. What would Mom say? "I'm very happy to be here."

It was a lie, but politeness so often was. Dmitri tugged at her elbow, Sam the bellboy glided past them towards a bank of brightly lit elevator doors, and Nat hoped she wasn't walking funny.

She also hoped Dmitri was going to tip the young man, because she didn't have any clue what the going rate was.

A HUNGRY GIRL

Whatever she'd expected, it wasn't a vast green-carpeted suite; the bedroom held a wide white damask bed on acres of thick emerald. Both sitting room and bedroom had enormous bay windows looking over a night-jeweled city skyline. A faint good scent of cut grass in the sitting room breathed over a white leather couch and two wide white leather chairs crouching before a glassed-in gas fireplace. All the furniture looked suspiciously like whole birch saplings trained into different shapes, solidly rooted in grassy shag, their papery boles glowing with health. There was no television, but she didn't mind once the door closed behind and she was left in blessed silence, all but duck-waddling for the bathroom.

A giant sunken tub with whirlpool jets just in case she needed drowning, shelves of toiletries she was fairly sure were charged for by the ounce, a vanity with rosy bulbs overhead to give a flattering light—that was nice enough, but she hobbled for the recessed commode and lost herself in sheer relief.

If she was a "divinity" why did she still need to pee? She didn't have anyone to ask, and by the time she finished she not only felt several pounds lighter but also strangely . . . cleansed, as if she'd taken a shower instead.

With immediate concerns taken care of, she edged through the suite. A small leather folio on the nightstand did list "amenities." Swimming pool, bar, room service. She didn't want to know what the Ring was.

At least she was smart enough for that, despite the fact that it rated a page of its own in the folio.

No prices listed, either. Apparently powers and principalities didn't look at price tags. Or maybe they paid in something else. Belief? Energy? Life-force? Jedi mind-tricks?

A series of knocks at the door set in the sitting-room wall opposite the fireplace thankfully wasn't shave-and-a-haircut, but her mouth went dry anyway. "Open up," Dmitri's muffled voice floated through, and she flinched.

I don't think I want to. There was no lock, and she stared helplessly at the door. "Come in?" The last word was more of a squeak, but the gilded lever serving as a doorknob depressed and she caught a glimpse of smoky darkness and deep wine-red before he nipped through, sweeping the aperture closed behind him.

Against the room's pale luxury he was a black blot, his boot-toes glittering sharply. Dima eyed what he could see of the suite and grinned. "You like it?"

"I wonder what it costs." There was, after all, no reason to lie.

"Costs?" He snorted, striding for the window; at least he didn't peek into the bedroom. "That's for the rubes, *zaika*." A slight hitch in his stride, then he halted, swung towards her. "She really told you nothing, eh? Your dear *Maman*."

"I'm not going to sneak out in the middle of the night, if that's what you're worried about." Nat folded her arms, thankful she'd had a chance to unload, so to speak, before this. "And I know you hate her, but she's my mother. Can you just . . . not?"

He stared at her, his dark head cocked, and his smile went through several different shades of feeling, most she couldn't decipher, before it settled on something that looked almost pained. Had he ever had parents? It didn't seem likely.

"Little girls love their mamas," he muttered. "You hungry?"

She was, but she shook her head, digging her fingers into her coat sleeves. Maybe she could drag one of the chairs against the door between their rooms, if it wasn't bolted to the floor. That sounded like a really good idea.

An uncomfortable semi-silence spread sharp feathery wings

between them. The gas insert's flames twisted, hissing slightly behind sparkling glass. Had Mom ever stayed here? She'd had to at least have gone to South Dakota to leave the items for this scavenger hunt, but she always made a point of saying how she hated travel.

After coming from the old country and making this kind of road trip, probably with Dmitri breathing down her neck, Nat could see why. Had Mom been afraid of him showing up on the yellow house's doorstep, or had de Winter held him back?

There was so much she didn't know, and couldn't trust anyone to tell her. Even her own mother, it looked like.

"You like the fights?" Dmitri turned away, strode to the window, examined the view like it had personally offended him. "I take you."

Fights? Probably that ring thing. Even trying to ignore it didn't keep the knowledge from seeping into your head; you couldn't escape anything cruel. It was just the way the world was set up.

"No." Nat's arms and legs weren't quite sure they'd stopped moving for the day; she could still feel the car's engine throbbing in her skeleton. "Thank you."

"Mascha liked the fights." One shoulder lifted, dropped; the shrug looked almost painful. Maybe he was sore from a day in the car too, though she doubted it. "A hungry girl, your mamma. We had some good times."

That's . . . unexpected. "Oh," Nat said, blankly. How did you respond to something like that?

He spun as if she'd shouted, and glared at her. But when he spoke, it was the same flat, mocking tone. "They got a swimming pool. Bring a bikini, *zaika?*"

Oh Christ, I should hope not. "Did you?"

A brittle laugh and he jolted into motion, passing her with a long swinging stride. But his shoulders hunched like he expected her to hit him, or say something nasty. "Rest up. Tomorrow we really drive."

"Great." Nat waited until the door in the wall swallowed him again, and let out a long, soft breath. Tiny tremors ran through her, and even her favorite knit cap felt itchy and strange, like someone else's clothing. The room was quiet except for the fire, eating whatever fuel it could find and exhaling heat. A ghostly reflection hung in the window's clarity, a pale face and a dark coat, just as insubstantial as she felt at the moment. Nat peeled the hat free and unbuttoned the peacoat, trying not to feel like she was taking off necessary protection.

Maybe dinner would be a good idea; she could certainly use a drink. And if there were other powers, or divinities, or whatnot in the bar . . . well, she at least *looked* old enough for booze, didn't she? And she didn't think they checked IDs here.

"Certainly old enough," she heard herself say, and wondered if she was going insane. "But *brave* enough? That's the question."

It didn't matter. De Winter, or Baba, or whoever the hell she was, would fix her mother. That was the goal; *keep your eyes on the prize,* they said.

The only trouble with that was you couldn't see what was sneaking up behind you.

PERSONAL, DIFFERENT

When a man was in a certain mood, drinking was only a prelude to a fight or a fuck. He didn't want one of Candy's girls, though all he had to do was pick up the phone and request; the thought of her smug smile when she caught wind of the event was intolerable.

No, there was only one thing that would do right now. Which meant Dima skipped any imbibing at all and rode the whisper-quiet elevator down, down, and down, snarling silently at his reflection in the polished brass doors.

She's my mother. Can you just not? As if a little bitch's sentiment could—or should—outweigh what Mascha had done. The *zaika* didn't even want to go to the fights, despite the fact that an invitation was highly prized, something she'd never seen in her mortal life.

Maybe letting Maschka eat her own spawn was fitting. Maybe it would soothe the prickling under his skin, the throbbing in his empty chest. She wouldn't even have *dinner* with him, as if she knew her place in the pantheon was so different than his.

Same old story, the rich girl looking down her nose at the thief in the shadows. Well, she would bleed just as well as anyone else, the minute his sharp little friends left their dark homes and glitter-glinted.

You could have done something.

Like it mattered, one rube more or less. Like *anything* mattered.

The elevator halted its plunge; when the doors whooshed reluctantly open a featureless black granite hallway receded into the distance. At its far end bloody neon glowed, flanked by two big slabs of muscle with shining-blank eyes. Purely for aesthetics; no rube would get this far even if one could be brought past the Elysium's hungry revolving door, and no true power would be troubled by mere soldier ants.

But appearances had to be observed. Dmitri Konets stalked down the hall, an unfamiliar tickle at his nape and his boot-toes shining.

The starving ones couldn't enter the Elysium. She was safe enough for tonight. If someone else swooped in to grab the *zaika*, if someone else trailed her or forced her to hand over what belonged to him . . . well, as soon as he didn't need her to show the way, he could pursue whoever acquired a bloody fist-sized diamond and let his vengeance upon Mama Dearest take a backseat like so many other enjoyable things, savoring the inevitable when he had the time to devote himself fully.

Assuming, that was, that dear Maschenka survived long enough to be punished.

"Good evening, Mr. Konets." Both soldiers bowed slightly, and Dima contented himself with a nod instead of a snarl. The door opened, bloody light spilling out with the formless mutter of an excited crowd.

He plunged into smoky dimness very much like the room the Elysium kept for him—or maybe they changed between every guest, because Masha wouldn't want white leather and birch bark. No, *she* would have a room with a rocky cataract in its center and a gray stone altar with the flint knife ready, no cozy fire or wide soft bed. She would want a pile of springy pine boughs and a jug of water-clear vodka, a steaming mound of winter-lean meat and tender little bunnies quivering in an osier hutch.

Or maybe she had changed when they brought her over the ocean in crammed holds and shipping containers. Had she taught the little *zaika* to crack an egg and suck it dry, or how to call up the black stinking mud to mire any pursuit?

No, she'd taught the girl nothing. A little shivering ball of fluff

trapped in wickerwork, ready for the black blade and possibly stupid enough to offer its own throat out of misplaced affection.

"Dmitri!" A rich, plummy baritone with just a hint of static-
scratch hidden in its flow boomed through the haze. Hash smoke,
tobacco smoke, the skunkier harsh tone of plain reefer, a thread
of sticky perfumed opium, all mixing together. The doors closed
behind him and Prommo appeared in his white coat open to the
waist, his hard little potbelly twitching. His white top hat was
furred, like his broad shoulders; his oiled moustache gleamed over
broad flat ruminant's teeth. "Heard you were in town. Come to
watch the show?"

The Ring, its borders festooned with chain link and barbwire,
held a fringed, spitting manticore and a youth in black leather; the
latter wasn't quite a power yet, his features blurring through several
copies of currently famous action heroes. A win here might keep
him solid for a few more weeks, and if one of his devotees managed
fickle stardom he might get enough of the short-term celebrity to
solidify yet more.

Although Arnie Sly might have something to say about that; he
generally liked to eat the newer ones to keep himself solid between
box-office morphs.

The manticore, pulled straight from a thundering, fevered mortal nightmare, hissed and squirted a bright jet of acid. The boy,
muscle moving in flat straps under bronzed skin—now he wore the
form of an Indonesian star achieving much stateside acclaim for
his photogenic savagery—flickered aside with disdainful ease and
stamped on one of the thing's fringe-tentacles.

It howled, the chain link rattled, and the crowd—familiar faces,
mostly, it was a slow night of second-rate principalities and powers instead of actual divinities—gave vent to its approval. Some
clapping, some cheers, one of Cashe's cousins at the bar giving
Dmitri a sour smile as if he suspected something, a few of Candy's
girls working the crowd with trays of cigarettes and other things.
One, a brunette with a cheeky grin and a pile of viands on her tray,
whizzed past on roller skates; there was the wrestler Nash at a table

surrounded by gleaming disposables, his aging body splinted and oiled, obviously having taken a few rounds in the ring and gotten his fill of physical pain.

Good fuel, in most cases. Nash had probably ripped one of the manticore's cousins into pieces. At least it wasn't a sacrifice night.

"Get me a match." Dmitri snatched a pack of crimson-banded hash smokes off a passing girl's tray and nodded at a far shadowed corner, where a placeholder for the Rumbler drew back into gloom with a viperish slither.

He was everywhere a fight was, like Dima was everywhere hunger and light fingers lingered. But the Rumbler wasn't the lord of just *any* fight, no—merely the ones where the blood was paid for.

When it was personal, well. That was different.

"Oh, certainly, but we have nothing to match someone of your . . . status." Prommo bobbed next to him like a fucking carnival toy as Dmitri strode for the Ring. "I'm afraid it won't be, ah, to your usual standard, Mr. Konets, sir, but—"

"Then put four or five bastards in the Ring and let's *go*," Dima snarled, tearing a smoke free, lighting it with a fingertip, and shrugging out of his torn, stained jacket. He let it fall—one of the girls would collect it—and his shirt tore free as well.

Cool air hit his torso, and the tattoos shifted. Hypersaturated koi swam across his ribs; the stars on his shoulders gave deep aching twinges; the onion-domed churches rose on his back. It was a pleasant sting, like a razor delicately caressing a sobbing rube's throat. His boot-toes spat sparks and he shoved aside a clot of barbwire, relishing the slices along his forearms. They sealed instantly; he lunged and leapt, and the manticore splattered in a tide of caustic goop and acidic venom, its deathscreech a nailbiting falsetto like golden needles piercing every eardrum in range.

Other tattoos shifted, numbers in gothic script crawling up Dmitri's neck, symbols clustering his heart. His nephews and uncles were busy tonight, probably feeling his fury in their own flesh. He wasn't like the pale bastard crouching in Protestant holes; no, Dima took the willing of any stripe. They paid their toll in watches ripped from cooling wrists or cargos subtracted from listing ships, wallets taken at gunpoint and knife-edge, with easy patter and a charming smile or with dead dark emotionless glares.

All of them were his, and they served their loving uncle well. What need for a disdainful little rube divinity and her snotty little nose?

"I was *fighting* that," the youth spat at him, bloodlust contorting his young face as he shifted into the form of a muscle-chunky blond youth with a string of B movies to his credit and probably a huge coke habit to pay for as well, clutching at stardom like the hungry rube he was.

"I'm better." Dima's smile stretched wide and white; he spread his arms. "Come and see, little boy."

Prommo cursed, then began the fight-patter in his rolling baritone as the barbwire twitched, healing itself in fits and starts. Maybe the youngling in the Ring didn't know who he was facing, or maybe it was simply berserker fury; he jolted forward, fists wrapped in dirty bandages coming up in an approximation of a savate stance, and Dima couldn't help but laugh.

He hoped they had more cannon fodder than *this*. He was going to need it, the mood he was in.

GOOD ADVICE

Riding the elevator down to the lobby was easy, no sweat. Nat made it to the smoked-glass door of the bar before her nerve failed and she had to stop, taking a deep breath and hoping nobody inside was watching.

Then she pulled it open, decisively, and stepped through.

Hotel bars were apparently all the same, even when they serviced "divinities." A scattering of drinkers—a platinum-haired woman in a violently glittering blue evening gown with a white fur stole over her shoulders, a trio of men in khaki with their shaven heads pressed together as they conferred, a lean copper-skinned man with a cowboy hat, its band starred with silver scallops, and others she didn't dare look too closely at—paid no overt attention to her advent, and she strode for the long, mirror-polished bar like she did this every day.

The bartender was thankfully not like the butlers at Jay's mansion, but he did glide behind the wooden edifice like he was attached to a rail. Probably a twin to the brass foot-railing on Nat's side; she settled on a leather-cushioned stool and tried a smile.

"My lady Drozdova." Under the bartender's big dark walrus moustache lurked a tinny tenor, and his shaved cheeks gleamed. His eyes were polished brown marbles, glistening wetly as he blinked. "What will you have?"

"Vodka, neat," Nat said. *I even sound normal. Great.* "Very cold. Can I order dinner here too?"

"Of course. One moment, please." There was a muffled musical clanking, and the man—dressed like an old-timey saloonkeeper, right down to his bowler and the black bands over the elbows of his snow-white button-down, his white apron and his round, jolly heft—turned to the serious business of getting a customer a drink.

Behind the bar, ranks of bottles on glass shelves watched their own reflections in bright, water-clear mirrored tiles. They also—solemnly, silently—watched the patrons. Double-faced, like the god of doorways—oh, all the Greek and Roman mythology the sisters had grudgingly taught was bleakly hilarious now.

Was there a god of bars? Would it be a he or a she? Did they get lonely in the afternoon dead time when all food service workers moved purposefully through the lull, knowing the dinner rush would start soon?

There was a faint susurration. She expected Dmitri to come sauntering through the doors, the vast lobby a dreaming figment of its own polished self trapped behind a cascade of dark glass.

Instead, it was the beak-nosed man with the silver conchas on his hatband. He arrived just as the bartender set a thick snowy paper napkin down with a sweating, narrow glass of clear vodka atop it, a paper-thin lemon slice artfully twisted on the rim.

"Well, hello." The man leaned against the bar, one elbow propped on its mirrorshine. The conchas glinted like Dima's boot-toes, but this guy's grin was only half predatory. The other half was sheer goodwill—a few crucial millimeters of difference, maybe in the laugh-lines around his eyes. "Did you enjoy the party?"

Nat could have pretended not to know what he was talking about. She returned her gaze to the vodka, wondering if getting drunk would solve anything about this whole insane situation.

Probably not. "You were at Jay's." It wasn't even a bad guess, especially if she tried to sound bored and world-weary, like she did this all the time.

"I'm everywhere, and nowhere at once." Intoned like a riddle while he shifted, some motion made to the round, mechanically grinning bartender. "Coffee, please."

"Yes, sir." The bartender's tone never changed. He glided away again.

Nat touched her glass with a fingertip. Icy condensation, just like any other cold drink in a warm room. "Let me guess, you're the god of air."

The man made a slight *tch* noise, like Leo decrying a child's impoliteness. "Spoken like a white girl."

What the fuck did you expect me to speak like, a cartoon rabbit? "Guilty as charged." Nat strangled the depressingly familiar flare of anger; it hurt to think of Leo. Was it too much to ask that even one of her parents cared about her? But every great love story left out everyone else in the world, she supposed. "And not in the mood for a lot of bullshit right now."

"Bullshit's at least warm when it comes out. And it's useful for some things, you know." The man stayed where he was, probably eyeing her curiously; Nat felt the weight of his gaze. Not precisely unfriendly, but not kind, either. "But I don't carry it around with me and you shouldn't either. Coyote." He offered his hand, a flicker of motion in her peripheral vision.

Is that your genus, species, name, or title? Realization arrived just as her mouth was opening to say *leave me the fuck alone,* and she turned, studying him afresh.

It wasn't the eyes, she decided. Nor was it his clothes, or the fringe on his jacket moving in slow, questing twitches like it wanted to grab any small animal unwary enough to step close. It was the *vitality,* a crackling sense of force only barely contained, an inaudible humming she couldn't find a source or comparison for. He just seemed more . . . *there.*

Like de Winter, and Dmitri, and Coco, and Candy.

Like Mom used to be, before she got sick. There hadn't been a sharp boundary, a dividing line; it had happened gradually.

Like a child growing up. They started out tiny squalling bundles, but then one day you looked and your kid was ready to go to college. Everyone said so.

Koschei didn't share that vitality, despite his rich voice and apparent durability. Jay did, but relatively weakly. Leo? Not at all.

So Nat shook his warm, strangely callused hand. Nothing but

skin contact, like a hundred other times she'd been forced to this social ritual. "Nat. Nat Drozdova."

"Pleasedtameetcha. Or whatever lie white people say."

She reclaimed her hand and shifted on the stool, leaning away. How on earth could you respond to that? "I can't say the same." At least she was absolved of the duty of politeness, however briefly.

"Then you're more honest than your mother."

It stung, but only for a moment. "You knew her."

"I met her. Big difference." He nodded as the bartender slid a white ceramic cup of strong black coffee into range; the man calling himself Coyote turned his back to the rest of the bar, hunching his broad shoulders and dropping his chin. Despite that, his eyes gleamed like live coals, and she realized he was using the mirror behind the bottles to watch the entire place. "She's sent you out for it, then. The treasures, and what she took."

Treasures? "Yes." Had Mom hidden more than the gem? Oh, what the hell, she might as well pump this guy for whatever information he'd give. "I'm going to save her. She's dying."

He shrugged—not Dmitri's fluid catlike movement but a canine ripple, his jacket twitching like loose, furry skin. "Everything changes." His teeth were just as white as the gangster's; apparently, divinities had good dental plans. "Didn't the cats teach you that?"

"They don't lecture me." The impulse to hunch her own shoulders guiltily and blurt out *it was just my imagination* was immediate, but Nat quelled it, picking up her stinging-cold glass. Maybe she was insane and gabbling on a street corner, lost in hallucinations. "I don't lecture them either."

"At least there's that." Seen in strong-nosed profile, he wasn't quite handsome or the opposite. Still, nothing in his face was apologetic. He looked, all things considered, very comfortable with himself indeed, and Nat longed for a sliver of that confidence. "You know he'll kill you if he can."

There was no reason to pretend to be shocked, or ask what he meant—it was, indeed, like talking to one of the cats. And now she remembered him, the memory like thunder after a lightning flash.

At Jay's party, in top hat with those silver conchas and beaded necklaces, carrying a pipe, he had given her a long appraising look. *I am where you least expect me.*

Nat suppressed a shiver. Of course Dmitri would kill her; he'd flat-out told her as much. It looked like others might be willing to help him or warn her, but nothing more. "So he informed me."

"It's a valuable thing you're after. Lots of other people wanting it. You know what happens if you eat a Heart, right?"

"You take his power?" It wasn't a bad guess, Nat thought. Cannibals did it all the time.

"Nice guess." His fingers drummed the bar in quick succession, tiny thumps much louder than they should be. "Suppose you could, if you tried. Give you a helluva stomachache, but might be worth it. Didn't tell you that, I bet."

"It didn't come up." Why would Mom have hidden it, then? Nat was, however, fairly certain she didn't want to ask this guy about that particular parental choice. "I don't suppose just giving it back with an apology will help anything."

"Would you?" Coyote studied her in the mirror; it was probably easier to talk about this sort of shit if you didn't have to look directly at the other person.

Like conversations on long car rides, maybe. "I . . ." Nat stopped.

Bring back the gem to Mom, take it to de Winter, or give it back to Dmitri? Agreeing before you knew the whole deal always bit you in the ass; she'd been working retail, not to mention call centers and the office at Humboldt Insurance, long enough to know *that*. She shouldn't feel guilty about it at all, either; the gangster was an asshole who had let a boy die just that afternoon.

Nat couldn't even go to the cops. Were her fingerprints all over the gas station? Dmitri's certainly were.

It would serve him right, and yet . . . a *heart*. She tried to imagine her own cardiac muscle pulled out of her chest and carried away. It must hurt. Returning it to de Winter would just put him back where he was before, right? Sitting up in the old woman's office waiting to be sent out for errands, or whatever she made him do.

If she took it to the hospice first, would Mom eat it? Or would de Winter, Baba Yaga, or whoever the hell she was, truly fix Nat's mother?

And then what? Go back to living in the little yellow house with Mom and Leo? Nat could move out, having done her daughterly duty, and then . . . go to college? Would she have to move to a different city, a different state?

A different country?

The idea of officially leaving home was both terrifying and enticing. Especially if she didn't need money.

But what if she did? What if the power, or whatever it was, depended on Mom's . . . well, the fading, the sickness that made her not-quite-*there*?

If Mom was healthy, Nat could go back to being what Dima called "a rube." Which might not be so bad—being a divinity looked like it sucked.

Bigtime.

"Oh, buffalo girl." Coyote laughed, a yip running under his very pleasant tenor. "You are fucked for sure."

It certainly looks that way. "It's no surprise, and no change." Nat touched the vodka glass with a fingertip again. Did this guy remember the Pilgrims coming over on big-sailed ships? It probably wasn't pleasant, if he did. "Are you here to help point the way?" *Or are you just talking shit?*

"Not yet. But when you got the Cup and that big blue beast, you come on up to see us, and we'll talk. Might even smoke a pipe or two."

That sounds incredibly unappetizing. "I know where to find the Cup." She studied his expression in the mirror, but it didn't change. "But I don't know anything about a blue beast. I suppose the next part of the scavenger hunt will happen on its own." *Maybe in your direction, unless you're just handing out an invitation?*

"If you're brave enough." Another canine shrug-flicker. "But I gotta tell you, buffalo girl, might be best just to go home and wait."

Well, that was unexpected. She didn't think Dmitri would go for it. "And let my mother die." Everyone seemed to assume that was the choice she'd make.

It made you wonder about their home lives. Was every divinity family unhappy in its own way?

Coyote turned his chin slightly, eyeing her sidelong. "You keep going, you ain't gonna like what you find."

"Yeah." Nat picked up her glass, tossed the vodka far back. It burned, hit her stomach and exploded with warmth. It tasted like it was from the bottle in the freezer at home, and she wondered if Leo was wearing his scarf, if he was visiting Mom, if he was salting the front walk enough. If he was wandering the house, his mouth tasting like dirt. If he was making borscht and freezing it so when Nat returned she could reheat a single portion carefully ladled into a margarine tub, because buying Tupperware was for rich idiots and in the little yellow house they knew the value of an American dollar. "It's called growing up, I guess."

"That what you think?" He wrapped his long copper fingers around his mug. "Just like your mama, won't take good advice."

Everyone had an opinion on Mom, but none of these assholes had ever lived with her. "She's my mother," Nat said, dismally aware she was repeating what she'd flung at Dmitri earlier. "Can you just *not?*"

"If you like." He lifted the white ceramic mug; the coffee had to be just this side of boiling to steam like that but he drank it like Nat had taken the vodka, a straight shot all the way down. His throat worked, and she wondered what other "divinities" ate. Would her own diet change the longer she traveled?

There was no one to ask. Not Dmitri, and certainly not *this* fellow.

What would happen if Mom died while Nat was still chasing clues?

"Ah." He set the mug down and exhaled hard, not quite a belch. "If you wanna see that thief get his ass beat you can go down to the Ring. Might even amuse you."

Is that where he is? She didn't want to ask how this guy knew, and in any case, it didn't matter. "I'll tell him you said so."

"Go ahead. He's too slow to catch me, and in any case, he's family.

I steal too, when I've a mind to." He smacked his chest with a fist, very much like Leo trying to dislodge indigestion when there were no radishes to put in a glass of milk, or Dima each time he finished a liter or two of Mountain Dew. "Coffee's a great invention, ennit? Not like that shit you're drinking. Anyway, come see us when you got to. We'll be waiting."

"Who's this *we*?"

"Come and find out." He touched his hat brim, and that hot, gleeful gaze met hers directly in the mirror. "If you won't go home, buffalo girl, you gotta dance."

"Thanks for the advice."

His laugh was more of a bark now, and his nose twitched. "Oh, man," he wheezed when the chuckles stopped. "You're a damn co-median, too. I'll tell you something, then, since you so funny."

Great. "Go ahead."

"That horsethief will kill you if he can, buffalo girl. But a lot of others will do worse. You're nice and young and tender."

I was a teenage girl in America, you think I don't know that? "So staying with Dmitri is for my own protection?" *Just like a battered girlfriend. Great.*

Coyote found that funny. At least, he laughed again, tipped his hat like a cowboy once more too, and did an about-face. He strode from the Elysium's bar like he had somewhere to be, and right be-fore he went through the smoked-glass doors he capered a little, dancing to music nobody else could hear.

Nat watched him go in the mirror, and it felt like everyone in the bar was looking at her now. Maybe they were, and if someone else wanted to come up and give a bunch more cryptic pronouncements or threats, now was as good a time as any.

But nobody did. The bartender glided back in front of her, a smooth motion like he was on rails. "Another vodka, please," Nat said, even though the first one was still stinging her throat and she should probably have something solid. Drinking on an empty stom-ach was bad for you, or so Leo said even though he did it at least once a week.

"Yes, ma'am." The marble-eyes didn't roll in their sockets, and the saloonkeeper's movements were just as robotic as ever.

One more, and then go to bed. It wouldn't do to skip dinner *and* drink all night. But Nat wondered if taking a bottle up to your room was allowed.

It might be the only way to get some sleep.

GODSAKE

She wasn't hungover, at least. Nat woke in a wide white Elysium bed, blinking against winter sunlight sharp as a thin yellow ceramic blade, the gas insert's fire pale and anemic but still hiss-devouring fuel and oxygen. The empty vodka bottle stood stiff and formal on the nightstand, and it was no brand she'd ever heard of, its label so faded from condensation and age it was just a rag of glued paper clinging to embossed glass.

It was nice to take a shower without worrying about the hot water running out for Leo or Mom, nice to poke at the white plastic coffee machine with its self-contained pods in fantastical flavors, and she was considering the prospect of breakfast when a thundering series of knocks on the door between her room and the gangster's brought her out into the suite's sitting room in a heart-thumping rush.

"Open *up*," he growled, and it sounded like he was as bad-tempered as Mom on Saturday mornings, when child-Nat wanted someone to turn on the balky old television for cartoons.

Nat folded her bare arms, staring at the white door with its golden lever-handle. Facing down Dmitri in her soft yellow pyjama tank top and boxers was *not* on the menu today.

Another thundering series of knocks, but he didn't just bust in. Maybe he couldn't?

Her heart was in her throat.

"Eh, *zaika!* Open the fuck up!"

"No." Her throat was dry, so she had to clear it and pitch her voice loudly enough to carry. The coffee machine made a soft series of beeps; she'd chosen a French vanilla pod. Maybe they'd charge her double for it. "No," she repeated. "I haven't even had coffee. Cut it out."

A crackling, dangerous silence pressed against the door. It groaned slightly, and she wondered if he was about to simply break it down.

All the same, Mom was lying in a hospice bed miles to the east, waiting for Nat to save her. She shouldn't be sleeping past dawn. She shouldn't have agreed to stopping last night, either.

With that cheerful thought pulling up her shoulders and settling like an icy bowling ball in her stomach, she crossed the room and yanked on the little golden handle. The door swung wide, almost hitting her, and she jumped nervously back, bare feet slipping on thick green carpet.

"I'll be ready in—" Words failed her, and she stared.

Dmitri's face was discolored, bruises puffing over both dark eyes and a slice along his cheekbone. The bruising spread down his neck and across his muscled, tattoo-writhing shoulders; he was in a black tank top and a pair of well-worn jeans, his forearms a mass of scrapes and cuts and his knuckles scabbed.

In short, he looked like he'd been put through a meat grinder, and Nat's jaw dropped. *What the hell?*

"Smells like coffee." He pushed past her, one bare shoulder almost striking hers, and the room behind him was almost too dark to see a rumpled bed, heavy red draperies, and a knee-high pall of clinging smoke that didn't smell like burned wood or tobacco. The smog trailed into clear air just before her door, and she caught a glimpse of a broad black leather couch crouching at an angle before there was a click and a sigh behind her.

He'd lit one of his incense-smelling cigarettes and ambled into the bedroom, heading for the small counter with the coffeemaker. "Sleep well?" He exhaled a cloud of thin grayish vapor and bent to look at the stream of coffee falling placidly into a pretty white mug. His back was a raw mass of injuries, tattoos vanishing under slices, scrapes, contusions, scabs, and one particularly nasty gash running diagonally from his left shoulder to right hip.

"Are you all right?" She flinched in sympathy as some of the scabs cracked; he glanced over his shoulder, not even bothering to wince. "What happened?"

"Oh, *zaika*, it almost like you care. Just had some fun, that's all. Storm's gone, we drive fast today." He grabbed the mug as soon as the machine finished, and slurped at it while he drifted to the window.

"Did it . . . the guy in the bar last night said other people are after it too. The Heart." Nat found she was hugging herself, cupping her elbows in her palms. "Was that it? Are they after you? Did you get into a fight, or—" It was probably that Ring thing. She was even more glad she'd turned down *that* little entertainment.

"Lots of questions." He halted, turned slowly on one heel; his boots were the same, and their toes glittered viciously. He didn't seem to notice she was in her pyjamas, which was probably a blessing. "So, you went downstairs. Who was it, eh?"

"Coyote. He had silver on his hat, like your—"

"Oh, him." He wasn't going to let her finish a sentence, it looked like. "Never mind him, *zaika*, he just a dancing fool. You hungry?"

Oh, for God's sake. The irony of the thought wasn't lost on her; still, it wasn't blasphemy if everyone said it on television, right? "It's fine." Miraculously, he didn't interrupt, so she continued. "Shouldn't we . . . isn't there a doctor or something?" *A god doctor? Hygieia? Hippocrates? Trapper John, M.D.?* "You look . . ." Words failed her as he glared from under a messy shock of dark hair, slurping at coffee that had to be too hot.

Just as the man in the silver-banded hat had last night.

"Look at you." He smacked his lips and grinned. "Pretty girl all worried for Dima. Maybe I show you so you forget just what we doing here, huh?"

Well, she had been feeling some sympathy, but if he was determined to ruin it, fine. "And maybe I can find another ride to where we're going."

"Oh, sure. Go on, see what happens. At least Baba keeping you safe until I get my hands on it, *zaika*. Old granny probably thinks you better for her than your momma Mascha. Ever think of that?" He bore down on her with all the fluidity of a jungle cat, one soft, heavy step at a time. "You trust too much. Better toughen up and start thinking how to keep me from eating you. Chomp, chomp." His teeth snapped together, a heavy click like billiard balls meeting.

"I heard someone could eat that Heart." Nat's chin lifted slightly. "What would that do, I wonder?"

He stilled, peering over the top of the mug. "You hungry as your mama, girl?"

"She could have eaten it before, right?" *Helluva stomachache, Coyote said.* "But she didn't."

"And smart little girl wondering why. It's no good to your mama; she need different food."

That was interesting, but Nat had another question. It bolted free of her before she could close her mouth, probably spurred by lack of caffeine. "So de Winter had it, and you did what she said. Right?"

"Oh, you think you hold it and make Dmitri little errand boy?" He lowered the coffee mug and examined her from top to toe, dark eyes burning behind swollen lids. "Maybe I do that. Bring pretty girl some pretty things, show you a good time." His smile widened, finally became lascivious, and Nat was hard-pressed not to shudder.

"I don't want anything you're likely to bring me." Stolen goods weren't her cup of java, and hadn't Bonnie and Clyde died in a hail of bullets? Some women might like that sort of thing.

But not Maria Drozdova's daughter.

The leer turned into a scowl. "Too good for me, eh?"

Isn't that just like a man? It was something Mom might have said, and Nat's pre-coffee temper threatened to break. "Is there a reason you're in here, Dmitri?"

"Coffee." He waved the mug, threatening to slop whatever was inside in every direction. "And maybe I wanted to see what you sleep in, *Drozdova.*"

She should have known he would turn out to be just like every other male except Leo. "Fine. I'll get ready and we can go."

"In a hurry now?"

"Will you just stop? For God's sake." Her fingernails bit her upper arms, and her legs trembled.

But he just gave a bitter little laugh and sauntered past, slurping at the mug again. "Exactly," he said, as he reached the door. "Egg-zack-ly, *zaika*. Godsake. Oh, you a funny little girl for sure."

Everyone was finding her hilarious lately. He toed the door as he passed, and it shut with a sound far heavier than it should. Maybe he just wanted to irritate her before the day's drive.

In that case, he'd succeeded. But it also left Nat wondering just why in hell her mother stole a god's heart and created a cross-country scavenger hunt.

It didn't seem very efficient, and not like Maria Drozdova at all.

RUNNING FROM SOMETHING

Asecond coffee pod, a quick shower, and a protein bar scarfed in the wide white luxurious bathroom readied Nat for another day of travel; the sleek silver room-service trolley that appeared while she bathed remained unplundered, though the gangster gave her plenty of curious sidelong looks once she was finished getting ready and knocked on the connecting door.

She'd done her best to block the bathroom door with her backpack, and kept looking through fogged shower-door glass to make sure it wasn't moving. Dmitri had also taken the opportunity to clean himself up, too, because he was in yet another suit a few shades away from true black, with sharply ironed creases and a tie the color of an oil slick.

The boots were still the same, though.

She was also prepared for an argument over the hotel bill, but Dmitri just took her elbow as they left the elevator, hustling her through the foyer. The man behind the desk—Priest, his shaven head gleaming—saw them and smiled encouragingly, waving a gloved hand; maybe Dima had prepaid? The bar was still the same behind its smoked glass, and there was a tall woman with a shock of bright thistledown hair, her ragged gray dress brushing neatly at pale ankles as she stood before the fireplace, wearing leather sandals with diamond-glittering soles.

Nat craned to look more closely at that gleaming, but Dmitri let out a soft short sound, more than an exhale but not quite a word. He hurried her through the giant, polished revolving glass door, and once more she was dead certain it would turn into a mouth and swallow them both whole until they burst into bright thin golden frostlight, shadows sharply defined on the cobblestones and the big black car rumbling a greeting under its shining hood. He all but shoved her into the passenger side, not even bothering to nod at the valet's greeting, and Nat watched the Elysium's spinning door.

It seemed ridiculously like the gangster was almost . . . frightened? No, but certainly cautious.

When he dropped into the driver's seat it was with a muttered word in the old country's language she was certain Leo would never had said in her presence, even if he'd just skinned his knuckles on an engine.

"What's wrong?" It was stupid to ask, she knew. Still, the glaring bruises on his face, and the damage all over his torso—at least he seemed to be moving all right. "We can get you some ibuprofen or something."

"What the fuck for?" he snarled, and the engine replied with an unhappy sound. The tires chirped, the hood ornament shifted as it clove freezing air, and she barely had time to get her seat belt fastened before they rocketed out of the courtyard and onto a snow-packed city street, just narrowly missing a big blue-and-white bus carefully picking its way between stratified snow-ridges.

At least he hadn't hit a pedestrian. Still, Nat almost grabbed for the dash, restraining herself just in time and clutching her backpack to her chest instead.

The gangster dug in the inner pocket of his black jacket, his lip still lifted slightly, teeth gleaming underneath, and extracted a somewhat prosaic pack of Camels. His frown was thunderous, but he tapped one coffin-nail up and lit it with a mutter; it smelled just the same as the others.

It didn't take long for him to find I-77; once they reached the freeway his knuckles lost their white tinge on the wheel-yoke and the incense-smoke, exhaled in long twin jets, was dragged out the crack of open window into the slipstream. No chains, again, but the black car didn't slide, and its low-throated growl had turned carnivorous. "Drive fast today. Might wanna tell me just where we goin', *zaika*." He checked the mirrors, probably just for show, before he turned the wheel slightly and they swung wide around a laboring semi. The tires grabbed hard, he pressed the accelerator, and for a moment the thought that she was going to die in a car wreck was either proof of sanity or completely irrelevant. "West, yeah, but north or south?"

"South," she managed. *Weren't you listening?* "South Dakota."

"Old ground," he muttered. "Don't get out that way much."

Do you have GPS in this thing? Somehow, she didn't think so. Nat hugged her backpack tighter and stared out the window, trying to ignore the slippery way mile markers were flashing past. Every other vehicle on the road was using relative caution, but the black car grumbled as Dmitri twisted the wheel, slaloming past snow-starred vehicles with fringes of dirty ice clinging to their mud flaps. Traffic was surprisingly heavy but then again, the entire economy couldn't shut down because of a little thing like the weather.

Was there a god of capitalism? Who was in charge of the snow, de Winter? Was she watching them now, every drift a listening station and every snowflake a tiny eye?

It sounded exhausting.

Dmitri didn't turn the radio on; the car might not even have one. The only sound was the engine's subterranean song and the crunch of tires on ridged, salted ice. It was oddly soothing, and if she could just relax, might even be fun.

And yet.

That horsethief will kill you if he can, buffalo girl. But a lot of others will do worse. "Who else is after me?"

"*Now* you askin'?" His laugh rode a cloud of that strange perfumed smoke; those definitely weren't Camels, despite the packaging. "Don't matter none, *zaika*. Dima will keep you safe and sound, so long as I don't get my hands on what your mama stole from me."

It was the first time he'd said it quite so directly, which would have been a small victory if he hadn't slewed the car from the far left lane all the way across to the right, almost onto the shoulder, and aimed at a ramp for I-76 South. It looked like he knew the local roads.

Probably for quick getaways.

"Technically she stole it from Baba, right?" She braced herself for an explosion, but all she got was a sideways glance from one bruised, blackened eye. He looked a little better now; maybe it was the light. "I'm just trying to understand."

"What you need to understand? It's *mine*."

"Oh." A laughably simple observation occurred to Nat, and bolted free of her mouth besides. "You were going to steal it back. She beat you to it."

"Do me a favor and shut up." Dmitri stamped on the accelerator, and Nat was pushed into her seat. "Today we travel like we should."

What, like we're running from something? Well, they probably were.

Silence ticked by, the sun glittering vengefully off snow-covered houses, filthy ice clinging to shoulders and curbs, a long line of darkness in the north that meant another storm but not quite yet. Once city faded into suburbia and the modesty screens of spindly bushes and saplings, naked for the winter and hopefully sleeping through the miserable cold, showed fields beyond, Dmitri eased up on the gas, and it wasn't her imagination.

He was looking better. The bruises retreated almost as she watched, cuts sealing themselves up in tiny twitching increments.

Now *that* was handy. She almost opened her mouth to observe as much, thought better, and swallowed the words. They hit crowding questions at the end of her esophagus with a plop, mixed with the coffee she'd bolted after the protein bar but before a quick tooth-brushing, and settled into a ball of anxiety.

Did she really have an esophagus? What was divinity biology, not to mention anatomy? How on earth was she going to find out? Why wasn't she hungrier?

And why hadn't she needed the toilet in the birch suit's luxurious bathroom this morning?

The car gulped miles and poured over the road-ribbon, rocking gently like a boat on calm water. Nat might have even liked the scenery, but a flash in the side mirror caught her eye, a glimmer of blue in the far distance.

"Oh, shit," she said, blankly, forgetting her resolution to stay strictly silent. "It's a cop car?"

"Fucking *Ohio*," Dmitri snarled, jamming a spent cigarette butt through the window's open crack. His hands resettled on the wheel, and his knuckles whitened again.

It went on that way for quite some time.

FRIENDLY LAW

Nat didn't know just how fast they were going, but the twinkle in the mirror never got larger or smaller. It just hovered, a vicious little stab of repeating light. The landscape
did funny things, streaking and foaming away on either side. Signs
began announcing the approach of Indiana much sooner than they
should have, and like they expected a tip for the information too.

Just over the state line was a rest stop; the gangster wrenched
the yoke at the last moment and sent the car up a long gentle slope,
speed bleeding away with eerie, stomach-lurching smoothness.
"Stay in the car," he said, his gaze flicking to each mirror in turn.

"I haven't done anything wrong." And really, Nat wondered,
what kind of cop would follow a car like this?

Maybe de Winter wasn't a legitimate authority. Maybe Nat could
appeal to something, someone else. It was certainly worth a shot.

"You think that matters?" The gangster shook his head; the rest
station was a whale of bleached, ice-starred concrete rising outside
the passenger window. "Think this fellow wants nice little tea party
with little Drozdova and her good friend Konets?"

Her stomach, so far, was taking this relatively calmly. "You
could can the sarcasm and actually explain. It wouldn't hurt you."

"You sure?" At least the gangster wasn't snarling anymore. Instead, he was coldly calm, his profile sharply severe, and the change
wasn't exactly pleasant. When the black car came to a full stop, the
sense of highway motion drained in fits and starts, her body re-
adjusting to stillness. Nat watched her side mirror; the bright blue

light acquired red strobes. Underneath both a separate ruddiness flickered, and she rubbed at her eyes.

"Is it . . ."

"Burning? Yeah, he in a helluva hurry." Dmitri reached for his door handle. "I tell you to stay in car, you won't listen."

No, I probably won't. "Maybe I can help you." Nat almost winced; it wasn't exactly a lie, even if she was halfway hoping otherwise. Of course Leo held that cops and criminals were virtually indistinguishable; the badge was only a cover for the bigger bastards, always in service to the rich. "I'd like to."

Leo generally recited his feelings on law enforcement when the level in the vodka bottle reached a certain shallowness, and missing him rose like a dry stone in Nat's throat.

"Sure." The gangster stared into the rearview, all trace of mockery vanished just like the anger. His eyes were dark and serious, his hair slightly disarranged, and the traces of battering were almost gone. A bloom of stubble crept up his jaw, darkening his cheeks, and his mouth was sculpted in repose. "I bet you do. Yeah."

Quiet bitterness rode under his words, but at least he wasn't sneering anymore. Could a divinity change? It probably wasn't like quitting one retail job and getting another. But even if you couldn't get another job, you didn't have to be a complete asshole while doing the one you had, right?

Was Mom the way she was because of divinity? It would explain a lot.

The parking lot was deserted, its fringes lost under a sheet of unbroken snow. At least the sanders and plows had come through and cleared a strip. Nat shook her head and popped her own door. "I suppose I should use the restroom."

The car didn't try to stop her, though Dmitri gave a sharp glance; she rose into a winter afternoon and stretched, watching the flicker in the distance as it swelled. A cold breeze bearing the metallic reek of incipient snow and an almost solid wall of freeway exhaust tugged at her knit cap and played with the hem of her peacoat; her damp braid, left lonely outside layers, would probably freeze.

"Eh." Dmitri emerged from his side of the car, shaking his head and digging in his jacket's breast pocket again. "You think I'm bad. I tell you, this one, he worse."

That's a big endorsement. "Duly noted." Nat set off for the big concrete block. Maybe the gangster and the divinity cop would be so busy with each other she could just . . . what? Wait for someone to come along and hitch a ride? Was there a divinity for hitchhikers? There had to be, although they probably lost a lot of followers when thumbing a ride stopped being safe and started being an open invitation to serial killers.

Nat had watched the documentaries. She probably should've been reading up on comparative religions instead.

The ladies' room was frigid, lit only by a single buzzing, dispirited fluorescent strip on the ceiling, and smelled rancid. She took one look at the stalls, decided the drain in the corner was probably the more hygienic option, and was glad she didn't have to pee.

In fact, she hadn't had to since yesterday afternoon. Her biological functions were all messed up.

She could have called someone, but Nat's prepaid phone was only for emergencies, and *hey how are you, I'm on a cross-country trip with a divine gangster* didn't really qualify, did it?

Especially since Leo already knew. Had known all along.

There was no water when she turned the sink taps, of course. Nat tried not to look at herself in the slice of fly-spotted metal passing for a mirror.

There was no point.

When she emerged, the black car was in the same place. A similarly dark blot leaning against its trunk was Dmitri, smoking as he watched a Crown Victoria, much whiter than the snow, cruise up the rest station's ramp. A shining gold shield on its side sent migraine darts of reflection every-which-way, hiding its true shape under dazzle. A plume of black smoke lifted behind the car, its tires wreathed in orange-and-yellow flame oddly pale under bright sunshine, and its top glowed with a long bar of bright flashing blue and red.

The tire-fires snuffed themselves as the vehicle coasted to a stop, and she didn't want to know what the siren would sound like.

The Crown Vic pointed its blunt white headlight-glowing nose at
an angle as it halted behind the black car, and while its windows
weren't tinted the day's glare on each made the driver a mystery.

When the driver's door finally opened, a tall bulky form in blue
serge swelled, one ruddy, meaty hand clapping a Smokey-the-Bear
hat onto a close-cropped, glistening head. The cop had mirrored
aviator sunglasses, spit-shining boots with heavy gripping soles,
and the blue cloth of his uniform paled like a chameleon's skin as
he moved, turning into the tan of a highway patrol officer.

Nat's mouth went dry. It was the cop from Jay's.

Florid, angrily shaven cheeks and a pursed-tight mouth com-
pleted the picture of ponderous authority, just like the holster on
a broad leather belt and a silvery winking from a tiny case also
attached—handcuffs, Nat guessed, and tried not to shudder, picking her way carefully along cracked, frost-heaved, icy sidewalk. She
set her chin and headed for the black car, hoping she didn't look
scared.

It was a vain hope, but all she had.

The ginger-haired cop from Jay's was the absolute incarnation
of every officer she'd ever seen on television shows or grainy news
footage, right down to the glittering badge pinned to his barrel
chest. Refracted darts hurt the eyes just like the jabbing light-bar
atop the Crown Vic's roof. The only strangeness was the fleshy pro-
tuberances on his gleaming forehead, and the pink dampness of his
nose. And that burning, buzzing sense of *there*-ness.

This, in other words, was a goddamn divinity too.

The cop took his time, bearing down slowly on Dima, who
smoked and gazed past the white car, his chin level and his dark
eyes smoldering. Even the air rippled between them, straining
uncomfortably between two chemicals so opposed their contact
would produce an explosion.

"Afternoon, Konets." The cop's voice was a deep rumble, surprisingly crisp consonants rubbing fruity vowels. "Don't suppose you've
got a license."

Another uncomfortable silence enfolded all three of them,
broken only by the highway's seashell groan in the near distance.

Finally, when he'd made the fact that he didn't *have* to answer adequately clear, the gangster spoke. "Don't suppose I need one."

Mirrored sunglass lenses turned in Nat's direction. The motion was oddly mechanical, well-oiled, and soulless. "And you? You got some ID, young lady?"

The voice wrapped around Nat, shortened her breath, turned her heart into the rabbit Dmitri was always calling her, and made her palms damp. She didn't start digging for her wallet only by sheer force of will, because Dima laughed, a harsh cawing bare of any amusement whatsoever.

"None you need to see. Go back to stepping on necks, Friendly. This ain't your time."

Friendly? As in Officer Friendly? A great swimming sense of unreality descended on Nat—not for the first time since she'd entered de Winter's building, and probably not for the last. *You have* got *to be kidding me.*

The cop's thin, prissy mouth twitched, and his flush mounted again. His nose twitched too, pink and gleaming-damp. "Why don't we let the young lady decide, Konets? I'm sure you've been your usual charming self."

"Fuck." Dmitri's tone hardened; the word rode a tide of incense-smelling, exhaled smoke. "Off."

The sky was crystalline, the snow-choked rest stop deserted, and Nat stayed where she was, her boots nailed to the sidewalk. A soft, terrible humming enfolded both men, like a power transformer buried under a sheet of ice; it was the same feeling she used to get watching the sheriff and the villain in old Westerns face each other early in the movie.

Leo loved old cowboy movies. *Now that John Wayne,* he would say. *He's a real bast—uh, a real fellow, eh, devotchka? Nothing like him in the old country, except maybe Cossacks. Go make some popcorn, we watch together.*

The cop's chin turned a little farther towards her. "You know, Miss Drozdova, you don't have to go with him. I could take you there."

Was he attempting to sound paternal? Nat's throat was so dry she doubted she could produce any noise, whether affirmative or not.

"Oh, yeah." Dima shrugged. "Clap on nice shiny pair of bracelets after he got no more use for you, *zaika*. Put you in little cell too, only let you out when *he* says."

"I operate in strict accordance with the Law." The capital letter was plainly audible. "You'll be safe with me, Miss Drozdova. And once you have what you're looking for, I'm sure you'll know the right thing to do with it."

"You think you can eat me, *politruk*?" The corners of Dima's mouth pulled up, a grimace not even attempting to impersonate a smile. "You choke on it, if I don't find you first and carve you like *matryoshka*."

So this guy could eat it, but Mom can't? Maybe they had to be opposing forces before they could consume each other? In that case, could de Winter eat Mom?

Nat had no idea and nobody to ask. Then again, so much of this was bonkers, it really didn't matter.

"Speak English, you fucking commie." Friendly's calm cracked; his own lips skinned back and his teeth were very white, and oddly blunt. They could probably do a lot of damage, crushing and tearing; they weren't sharp, but they looked very strong indeed. "You're in our house now."

"Your house is a shitpile, *pig*." Dmitri's left hand rose; he pinched the cigarette's filter between two fingers. His right, though, hovered low and tense, and Nat was suddenly, deeply, mortally certain the two of them were about to pull the most classic of Western-movie clichés right in the middle of an Indiana rest stop. "You think I don't know you of old?"

Oh, God. If this was authority, she didn't want it. Nat cleared her dry, aching throat, and both men looked at her, the cop with some visible surprise and Dmitri . . .

Well, he looked vicious, his sharp face feral and contorted. The resemblance to a hungry street cat expecting nothing good from anything human-shaped was overwhelming, and her chest hurt, a familiar pain.

"Excuse me." Her voice wouldn't quite work right, high and breathy as if she was trapped in Koschei's mirror-maze again. "Are we under arrest?"

Dmitri snorted, his expression barely easing. Friendly stared at her, a brick-red flush rising up his painfully bare cheeks. It looked like he shaved with a belt sander.

That was a vivid mental image Nat didn't need.

"I don't need to arrest you—" Friendly began, and a great surge of pointless anger arrived out of nowhere, settling in the pit of Nat's stomach, rising to her throat like vodka fumes, and pouring between her teeth in a reasonable imitation of her mother's *I am being patient but that might not last* voice.

"Then we're free to go." Her hands had curled into fists, and she wasn't even cold now, she realized. "That's the law." *If there's a god of the Constitution, I bet they'll be along any minute.*

Friendly studied her for a long moment. That brick flush deepened into maroon, the very picture of a petty Napoleon denied the pleasure of squatting over someone else. It was stupidly, deeply familiar—who, after all, hadn't suffered a boss like that?

You could smile and play nice and go along, if you had to. But sometimes, you could stick it to what Leo called *gaets* and others called *The Man*.

The only thing more satisfying was getting away with it.

Of course, if they caught you next time, you'd suffer double. Still, this was an old game, and Nat was reminded of the headmistress of Sacred Grace Middle School, a holy terror to all the girls she was supposed to teach and guide but a deflating black-and-white balloon when Mom appeared, Maria Drozdova finally prodded into action by Nat's pleading and whatever Leo had said to her during that one terrible fight.

That was a bad memory, full of the scent of her closet as young Nat huddled in a corner with her hands over her ears, but she wasn't thirteen anymore. She set her chin and gave Friendly—dear God, what a name—her best *fuck you* look.

"Little girl." The cop's tone turned stentorian, a judge expressing his just displeasure from a high bench. "You know nothing of the

Law. *That* is a thief, a murderer, a despoiler and robber, and he will turn upon you the moment you don't serve his plans."

"Yeah." *I listened the first time he told me, thanks.* "At least he's honest about it."

She'd never seen a cop deflate before. It did look an awful lot like the headmistress almost quailing in front of Mom, and a sudden, almost alcoholic sense of heady power filled Nat's skull.

If Mama got better and her daughter lost this . . . this force, this sense of calm warm strength, what would she do?

"You'll regret this," the man named Friendly growled in her direction, but his thunderous mantle of overwhelming dominance was gone. Now he was just a portly man in Highway Patrol khaki instead of a massive monster in blue serge, and his hat's brim actually drooped at the edges. He turned on one waffle-stomping heel and strode back to the Crown Vic's open door. The car's springs didn't quite groan when he dropped in, but she thought it was probably close.

A chirp of tires, a cloud of noxious smoke, a howl like a jet plane taking off in place of a siren—it threatened to rupture Nat's eardrums—and the white car lunged forward, narrowly avoiding clipping the black car's rear left quarter-panel. Dmitri didn't move, tense and ready, and when the screaming noise faded in the distance he regarded Nat, taking the long last final drag on whatever he was smoking.

She decided she could live quite comfortably without knowing what was packed in his cigarettes.

"He right," the gangster said, finally. "You shoulda listened."

What could she say to that? "My father's an immigrant too." It wasn't really an answer, but then again, the gangster hadn't really asked a question.

"Get in." Dima flicked the spent filter away. It hissed as it met icy concrete, a tiny, lonely sound. The freeway noise returned, folding seamlessly over a hole in the world. "Still far to go."

"Yeah." Nat's legs were a little rubbery; she shuffled for the black car.

Dmitri glided for the passenger side, his boot-toes winking. He didn't look happy, but then again, she figured it really wasn't in his nature.

He held the passenger door open, though, and when she slipped her backpack off her shoulder and dropped into the black car's now-familiar interior, he closed it gently behind her instead of slamming.

Nat fastened her seatbelt, hugged her backpack, and stared out the crystal-clear windshield like she was watching the most interesting movie in the world. She didn't have to ignore him very hard at all, though, because when the gangster got in he didn't speak, just roused the car into purring life and swung the wheel, pointing them westwards.

WILL OF IRON

It was good to drive, but each mile was an itch of anticipation and the girl didn't help. She did, however, dig a sheet of paper out of her silly bag after a hundred scorching miles passed underneath the car's angry-muttering tires.

"Dmitri?"

Better not, little girl. "What?" He couldn't quite snarl; after all, she had given Friendly a kick right in the stones, and that was something to warm a thief's heart.

If he had one, that was. If it hadn't been stolen by her fucking mother.

"This is where we're going." The sheet trembled in her fingers, maybe because of the vibration of travel—he wasn't bothering to keep their speed below a certain mortal threshold since she had been burnished by a night spent among her own kind, and the flashing of small towns or the streaks of longer gray cities outside the windows blurred and ran in a way that would give one of the rubes nausea fit to kill.

A simple piece of lined paper, three holes for a binder's rings on its side, like a schoolchild might use. Written upon it in a fair, likewise schoolgirl hand were highway and exit numbers. He glanced at the end—some no-name town in South Dakota; at least she hadn't been lying.

Did this girl even know how to mislead? Even her silences were telling.

"That where it is?"

"That's step one," she corrected, still cautious but not quite fearful. "Whoever's there will tell me the next step, I guess."

"Your mama took no chances."

"Yeah, well." The paper quivered. "Do you want it or not?"

"Got it right here now." He tapped at his temple with two fingers, and returned his itching, aching, burning hands to the yoke. The car, sensing its true speed might be called upon soon, gave another restless thrumming mutter. "So, we get there before she die, what you gonna do?"

The paper retreated; the girl folded it again, sliding it into that silly kid's backpack. If she was going to learn to lie, well, now was a good time.

Instead, the *zaika* zipped the bag closed and hugged it again, her gaze fixed out the windshield. The farther she got from Mascha, the more the process of burning away the dross of rube camouflage would accelerate. It was already well underway, and no doubt Matchenka felt it in the root of her own being, a terrible draining lassitude gaining speed, the thing that made her what she was slipping away bit by bit.

She'd held on this long, though. A will of iron had Maria Drozdova, very much like Dima himself. Her daughter was too soft; it was going to get her killed.

Those who eat had noticed this tempting meal. He could feel the pursuit, their blind, grasping, maggoty interest.

Not his problem, right? His knuckles were white again and he exhaled, the car leaping forward now that it knew its true destination. A low roar like a plane's breath curled away on either side and the ride smoothed, the road shaking off a crust of ice as it arrowed west. Indiana's pavement arteries unreeled while the light took on a strange depthless cast.

Chasing the sunset could even be fun. It wasn't like the thiefways, but he would not take the girl *there*.

Not unless forced to.

"I don't know," his *zaika* finally said, softly. "If I take it to de Winter it saves Mom—*if* Baba's telling the truth. But she stole it from you. Right?"

"Took it from Baba's cabinet."

"But if it's stolen, don't you . . ." She trailed off, stealing a little sideways glance at him. The trepidation might have been pleasant, on another day.

"Some things not so simple." Normally a stolen item would cry out to him in its own deep, brazen, wordless voice, but the turning of seasons was an even more powerful force than greed, and Mascha had hidden the item well.

It rankled to have to admit as much, even if only to himself.

"Did it hurt?"

What kind of a fucking question was that? "Life hurts, *zaika*. Any other stupid questions?"

"I guess not." She huddled as far away from him as possible, almost pressing against the door. He tried to imagine being raised as a rube and thrust into the first stages of incarnation when your mother sickened, tried to imagine a rube threading through one of Koschei's little traps, a young rube girl meeting the Cold Lady and seeing the Elysium for the first time, not to mention facing down Friendly and climbing into a car with Dima himself.

A brave little bunny, and what did that make him? Shame was familiar to some of his nephews, but he didn't like its bite.

"Stop cringing," he spat, harshly. "You toughen up, and *stop cringing*. Or you die before you bloom, and then neither of us get what we want."

"You want to kill me anyway."

"Not before the right time." *Whenever that is.* His irritation mounted another notch. "Let me ask you something, little girl. You think Maria Drozdova would do this for you, huh? Little *zaika* in hospital bed, you think dear little mamma get in car with Dima and go riding to fetch what she stole? *Do you?*"

He waited, but she said nothing. A tightly closed rosebud, refusing to peek its petals free while frost was still thick on stem and leaf. The car took another deep breath and arrowed forward, rising over a slight hill; the glitter of Indianapolis blurred on the northwest horizon.

A nice town, but they were going to drive straight through. The hunting-thrill was upon him now, and the emptiness behind his strong flexible ribs twitched.

What would it be like to hold that bloody gem in his fist again? To feel that pulse, the warmth that had left him when Baba shook her head and closed her own thin, iron-strong fingers inside his bony chest-cage with that sickening, tearing sound? To feel the black ice settling in his bones again as his adopted land ceased its struggle to eject or remake him, but also to feel . . . what?

When he stole a hateful glance at the girl—for no real reason, he told himself, just to check if she was about to do something stupid like open the door and spill out onto the freeway—she had closed her eyes, and there might have been a damp gleam on her soft, lucent cheek. She hugged her idiotic backpack like a baby with a rag doll, and why, in the name of every fucking divinity, power, principality, or other Endless Being, would Maschka have raised her daughter like a rube?

He knew why. The only surprise was that the hungry Drozdova had waited this long to make the finest meal of all, but of course the closer to full incarnation the more powerful the morsel would be. The cold calculation that could raise and fatten for consumption wasn't the province of any one divinity; sacrifice was, after all, good fuel for any of their kind. It wasn't even unusual for a divinity to eat their own get.

Look at that gaunt gray fuck Kronos, after all.

Stealing Dima's property to reserve as Baba's bribe for looking the other way during eating your own soft, innocent spawn was something else, though. The loathing sliding through his belly at the thought was a direct result of the *zaika*'s fragrant, helpless presence in his car, and he hated it.

His boot-toe pressed the accelerator harder.

It was no use. The knowledge could not be left behind. It rode in the car with them, tickling Dima's ear, swelling between him and the achingly vulnerable creature trembling on the cusp of its own unfolding while she shivered once, convulsively, and swallowed silent tears.

TRY AGAIN

Maybe semi-fasting meant you didn't have to pee, or maybe the sheer unreality of current events was keeping her from feeling biological imperatives. In any case, Dmitri didn't stop for gas or more snacks, just hunched slightly in the driver's seat, his hands lazily clasping the yoke and his mouth set, his eyes almost black from lid to lid, tiny crimson spatter-sparkles burning amid the darkness. The sun descended from its apex as highway signs flickered past too quick to read, the car thrum-hummed in Nat's head until she was sure she was going to throw up before the pressure suddenly eased all at once like a fever breaking, and the landscape began to fold away into sere fields and rolling hills on either side.

She fell into a thin troubled doze as afternoon wore on, and slept through sunset filling the windshield with orange glare so thick nothing of the road could be seen. When she woke with a jolt, lit streetlamps leapfrogged by on either side, dusk was purple and gray in every corner, and the shape of the signs had changed once again. Her neck wasn't too happy, since the engine-sound slid from her temple—pressed against the window's thin glass skin—all the way down the right side of her body, taking a powder in her hip before jabbing down her right leg like the sciatica Pat the Humboldt office admin was always bemoaning.

They probably didn't even notice she was gone; turnover was high in retail and call-center trenches. She'd never gripe with Sandra at lunch again, or meet Jon's wide hazel eyes across the room and exchange a shrug, corral one of Bob's lunatic managerial impulses, or be invited out for a beer—not that she ever went, wanting to get through any shift as soon as possible in order to go home, or to the hospice.

She almost winced. Thinking of Mom in the hospice was reflexive, and now she couldn't do it without hearing Dmitri sneer.

You think Maria Drozdova would do this for you?

The car bumped, floating as the world sped away underneath. Its tires touched the road again, their hum changing, and she realized the black beast was slowing. Streetlights stopped smearing against the windows, separating into distinct glowing globes, and either traffic was thickening around them or they were sliding back into the dimension where normal people drove at normal speeds. Headlights glared, brake lights popped into view, and she braced herself for a fresh jolt of strangeness or more of Dmitri's hateful bullshit.

They finally slowed enough for her to read the signs, and she let out a soft breath. "Waterloo." Her eyes refused to focus for a moment, then the shapes made sense. "We're in *Iowa*?"

"You even slept through Chicago." The dashboard lights turned Dmitri's face into a much older man's for a moment, hollows under his dark eyes and his hair gleaming. His mouth turned down bitterly at both corners. "We can stop here, or in Sioux City. If you want."

"What time is it?"

"Just after dark." One shoulder lifted slightly and dropped; he was, the small movement said, not wearing a watch and didn't feel the need to start.

Watches were probably for "rubes," though he'd had one the night of the party. Apparently he didn't have a smartphone to check the time, either.

Nat pointed her toes, stretching as the car slowed to regular old freeway speed, and the strange floating feeling behind her breastbone vanished. Her head was a lot clearer now. "Can't believe I slept through Chicago." Here she was, out of the Big Apple for the first time, and she'd missed one of the more important sights along the way.

She probably wouldn't have been able to see it with the car moving at warp speed, though. Just how fast could he travel?

And could she do the same?

"We could go back." Dima grinned, but the expression lacked its usual edge.

She dropped her feet, trying to stretch her back without moving enough to draw more of his attention—or his ire. "I'm not complaining."

"I know." Did he sound aggravated? Road trips were supposed to be hard on the temper, and his wasn't too patient to begin with. Maybe it came with being a divinity of gangsters, or thieves. Did he have an older brother who did assassinations?

It was a terrible thought.

"I just think maybe *zaika* like to see the sights is all," Dmitri continued, and glanced at her. "Bet you feelin' good. Not hungry, not thirsty, eh?"

How did you know? "Is it the car?" It didn't qualify as a stupid question, she hoped. Even her fingers felt better, humming with energy as if she was a kid again, a restless ball of curiosity with her hands caught in Leo's as he taught her to walk.

"Incarnation." Another sideways look, his long nose wrinkling a little. "Little *zaika* must be confused."

"I'm trying to keep up." She aimed for Mom's dry, ironic tone when Maria could be persuaded to play gin with Leo at the kitchen table. *Incarnation* sounded very Catholic, and if she ever went back to Mother Mary Elementary again, she'd tell the sisters a few things.

"I take you to place I know. We get a drink." The car bounced again, engine noise dropping into an even deeper register, and he swerved for an exit.

Again, she didn't grab at the dash, but it was close. *I don't want a drink, thanks.* If his car could all but fly and neither of them needed the bathroom, they could just drive right through.

But if she could lock herself in a bathroom for a few minutes maybe she could call Leo, even if there was nothing to say. As long as she kept it short.

Mom might never sigh heavily at another Nat-induced bill, phone or otherwise, ever again. But divinities didn't need money? It was confusing, and even the deep new eerie sense of well-being didn't help, just gave her more questions.

Dmitri hit the brakes, the exit curved under them like a startled cat's back, and the seatbelt grabbed at her hips and shoulder. Nat clung to her backpack and waited for him to say something cutting or nasty, but instead he simply jabbed a finger at the traffic light at the end of the off-ramp.

It turned green, and her jaw threatened to drop. *That's a nice trick.*

"First lesson, *devotchka*," Dmitri said conversationally. "World wants to obey, all you gotta do is ask. Even the rubes wanna do what you say, more so because of who you are. Drozdova."

But I'm not . . . Nat stared at the dashboard. Was he actually trying to be helpful, or was there a sting in the words? "So I just ask?"

"It's a muscle, you gotta find it. First time's hardest." The car banked into a left turn, and a long hill swung into view, starred with traffic lights and orderly rows of cars. "Point at the road, *zaika*, and get them out of our way."

Just point at the road? "I'm not sure I can—"

Dmitri gunned the engine, the car leapt forward, and Nat yelped. Two blocks of clear road ran out at high speed as the black car made a low evil chuckling; Nat's hands threw themselves out, fingers spread and palms throbbing as a semi's hind end loomed before them.

There was a deep grinding, felt more than heard, and the black car slewed wildly as Dmitri twisted the wheel. "Close," he said, calmly, as the tires smoked and they zoomed into oncoming traffic. Headlights gleamed, bright blaring diamonds. "Try again."

Oh for Chrissake I just woke up! A trapped scream burned Nat's throat, her fingers flexed, and suddenly a great painless gout of force bloomed in her middle, bubbled past her breastbone, curved her shoulders forward, and snapped through her arms. A stinging ran down her back, like a broken rubber band recoiling against skin; the scream turned into a ringing "—*fuck* you, you gangster sonofabitch!"

A crash and tinkle of broken glass, another tire-smoking fish-tail, and they were back in the right lane. Cars jolted aside, the traffic lights swaying on their poles and blinking red, yellow, green with no discernable pattern. Nat swallowed another cry and Dmitri laughed, a harsh cawing of effort and amusement at once as he spun the vehicle through the tangle with bare centimeters to spare on either side.

They crested the hill, sparks flying, and Nat was swearing as she had only heard her mother swear once or twice in her life, both times while hiding in her closet, breathing the fusty muddy smell of shoes and her school uniforms, hearing the faint mutter of Leo's voice as he tried to calm the sudden storm.

Other mothers didn't smell like ozone when they were angry, and some of them didn't ignore their children or heave deep pained sighs when the kids grew out of their shoes *again, Natchenka, why do you do this?*

It wasn't like she could help growing or breathing or needing things, and the old familiar hopelessness filled Nat's skull like colorless gas fumes.

"Try it again, *zaika!*" Dmitri gave another sharp yip-laugh. More traffic lights bloomed on the hill's downslope, a very busy intersection. Cars were shining metal beetles, a popslither spatter of sleet smacked a crystalline windshield, the hood ornament twisted to snarl over its fluid silver shoulder, and the fumes in her head ignited.

Easy, devotchka, Leo's voice said in memory as he held the back of the bicycle seat. The big rusting pink contraption hadn't looked like much, but once he finished oiling and sanding and repairing it was *fast,* and he even found a little bell to clamp to the handlebars. A press of her thumb on the lever and the bright silver ratcheting sound would warn people out of her way. *Don't you go out into traffic, or Uncle will have to come get you from hospital.*

A glass bubble of silence descended on her, and the bell rang again. Nat blinked, a deep endless breath filling her lungs, spreading her ribs so hard they creaked. The moment riding a bike really clicked and she found her balance, pedaling furiously in Princo

Park's green blur while Leo yelled and cheered behind her and the sweet song of wind began in her ears—oh, she loved that sound, because it was almost flying, escape and freedom and a high sweet spillskin ecstasy like a ripe fruit just on the edge of bursting all at once.

The car's engine settled into a sweet soft decelerating purr, and a warm breeze touched Nat's face.

"And there you are," Dmitri Konets said quietly.

The traffic had cleared, the lights were green, and the black car flickered between other vehicles trapped in a curious stasis, pedestrians caught in the act of turning to look at the source of a long howl of abused tires or the jolt of crumpled metal and broken glass. People paused like a special effect, their feet hanging between one step and the next, their winter coats flapping at the hem, or their mouths slightly open.

Oh, wow. It was the only possible thing to think. *Oh my holy wow.*

Nat's hands were out as if ready to catch a dodgeball in gym class. Golden coruscation slipped over her spread fingers, gloves of living light. It was warm, and for a moment something else trembled just on the edge of understanding inside her skull.

Of course she's sick, Nat thought. *Losing this would be like dying.*

Then they were through the intersection, a big green SUV a few inches from her left window held in an invisible cage, and she wondered blankly if anyone had been hurt in the accidents left behind.

The light on her fingers snuffed, darkness swallowing the interior except for the dashboard instruments and the gleam of Dmitri's teeth. His smile was wide, gleaming white, and full of carnivorous good nature.

"Not so hard, eh? But now you really need drink, *zaika*. I take you to a place, and after that, we talk."

RANDOM DISAPPOINTMENT

When he cut the engine in a weedy dirt lot overlooking a dark river fringed with fingers of rime-ice, the headlights died. A ramshackle building cobbled together out of plywood and spare oil drums crouched on the other side of a row of shiny vehicles; the black car surveyed them all and the river itself with a satisfied air, metal ticking as the engine and hood cooled.

Whatever it ran on, it had probably used a lot today.

Nat studied her hands. They looked just like they always had—Mom's long fingers, a ghost of clear nail polish because Maria Drozdova said anything else was for streetwalkers, a cupped palm that was very much like Leo's too, now that Nat thought about it, and her wrists fine-boned and slim like Mom's as well.

The lines on her palms were the same. Or were they? She'd never really looked at them before. Who memorized their palms?

"First time's hardest," Dmitri repeated. "Sometimes it happen before you know it too. Like riding a bicycle, *da*?"

She almost flinched. But it was a cliché, he probably couldn't know about Leo and the Pink Princess bike.

Or could he?

He waited for an answer; when none came he continued, soft and reflective. It was a new tone, and one she wasn't sure she liked. "Gets to where you get used to it, then you hit something can't be changed and . . . well, the bitter with the sweet, *zaika*, no vodka without the sting. Then you make bargain."

Is that what happened to you? Nat cleared her throat. "The cats," she managed, dryly. "They told me things, but Mom . . . she pretended I was lying."

Said like that, it was a horrible thing. Getting upset over it didn't help. Besides, you weren't supposed to get angry at your own mother. There was even a whole commandment about it.

What divinity, she wondered, was in charge of that one? Was Moses's God still alive? How about the sisters' Mary, looking down with her vacant smile, promising intercession but never quite delivering?

"Now why she do that, you think?" Dmitri didn't look at her, staring at the wintry river. No chill crept inside the car, but then again, it was magic, wasn't it? Or damn close.

This divinity thing wasn't waving wands and glittering bibbidi-bobbidi-boo. It was huge, overwhelming, and flat-out terrifying.

Just like everything else in the goddamn world. *Goddamn,* what a word. If one god damned you, did you just find another?

Now why she do that, you think?

Mom was dying as Nat used the divinity-stuff. Getting the Heart would stave it off—but if that was true, why hadn't Maria Drozdova just consumed the damn thing, standing in the office with that little baby bump and her pretty bare feet? She couldn't eat it, but she could trade it back to Baba, maybe?

But why not just *do* that, without all the fuss? Why this giant production? There had to be a reason; Maria Drozdova didn't believe in wasted effort. Charged silence filled the car, touching Nat's hair, filling her with the nervous desire to fidget. It was like missing something in math class; she knew the hole was there, but not what shape or number would fill it.

"I am biggest uncle," Dmitri said heavily. "The nephews and other uncles, they come to me for . . . things. I rule what is stolen, by greed or by desperation. They invoke me, and I keep the wolf from the door. But sometimes, *zaika,* I *am* the wolf. You, now, you are the Drozdova. Nice baby lambs on green fields, *da*? But you also the storms and the deep black mud. Everything got a cost."

"So . . ." Her throat was so dry. A drink suddenly sounded wonderful, just the thing to stop the merry-go-round of carnivorous questions inside her head. "But Mom stole your heart. Doesn't that . . . isn't that something you have, you know, control over?"

"Oh, you'd think, eh? But spring came before the rubes—before the animals at all, you know—and spring be here long after all the rubes gone. She *endure*. I follow nice juicy little *zaika* who doesn't know to protect herself from me, and maybe I get it back, you see? Baba tell me *look after her* because you still growing, and others maybe not so nice as Dima. In a little while, nobody be able to do shit to you. But right now, you bloom while Mascha Drozdova fades, and you a little snack. Nice and juicy."

I bloom while Mom fades. But spring endures. That had a hopeful sound; maybe she could fix Mom and move out into a place of her own. "So you couldn't find it because Mom's a bigger, uh, deity? Divinity?"

"Not bigger, *zaika*. Different. Your mama have hiding place even *I* cannot find, that's deep magic. Could be dangerous for little you, so if Dima doesn't follow, no chance of getting heart back at all. Other way . . ." He shrugged. "Who knows? Chance is there, that's all."

"So you're playing the odds." *And Baba's betting I'm smart enough to find it and keep it away from you, but not smart enough to take it directly to Mom?* That didn't sound quite right either, and Nat longed for a room with a nice solid door she could shut and just *think* about some of this bullshit.

"You could say that." He lifted an admonishing finger, wagging gently. "But remember, *zaika*, you talking to a thief. *The* thief."

Well, wasn't that comforting. "The convenience store." She stole a glance at his profile. "Because the guy was a robber, you helped him."

"Maybe." A slight shrug, his jacket moving against the leather seat with a whisper. "Another day, I let him get caught. If he sloppy, or don't give his nice loving uncle a slice, you see? I give, or I don't. *They* pray to *me*." His tone shifted to a quivering falsetto. "*Oh, Uncle, don't let me get caught; oh, Uncle, let me kill this fucker; oh, Uncle, get me out of this cell.* Sometimes I do."

"So it's just . . . random?" Finally, someone was explaining basic precepts—if she could trust his explanations. "Or it depends on your moods?"

"Summer, fall, winter—*that* random? Friendly and his fucking Law, that random? The Cold Lady, well, maybe she is, maybe not so." Another shrug, and he dug in his breast pocket again, extracting what looked like a pack of Pall Malls. "Come on. Safe for a little while; I get you drink." He reached for the door, a cold mineral breath of winter evening filling the car's interior, chasing the warmth away.

Nat scrambled out on her side, ignoring his aggravated sigh—the god of chivalry was probably good and long dead, trying to open her door all the time wouldn't bring it back—and followed him across the parking lot, her peacoat pulled close even though the cold didn't bother her.

Oh, she knew there was ice, but it didn't matter. Her backpack rode her shoulder, a familiar weight, and her boots crunched gravel and frostbitten weeds. Her fingers tingled. Mom could make anything grow; why did she let the garden die back every year, if she was . . . what she was? Could she violate the laws of seasons?

Could Nat? A galvanic shiver went down her back, and the breeze from the river turned warm.

"You see?" Dmitri had lit another one of those cigarettes; he exhaled a cloud of incense-spiced smoke. "Feels nice. But come on." He hopped up two steps that looked nailed together out of lath and plywood, and Nat was surprised the entire edifice didn't sway and tremble. Frankly, the place looked condemned, but a thump of music came from inside, and there was a row of motorcycles parked around the side.

Oh my god, a divinity's taking me to a roadhouse. It sounded like a Monty Python skit. Leo didn't really understand their stuff, but he laughed when she tried to explain it.

Nat had to swallow, hard. "Is this place safe?"

"You with *me*," Dmitri said, and knocked on the door.

A rectangular slot opened, a pair of bloodshot blue eyes peering out. "Fuck off," a man growled.

"I strike you blind, you talk to me like that," Dmitri said, pleasantly, and the menace under each word could have stripped the peel-bubbling paint from the entire wall. "Open the fuckin' door and watch your shit-filled mouth, I have lady with me."

There was a clanking of locks being thrown, and Nat tested the steps gingerly. They were solid. This place was maybe more than it appeared.

Looked like Nat Drozdova, her mother's worst disappointment, was too.

LITTLE BROTHER

For all the urban legends and television jokes about biker bars it seemed pretty tame, though the jukebox music died as the door closed behind them. It certainly wasn't the Elysium's polished splendor; every surface looked sticky with neglect, even the pool tables crouched in cones of golden light under hanging green lamp shades. A thick fug of cigarette smoke—regular tobacco, worlds away from Dmitri's almost sweet-smelling vapor—clung to every surface, and the floor was slightly gummy as well. Most of the booths were empty, all the other tables were chest-high, and the stools were particularly flimsy. A few neon beer signs buzzed dispiritedly on the walls, the only windows were boarded up, and the bar listed like a Fleet Week sailor trying to prove he wasn't drunk by enthusiastically saluting while he swayed.

The bartender, a big balding beer-bellied man wearing a patch-festooned leather vest and a long gray beard, stared balefully at Dmitri as the gangster strode straight for him, and everyone else in the place, from women with teased hair and spike heels to men in leather-and-denim jackets and engineer boots, eyed Nat like a church full of widows with a drunken obscenity-yelling soldier in their midst.

In other words, it was definitely not Nat Drozdova's usual scene, but she followed in Dmitri's wake, trying very hard not to look at anyone directly and wondering if this was a divinity bar. Was there a god of bikers? If so, would he look like one of the men playing pool, or maybe the cocktail waitress hefting a tray crowded with brown beer bottles, her gaze avid and her bright red lips curved in a half-familiar grin?

She looked a bit like Nurse Candy, and now Nat wondered if that divinity could, well, look through any of her "girls." It sounded, like the prospect of Baba peering through snowflakes, incredibly exhausting.

The waitress even tipped Nat a heavily mascaraed wink, and Nat couldn't help but smile a little and give a halfhearted wave, like greeting a school friend in a crowded hallway during the inadequate ration of passing time.

God forbid kids should have any time to think, or even walk at a normal pace between classes.

Dmitri chose a stool at the bar, glanced over his shoulder while indicating the seat on his left for her, and settled with the air of a man reaching an easy chair in his own living room after a long day at work. "Vodka," he said to the bearded bartender, and tipped his head in Nat's direction. "Two."

The 'tender looked like he wanted to ask for her ID, and she was suddenly sure she liked this place better than the Elysium. It was grungy and the hall past the pool tables leading to what was probably the bathroom was full of deep gloom and likely more than one titanic, nausea-inducing smell, but it was . . .

Well, it was *human*.

She should brave the bathroom, no matter how it smelled, and call home. But what would she say? *Hi, Leo. I know everything, or at least the biggest things. All those times Mom said I was lying, all those times she said it was my imagination, and you just stood there. What was that? By the way, how's she doing in the hospice? They won't be able to help her, but you probably knew that, right? Anyway, nice talking to you, I'll call in another day or so.*

It wasn't a conversation that would do any good.

So she eased herself onto the stool, one of its legs a little wobbly, and did *not* rest her elbows on the bar. She even tried an apologetic smile at the bearded man, who flushed and coughed, turning hurriedly away to select a bottle from the mirrored shelves behind him.

All bars had glass behind the liquor. Maybe it was a cosmic law, divine regulations.

A laugh hit her sideways, got caught in her dry throat, and died. She shuddered, and Dmitri eyed her sidelong.

"Helluva kick, eh?" He wasn't shy about putting his elbows on the tacky-sticky wood, and his dark hair gleamed in the dimness, combed back again, not a single strand out of place.

"You could say that," Nat managed, each word scraping-dry.

Two indifferently wiped glasses were thumped atop square white napkins, and a generous measure of tepid vodka cascaded into each. Leo would have been scandalized; even Mom admitted vodka had to be *cold*. Still, Nat barely waited before picking hers up and tossing it far back, hoping the booze would kill whatever germs were riding the glass.

It tasted just like always, hit her stomach, burst into forgiving warmth, and her eyes watered.

Dmitri made a small scornful sound. He touched his drink with a fingertip, and condensation bloomed on the glass. There was a thin singing sound of strain as the temperature shifted.

Nat swallowed, blinked several times, suppressed a burp, and felt much better. "Neat trick."

"You like? I teach you." He took another drag, twin threads of heavy white vapor curling out through his nose. "Want a smoke?"

She shook her head. Who knew what he had rolled in those shapechanging cigarettes? Maybe Nat could take up smoking. What about other drugs?

Did divinities do cocaine? Now there was a question the gangster would probably love to answer.

The bartender cleared his throat. Dmitri's gaze swung slowly to him, and the gangster god smiled. It was a slow, terrifying grin; the man, though he was a good head taller and probably twenty pounds heavier—at the very *least*—stepped back, a floorboard creaking sharply as his weight shifted. He found something to do at the far end of the ramshackle bar, a puddle of deep shadow swallowing everything except his pale, stained apron.

Conversation at the pool tables resumed, the clack of balls hitting each other, a low laugh. The rest of the place sank into profound apathy. The waitress's shoes—thick-soled numbers that wouldn't be out of place on a nurse—made soft sounds as she prowled, and bottles clinked.

"There's no music now," Nat said, staring at her empty glass.

"Jukebox over there." Dmitri tipped his head again, indicating the pool tables. Snugged next to a dark archway—there was indeed a faded RESTROOMS sign overhead—was what looked like an honest-to-gosh Wurlitzer, with bubbles rising through the glowing tubes on its face. "Just ask it nice, *zaika*."

The prospect of walking past the men at those green-felted tables was only slightly more appetizing than the likely state of the bathrooms. "Can I do it from here?"

"Try." He lifted his drink, took it down in one go, and exhaled hard, smoke rising from the paper-wrapped stick in his hand.

How do I say "Excuse me, I'd like some music?" She stared at the jukebox, letting her eyes unfocus, and a few moments later, a sharp click like a revolver's hammer drawn back cut through the pool-playing mutter.

The first few bars were familiar; George Harrison began to sing "Here comes the sun . . ." and Nat was suddenly young again, standing in the kitchen while Leo and Mom danced, Maria laughing and all right with the world for a few moments as she swayed and dipped in his arms.

Tears prickled behind Nat's eyelids.

Sometimes Mom would hug her and whisper *my little one, hush now my little one,* stroking Nat's hair that wasn't as bright as hers. She was golden-warm and beautiful, a sun in the little yellow house, the glow Leo and Nat revolved around. She'd taught Nat to cook and how to clean, how to weed and what to leave, how to loosen earth with a whisper and how to layer a compost pile, how to whistle like a bluebird or fill a feeder so the hummingbirds would find it acceptable.

And she had lied, relentlessly, for as long as Nat could remember. She resented her daughter's sticky, grubby hands on clean linen, Nat's need for regular mealtimes, the way Nat grew out of clothes or shoes.

All mothers got tired though, didn't they? And Maria was never truly, actively cruel—at least, not for very long. Lots of kids had it worse growing up.

You bloom, she fades.

The thought she'd been trying to avoid walked right through her skull like a cat deciding it wanted attention, presenting its hindquarters with an arrogant tail-flick. What if, Nat wondered, there was only so much divinity power, and she was taking more than her fair share by just *existing*?

The song stretched, the entire bar caught in hardening honey. The lights turned mellow; a brief warm breeze whirled through, ruffling every napkin and rustling across leather, denim, T-shirts, scarves, gin-blossomed noses and hard hands, bright earrings and knotted bandannas.

Dmitri beckoned the bartender. "Another," he said, and the word cut the glow in half. The good feeling drained away, and Nat hunched her shoulders.

"You gonna pay?" The bearded man had recovered his bravery, it looked like, or whoever was down at the other end of the bar had bolstered him.

"Fuck your mother," Dmitri said, quietly, but every syllable was clearly audible all the way to the front door.

Oh, boy. Apparently she was stuck between *oh God* and sounding like a pearl-clutching old lady. "Please can you just—" Nat began, but there was a gleam at the other end of the bar, and another man melded out of the deep well of shadow.

He wasn't quite mountainous but his shoulders gave a good impression of it; his raven hair lay under a red bandanna and his leather jacket was at once shiny and well-broken. His nose was a sunburned blade matching rosy windburn on his stubbled brown cheeks. An unlit cigarette hung from the corner of his sculpted mouth, and his engineer boots were just like Leo's but lovingly polished. Nat figured the biggest, shiniest motorcycle outside was his, and it probably sounded like thunder when he kicked it into life. The same buzzing, blurring sense of *presence* Dima carried hung on him too; his belt was large, leather, and buckled with a giant sterling-silver eagle.

In short, he was the epitome of *biker*, even wearing leather chaps over the pegged jeans clinging to legs packed with well-delineated muscle. Dark eyes peered from a network of fine lines that came from squinting against roadglare. He paused, his hip bumping one of the barstools, and regarded the gangster steadily.

The clatter of pool balls and low male voices halted. Breathless tension took its place.

"Been a while, Dima." A deep, resonant baritone that could probably cut through the roar of going seventy on the freeway without a windshield lingered on each word.

"Not long enough, little bro." The gangster turned slightly on his seat, cocking his head. Nat couldn't see his expression, but she could imagine the slow, insouciant study of the other man from boot-toe to bandanna-top. "You hiding out here?"

"Nah." The Biker's gaze slipped past Dima's shoulder, glided over Nat in a brief sweep. At least he didn't stare at her chest, but she was in so many layers it probably would have taken X-ray vision or a prospector to find anything there. "Whatcha want?"

"Friendly getting above his pay grade again." The gangster said it carelessly, but with an edge to his tone, and now Nat knew why he'd stopped here. "He coming through after me."

"Is he now." The Biker nodded, and one large, hard, callused hand rose to scratch at his bristled chin. "Well, we'll get out the welcome wagon." He indicated the bartender with a swift, economical motion; it beggared belief that someone so muscular could move with such fluidity. "But honestly, Dima. Mortals gotta live too."

"Then they oughta know better than to disrespect me."

"True, true. Suppose we call it on the house, this being her first visit and all." The man's gaze swung to Nat, lingered. "So. Mascha's dead."

Nat suppressed an uneasy flinch, wanting to correct him but not quite daring to speak. Apparently everyone knew what her very existence meant. Maybe Mom had thought she could raise Nat and not have this happen?

The simplest answer was probably the right one: Nat had done something terrible inadvertently, and—true to form—triggered her mother's illness. Which didn't explain why Mom stole the Heart in the first place, unless she'd suspected her child would fuck everything up and make her sick?

Nat's gorge rose. A sick, feverish flush passed through her, with a chill as deep as Baba Yaga's snow in its wake.

"Not too soon, you ask me." Dima's shrug was smaller than usual, and he was, Nat realized, carefully keeping himself between her and the other divinity. Probably for a reason.

"So. You gonna get on her next incarnation's good side?" The Biker's eyebrows rose, not quite a caricature of surprise but close. "You two were pretty tight, back in the day."

"She had things she wanted." The gangster couldn't sound more dismissive if he tried. "So did I."

It wasn't exactly a surprise—after all, Mom had to know Dmitri to know about his heart, and both "worked" for de Winter in some way. It only made sense. But the way the other divinity said *pretty tight,* with a lascivious curl to sculpted lips, was sick-making.

"And this charming young lady?" The Biker's grin stretched. "Does she have things she wants too?"

Not sure you're in a position to give them. Nat had to suppress another guilty movement as the bartender, with a mutinous glare in Dmitri's direction, poured another generous measure of vodka into her glass. She folded her hands in her lap, wishing she wasn't perched on a tottering seat, and squeezed her fingers together until they hurt.

Everyone assumed Mom was dead and she was the replacement. But if Mama wanted to trade the Heart so Baba made her better, why did she wait until she got sick? It just didn't add up. Nat was no champion in the brain department, or so Mom always said, but she'd been doing all right so far.

Hadn't she?

"Don't they always?" Dmitri's laugh was just as bitter and caustic as ever. "Baba likes her. *You take care of my granddaughter, Dima.*" The impression of de Winter was impressive, right down to the older woman's dry, ironic tone. "She be very upset if her little girl gets any grief."

The Biker's expression hardened. "Old bitch choosing sides, huh?"

"Something like that." Dmitri reached without looking, his left hand snagging Nat's full glass. His cigarette was still fuming; ice bloomed on the glass and that faint singing sound as the temperature shifted again, a tiny crystalline scream. He downed it, but didn't tip his chin up; Nat realized he was holding the Biker's gaze while he drank.

It was like seeing two lethal prehistoric beasts engaged in a pissing match, and Nat nervously calculated how far it was to the door.

"You've given your warning, and I should probably thank you for it." The Biker stretched his beefy neck, head tipping to one side, then another. Tiny cracking sounds were loud in the stillness. "But maybe we should find out what the girl thinks."

"Her?" Dmitri lowered the glass and made a small scoffing noise. "Bitches don't *think*, Barry. I keep her nice and safe, don't you worry. When she get home you can bring a nice bouquet to her door, though, see if she give you time of day."

You misogynistic fuckwads. Don't make me part of this. "I'll just wait outside," Nat managed faintly, and slid off her seat. Neither man appeared to notice.

"You come here to give a warning, or lookin' for a fight?" Barry the Biker—and oh, good *Lord*, what a name for a divinity—smiled, a ferocious grin just as wide and unsettling as any of Dmitri's.

"If any of you corncob motherfuckers worth fighting, I'd do it." The gangster dropped his cigarette into Nat's glass and set it carefully on the bar. "But the girl wanted a drink, so I thought I'd play nice. Maybe she like to see me beat your ass, though."

You'd think gods would act a little more mature. Nat performed an almost military half-turn, fixed her gaze on the door, and set out on trembling legs. Divine boys were just like human ones, and why should that surprise her? The toxic masculinity went all the way to the top. Of-fucking-course it did.

"That's right," Barry said quietly. "Walk away. Some big brother you are."

"You keep saying, *don't want to be outlaw no more, just want to ride*. Some day I even let you, *moj malenkiy brat*." Dmitri laughed again, but this time, it didn't sound pained. No, he sounded genuinely amused instead, and Nat sped up, the door almost swelling as she focused entirely on it.

Do whatever you're going to, guys. I'm out.

"Asshole." Glass shattered.

Nat's shoulders hunched, and she was almost certain the door wouldn't open. The guy who had let them in, a pair of aviator sunglasses tucked high up on his forehead, eyed her as nervously as a fellow at least a foot taller and plenty of muscled pounds heavier could.

"You forget who taught you how to ride, *Barry*." A harsh thump, meat striking meat, and Nat tried a smile on the doorman.

"Excuse me," she managed, and watched his pupils swell. "I'll just be going now." The locks looked complicated, but there were tiny metallic sounds as they shifted under some invisible pressure. Maybe she was doing it, maybe Dmitri was.

Is it really just that easy?

The doorman slid off his own rickety stool, standing almost to attention, and she wondered if the seats were all crappy so they'd break easier during fights. You could hurt someone more with a solid piece of furniture, she supposed.

The door creaked; she pulled it open and stepped out into a dark, frosty Iowa night. Maybe she could even start running, make it to a well-traveled street, flag down a car? Ask someone nicely to take her to South Dakota, no matter what they had waiting at home?

What were the ethics of this sort of thing? Were there any?

Had Mom ever thought about them?

There was a crashing behind her, a sound of male pain. Nat put her chin down, wishing she could cover her ears, hopped off the steps, and kept walking.

DONE DEAL

The black car pulled up beside her barely a block away, its engine purr familiar now and the passenger window rolling down. "Eh, *zaika*." Dmitri was familiar too—you could, apparently, get used to anything even in a short while. "Get in."

She didn't even know what day it was; hanging out with divinities messed up your circadian rhythm something awful. Or maybe there was a divinity of time, and he was mad at her for some reason.

Nat pulled her backpack higher on her shoulder, focusing on the far glow of an intersection where the dirt road turned to pavement. "I should have known you had an ulterior motive."

"What? Get in." The engine revved; either he'd done it out of pique or the car itself was impatient. "We get some snacks, drive all night. Or we stay at Elysium again." Did he actually sound anxious?

Just how many Elysiums are there? "All I've got to do is ask someone for a ride, Dmitri."

"Oh, you think it so simple? Get *in,* I'm not asking again."

He wasn't asking in the first place, but Nat didn't bother pointing it out. "Are you going to beat me up if I say no?"

"What? That's just play, *zaika.* So he knows I care." The engine revved again, sharper now. "And now that *politskei politruk* motherfucker get a nice warm welcome when he come through sniffing at our trail." The car edged forward; he cut the wheel to the right so the front fender edged into the icy shoulder, effectively blocking her. "Not every family nice and happy like you and your mama."

For fuck's sake. "You think I'm happy? You think I like this?" Nat's hands curled into fists; her backpack slipped on her shoulder and the wind, freighted with icy riverbreath, tugged at the green knit cap and hem of her coat. "Every time I turn around someone's reminding me they hate my mother and she lied to me, or that I'm killing her just by existing. And *you,* you hate me for something I never even did. All I want is to be left alone!"

The dome light came on; Dima rose from his side of the car. He peered over the shiny black roof at her, and a soft chiming was the *hey dipshit, door's open* standard on every model.

Even this one.

The gangster didn't have a pithy comment or a hateful little speech ready. Instead, Dima stared solemnly at her, his dark eyes narrowed and his hair gleaming. The shadows thickened, turning sharp; she could swear some of them almost twitched, like the mummified sorcerer's little helpers.

Surrounded by acres of sleeping farmland, Waterloo still sent an orange stain into the cloud-lowering winter sky. Nat was frozen too, but not from the weather. The breeze held an iron tang of snow on its back; maybe de Winter was watching.

I hope she is. I'd like to flip her off, so help me, I'd just love *to tell her a few things. At top volume too.*

They stared at each other, mobster and girl, Nat trembling with what couldn't be anger because good girls weren't supposed to feel rage, were they? Society, not to mention the sisters at school, were both very clear on that point indeed, and Mom . . .

Your little temper, Natchenka. And that slight disdainful sound Maria Drozdova made, not quite a huff. *Go clean your room.*

Childhood was knowing your own mother hated you, but accepting it as natural. Adulthood, Nat realized, was the moment you figured out it wasn't just an unchangeable fact but also how fucked up it was, and how much it hurt.

Dmitri nodded a little, as if she'd done something surprising but pleasant at the same time. He still said nothing, but his expression changed—though in precisely what way, she couldn't tell.

Oh, for fuck's *sake.* Nat reached for the car door, yanked it open, and dropped into leather-scented warmth. She slammed the door, hugged her backpack, and didn't reach for her seatbelt.

If they got in a crash, what the hell would happen? Would Mom suddenly be all right again? What if Nat sliced open her wrists in a hotel bathtub?

Dmitri had a nice big black gun, too. Would *that* work?

He settled in the driver's side, and his own door closed. He turned the wheel and popped the emergency brake, dropped the big black car into gear, and feathered the accelerator.

At the end of the dirt road they bumped up onto pavement. No tricks, no zooming, he drove sedately as a grandma out for a Sunday tour.

He worked them back towards the freeway, following signs different than the ones at home. The variance wasn't huge, just enough to make her head hurt and her nose fill up. Nat wiped at her cheeks, surprised to find them dry. Maybe she was too tired, or too furious, to really cry.

They stopped at a red light, the left turn signal blinking steadily. The freeway on-ramp swallowed right-turning oncoming traffic with no demur, and his hands were loose on the yoke.

"Sioux Falls," Dmitri said finally, quietly. "If you want. We get snacks. This time you choose."

"Can we just we drive straight through?" She shouldn't push, Nat supposed. She should play nice, get along, keep her head down and her eyes open. "To Hardesty?"

"*Da, zaika moya.*" Dima nodded, and just like that, it was a done deal.

She couldn't figure out just what she'd bought, but it was hers now. Both the knowledge, and the new, tentative silence in the car as it hummed over cold pavement, just short of flying.

DELAYED ENOUGH

Early on a strangely dark afternoon, while a black car roared relentlessly west seeking a small town, New York lay under a stiff iron blanket of cloud. More snow coming, the weather report said, and those whose lives depended on the water sought whatever port they could find because their bones warned of a real howler coming from the north. Pedestrians bundled into beetle-shapes hurried, the homeless sought shelters, warming stations, or the imperfect safety of the subway; every tow truck and plow in the city was pressed into service, working double shifts.

It was not a day for visiting, but the old man opened Laurelgrove Hospice's front door. An ancient furry steppe hat was pulled down to his eyebrows, his hand-knit red muffler wrapped up to his nose, and normally he wore an old navy peacoat. Today, though, Leo Mishkin—no patronymic needed in America, left behind like so much baggage—wore a heavy striped cardigan over three thread-bare flannel shirts, jeans almost wet to the knee with slush-splash, and heavy engineer boots a honey-haired girl used to shuffle across a yellow house's back garden towards garbage cans chained to the fence.

He stamped his boots dry while eyeing the brightly lit Christmas tree in the foyer and unwound the muffler, changing from a masked intruder to an elderly fellow who might be a patient himself in the near future. He wasn't recognized quite as readily as some of the younger visitors, but nobody seemed to notice as he set off with a determined shuffle.

After all, he knew the way. Signing in would waste time, and he suspected he had little enough of that.

The room he wanted was on the third floor and today the lift was working, albeit as slowly as he himself felt. Growing old was a man's lot, all the books agreed.

Leo knew books lied. Wasn't he living proof? Then again, they did it to show other truths, buried shapes and guessed-at contours, archaeology of the truly real. He was Russian, though he had come to the shining wasteland of America by choice; he could argue about literature all day.

He remembered teaching a little girl to read, holding her small hand around a chubby pencil, helping her trace a stark graceless alphabet entirely unlike the flowing script of his homeland. Holding the back of a bicycle seat as she wobbled, then the bright silver bell ringing as she shot away, pedaling furiously, her honey hair flying on a lucky breeze. A pale young woman in green and gold, so beautiful it could make a heart break or mend in a single instant, her hand palm-up on tacky plastic sheeting covering a table's linens.

Mustn't spoil the cloth, after all.

He stopped in the hallway once, resting next to a brightly crayoned sign bearing a useless mortal name. Coughs and murmurs of conversation throbbed through the entire building, its sad bones from another era peering through bright antiseptic modern use. Leo's chin almost touched his sunken chest; he'd lost weight in the few days she'd been gone.

Why bother eating? Everything tasted of earth, even the ice cream he bought them both with couch-cushion change or small bits wrested from Maria when he behaved well.

When he *pleased* her.

He set off again. Not so long now, a journey almost done.

The room was full of slumberous snowlight; Maria was propped up in the expensive bed. The oxygen machine gave a soft whoosh, and the tangle of tubes leading to her body might as well have been paste jewelry for all the good they'd do her. Leo's sunken chest gave another deep twinge because the box of crackers, opened by Nat's careful hands, stood sentinel on the adjustable bed table. It hadn't been otherwise touched.

"Finally." Maria's large blue eyes were bloodshot, the whites yellowing. She was a straw-haired skeleton now, staring from under a black kerchief blotted with violently red flowers. Her bed jacket was awry—of course, her daughter hadn't been in to button it properly, to comb her mother's thinning mane, to stand patiently head-down while Maria lashed out. "I should have brought Raskolnikov instead."

"*Da,*" Leo murmured. She probably should have. He looked around for a chair, found the one Nat perched in when her mother didn't send her around the room on tiny errands—*get me water, no with ice, fetch my bag from the closet, close the drapes, open them a little I can't breathe, give me this, give me that.*

And each time, her daughter did.

"You took your time," Maria continued, the language of the old country rushing out of her thin mouth. No crimson upon plump pretty lips now, no soft pale cheek, no low laugh as she uncovered twin pale breasts, dusky-nippled, sweet as apples. "Is she gone? Did she take the car?"

Now she was a raddled *baba* in her own right, just the same as the old women she disdainfully sniffed at for so long, secure in her unassailable beauty. Leo, a fool like all men, had thought the loveliness meant a kind heart, or at least a willing one.

He finished unwrapping the muffler, took off his hat. His hair was gray as the oncoming storm, but still vigorous; he was rather vain about that, and combed it twice a day with a little oil. He set his hat on the swung-aside bed table, bumping the cracker box, and his old knob-knuckled hands—still strong enough, he hoped—occupied themselves with folding the scarf.

After all, Maria's daughter had bought it for him.

"Leo," Maria snapped. "Look at me."

He didn't want to, but he obeyed. A nurse in the hall might peek in and think them an ancient couple, perhaps still in love or the facsimile of it granted by time and mortal habit. He gazed upon the woman he had adored enough to follow across a foaming sea-desert, enough to eat black bread with strange grit in its crumb, enough to push his body repeatedly into hers until a quickening kindled.

I know you love Mom, Maria's daughter said, her arm outstretched and her dark eyes pleading. *That's a good thing.*

"*Nyet,*" Leo mumbled, a cricket's whisper. "It isn't."

"What? Speak up." Maria made an irritable movement. She was furious, of course—the rage glittered in her blue eyes, wrinkled her nose, and made her thin bony hands clench against the tan hospital blanket. "Did she leave? She took the car?"

"She left." Now Leo enunciated clearly. Standing in the window, watching the girl follow the dark man—oh, Leo knew who *he* was.

He knew far more than Maria realized.

"Did she take the car?" His darling Maschenka bared her yellowing teeth. "You were supposed to fix it, or get a new one. I told you how."

"Oh, *da, da.*" Leo nodded. "You told me, yes."

Maria stiffened. Normally, when she was this angry ozone would crackle in the air and the smell of evil black mud would rise from her in waves. Her golden hair would lift on its own personal breeze, and though she was always lovely, she was also terrifying in those moments. "You silly old man," she hissed. "I told you to get her another car. It should have been easy."

"Why, Marischka." He finished folding the scarf, laid it aside. "Cars are so expensive. She had a friend to ride with, and your precious money is safely where it should be."

A dangerous silence expanded like a soap bubble. Sleet rattled against the window with a tiny hollow chuckle, the storm's precursor. There were few warm places in New York, even with heaters turned up and blankets piled on.

A secret glow had left the warren of concrete canyons, the subway's thumping and screeching, the jammed-together storefronts and leaning houses. Even the rats were hiding deep in whatever hole they could find, pressed against each other to find some manner of warmth.

"I. Told. You." Maria's rage pushed her upright a few inches, her back leaving thin, stacked pillows she had probably bullied a mortal nurse into bringing. "I *told* you what to do."

"You always do." Leo's hands twitched. If he were his old self he might wrap them around her scrawny throat and squeeze. He had worked on the Léon Bollée for months, but for every problem he fixed, he created two more. It was the kind of job a crafty *zek* would recognize. Keeping the car from suckling at the new force in the house had cost him much of his waning strength, but each day he had shuffled into the clean kitchen and smiled as he washed his hands. "Our Natchenka is out in the world, Maria." He drew in a deep breath, staring at her mad, burning eyes. "And I hope she stays gone."

He had done all he could, hoping his little Natischka wouldn't visit the old lady. Finding reasons for her not to go, not yet, spending days alone wandering in the little yellow house while the honey-haired girl was at work, wringing his hands and waiting for her key in the lock and the soft *Leo, are you home?* Keeping the old car decrepit despite its urge to wholeness, cooking dinner, pouring the vodka with a silent prayer that she would stay just a little longer, just a short while, since Maria was now, after her collapse, too weak to pounce.

That very morning the old black car had sagged on flattened tires, rust racing through its once-shiny sides in hungry rivers. It had made a sound like a disintegrating parachute when he touched the hood, and the fender clanged to the garage's floor with a sound far too light and chiming for such a big piece of metal.

It had broken into three pieces, too.

The houseplants were withering, and each one's tiny dirtbound death pleased him because it meant Maria's daughter was safely away from her voracious mother. The dinginess in the walls, mildew spreading and paint peeling, was a blessing. He didn't mind the cold; some of Maria's favorite furniture burned very well indeed.

Maria choked. Her blue eyes bugged. She fell against the pillows, making noises mortals might mistake for distress. Leo rose slowly—after all, he was an old man—and shuffled for the door to call help.

She hated the nurses poking and prodding, the doctors' cheery bluster and refusal to treat her with due deference, the orderlies' sneaklike thieving. Her hatred brushed against his back, a dying breeze instead of a hailstorm, and Leo sighed.

No, he could not strangle her. He was as he'd been created, that first sharp birth from a swiftly flying pen all but forgotten in the crowd of impressions afterward. Besides, her end meant his own.

He had no illusions about that.

"Excuse me," he quavered in English at a passing nurse, a young white-sheathed woman with dark eyes very much like his little Natchenka's. "My wife . . . my wife is having trouble, you see? With the breathing."

A man with dirt in his mouth could not speak very loudly, after all.

He lingered in a corner, forgotten while medical professionals clustered Maria, who choked and raved in the old country's language, swearing she would cut his throat with the flint knife.

But that knife was in her daughter's hands, and both he and Maria would be past saving soon enough. He felt the approaching event as he'd once sensed a divinity's warm interest, looking up to see a pair of bright blue eyes across a crowded hall in Saint Petersburg, a man caught as surely and swiftly as a rabbit in a country girl's trap.

Soon Nat Drozdova would have her mother's treasures, all of them. And Leo Mishkin, once a prince who had given his heart to springtime, hoped he had delayed his daughter long enough.

I love you. The words beat behind his breastbone as they had for over two mortal decades. *I love you, my little one. I love you, I love you, and I hope I am dead before you return.*

For that would mean Maria Drozdova was too.

THE
CUP

FINDING HARDESTY

E ven in winter, South Dakota is beautiful.

Sere snow-swept prairie rolled by, changing only gradually as rivers came from the north to cut under the freeway, pavement bridging their icy foaming. The roads were mostly ruler-straight, mostly joined at right angles, and the endless vaulted sky might have been terrifying for a girl raised in close, confining concrete canyons.

But when the land stretched away in every direction, blurring to an infinite horizon, Nat's lungs loosened and she took deep breaths for what felt like the first time in her entire life, staring at the immensity. Every once in a while—just often enough the space wouldn't drive you mad—trees both evergreen and deciduous-naked softened the stony shores of a river or rose above some other secret water-vein. Sometimes the clouds broke and scudded over a sky full of thin, aching winter blue.

You could see the weather coming a long way away out here. You could see *anything* approach, but the prairie wasn't completely flat. It undulated, especially as they drove west, and even though she wasn't hungry Nat still had a bag full of road-trip munchies sitting in the back seat.

At her tentative suggestion that maybe they could stop for snacks after all, the gangster even produced a few bills at another brightly lit gas station to pay for a load of road-food, and nobody had died.

Dima said barely anything, which was a mercy all its own. The car didn't use that strange floating speed again; was he really so afraid of Friendly following? The cop had peeled out of the Iowa rest stop *ahead* of them, but would that really matter when dealing with a divinity?

A rough brush of wind traveling across miles of empty openness licked towns made of huddling-close hearts and sprawling limbs. Even the cities, their downtowns full of skyscrapers to match Nat's home, only sent their tentacles out along pavement ribbons.

Then there were the smaller human accretions in river valleys, barely raising their heads to look at the vast outside sweep. Sometimes collections of trailers flickered on the other side of a forlorn ditch and gravel shoulder, held back by everpresent three-strand barb-wire fence keeping the freeway from escaping its appointed path.

The rumble strips surprised her too, their edges filling with ice. At first she thought the divots were damage from chained-up vehicles, but they were too regular.

Dmitri drifted the right-side tires across them, a feral smile lighting his sharp face when she flinched. "Keep you awake, driving at night," he said, with no mocking edge to the words for once. "Get me Mountain Dew from back, eh?"

The storm lingered behind them, gloomy clouds with grasping westward feathers, but soon enough it was penned by a steady headwind. Signs cropped up for the Black Hills, but Dmitri kept them on more northerly roads as Nat tried to remember school history classes and documentaries.

The sun fell towards a distant purple smear on the horizon, and Nat should have known better than to enjoy herself even the slightest bit. Like everything else she'd ever found pleasant, the drive was over far too soon. They coasted off freeway onto two-lane highway, and from there onto another even smaller road parallel to a thin river that lunged for the road to shy away at the last moment, miserable scrub clinging to its uneven sides.

Dmitri pointed, a brief economical movement, at the first sign for Hardesty.

X

A small town, as advertised, with its back turned to the north wind and its downtown just a strip of storefronts crowding anxiously around a single stoplight. It looked deserted, though electric light shone through store windows—two gas stations, an auto mechanic with ancient, probably dry gas pumps outside as well, a quilting shop, a supermarket with a lone string of gap-toothed Christmas lights across its front, a laundromat, and a diner with faded gold lettering whispering CIGARS.

"He said I'd know it when I saw it," Nat repeated. "A bar. That's all he told me." The Knife was safe in her backpack. Maybe she should get it out, and it would point the way like a compass?

"*Something* here, that for sure." Dmitri sniffed, one of his cigarettes burning between two fingers as he clasped the yoke loosely with his other hand. He leaned forward a little, his face in the stream of cold air from his cracked-open window, and inhaled deeply again. "Yeah. Beer and horseshit."

I haven't seen a single horse. But what animal would be out in this weather? Maybe only bison, but those were dead, weren't they? All killed so the tribes depending on them could be starved out. She remembered that much from history class, at least, and also the faint worm of disquiet in her ribcage when the history teacher said it was a good thing, because everyone had to be civilized.

Asking questions—pointed or merely honest—about things like that got you labeled a troublemaker. Child-Nat had all the trouble she could handle, so she did her best not to look at the slides with mountains of buffalo skulls or other bones piled next to grinning, mustachioed white men in old-timey clothes. Now she was a grown-up, and couldn't look away ever again.

What were the divinities out here? Did they remember those days?

There wasn't a single vehicle moving on the street. Dmitri slowed down anyway, his eyes half-closed, taking deep sniffing breaths over and over. His snuffling would have been funny, except for the chill down Nat's back.

She'd never been to the zoo, since Mom hated seeing animals in cages. Nat had only ever seen wolves in pictures or on television; being trapped in a small space with a divine gangster who reminded her so forcibly of one wasn't comforting.

A lonely listing stop sign two miles from the tiny downtown brought them to a halt, and the black car grumbled softly. "Which way?" The gangster's tone was another surprise, quiet and business-like, as if he expected her to know.

Nat opened her mouth to say she didn't. And heard herself say, "Left. About a mile."

He didn't argue or question. The car turned on a dime, leaping forward. She couldn't remember anyone believing her so immedi-ately before, and hoped she wasn't wrong.

Another old-fashioned roadhouse came into sight, set in a wide graveled parking lot. The sign on its rusting pole was too faded to make out any sort of name; the building itself, under a steeply pitched roof, bore a kissing-cousin resemblance to the oil-drum-and-plywood bar in Waterloo. Neon buzzed in a darkened window, the bright red OPEN sign a beacon in monochrome landscape. Pickup trucks, old gas-guzzling sedans, and one or two shiny SUVs parked in neat rows as close to the long, brooding shack as possible.

It looked, in short, like a real old-timey honkytonk. Its other ration of neon was blue, and simply stutter-blared BEER at anyone passing by, twice as large as the open sign. A few strings of multi-colored Christmas lights clung to the gutter-edges, and the front doorway was lined with their cheerful multicolored sparkle.

You'll know it when you see it. The feeling of rightness was just like finding a cat who would speak to her, a stray dog needing to be led home, a wounded squirrel, a ring of softly singing out-of-season mushrooms, or a weed forcing its way through cracks in forgotten sidewalk. An electric thrill shot down her arms and legs as if she was in Baba's wooden chair again, struggling against an invisible weight.

Would she learn how to invisibly hold someone pinned like a butterfly, too? Just how old was Baba? Had even *she* been a young divinity once? How had a Russian winter poured into bodily form arrived in America, anyway?

Probably on a ship, like many other European immigrants. There was no way to ask without risking more of Dmitri's uncertain temper. Nat studied the roadhouse instead, her hands clenched in her lap. The structure grew bigger and bigger as the black car slid towards it.

There wasn't much snow with the wind sweeping everything clean; still, plenty of gleaming frost lay in the building's shadow. "There's supposed to be a man inside." *Another divinity. Probably one you'll pick a fight with.*

"Oh, *da,* someone's in there." Dima's teeth gleamed in the failing dusk. "Don't worry, *devotchka.* Dima keep you safe and sound."

Until you've got what you want, sure. It was just like Mama calling her "dumpling" when she wanted Nat to perform a particularly dirty or unpleasant task. Everyone was nice when they wanted something from you—was it a divinity thing, or just a basic natural fact?

When Dima cut the engine, a faint tinny thumping drifted through the sliver of open window on his side. "Fucking shitkickers," he muttered.

Nat had to lean uncomfortably close to reach for her backpack in the footwell behind her seat; she was getting used to the confined space. It seemed almost natural to brush against his suit-clad shoulder, and the gangster stayed very still. At least he wasn't trying to poke or pinch her; she'd probably scream if he did.

For all the good it would do.

Still, she'd driven off Friendly, right? Except maybe that wasn't an achievement. She had the sinking feeling she might see him again, just like she'd known about Sister Roberta's stroke.

Witchgirl, creepy Natty. Freak!

"I liked the Elysium better." She wriggled back into her seat, reaching for the door handle.

"Eh." It was a very male sound, just like the one Leo made when he didn't agree or disagree, just wanted to let her know he'd heard. "Stay put. I come to your side."

Nat's unease deepened. "Okay."

"*Now* you a good little girl." Dmitri snorted, and opened his door.

I was certainly raised to be. Nat watched him stalk around the front of the car, his head up, still inhaling deeply. His sharp nose twitched, and his suit was far too thin for this weather.

Dumpling. Mind your mama. Do as I tell you, Natchenka, and do it now.

So far, being a good, obedient little child hadn't done a damn thing. Maybe it was time to change.

RANGER

The place was packed; hard to believe such a tiny town could hold this many people, even with beer on tap.

It smelled of sawdust and fermenting yeast, the close fug of winter-damp woolen jackets steaming when they were brought inside, and black earth stamped from hardworking boots. There were two jukeboxes, but only one was playing—she thought it was Hank Williams, who Leo called *real American music* and sometimes found on the ancient Bakelite radio when Mom was out shopping.

Of course, Maria hadn't left the little yellow house for a while, Nat realized, not until the night she collapsed and the ambulance had trouble finding their address. Since Nat's last year of high school, Mama'd been practically a shut-in.

Hank was moving the little dog over; the interior of the bar was a sea of heads with slicked-down hair bearing the indentation of cowboy hats—said headgear occasionally placed on tables or held in work-roughened hands—flannel-clad shoulders, and women with no-nonsense ponytails and dainty point-toed boots.

Every eye in the place settled on them, but it didn't go quiet. In fact, though there were several hard stares from men in denim jackets or apple-cheeked women holding bottles of Coors, the hum of conversation continued apace. A shiny brass rail ran under the bar, which looked solid and true as a deep-root oak. Even the mirror behind the shelves of liquor was polished, every reflection a glowing jewel.

There were pool tables here too, a drift of cigarette smoke hanging around them, but the clack-clatter of balls didn't go straight

through Nat's head and the men playing took pauses to consider
the fields of green felt, conferring in drawled syllables between long
shoals of quiet attention.

Two waitresses moved like small tropical fish through the table-
reefs, both wearing knee-length denim skirts. One had black tights,
the other striped blue and green; both had shirts with piped yokes
as well as high-teased bangs frozen with hairspray. The crowd only
appeared a homogenous mass; as Nat got closer she picked out short
or tall, stocky or rangy, cowboy or hiking boots, jeans or Carhartts.
Most of the faces were brown; threads of Spanish slipped through
the conversation, sharply accented.

Dmitri glanced at Nat, his eyebrows up. Clearly she was supposed to know what to do here, and maybe she would have figured
it out if a cheery "Well, hellooo there," hadn't pierced the crowd's
murmur like a silver needle.

The greeter was wearing a cowboy hat, and it was a real ten-
gallon number in dove gray. Maybe it had been white once, but
hard use had turned it soft and rain-colored; broad shoulders filled
out a red flannel shirt under a hip-length, dun-colored rancher's
jacket. Ebon skin gleamed, a faint roughening of windburn on his
cheeks, and he was lean-hipped in butter-soft, hard-broken jeans.
His boots were only slightly like Dmitri's, their toe-caps dull iron
instead of burnished silver, and his belt buckle was a plain iron oval.
Still, boots and buckle were both heavy, and probably antique.

A broad white smile bloomed on the cowboy's face; the crowd
parted for him. He came to a stop just before Nat, burning with
that vitality that shouted he was like Dmitri, like Mama used to
be. He even doffed that gray hat, swinging it gently between two
fingers, and his springy, close-cropped hair was sable too. "Last
time I saw, you were just a glint in your mama's eye." He had a
nice, cheerful, ringing baritone, but slung low on his hips was an
honest-to-gosh gun belt, and two revolvers nestled in leather holsters. "Drozdova, right? Or are you takin' another name now?"

The guns made her nervous, but then again, what else did a cowboy wear? "Nat," she said, cautiously, and held out her hand. "Nat
Drozdova. How do you do."

"Ranger." His grasp was warm and firm, and an electric thrill slid up her arm. "At least, for the last fifty years or so. I'm sorry about your mama."

"She's sick." Nat's throat threatened to close around a lump. "That's why I'm here."

"That so?" The cowboy glanced at Dmitri, and though his expression didn't change, his hazel eyes held a steely glint. "Well, come on in. Let's get you a drink, ma'am."

Iron spurs clung to his boots, solid and well-used like the rest of him, but they didn't jangle as he turned, a little stiffly, and offered her his arm. Dmitri said nothing, so Nat tentatively took hold and found herself whisked through a crowd of drinkers suddenly paying no more attention to her than they would a fly buzz-staggering well above their heads. A rill of laughter started near the pool tables, but for once it didn't feel like it was directed at her clumsiness.

Ranger aimed for the right of the bar, where an arched doorway was masked by a dusty red velvet curtain. He swept it aside with a flourish; the room beyond was bright and cozy, not to mention antique as his belt buckle.

Stepping over the threshold gave her the same strange internal hiccup as Coco's boutique, Jay's mansion, or Dima's black car bumping from dirt road to pavement, a small inward jolt like the thump of ear-cracking bass from a passing vehicle.

The room behind the curtain had clapboard walls, fitted together with neat precision; a well-scrubbed stone hearth held a crackling blaze. Suspended over the fire was a blackened iron cauldron; a brass poker, shovel, and brush sat on a trim little rack to the right. A wooden table, looking handmade, stood along the left wall under a window curtained with red check gingham. The back right corner was hidden by a colorfully striped wool blanket held by bone-colored rings on an age-polished rod.

It looked like a tiny apartment, right down to the freestanding sink in the front right corner, an old-timey pump handle poised above it like a sleepy snake. Next to the window and the table, its three wooden chairs all different styles, a big maple bookcase held a collection of spines—some old and leather, others cheap paperback, all apparently well-loved.

Nat liked it immediately. The warmth loosened her arms, made her backpack lighter, and she knew that behind the curtain would be a single iron bedstead, the covers so tight you could bounce a quarter. It would be nice to live in a room like this, especially once the bar closed down and you could open the window-curtains, looking out on snow. You could sit at the table and read, or just listen to the creaking and sighing of a solid wooden structure as it breathed.

There was no sound from the other side of the red velvet. If this was magic, it was *great;* making a warm little nook like this would be well worth knowing how to do. A faint tang of woodsmoke, the smell of clean sawdust and a thread of bleached, sun-dried laundry—every bit of tension fled her aching shoulders.

"It ain't big, but it's quiet." Ranger led her to the very center of the room, stepping onto a rug patterned like the hanging blanket curtaining the bed before letting go of her arm. "You, sir, can take that chair and set it near the fire." He pointed, and there was that glint in his hazel gaze again. "Y'all behave yourself while you're on my ground."

"As if you have anything I want." Dmitri made a short, scornful noise, but he also took the chair and dragged it, bumping carelessly, over the wooden floor.

Ranger shook his head. "Ma'am, come on in and sit down. What would you like? Coffee? Scotch? Or if you're in the mood for something more substantial . . ."

"Coffee would be great." Nat let her backpack slip, dangling it from one hand as she edged toward the bookshelf, suddenly longing to see the titles. "So . . . I guess you're a divinity, right? Is that the word?"

"One of 'em. Used to have a quick temper and a quicker gun, but nowadays I'm more of a keeper, like. I keep track of things." Another dark glance at Dmitri, and the man moved with swift, economical grace to the fireplace. Two speckled blue enamel cups appeared in his strong hands; he dipped them in the bubbling cauldron. "And sometimes I ride, or roughneck a bit when I've a mind to. Always glad when you come around, though, Miss Drozdova. Your mama's poorly?"

Dmitri muttered something; Ranger didn't even glance at him. Nat set her backpack carefully on the chair with its back to the bookcase, studying the titles. Mostly field guides, though there were a fair number of old medical texts, mostly veterinary, and a whole shelf of Westerns with lurid titles. It was warm enough she could unbutton her peacoat, and she found herself doing so. It was impossible not to like the man, he radiated such calm goodwill. "She's really sick." Nat glanced over her shoulder, gauging the gangster's reaction.

Dmitri spun the chair around and dropped astraddle; then he stared into the fire, his profile hardened into granite, his black-clad arms crossed on the chair back. Orange firelight played over his hair and suit jacket, burnishing every sharp edge and making his boot-toes glitter balefully.

"Have a seat." Ranger brought the two cups to the table, edging sideways with balletic grace. He was, Nat realized, very pointedly not turning his back to the gangster. One cup went in front of what he obviously considered Nat's chair at the moment, the other settled on mellow wood in front of the other. "If you like, ma'am, he can wait outside. You're safe here."

It was almost ridiculous, those last three words. Nothing was *safe*, especially not when you were driving cross-country with a man who carried straight razors and a silenced gun, not when you visited a woman named de Winter and agreed to fetch a bloody diamond from wherever your cancer-ridden mother had hidden it, not when "divinities" and "principalities" were doing things that violated every rule of the safe, sane, normal world Mom kept insisting was real all Nat's life.

Constantly calling your own daughter a liar wasn't really protection. There was another word for it, one Nat had been trying not to think.

The lump in her throat had swelled. *Oh, for God's sake. Please don't.*

It was ridiculous to say *God*. Who knew what would answer? It was even more ridiculous to feel so sheltered while sitting in a room with two virtual strangers, especially when one of them was quite clear he was going to try to kill you. But the feeling was deep, undeniable, and her eyes smarted. A single hot fingertip traced down her cheek.

"Oh, hell," the cowboy said, digging hastily in his right coat pocket and producing a crisp white cotton handkerchief. "Pardon my French, ma'am; it's gonna storm tonight for sure. Take this and do what you need to—and you, horsethief. Go on out and drink at the bar, the lady needs a moment."

"*Nyet.*" Dmitri didn't move, gazing at the fire like it held some sort of secret text. "I stay with little girl, *cowboy*. Lots of people like to get their hands on her during incarnation."

"During . . ." Ranger's chin swiveled toward Nat, his hand offering the hankie hanging in midair. "And Maria's still . . . huh."

The silence turned uncomfortable. Nat's heart wrung itself into a tight, painful fist. Of course she'd walk into a nice, homey little room and completely ruin the atmosphere. "I'm sorry," she repeated, dismally aware it made no difference at all, and accepted the scrap of cloth. "I'm kind of new at this."

"Take your coat off, sit down. Tell me what you've got a mind to." He settled in his own chair, a slow graceful coiling. His back rested against the wall near the window, and his gaze moved restlessly from the fireplace to the red velvet over the archway.

Nat lowered herself gingerly; the chair was solid, and it was a relief not to be trapped in the car's confines or on a teetering barstool. She settled her backpack in her lap, touched the blue metal mug. "These are like the ones for camping, right?"

"I like 'em." Ranger smiled with one side of his mouth, a quick warm glance in her direction before he returned to watching the room like he suspected Dmitri would do something . . . well, something violent.

It wasn't a bad guess.

The mug was warm; a hot comforting wire slid down her arm

when she cautiously hefted it. She gave the dark liquid a token sniff, caught between the urge to smile and the lump in her throat.

It smelled exactly, but *exactly* like Leo's coffee, with just enough vodka poured in to make it respectable. Nat realized she was still holding the man's handkerchief when the tears overflowed again, and she sniffed heavily, dabbing at her cheek. "She never told me about any of this." *Stop that silly crying, Natchenka. Or I give you something to* really *cry for.* "Maybe she was . . ."

Ranger lifted his own mug, took a sip. His quiet was almost tangible, but not like a classroom with a towering nun by the chalkboard or a little yellow house full of displeasure. Instead, it was a soft, considering unsound, granting space like the wide prairie outside.

"Maybe she was trying to protect me?" Nat continued, hating that she sounded so tentative.

Dmitri's snort sliced through the fire's crackling breath.

Ranger frowned. "If you can't keep your mouth shut—"

"Why should I?" The gangster stared at the fire like it had made a rude noise instead. "Only thing Matchenka Drozdova want to protect her own sweet self. Count on that, *zaika.*"

"That's one," the cowboy said mildly, yet with an edge of menace under the words. The entire room creaked, a shadow passing through directionless golden light. "Don't make it two, horsethief."

That was when Nat realized there weren't any electrical fixtures, just the fire and that gold glow. It was the thick syrupy light of a desert afternoon in certain movies, when the stagecoach came rumbling around a bend and the title music faded.

Come on, Nat. Maria Drozdova was lying in a hospice bed, struggling to breathe, counting on her daughter. She wasn't perfect—but who was? And she was Nat's *mother.* That had to come first.

Right?

"She sent me for the Cup." Nat tried a sip of the coffee. It even tasted just like Leo's. "In a well to the West," she continued, reciting the lesson she had no trouble remembering because Mom wasn't pinning her with the bright blue stare that made words jumble together in her throat, and didn't miss Dmitri's sudden tension.

"Oh, ayuh," Ranger said. "What she left with me is safe, a'course. And I'll tell you what, Miss Drozdova. You spend the night with me, and I'll lend you the iron horse to get there."

DIFFERENT HURTS

The sky had cleared, and hard diamond stars shimmered in dry darkness. The wind was up, though, and it smelled of thick cold precipitation; a void hung on the northern horizon, clouds massing to blot out tiny shimmering points.

It was indeed going to storm tonight.

The bar's back porch held one faint incandescent bulb trapped in an old-fashioned iron lantern fixture; with so little in the way of light pollution the Milky Way could be seen spilling across heaven's vault. Nat pulled her peacoat close and pushed her hands into the pockets, though the cold didn't bother her. Maybe the vodka in the coffee was keeping it at bay. She stood at the top of the porch steps, a strip of gravel fringing into prairie sod a stone's throw away, vanishing into the dark. Even with the cover of night, the sheer physical immensity of the landscape could make anyone uneasy.

Was there a divinity of stars? Of weather in general? Where did they live, and what did they look like, and would Nat ever find out?

If she could get a car like Dmitri's maybe she could travel, once Mom was well again. It sounded great. "I don't really have a choice." Which was true all the way through this thing, really.

Music thumped faintly inside the bar. The night was just getting started in Hardesty's only bar.

"I don't like it." Dmitri took a long drag on his cigarette, the cherrytip glowing, a baleful eye. He stood on the step below her, so their heads were almost—but not quite—level. "He dangerous, *zaika*."

Well, everything about this was. "Like you." Still, Nat was pretty sure Ranger wasn't intending to shoot her, or use a straight razor.

The thought that Dmitri might simply *bite,* with those very white, very sharp teeth, was not comforting at all.

He made another short, dismissive noise. "Dima has vested interest in keeping you alive."

For now. Getting into that argument wouldn't solve anything. Nat's shoulders ached; it was a conscious effort to keep them from hovering near her ears. What was Mom thinking right now? Did she know Nat was doing her best?

Probably not. She never had before. "I don't think he's going to hurt me." *And even if he did, it's worth it if it helps Mom.*

There it was, the entire problem reduced to its barest simplicity.

"Lots of different kinds of pain." Dima's expression turned stubborn, and he scowled at her.

Did he think she was unaware of that single, stark fact? "I know."

"Fine." He turned away to glare into the night, a short sharp movement. "But if he *do* hurt you, *zaika moya,* I make him pay."

"You'll just be mad you didn't get to it first." It leapt from her lips, a stinging truth, and Nat crushed the sudden urge to clap a hand over her mouth.

The gangster's shoulders hunched as if she'd struck him, and he swung back to face her, snake-quick. His right hand, half-curled, lifted slightly, and for a moment Nat thought he was about to hit her.

She stepped back hurriedly, onto the creaking porch, and Dmitri studied her. His dark eyes glittered under the incandescent bulb's weak golden shimmer, shadows gathered behind him, and the wind rose sharply, tugging at her coat and ruffling his dark, slicked-down hair.

He didn't speak for a long moment, eyeing her like she'd grown another head. "You think so?" When he moved again, it was to dig in his jacket pocket with his right hand, cupping his left around the cigarette and lifting it to his mouth. "Here." He fished out a small glittering thing, and offered it to her.

Nat peered at his hand, finding only a silvery, metallic oblong. "What is it?"

"Zippo." His fingers flicked. The top of the rectangle opened and a bright brief star of flame bloomed, then died as he snapped it closed. It looked vaguely like Leo's ancient, foreign lighter. "You take it. If you need Dima, you just *poof.*"

Oh, hell. That was worse than *oh, God;* if divinities were real, could some kind of hell be far behind? "That's very nice," she hedged.

"Take it." Another brief beckoning motion. "Christmas gift, *da*? Very useful. Light cigarettes, candle for birthday cake."

"It's really nice of you." Nat jammed her hands deeper in her peacoat pockets. "I'm okay, though."

"*Fuck*sake." The lighter vanished. He was back to snarling; the sudden change was almost comforting. At least when he was being an asshole she knew how to deal with him. "You take cup of coffee from him, but nothing from Dima, huh? Stupid little girl."

"Yes. I really am." If this was what being a divinity was like, Nat didn't think it was such a hot deal. She just got more emotionally exhausted the longer this trip went on, and it wasn't anywhere near finished yet. "But it's not entirely my fault. I know you hate my mother, but she might have been trying to protect me in some weird way. And I can see why. I'm sorry you'll have to find a hotel for tonight, but it's going to get you what you want, right? A chance to kill me and take your heart back. So just go, please."

The stars faded one by one as the weather to the north moved in. She liked that, how you could see something coming out here even at night. The nail-paring moon slipped behind a veil. The metallic tang of snow sharpened, and somewhere close by were naked branches rattling together. That probably meant water; on the prairie, everything dug in to find moisture and hide from the wind.

"Fine." Dmitri took another drag, and a plume of smoke was torn into pieces, snatched from his mouth. "But I come back at dawn to fetch *zaika moya*. And if you not with him all safe and sound, I burn his place down. *All* his places, and him inside them."

The gangster hopped down the steps, landing stiff-legged, and stalked for the corner of the building. Nat pushed her hands even deeper into her pockets, and shivered. Not with the cold, no.

Because she believed him.

YOUR OWN GROUND

Inside, it was much warmer. Ranger leaned hipshot against the wall near two pay phones that probably even worked; the arched doorways to the restrooms past him were stenciled neatly with BUCKS and DOES. The light was kind, burnishing a ghost of stubble on his dark cheeks and catching in his short springy hair. "Guessin' he ain't happy."

"I don't think *happy* is a word that ever applies, to him." Nat's lower back was damp, despite the cold. Maybe divinities only sweated when stressed. "Was he always like that? Or do you know?"

He nodded. "Never did meet a contented horsethief. You ready?" *I don't think I am.* "Of course."

"You can relax." Ranger didn't move, still eyeing her. "I ain't gonna do anything ungentlemanly. I just figured you'd have a question or two, since it's not your mama comin' out to collect. And, well." A slow grin stretched his sculpted lips. "A man always likes welcomin' springtime."

Oh, boy howdy and beans. Was she blushing? Nat hoped not. She settled her backpack strap a little higher on her right shoulder. "I guess that's more my mother than me. Once I get what Baba de Winter wants, she'll make Mom better. At least, that's the deal."

The song on the jukebox ended, and a hush settled over the bar's interior. It happened sometimes in crowds, but raised gooseflesh on her every time.

There was a hiss of static, the juke changing songs, and a woman began crooning about who was sorry now. It sounded like Connie Francis, or maybe Patsy Cline.

Did country singers have a divinity?

"That the deal?" Ranger's eyebrows had lifted. "Huh. I see."

Did he think she was lying? "Unless Dmitri kills me first, I guess."

"Now that ain't right." He peeled himself away from the wall, a restless, liquid movement. "Man ain't a man if he goes liftin' a hand to a woman. Not that I ain't but met some what deserve it, but still. Now tell me, Miss Drozdova, do you like drivin'?"

"I'm not that good at it." She had her license, sure, but Mom's old Léon-Bollée wasn't exactly modern and why bother wheedling permission to take it anywhere when there was the bus system, let alone the subway? Not to mention it had been out of commission for at least a month before Mom's collapse, despite all Leo's babying. "But I can. If I have to."

The fact that she did like it, and maybe secretly longed to get behind the wheel of Dmitri's car just to see how fast it could really go, was beside the point.

"You just sit and look at the scenery, ma'am." He tipped his head, turned smartly, and set off; there was a small soft sound and that dove-gray hat appeared, swinging from his hand. "I'll do the rest."

They plunged into the crowd; the bar was still full and conversation reaching highway-roar levels. Nobody paid any attention to him or Nat, but nobody jostled them either. There was probably some sort of magic involved in that, too, and suddenly Nat's head hurt. Stumbling from one place to the next, trying like hell not to put a foot wrong—oh, it was what she'd been doing all her life, but this time the stakes were so high and she was already so tired.

Not physically, though. Her body blurred and buzzed with bright good strength. She was exhausted *inside,* and wondered if Mom's illness was infecting her too.

By the time Ranger opened the front door, ushering her out with a slight bow, the black car was nowhere to be seen in the parking lot. There was an angry screech in the distance, rubber tires smoking on pavement, but the wind whisked the noise away. Cold winter night swallowed her and the cowboy, who jammed his hat firmly atop his head. It didn't look like it would dare come off even in a tornado, he was so self-possessed.

Boots crunching in gravel and frozen weeds, he headed straight for a cream-colored pickup just this side of antique. Heavy chrome fenders glowed under the failing starlight, its bed was a wide pale plain, and its wheel wells bulged cheerfully. The passenger side door opened silently; he didn't need to unlock it.

Who would steal a divinity's car, after all? Nat clambered up onto a seat upholstered with faded blue stripes, glad she didn't need help.

Although old, the truck was lovingly maintained. It probably ran on the same thing Dmitri's did, and she wondered why Mom's Léon-Bollée needed gas and Leo's constant fixing.

Ranger climbed in, turned the key, and the engine woke with a deep happy sound, much softer than the black car's aggressive purr. The dash was simple—an old-fashioned button radio, speed and RPM dials, no odometer, and an orange bar to show which gear it was in.

"She rides smooth," Ranger said. "Sometimes I miss wagons, but not often."

Just how old are you? It was probably impolite to ask. Probably stupid to ask where they were going, too. There weren't seatbelts, but it wasn't like it mattered, was it? She folded her hands in her lap and watched the headlights blaze into life; the edge of the lot was revealed in pitiless detail, sad weeds straggling to reclaim the space where heavy human traffic wore everything down.

He cut the wheel hard right, they bumped onto pavement, and she tried her best to stare straight ahead. *Spend the night* covered a lot of ground. He wasn't going to be "ungentlemanly," but what did that even mean? She'd agreed to it, though, and it was for Mom.

She just hoped it wouldn't hurt too much. What else would she have to pay to collect after this?

"Not one for talkin', are you." Ranger's tone was thoughtful.

"Mouth shut, ears open." One of Mom's favorite sayings, whenever Nat had questions. "Especially since I don't know what I'm doing."

"Nobody really does, darlin'. Not even us. Ol' Ma Winter has you thinking she'll fix your mama? She said that specifically?"

Thinking she'll fix her? "That was my understanding," Nat said, carefully. "I get what Baba wants, and Mom gets out of hospice."

Ranger glanced at her, back at the road. "Hospice."

"It's where they stick you when they're sure you'll die." It was a night for being horrified at her own words; Nat had to squeeze her fingers to keep her hand from flying to her mouth to trap them.

"But . . ." A sidelong glance, his eyes gleaming like Dmitri's. He wasn't overpoweringly dangerous in the way the gangster was, but that contained, quiet thoughtfulness was far more concerning. It could break at any moment. "Maria ain't been teaching you what to do? She ain't told you a thing?"

"No. I think she was trying to protect me." As soon as she said it, Nat was painfully struck by how illogical it sounded. Dmitri was an asshole, but he was right; if Nat was in the hospital, she couldn't see Maria Drozdova taking the time to visit more than perfunctorily, let alone go on a cross-country road trip. "All this is terrifying, you know?"

"It's *natural*. And it's a mama's job to make sure her daughter's ready. 'Specially when it's one of ours." He shook his head, his hat a pale blur. "Still, I ain't got no children yet and my own daddy wasn't no prize, so reckon I can't throw stones. But your mama's from elsewhere, miss. She ain't gonna get better."

Thanks for that vote of confidence. "I haven't done too badly so far." Which was true, at least so far as Nat could see. "I went to a party at Jay's—"

"New York Jay?" Ranger's laugh, deep and soft, filled the truck cabin. "He still givin' parties? Well, wonders never cease."

"And I dealt with a flying van and a sorcerer, and then we were driving and there was a robbery in a convenience store—" Nat shuddered. Mom would have known what to do with the poor bleeding store clerk. "And then there was Officer Friendly, but I took care of him."

"Oh, Friendly? He ain't nothin' like his name, the old . . . Well, he's been after that horsethief forever, like that damn coyote after a roadrunner. Not gonna catch him anytime soon." Ranger feathered the brake as they approached a shallow curve running alongside what would be a creek in summer but was now merely a deeper collection of branch-choked shadows. "You're doin' right well, I didn't mean to imply otherwise. I just gotta say, Maria ain't gonna get better. It ain't the way of things, and standin' in the way of things never did nobody no good."

Nat stared at the cone of headlight glow, wondering if the entire trip was going to be riding in cars with strange cryptic men. Faded yellow dashes stuttered by on one side, a faint ghost of a white stripe on the other, worn away by time and almost lost under hard frost.

What if . . . just say, as a thought experiment, what if the Heart wasn't enough, or if Nat was too late? Mom was already so thin, and Nat had put off visiting Baba for two whole months.

Not only had Nat ruined her mother's life by being born, but she might have outright killed her just by being stupid and afraid. And what did it say about Nat Drozdova that the prospect of being too late filled her with horror, yes, but also with a deep rose-red stinging feeling that could only be described as *relief*?

"So you're here for what your mama left." Ranger nodded, the crown of his hat almost brushing the top of the cab. "Can't say as I'm sad to get rid of the bargain. Man keeps his own secrets, a'course, but others' tend to weigh on you. Come morning I'll lend you my horse, and he'll take you to the Well."

Is that an euphemism? "Okay."

He studied the road as if it were the most interesting thing in the world. "You're mighty agreeable."

"I'm trying to be."

"Are you? From over here it looks like you're scared stiff." His chin dipped slightly; the whites of his eyes glowed in the dashboard light. "Not that I blame you. Horsethief ain't easy company."

"Why do you call him that?"

"Used to be that's what his kind was. Not even an outlaw, 'cause outlaw's got a code." Ranger gave her another one of those sidelong, considering glances. "Shot more than one in my day. That bother you?"

Everything about this bothers me. "No."

"Friendly's worshipers probably put a bullet in man who looks like me without pausin', and feel just as easy about it." For the first time, a harsh edge of anger crept into Ranger's tone. "Sometimes I think about that while I'm ridin'."

"*That* bothers me." Nat couldn't think of what else to say. Staring your own moral relativism in the face left little in the way of polite conversation or stones to throw at other people's glass houses. "It shouldn't be that way."

"But it *is*. I could wear another body. I could look like gat-damn Gary Cooper, pardon my French, ma'am, but I keep this form because back then on the range, most of my boys looked just like this; plenty still do. They didn't ask for much, still don't." He moved slightly, rolling his window down a little. The familiar wind-rush rode a trickle of fresh cold night air into the cab. "Just a place to stand. Not in the way of things, but on your own ground."

Wear another body sounded kind of gruesome. "So nothing ever really changes?" It was easy to talk to this guy, she realized.

Terrifyingly easy.

"Things change all the time." One of his fingers lifted, brushing the truth aside like a windshield wiper. Snowflakes began to star the truck's pale, glowing hood, vanishing almost immediately. "Buffalo get murdered, railroad comes out west, cities grow up, a man marches on a bridge and the whole world shifts a little. Trees get green every year, but it ain't the same green. *They* do the changin', we do the catchin' up."

They probably meant . . . well, humans. Worshipers? Believers? Or, in Dima's terms, the rubes. "But spring was here before."

"Oh, yeah. But your mama's people weren't. Now they're here, and so are you. You're native-grown. Child of the times, Marisol's little sister, Flora's cousin, Eostre's elder, related to White Deer Woman. Many names. Y'all might meet some of your other forms someday." He shrugged. The road looked like it went on forever, but the sky was a lowering lid now and a spatter of sleet touched the windshield. "I ain't like my daddy. You ain't gonna be like Maria."

The only thing worse than his calm certainty was the relief

pouring through her at *that* particular assertion. The snow mixed into sleet, turned to fat driving-hard drops, and he flicked the wipers on.

It was probably time for a subject change. Nat swallowed the lump in her throat. "You keep saying 'your boys.'"

"Oh, Calamity's got the girls." Ranger laughed, a nice mellow sound. "She'd skin me alive, I took one."

Calamity. Well, there was a name. "Does . . . did my mother have them? Followers?"

"Force of nature don't need 'em, not the way I might, or New York Jay might. Though they're nice enough, everybody can use a little extra pep every now and again." The truck slowed; a white stone fence post loomed in the darkness and they banked, taking a turn so smoothly she barely felt the deceleration. "Here we are."

The headlights splashed across a small blue ranch house, touched the edge of a red-painted barn with white trim. Split-rail fences stood patiently under cold rain fast mixing with snow again. There was a line of cedars marching along one side of the house, probably a windbreak; it even had a wide white wraparound porch.

"It's pretty." And it was; she could even see window boxes covered for the winter and large pots that probably held ornamental plants in the summer. "What's in the barn?"

"Horses, of course. And *the* horse. But that's for tomorrow." He parked neat as you please near the porch front, where the cracked driveway turned into repaired wooden steps. "I gotta ask you, though . . ."

Here it comes. Nat braced to pay penance for the sin of thinking maybe it would be a relief if her mother died. "What?"

Dmitri might say atonement was for the rubes. Maybe a divinity of gangsters was a sociopath who didn't need or want guilt, and Mama had sent Nat to the sisters and priests to keep her from turning out that way.

"Well, it's been a long time." Ranger paused, cutting the engine and pulling the key free, scratching at his forehead under the hat brim. "Do you—now, you can tell me no, ma'am—but do you play Scrabble?"

What? "I never have," Nat admitted. Mom didn't like games she couldn't easily win, even if she could be persuaded to play gin sometimes, and Leo preferred chess to just about anything else. "But I'd love to learn."

NIGHT DRIVING

He fucking hated the sticks, but at least on the long straight roads Konets could open up the engine and scream along blacktop, headlights a violent white smear and the wheel-yoke vibrating against his fingertips. And at least he could nestle a bottle of Southern Comfort in his lap while he smoked and pressed the accelerator even harder.

No little girl in the passenger seat, hugging her backpack and radiating that tempting scent of prey. No disdainful little silences, none of her cold shoulder, none of her visible, vibrating unease.

When she relaxed he had to keep the window open and the smokes burning, because the scent of small white flowers and fresh green threatened to make his face crack into a grin. Masha's breath had been almost torrid, heavy with black mud and callused hands against a plow's handle; her daughter was gentler.

Still, there was a little fire in the girl. *You'll just be mad you didn't get to it first.*

Dima snarled, the yoke slipping and the tires grabbing as he passed an arthritic red pickup truck on one of the ruler-straight roads, probably scaring some cowshit-covered rube into cardiac arrest. There were a surprising number of prowlers out at night in the country, even in foul weather—nothing else to do but drink, drive, and tip large sleeping mammals left out in cold fields, after all.

So high and mighty, her hands in her pockets like even a cigarette lighter was below her notice. No matter that it was an honor any of his nephews or uncles might kill for, a way to summon the luck of the best thieves.

In a mood like this he could easily visit one of his silent ones, the nephews who took payment in gold for the biggest thefts of all. Rifle, garrote, knife—those were acceptable, and then there were the *crème de la crème*, the ones who could make it seem an accident. A slip in the shower, a gas leak, the prick of a hypodermic between toes, there were a thousand and one ways to remove an obstacle and collect payment for the theft of a life.

Even among Friendly's followers—or Ranger's—there were those who paid him secret homage, and normally Dima was gleeful at the thought. But it stood to reason they could report back to their *other* masters, and the thought that the fucking cowpoke with his drawl and his aw-shucks façade was probably making a girl laugh right now, or holding her hand, or doing any of a hundred other things did not please Dima Konets.

Not at all.

He drifted into the oncoming lane, staring at bright diamond jewels. The approaching car swerved, lifted as if it meant to fly amid silver flashes of freezing rain, and he caught a glimpse of the Cold Lady walking along the shoulder, her fishbelly skin bright but her great shock of dark hair blending into the night.

Maybe she was watching. Waiting to see what he'd do.

So just go, please.

Stupid, cringing girl. Stupid Dima, offering something for free. Or maybe she was a wise little girl, knowing there was a price for everything.

Even for dreaming.

His lip lifted again as he streaked onto the interstate, frozen droplets hammering the windshield, and on a far hill a flash of drenched starlight showed a dim shape standing still, back turned to the wind. A man on a horse, his hat pulled low and his fringed jacket running with rain, the big black horse with its hellfire eyes flicking its fine plumed tail. Holding the high ground, watching the flocks of cars move through the secret veins of night. And in every icy pellet striking the car there was a fingertip-scratch of an iron-haired beldam, an impatient drumming.

Others were watching, too. Dima's smile stretched, turned lipless. The girl might well scream if she saw him now, the least attractive of his faces turning savage as he flickered through his many forms, jammed the accelerator to the floor, and bit the glass neck of the bottle, crunching slivers between his teeth before taking another hit from a cold, burning mouth as sharp as his own.

DANGEROUS GIRL

Sleet and restless almost-snow rattled in soft waves against the windows while Ranger made hot chocolate in a dented tin saucepan and Nat read the Scrabble rules. They played for hours at a kitchen table covered with yellow gingham cloth; Nat took off her peacoat, hanging it on the back of a wooden chair while her backpack rested at her feet. The house was roomy enough, an open floor plan and big bluff wooden furniture grazing on mellow hardwood starred with antique throw rugs.

Another fire pop-crackled in the living room's big stone fireplace, and sometime past midnight he pointed her down a hallway.

"Couple rooms and a bath, sleep where you like." He paused, a shadow of stubble growing on his ebon cheeks. "All the doors lock, ma'am. I'll be on t'other side of the house, unless I go out."

A yawn teased at Nat's throat; she denied it. "Did we just have to wait for daylight?"

"You looked like you could use some real sleep." His smile was slow and conspiratorial. "And maybe it'll do that horsethief good to roam the highway and think about things a bit. He's dangerous, but you ain't no slouch yourself."

"How many points would *horsethief* get me?" Nat shook her head. It felt good to smile, as if he was a friend. "I'm not dangerous, though."

"As many points as you want, ma'am. Ain't been beat like that since the Scribe came through last; good thing I'm not a sore loser."

"Good thing." Nat found herself grinning like an idiot, and she offered her hand once more, unsure of the etiquette. "Thanks. I mean, I just . . . thank you."

He shook gravely, his broad pinkish palm warm and sure against hers. "Wasn't what you were expecting?"

"Not really?" She might have winced, but it was impossible to doubt his calm. "Everything so far's been awful."

"I'll bet." He nodded, examining her face, and let go, stepping back. "But, little Nat, you *are* dangerous. Want to know why?"

"Certainly." Her other arm was full of her peacoat and backpack; she shifted them as she leaned against the wall. "If you can tell me."

"Springtime." He scratched at his forehead again; a faint indentation showed skin remembering where his hat rested. "Prettiest bit of the year, everyone says. New green, new life everywhere, sap risin' and the foals friskin'. But spring's also when a man gets tempted to thinkin' he can be somethin' he ain't. And say a girl comes by—a pretty girl, almost a woman, with that flash in her eye and that certain way of talkin', and a man with black and bloody hands starts thinkin' he can be somethin' else."

Was he talking about Dmitri, or himself? Or Leo? Or any guy? "Can't you?" She kept coming back to that same essential question. "Or, you know, can divinities? Be something else?"

"Maybe, darlin'. With enough reason, I reckon anyone can. But what's enough?" Ranger shrugged, easily. "You remember that, dealin' with that horsethief. He got his temper, and it's a foul one. But you ain't got to put up with it."

It would be nice not to, yeah. "It's just for a little while." Nat hugged her coat. "Did you play Scrabble with Mom?"

"Oh hell no, pardon my French, ma'am. Maria never slowed down long enough for that. Don't take it wrong, but I like you better. Good night, Nat."

"Good night, sir." A weight she hadn't even known was still present fled Nat's shoulders.

I like you better. There was a first time for everything.

She couldn't stop smiling while she brushed her teeth—did divinities get cavities?—in a painfully clean bathroom where the mirror was losing its silver. The good feeling didn't fade when she carefully turned back the pine-log bed with a red checkered counterpane in the smallest bedroom at the end of the hall, though she did make sure the door locked, just as he said it would. She curled up under blankets, her head on a cloud-soft pillow, breathing in a ghost of someone else's fabric softener, and might have listened more to the freezing, hissing, pouring rain.

She wasn't really tired. Not physically.

But sleep came like a sinkhole suddenly swallowing a busy street; Nat Drozdova dreamed of galloping hooves, rolling grassland, and thunder sweeping before storms that filled gullies with foaming water.

And that wasn't all.

She dreamt the acrid scent of gunsmoke, too, lingering among the lowing of terrified animals and thin threads of blood from gaping wounds; somewhere in the night a man with gentle hands was riding while the storm brushed hard against the prairie, and anyone out in the dark taking what they shouldn't felt a cold barrel-end pressed to the back of his skull.

NO HELMET

Freezing rain turned to sleet and then to a cold, driving drizzle that took the edge off the ice before sunup. It was uncharacteristically warm for near-Christmas on the prairie—but only by a few degrees.

Dawn rose bloody through freezing veils; a black car growled up a long paved driveway with gravel at its edges, sliding sideways to a tire-smoking stop before a trim blue ranch house and its big red barn. A sleek dark shape rose from the driver's side, and as the gangster slammed the heavy door he lit one of his cigarettes with a fingertip flicker, exhaling a cloud of perfumed smoke.

The barn door was open, and there was a gleam in the hay-scented dimness that resolved into Ranger, his gray hat tipped slightly back as he pushed a gleaming, low-slung black motorcycle into a chilly winter morning full of thin gray light. Chrome gleamed on handlebars and exhaust pipes, but even the most ardent historian of two-wheeled beasts would be hard-pressed to name its make or model.

Dmitri leaned against the black car's trunk, a sardonic smile lifting one corner of his thin mouth. "Now *this* the kind of horse I know all about."

"You ain't gonna ride him, sport." Ranger heeled the kickstand down with a heavy click and straightened, wiping his lean dark hands on a bright red shop rag. Behind him, an equine mutter rose, animals scenting something inimical on the breeze. "Have yourself some fun last night?"

Dmitri's shrug was loose and catlike; still, he made sure both his hands were kept plainly in view. "Where is she?"

"Probably finishin' her coffee." Ranger folded the rag, neatly and exactly, and used its pad to buff an invisible speck of dust from the motorcycle's shining flank. "Nice girl. Nicer than Maria, that's for damn sure."

The gangster's nostrils flared slightly. The cigarette's burning tip, pale in fresh daylight, brightened as he inhaled.

"Only gonna say this once," the cowboy continued. "You do that lady any harm, horsethief, and your kind won't be welcome anywhere I have a say."

"Not welcome in cowshit country anyway, *Ranger*." Heavy sarcasm tinted the last word. "You think you dazzle little Drozdova into giving you a pretty jewel, eh?"

"I wouldn't take that gewgaw if you paid me." Ranger finished his cleanup, tucking the rag in his jacket pocket. "Not worth the belly-gripe, and not worth the effort either."

Dmitri straightened, dark eyes burning coal-hot and his shoulders swelling like a cobra's hood, but there was a faint sound and the blue house's door opened.

Nat Drozdova stepped onto the white wraparound porch, buttoned into the too-big woolen coat, her green knit cap pulled firmly over shower-damp buckwheat-honey hair and her wide, slightly cat-tilted eyes glowing. Her ever-present backpack was snugged high on one slim shoulder. There was a faint happy flush on her smooth cheeks, but it faded when she saw Dmitri, and her mouth drew down at each corner. Her breath touched winter chill, a gift given to the world, and the raw edge of the northern wind, meeting no obstruction as it poured for miles across saturated prairie enjoying a sudden thaw, softened just a touch more.

Just enough.

"Hey." She hopped down the steps, light as a linnet, and gave Ranger a tight smile as she edged in his direction. The cowboy even tipped his hat, a slight reflexive movement. "The dishes are drying. I seasoned the cast iron, don't worry."

"I done told you not to worry about that." The cowboy shook his head slightly, and half his mouth tilted up in a smile. "Come on over and meet this fellow; he's ready for a run."

"Wow. He's gorgeous." The sight of the motorcycle brightened her, but she still observed a cautious distance from Dmitri, clearly gauging his mood while he stood very still, the cigarette loosely cupped in his right hand. "Good morning, Dima. Did you find a hotel?"

The gangster's lip twitched, lifting slightly. "It was a good night, *zaika*. I think I take you in *my* car today, though."

"Can't." Ranger trailed his fingertips over a handlebar, a gentle, calming touch. "This fellow will take Miss Drozdova where she needs to go. That was the agreement with Maria. Nothin' in it about no horsethief hitchin' a ride."

"It's what he agreed to with my mother." Nat stopped dead, watching Dmitri's face. "And what you want isn't there. It's just the next piece of the puzzle."

"You expect me to believe that pile of—"

"Horsethief don't believe nothin', since he can't be trusted." Ranger eyed the gangster, narrowly. "You watch your mouth, Konets."

The gangster's gaze rested on Nat. She hugged herself, a little girl lost in that coat—a man's jacket, blurring her outline. It probably felt like protection; growing up in that little yellow house with Maria, she'd need all the safety she could find. Oh, there were no marks on the girl, certainly.

Not physical ones. But a thief's gaze was sharp, especially when there was a secret to be ferreted out or a treasure discovered.

Dima stalked away from his car, bearing down on her with catlike, weaving steps. Ranger tensed, but Nat stood very still, chin lifted, the breeze warming as he approached.

A long drag on the incense-smelling cigarette, and when he spoke, the words rode stinging smoke. "You think you escape Dima, huh?"

"My mother did." She shook her head, a quick flicker of movement. "But I wouldn't try right now, Dmitri. It would be stupid, and I'm not."

"No. You are smart little *zaika*." His nose wrinkled slightly. Bright clear dawnlight showed traces of bloodshot in his gaze, and his jaw was rough with dark stubble. "Lots going on behind those big eyes, *neh*?"

"I promised to bring something to Baba de Winter." Nat took a deep breath. "But I didn't promise to *give* it to her, you know."

His stillness was absolute for a few moments. When he spoke, it was softly. "Careful. You sounding like me, now."

"It's yours, isn't it? It's only right." She studied him earnestly, and Ranger coughed, turning his head to scan the horizon. "I know you hate her. But *I'm not her.*" There was a faint edge of surprise to the words, too.

Knowing the truth was not like speaking it. "No." The gangster nodded, a fractional movement. "No, *devotchka moya*. You are not."

"Okay." As if that settled anything, she took a sideways step, then another. Dima was a statue again, only the drifting smoke betraying any life. "I, uh, I've never driven a motorcycle before. But I'm thinking that probably doesn't matter, huh?"

"It don't." Ranger didn't look at her, watching the gangster for any twitch, no matter how small. "Just get on, ma'am. He'll take you where you need to go and bring you back. That's the deal."

Dmitri turned on his heel, stalking back for his car. "He better." It was a soft, vicious mutter. "In one piece, too."

"Okay." Nat shrugged, loosening her backpack, and had a little trouble getting her left arm through the opposite strap. Ranger helped, then lifted the 'cycle and popped the kickstand up. "No helmet. Great."

"Don't need it, Nat. Won't let you fall accident-like." Ranger held the bike steady while she swung one long lithe leg over, and Dmitri settled against the back of his own vehicle again, making a small scoffing noise. "You'll do just fine."

The motorcycle shivered, accepting her slight weight. Its engine caught with a deep throbbing, settling into a chained growl. Nat flinched but reached forward, slim fingers clasping the handlebars. Her boots—too heavy for such graceful feet—settled in their proper places, and Ranger leaned forward, his mouth moving. Encouragement or last-minute directions, who could tell?

The man in the fringed dun jacket stepped back. The motorcycle rolled forward, glossy tires pawing lightly at cracked driveway. Nat bit her lip, and she glanced at Dmitri, a flash of wide dark almost-terrified eyes.

He tensed, but the bike took a deep coughing breath and picked up speed. Now it blurred, flickering; chrome, wheels, and glossy low-slung sides stretched like taffy. A proud black head lifted, a white blaze like lightning glowed between two intelligent eyes sparkling with red hellfire; long clean limbs stretched and iron-shod hooves bit, striking colorless stars from pavement.

The girl's body dropped into the rhythm of a canter—and what girl doesn't love a horse, doesn't already know how to ride? The knowledge lurks in them, breath and bone, part of an ancient compact between big grazing beasts and the women who patiently tamed them, knowing brutality might work for a short while but true partnership can never be forced.

Horses remember, too.

The canter became a gallop. There was a roar of displacement, shining black flanks bunched, and the stallion lunged forward. A black streak boiled innocent air, bearing away a slight figure, honey hair streaming from under her cap.

They vanished with a sound like tearing cloth. Ranger hooked his thumbs over his belt, a tuneless whistle escaping his lips.

Dmitri finished his cigarette, dropping the filter. A boot-toe glittered as he ground it out, a ruthless twist of his ankle. "You let Mascha ride your horse?"

"No," Ranger said quietly. "Can't say as I did." The two men were silent for a long moment. "Might be a while. Y'all want some coffee?"

There was no such thing as peace between two such diametrically opposed beings, but a cease-fire was sometimes possible, sometimes allowed.

Dmitri nodded. "*Da.*" Then, grudgingly, he added one more word. "*Spasiba.*"

BLACK HORSE, CHERRY TREE

The handlebars stretched into reins, but were stiff metal at the same time. It was unsettling, feeling two such different things at once. There was the steady hum of an engine and the low sweet wind in her ears like riding her pink childhood bike; at the same time there was a gallop, jarring until something deep in her bones woke with a twitch and the rhythm of hoof-fall and brief lift melted her into a steady, ever-changing equilibrium.

It was just as wonderful as her voracious childhood reading said it would be. *Black Beauty*, *Thunderhead*, even *The Black Stallion*, not to mention the magazines at the library with red-jacketed girls in jodhpurs smiling as they clung to saddles.

Don't be silly, Natchenka. No horses in the city.

Oh, but she'd dreamed, and she'd longed, and once she was done with all this, maybe she could return here and learn.

The black horse ran as if he felt her joy; he tossed his head and uncoiled in a leap over strings of barbwire holding the road back from prairie. Under an endless winter sky they galloped, clods spattering from those sharp, sharp hooves; the horizon blurred and green raced under iron shoes. The cold wind turned soft, then warm, and Nat's lungs burned as the sunlight changed, a flood of gold.

The horse wheeled to the right, and there was a valley with bright icy-blue water foam-chuckling over rounded stones at its bottom. Willows reared on either side, their long winter-bare branches whipping past; one cracked close to her cheek and Nat flinched. But the horse neighed like an engine revving and tensed before bulleting forward. He followed the river, leaning first to one side then another to keep his rider from the clutching branches—and that was wrong, it was winter, but now the trees were green.

A stony slope rose before them, the horse leap-climbing surefoot as a shaggy mountain goat, and now the prairie had turned green as well. Tiny dabs of blooming color spattered by too quickly to name the flowers they belonged to. Nat clung to the beast's back, bending low, breathing in a good scent of hay and simmering heat touched with a tang of wild fur and freedom. Strands of black mane brushed her cheeks, a rough caress, and the rhythm wasn't just under her now. It was in her breath, in her bones, in her pounding heart.

Her tiny bipedal self melted into something bigger, becoming a single creature with four hooves thundering as a massive heart churned, her vision flattening until there was a blind spot directly before her and the horizon widened on either side. A tail lifted high and proud, a sweet strong wind combing a long mane—her ears flicked, laid flat, her nose untangling a thousand different shades of grass, brush, flowers, the breeze bringing tales from far away where herds of her kind galloped for the joy of it, knowing no bridle but their own whims.

The footing changed, hoof-falls no longer sinking into sod but cushioned by dry, crumbling stuff. The prairie blurred, bleached and widening until there was nothing but rolling dun sand, the sky bright hot blue with a white coin hanging in its arms.

Now the scents were harsher—the water dove deep, hiding, and there was no grazing. The specter of starvation loomed rib-sharp, an ancient memory in a creature who lived on grass and could find none. Hot sand tickled her nose, burned her deep-heaving lungs, and foam streaked the great beast's glossy black flanks.

I'm sorry, Nat thought. *Oh, I'm so sorry to bring you here.*

The horse arched his neck, slowing to a canter; *he* wasn't sorry. This was the road, this was the journey; besides, there was a dark spot far away, a single break in the monotony of sand and glare.

It hurt to separate. She wanted to stay in that thumping bass forever, a single mote on the back of a rocking sea. There was no isolation among the herd, just the thunder of running and the sudden terror of predator-things with sharp white teeth and cruel slashing claws, the fear of lightning-crack when storms swept the grasslands. And over it all was the deep warm comfort of others like her, pressed flank to heaving flank.

She didn't want to be lonely again.

Now the air was hot, and every step muffled in wind-rippled sand. Nat straightened, regretful, and shaded her eyes with one aching hand. There was a thin pressure-stripe across her palm—not quite a cut, but a deep indentation.

The horse shook his massive head again, and she hurried to clasp the reins again. He turned slightly, approaching the shadow in a curve rather than head-on, and after a short while of jogtrot she realized it was a tree.

A cherry tree, to be precise, its blossom-laden branches raised in heavy defiance of this sudden desert and its blurring, devouring heat. It was the only shade around, and the horse smelled a deep mineral tang of water.

Or did she? Impossible to decide.

He slowed to a walk. How long had she clung to his back? There was no telling.

The cherry tree shadowed a small curved stone wall. No, it was something else—a well, hiding in the liquid-lacy shade. Pale blossoms moved gently, releasing tiny petals; the horse melted underneath her until a motorcycle's tires dug into sand and he plunged into relief under the branches.

The well was a ramshackle affair, its red shingled roof slightly tilted off-true. A winch, probably rusted into immobility, stuck drunkenly from one side, and dried moss clung between the stacked gray stones.

The motorcycle bumped to a stop, and sagged on its springs.

They had arrived.

DESERT WELL

S he was almost afraid to dismount, and it took two tries before she could figure out how to make the kickstand go down. Her arms ached, and her thighs quivered slightly. Cherry petals melted in midair or vanished into the sand. It was like standing inside a snow-globe, except for the dry heat reaching into her sinuses and rasping at her throat.

Magic. Right? She turned, peering out of the tree's skirt-shade; nothing but more sand, as far as the eye could see. Bright yellow dunes, starving-blue sky, the sun a fierce white circle, and the tree with its almost-black bark and creamy blossom. Everything so bright, so intense, so *real* like the heavy energy hanging on Baba de Winter, on Coco, on Dmitri and Ranger.

And on Mom, before she got sick. Nat was just a pale copy, but that didn't matter. She stuffed her cap in her peacoat pocket, unbuttoning the heavy wool. It was too hot.

"Well," a deep soft voice said, quietly. "Here we are."

Nat whirled, her hair falling free and tumbling in waves. No time for a braid, too busy washing the dishes from Ranger's breakfast—crispy bacon, fat-rich sausages, melting tomatoes, golden cornbread, thick black coffee, whole milk, bright tangy orange juice, too much food for two people to consume. Strangely, though, there hadn't been any leftovers.

And she hadn't been truly hungry, though the *taste* was good, and filling in its own way.

I read about fairy food. Was it all rocks and twigs? She stared at the motorcycle.

He'd shifted into a horse again, the reins caught on the saddle's high pommel, and regarded her sidelong. The red pinprick in his big dark eye was bright and rich as the rest of this place, and his sweating flanks gleamed just like the cherry flowers.

A talking horse. Okay. "Here we are," she echoed, and almost cringed at her own stupidity. "Thank you. For bringing me."

"An honor to bear the Drozdova." His lips moved, but they bore no relation to the voice, and she wondered if she was just on a really intense drug trip brought on by stress and the alcoholic bite in Ranger's coffee. "There's the Well. Haven't been here in a long time."

"Did you . . . did you bring my mother?" *Before I was born?*

"Her? Oh, no. Not at all." He shook his long equine head, a braying laugh escaping those flexible lips. His mane floated and his tail flicked, settled. "But I know what she left here. The Cup is in the Well. You'll have to drop the bucket."

Bucket was clearly not capitalized. The stress laid on certain words was audible, and she wondered how a horse could make it so clear. "If you know what she left here, then you probably know—"

"Where you should go next? Oh, yes." An equine snort somehow managed to convey amusement. "But you should look into the depths, and bring out what she left before I tell you what I know."

When you say it that way, I'm not sure I want to. The sheer unreality—here she was in the middle of winter, in a shimmerhot magical desert, talking to a horse that was also a motorcycle— threatened to pound her heart into pieces and her hands into shaking. "I'm going to see something there. Right?"

"Silly question." The horse's tail flicked, and that red gleam in his pupils strengthened. "It's the *Well*."

Yeah. She wished she hadn't worn Leo's coat now; the breeze was like standing next to an open oven despite the tree's shelter. "You realize all of this is really weird, right?"

"What's normal?" The horse's withers twitched, and he shook his glossy, cascading mane, obviously impatient with her reluctance. "Do what you came to do, Drozdova. I long to run again."

What *was* normal, indeed? Especially for a girl raised in a little yellow house by a divinity, a girl the cats talked to, a girl who was dressed by Coco and who danced with Jay, a girl who took a ride in a flying van or a low-slung black car driven by a god of gangsters and thieves? A girl who had basically told Officer Friendly, with the fleshy bulbs on his forehead and his big pink nose, to fuck off?

A girl who had played Scrabble with a god of cowboys and ridden a big black horse-motorcycle to this magical fucking desert, too. Couldn't forget that.

So Nat squared her shoulders and cautiously approached the Well. The closer she got, the more disrepair she saw. There were gaps in the curved rock walls; the winch was almost a solid mass of rust. The wooden bucket dangling above its throat was pierced by daylight; it couldn't possibly bring any water up.

Maybe it's not water down there, Nat. A shiver ran up her sweating back; the backpack straps dug into her shoulders even through the coat, as if everything in there suddenly weighed more.

The prepaid cell phone might short out around magic, who knew? She probably wouldn't get any service bars out here, either.

Wherever *here* was.

She laid her hand on the well's stone lip. It was disturbingly warm, smooth as satiny flesh, and the horse shifted behind her, one hoof digging through sand. Nat risked a glance over her shoulder, but the big beast was in the same place, still watching her sidelong, tail moving lazily to ward off nonexistent flies.

There was a metallic screech. Nat flinched, but it was just the handle attached to the crossbar, flakes of rust falling like the cherry petals as it ground into motion. The bucket dropped, air whistling through its holes—it would probably disintegrate when it hit.

Nat leaned over the waist-high lip, and peered into the Well.

The shaft went down forever, but there was a circular blue ripple at the bottom, a growing, glowing lens. Her eyes stung briefly, whether from hot sand or something she wasn't supposed to see.

This time, Nat decided, she wouldn't shout a silly question. She'd simply watch what was shown. The blue circle swelled, rushing up the sides of the well. Either that or she fell in without moving.

It was, she found out, terrifying either way.

STORM-BORN

Maria Drozdova, *propped on a mountain of snowy pillows, hunched over her distended belly. Her cheeks gleamed with water-beads, golden curls stuck to her damp flawless skin, and her bare knees, pale-soft and dimpled, trembled as she clasped them.*

A man hesitated, hovering uncertainly at the bedside. It was indeed the largest bedroom in the little yellow house, but there was no collection of bright glass bottles on the windowsill and the potted orchids were not yet tangling over the dresser. The plants hanging from ceiling hooks had not achieved even half their current luxuriousness, and were not starred with eternal blossom either. The window was full of the thin pale light of first spring, fairest and coldest, and cords stood out on the Drozdova's slim neck as she pushed, *a massive effort wringing a body too small for it.*

A steady stream of imprecations in the language of the old country fell from her ruddy lips, and that great belly twitched like a live thing.

Strictly speaking, it was. Or at least, it contained one.

Leo—for so it was, much younger and with a full crop of dark hair, stubble upon his handsome cheeks—leaned over to help, to bring a pillow up, to do something, anything for her, but one of her narrow pale hands flashed and he staggered back.

"You," she hissed, panting between great wringing efforts. "You did *this to me."*

He could have pointed out that it took two and that she *had selected* him, *but Leo Mishkin's mouth was sealed, and he could only rub at his reddened cheek where the blow had landed, staring reproachfully with eyes dark and wide as his daughter's would prove.*

Maybe that gaze was the final straw, for Maria Drozdova screamed, her body twisting against itself once more. The pain was like nothing she had ever experienced, even when invaders tore across her lands and left not only murdered bodies to enrich green life but also scattered metal conveyances and toxic elements rotting in great rusted piles. Her power would cover those terrible twisted hills with vines in its own time—but she had been brought unwilling to this place where the earth itself resisted her, waiting for the one who would come.

The mortals who loved spring in their native land had dragged her across an ocean, selfishly not heeding the pain their faithfulness caused. She longed to strike them down with the fiercest storms she was capable of, howling wind stripping boughs heavy with new leaf, lightning striking over and over, harvests rotting in black mud.

Summer could not ripen what Spring did not allow to germinate. Famine was the least elegant of her weapons, but she was enraged enough to use it.

Another great paroxysm followed upon its siblings' heels, and Leo reeled from the room as the Drozdova's massive, wrecked scream rose afresh.

Daylight thinned, heavy black clouds racing across the sun. Mortals fled the city streets, something older than roads or language speaking in clear imperatives.

Hide, *it whispered,* hide now, for one of the Eternal is angry.

Thunder lumbered after diamond lightning, hailstones formed in the sky's coldest reaches tumbling through successive moisture layers, hard kernels swelling until they were too heavy to fly, icy fists falling earthward to smash whatever they could.

Leo crouched in the kitchen, his big capable hands laced over his head. He cowered against the old oven, cabinets opening and closing like hungry toothless mouths, drawers shaking as their cargoes clattered, voracious blue-white sparks popping from antique outlets, the entire yellow house shaking as its mistress raved and cursed, her voice finally breaking in a long final trailing howl of effort.

The last scream was the most terrible, and hail pounded the Drozdova's new city. The mortals had names for every great storm, of course, but christening came later.

After they had survived its fury.

Silence fell. Leo, trembling, peered upward as if a mortal gaze could pierce the ceiling. His dark eyes rolled like a frightened animal's, and he was sweat-sopping as well. In that thick, exhausted quiet, even the rain did not dare whisper as it fell against the Drozdova's windows.

Not until another cry rose, thin and reedy, carrying the greatest of mysteries from a pair of tiny, brand-new lungs.

I am, the infant proclaimed. I am, I am, I am.

And so it was.

In her bedroom, alone except for a tiny squalling bundle, its tiny legs stiffening and its face purpling with exertion as it howled, Maria Drozdova sagged against the pillows, her eyes burning-full of throbbing red. She stared at the object that had come forth from her, and her fair face was just as ravaged and twisted as its own. The maggot screamed as if it sensed the hungry thing now watching, as if it understood there was no safety in a cold, starving world, as if it already knew what she planned for its tender fragility.

Maria Drozdova reached for a pillow, staring at the tiny, plump-bellied child, perfect and ivory-pale though golden ichor clung in its deep creases. Maria's belly deflated, sealing itself in triangular slices, and at least she did not have the detritus of mortal parturition to deal with.

All she needed was a few more moments. She lifted the snowy-white stuffed square, its linen woven in the old way from clouds and belief.

But there were unsteady footsteps upon the stairs, a man coming to see what his love had wrought. The Drozdova hesitated, shortsighted but intense hatred wrestling with a cold plan promising far more than temporary relief.

When Leo peered through the bedroom door he saw his beloved cradling a small howling child, staring at its furious little face with a curiously blank expression.

"It's a girl," the Drozdova said hoarsely. Her lover staggered, grabbing at the doorway to steady himself. A fear he had not been aware of carrying fled, for who can believe ill when gazing at mother and newborn?

Even one of the Eternal might well hold such a sight sacred, and suspect nothing.

DIFFERENT PROPOSITION

Nat gasped, her thighs hitting the crumbling stone wellside. Bright metal skated under her fingertips, the bucket swung crazily, and her throat was on fire. A flat metallic reek rose from whatever lurked in the bottom of the Well; its gleam brought a mental image of wide shimmering alkaline lakes that would either poison unto death or gripe a mortal so badly they longed for the Cold Lady's touch.

You keep sending me gifts . . . you know I haven't returned a single one, dearest.

The glittering golden goblet shrank as Nat touched it; she grabbed at the Well's crossbar with one hand, leaning on tiptoes. The horse made a low chuckling noise, and as she snatched a golden gleam from the wet, wildly swinging bucket, its shadow fell over her.

Nat stumbled back, vaguely glad her ass was large enough to prove a counterweight. She brought what she'd come to find towards her chest, where its metallic sides quivered like a trapped bird. It changed shape, melting from a gem-encrusted chalice through a few other container-forms before settling in a speckled blue number very much like Ranger's camping gear. Its glaze thickened, the cup became heavier, and glowing golden writing blazed across its side like a cheap special effect before it settled, with an almost-audible thump, into a familiar white coffee mug, its handle a gilt-gleaming unicorn's head, white china sides painted with its golden body.

It's my Cup now, she thought, deliriously, and flinched away from the horse's shadow. The big black beast peered into the well's throat, making a soft *hoom* that echoed all the way down to whatever rippled at the bottom.

Had it been trying to knock her in? She was fairly sure she could climb the crumbling sides, but still. If she hit her head on the way down, it was *goodbye, Nat, don't bother to write.*

Was Leo worrying about her? Was he visiting Mom right now? *You could look again. It would probably tell you.*

Nat clutched the mug close. Her knees failed and met sandy dirt with twin thumps. She wheezed, her lungs deciding they were definitely not okay with this goddamn program, and the golden afternoon turned into stutter-strobes as her eyelids fluttered.

Hoo boy. Helluva ride. "Wow," she managed, turned her head aside, and retched.

"First one's a lulu," the horse agreed. "I thought I was going to have to drag you back."

Sure you did. It wasn't worth arguing about; it just went to show that even if you liked a guy, his horse was a different proposition altogether. "I'm fine." The words wanted to produce another retch, repressed with an acidic burp containing a ghost of Ranger's thick fragrant coffee. "Just a little . . . wow. Huh."

"Good girl." Still, the horse sounded disappointed. "Did you get what you came for?"

More than that. Which I suspect is going to be the rule from now on. "Yeah." She'd read about hypnotic regression and people paying big bucks to supposedly witness their own birth; lucky her getting the show for free.

Her mother's belly torn open in triangular segments, tiny baby-Nat wrenched free, and that familiar cold stare her mother wore . . .

I do not want to fucking think about that right now, thanks.

Nat's arms relaxed; she studied the cup. Nurse Candy's version of her old, smashed-in-a-landfill mug had been exactly right down to the chips and cracks she remembered.

This one was new and utterly unstained, not just a unicorn mug made in a factory somewhere but the very *quintessence* of unicorn mugs, its reality burning like a divinity. There was a stirring in

Nat's backpack, and she knew without having to look that the knife was quivering in its wooden case, sensing another powerful object nearby.

Had Mom stolen them from Baba de Winter too? The cup felt impossibly right in Nat's hands, though, impossibly *good*. And strong.

"Who does this belong to?" She didn't mean to ask aloud, but the horse apparently didn't consider that question stupid. His big, iron-shod hooves landed delicately as he paced towards her; his nose dipped. He sniffed, deeply, warm velvet breath pouring over china mug and trembling hands.

"Smells like yours." There was the equivalent of a shrug in his tone, and his withers twitched to underscore it. "Now we run again. Come, hurry."

Give me a minute. Her legs were still noodle-soft. She traced the small gilt horn rising from the handle with a trembling fingertip, plain uncolored polish chipping free of her nail.

So Mom had hid *Nat's* stuff? Or her own, and now that she was sick it was her daughter's?

You know better, Drozdova. A swift spike of pain lanced Nat's head; she didn't want to think about the implications.

Unfortunately, she was probably going to have to face any and all of them, sooner rather than later.

The backpack's zipper made its old familiar sound and she rummaged, finding a safe place for the mug, wrapped in a pair of clean panties. She was going to have to do some laundry soon—or would she?

Did divinities have laundromats? If she found another Elysium would they wash her underwear? Was the divinity hotel a franchise?

She didn't even know what day it was. Was it Christmas yet?

"Are you finished?" The horse's tail lashed, and it put its head down again to eye her sidelong. "We should run again. Soon. Now."

Christ, give a girl a chance to breathe. Nat's shoulders hunched—what if she saw the man from Jay's party, his nail-punctured hands and feet weeping, striding through this desert? Spending forty days out here might force you to turn sand into bread, or rocks into fish for a hallucinatory crowd.

"I'm going as fast as I can." She was going to have to find a different way to blaspheme, that was for damn sure. "This isn't exactly an everyday occurrence for me."

"Not yet." The horse's laugh was cold foam under a bridge, gathering in rank gobbets as the current swirled.

Nat shivered at the mental image. She zipped everything up, shook the backpack slightly to make sure the contents would settle, and then had to work her clumsy peacoat-laden arms through the straps again. It wasn't a bad bag, and was still giving signal service.

She'd thought of taking it to college, even. But Mom said *what do you need more school for, Natchenka,* and so Nat stayed home.

You agreed to shut her up, Nat, and started saving up for an apartment on the sly. That's when she got sick. You know it.

Did the Cup just belong to the closest Drozdova? Would bringing it back help her mother somehow; was the Heart just something to trade to Baba for . . . what? Protection, maybe against the Cold Lady?

Nat shuddered at the thought. Once she had everything settled and zipped she rose, telling her legs they were just going to have to deal with whatever bullshit was going to happen next since every part of her was along for the ride.

Quite literally.

The horse stamped. His hooves were really very big, and edged with sharp iron, too. One of those heavy feet, thrown out with the force of a long limb behind it, could cut through a skull like a hot blade through butter. His strong, sharp teeth glittered as he pulled back his lips and eyed her, a prey animal with a disconcertingly direct gaze. "Climb into my saddle, Drozdova. There is so much to see."

Nat bounced on her toes slightly, making sure her bag was firmly attached. At least she didn't have to worry about her feet; the boots were holding up to all this bullshit just *splendidly.* "The way out here was pretty," she agreed. "Does it look different going back?"

Another soft, flowing, inhuman laugh. A red spark lit in the horse's pupil again, very far back. It was disturbingly like Dmitri's gaze; if the animal called her *zaika* Nat might very well scream.

"I don't know yet," the horse finally said. "We haven't been. But why go back? I can take you anywhere, beautiful one. All you must do is climb into the saddle and whisper in my ear."

There has to be more to it than that. "That's all?" Nat's forehead wrinkled; she could feel her eyebrows reaching for her hairline.

"That's all." The horse's tone took on a hard edge of glee. "Come, put your foot in the stirrup. I have such sights to show you, Drozdova."

She approached cautiously, hot wind teasing at stray curls falling in her face. Was the horse bigger? How did you ask a magical conveyance to turn itself back into a motorcycle because you were scared of attempting to clamber into a saddle? "You'll have to, you know, bend down a little, please. I'm short."

"Oh, of course." The horse sighed, a strange reverberating noise, and bent its black knees. It lowered itself with ungainly grace, settling with a sound of mechanical springs taking a heavy weight. "Climb aboard and whisper to me. I *long* to run."

Who wouldn't, built like that? Still, Nat hesitated. "Ranger said we come out here, get the Cup, and go back." *That was the deal, right?*

"Certainly." The horse's head bobbed. It watched her very carefully, moving leafshade dappling its coal-gleaming flanks. The sweat was gone; he'd recovered from their initial journey beautifully. "But you are here, and he is *there*. Besides, you need me. I can show you shortcuts."

The heat pouring from the horse was different than the desert's breath—damper, more clinging. The tree's shadow shifted, soft petals sliding lazily on updrafts before descending in slow, gentle arcs.

Great clumps of blossom clung to the dark branches, but she could see no leaves. Outside shady shelter there was nothing but bright yellow sand rolling in waves to distant horizons, a single purple smudge that might be mountains. Was that north?

She couldn't tell. The sun hung almost directly overhead, its gaze hammering endless dunes into submission.

The horse's ears pricked; the bright bloody spot in his eye dilated. "Many shortcuts," he continued, meditatively. "I can show you the edges of the stars' own country, where not even the Eternal have walked. I can show you the past—the rise of empires, great battlefields sown with the dead. I can even show you the tiny events History depends upon, the things only known to the Scribe and his ilk. I can take you anywhere, Drozdova. Simply climb into my saddle, and I will be happy to."

It sounded awfully enticing. She could be part of that galloping herd again, heart almost bursting with joy, loneliness a distant memory. The thunder would swallow her, and who knew? She might slip free and change in midair, her spine extending as her arms creaked and stretched, her face growing longer, longer, and brand-new hooves digging into dirt or flinging small rocks aside as she raced, forever a part, no longer separate.

She took another small, uncertain step towards the horse.

"That's right. Come, escape the pain of your mother's hatred." His lip lifted slightly, and his teeth were just as painfully bright and sharp as Dmitri's.

So even a horse knew Maria Drozdova hated her daughter. Nat inhaled sharply, as if struck; secrets children thought kept forever slice deep when articulated by a stranger. "My mother . . ." The words died in her throat.

"She will eat you, Drozdova. After you bring her what she wants so she can bargain with Baba Yaga to allow the theft of a native-born child." The horse's laugh was low and bitter, its lips moving rubbery over those razorsnap teeth, more fit for shearing flesh than grass. "Nobody told you, and you would not hear if they did."

"You're lying," Nat whispered. Or perhaps she merely thought she did; her lips were numb.

"Besides," the black horse continued, pitilessly, "the starving ones are gathering. And that thief won't hold them from you forever. He might even give you to the hungry shadows, if he gains your trust and the Dead God's Heart."

Starving ones? "Gathering?" The word slurred; Nat sounded drunk. Vodka was a curative in the Drozdova household, but Nat had never been tempted to excess.

Everything lied. Why should she expect a motorcycle-horse with predator's mouth to be any different? Nat swayed. *Don't believe it. Don't believe anything.*

The sense of missing part of a math problem was gone, though. The solution was there, staring smugly at her. A fact laid bare, as big and glossy and real as the horse sidling towards her, its heavy hooves soundless on the grit-sand of centuries.

"The starving ones are like black paper, lacking weight and substance until they feed. Koschei the Deathless has an ancient compact with their cousins, and he feeds them well." The horse chuckled, a slow deep whinny. "*Better consumed than weak,* some say. But you won't have to worry about that with me, little godling. I am of a different breed. Though . . ." He champed, teeth snapping together with deep clicks like billiard balls smashing each other on a field of green felt. Like Dmitri's, in fact; the gangster-god made the same sound when he bit empty air. "I am hungry too. In my own way."

I'll just bet you are. The thought was a slap of cold water, and Nat shrank back, suddenly aware she had drifted close to the beast without meaning to. Her boots crushed the ghosts of spent blossoms; they faded with tiny puffs, melding into the sand. Had this tree filled the entire desert with its shed flowers? Did its roots reach whatever quicksilver fluid was in the Well?

She had the sinking feeling she didn't want to know the answer to either question. "Dmitri said the ones who eat leave divinities alone."

"They know when to fear, yes." The horse shook his large, bony head, and it had stopped sidling. "But you are not quite divine yet, little Drozdova."

Well, that was a relief. Sort of. "What are you hungry for?"

He laughed again. "Climb into my saddle and see. You are small and light, barely a mouthful. I will carry you far indeed."

It would mean she didn't have to ride in the gangster's big black car. But it would also mean taking Ranger's horse, and that would be an ugly way to repay Scrabble at midnight, not to mention cornbread and good coffee in the morning.

Don't take it wrong, but I like you better. So far, Ranger was the only one who ever had. Dima, after all, hated Nat just as much as he hated her mother. Which was at least democratic of him.

Nobody told you, and you would not hear if they did. Well, Dima had asked if Nat thought Maria Drozdova would do this for her daughter if the positions were reversed. Maybe it had even been his edged way of hinting at . . .

It can't be true. Nat's shoulders stiffened. "You can take me back to Ranger. That was the agreement."

The horse's head dipped slightly, rose again. It looked an awful lot like a nod. "He is there and you are here, little one. Surely you realize such an agreement is easily . . . altered."

You know, Darth Vader thought that way, and it didn't work out well for him. Nat found her hands had turned into fists and the sweat was all over her back now, collecting under her arms; even her ankles prickled. Her nape was uncomfortably damp, and her hair, while dry, kept trying to stiffen at the roots.

She'd always thought that was hyperbole. It was another thing entirely to feel her skin crawl and tiny strands all over her body attempting to stand up. They said it was to make you look bigger when faced with a predator.

Her backpack was heavy. A tiny quiver near its bottom was the Knife; the Cup was a steady warmth different than the desert's.

"The agreement was for you to take me back to Ranger." It was a good impression of Mom's *don't you dare try to overcharge me,* deployed on hapless retail workers every time Maria Drozdova wanted to argue the price of something down. Nat's own squirming embarrassment at witnessing each incident was only rivaled by astonishment that it inevitably worked.

But Mom had stopped shopping, retreating into the little yellow house. Growing tired, growing weaker, growing *old,* and watching Nat whenever she was home from work.

Watching her closely. As if waiting for something.

"Are you certain?" The black horse blew out through his lips, and their elastic writhing would have been funny if she hadn't glimpsed the teeth shifting behind them. The horse's head was subtly changed, too, and a shadow of great branching stag-horns lifted into liquid shade. "I can show you so much more, Drozdova. You need not worry about the path before you, or about your mother, ever again."

Nat folded her arms. "I think I'll keep worrying, thank you. Will you honor our agreement?"

"The agreement was between you and He Who Rides, Drozdova. Not with *me*." Another teeth-snap, but the horse was thankfully looking far more horselike again, and less like . . . something else. "I merely do as I'm bid. Come, into the saddle. All you must do is whisper where you wish to go."

Not sure I believe you, thanks. But what else could she do—walk across the desert? She couldn't even guess which direction to start in.

The sun, after all, was stuck at high noon. She didn't know quite how she knew that, but the knowledge was deep, inescapable, and would have been terrifying if she hadn't had so much else to be scared of lately.

Was it bravery if you simply didn't have any choice but to continue?

Nat edged for the beast again. One bright stirrup lay against its glossy side; she kept a nervous watch on the horse's head, but those shadowy horns didn't reappear. A rustle went through the tree, hot silken air caressing its branches. The Well made a soft low sound too, the wind brushing across its top like Leo's trick of making a half-full pop bottle sing two different mournful notes at once.

Nat mounted with a lunge. The horse made a fluid movement; she had to grab for the reins. He didn't quite shake, but he did settle himself with a bruising jolt. "Well?" He turned his head, his long neck a sweet curve, and regarded her with that sly sideways glee. "Where goeth we, little Drozdova?"

"Take me to Ranger." She tried to sound definite instead of just quivery-scared. "As was agreed."

"Are you *sure*? I know shortcuts. So many of them, and rivers none of your kind or mortals have ever seen . . ."

That would be stealing. "Take me to Ranger," she repeated. "As was agreed."

The black horse stiffened, a low angry grinding beginning in his chest. He wheeled, caracoling, and arched his neck afresh. There was a puff of smoke, a rattle like chains, and Nat clung to the reins as the beast shot away from imperfect shade, into the burning sands.

NO MOUTHS

Waiting on a porch and drinking coffee wasn't quite the worst way Dima had ever spent a long sodden winter morning stretching into cloudy, iron-colored afternoon, but it wasn't very exciting either. Especially when your companion settled in one of the wicker chairs, his boots propped on the porch railing, and pulled his gray ten-gallon hat down over his eyes, appearing to nap for hours except when he reached for a tin cup of constantly steaming coffee settled on a tiny wicker table to his left.

Ranger's right hand rested very near a gun's butt, though, and Dima's own fingers itched. He paced across the front of the house, slow even clockwork steps, not bothering to make them cat-quiet.

Sometime after the sun began to fall from its noontime height, the Cowboy stirred. "So." Ranger's voice came from deep under the hat's shade. "That's Maria's game, then."

"Near as I can tell." The gangster had not made the mistake of thinking the cowboy asleep or unaware; nor did he bother pretending not to understand. Both were a compliment from one antithetical but not quite opposed creature to the other, Dima supposed.

Respecting your enemies meant you did not underestimate them.

"And you're . . . gonna let her do it?"

"Why interfere?" The gangster gave a tiny shrug, making his turn at the far end of the porch, pacing back. "No profit either way." His boot-toes glittered angrily.

Ranger didn't move. His left hand moved for his coffee mug again; Dima cradled his own cup in both hands, glad of the warmth like any rube. It wasn't a sweet potion, but it was strong, and at least the cowboy put enough bourbon in it.

Vodka would have been a step too far, from *him*.

"It ain't right," Ranger said heavily. He picked up his drink and took a moderate draft, setting the mug back down without looking. He tipped his hat up slightly with two left fingers, and his gaze glowed piercing from its brimshade.

The shadows were lengthening, and some of them sharpened at the edges.

Just a little.

"You sound like a fuckin' rube." But there was no heat to the insult; Dima was just keeping up his end of the conversation. His pacing didn't alter, but his left hand dove into a pocket, closing around a warm, worn handle. "How many, you think?"

Ranger considered the question. "Enough," he said, finally. "Don't take it the wrong way, but I'm glad you're here."

"If you'd let me drive her, they would pass by." None of the starving ones would catch *him*, after all. No, Konets was too spiky a morsel to tempt the scavengers, even in the old country.

Even in his youth.

"So you're protecting her." Ranger's full, sculpted mouth twitched. It was as close to a laugh as he'd dare.

Dima shrugged. His footsteps halted, and he drew out the black-handled straight razor, his fingertips gentle. The pearl-handled one was meant for other work.

He wouldn't use a silencer for the gun, though. Not out here. He set his mug down on the tiny wicker table, its warmth slowly leaching from his palm.

"Ways away yet." The other man stretched, feline-supple, and brought his booted feet down with a thump. "But I suppose we'd best get ready."

"You may sit on ass if you like." Maybe Dmitri even hoped the other man would. "But when little Drozdova come back, best if none of the bastards are here to greet."

The Cowboy unfurled, his broad shoulders swelling under the

fringed jacket. He pushed his hat back a bit further, steely gaze
roving the far hills. The sun, that ancient enemy of all darkness,
drifted even farther into the west; shadows on the ridge turned
fully knife-sharp and ink-glistening. They flitted from one spot to
the next, following the trail of a tempting, tender, delicious thing
not yet grown into its full strength.

It might even be a kindness if he let them rip the girl's fragrant
flesh and absorb her wine-sweet blood. It would certainly put Masha's plans all awry. She would wake to find Baba at her bedside,
perhaps with the scavengers pressing close, and though the old
snow-riding beldam could make it painless, Dima had the idea she
wouldn't.

Not this time.

Ranger's spurs were silent as he drifted down the stairs. He
didn't draw yet, watching the shadows as they crept closer, in their
blind witless way. Like maggots in a wound or hyenas pulling down
a sick antelope, they were simply doing what they were made for.

And, Dima thought, neither he nor the Cowboy were any different. Nothing ever changed, certainly not rubes and divinities
least of all.

He eased the gun free with his right hand, its finish dull matte
instead of stupid-shiny to present a target. The razor flicked free
in his left, its blade giving a venomous flash as it blurred through
a complicated pattern, and he hopped down the steps himself,
his stride lengthening on cracked, gravel-scattered driveway. He
headed for the lengthening darkness near the barn; his breath
plumed in the sudden chill.

When the starving ones drew closer living air would freeze as
soon as it left his mouth, falling to shatter on iron-hard ground. But
he was a creature of cold in unheated prisons, of shivers quelled by
sheer will, of tubercular coughs and clinging to impossible, grinding
life.

The space in his chest where a steady pulse should beat held only
a vast icy emptiness, and the numbness was kind. *There's nothing I
can do,* Baba had said long ago, while he writhed on a cheap striped

cotton mattress and raged against being brought to this new continent. *Unless* . . .

"Then do it," Dima muttered, as he had once before. "Get on with it, bitch."

He melded into the barn's shadow. It was a tepid bath, and he had never shivered when clasped in such gloom.

Much of a thief's best work was done in the dark.

Ranger stood in the middle of his driveway, his hat pushed back and his hands dangling loose. The idiot could draw them onto the battlefield, yes. He might even do a great deal of damage, thinning their numbers while the day lasted.

But it would take the ruthlessness of an old steppe wolf to cut off their retreat, to destroy them utterly. And if the sun sank before the girl returned, Dima would hunt them through midnight, through nightmares, through the empty hours between 3:00 and 4:00 A.M. when the elderly often loose their hold on life, giving way with grateful sighs as the Cold Lady smiled at them.

Sensing opposition, the shadowy scavengers thickened, swirling around Ranger's house. Drowsing beasts in the barn's warm safety made low sounds, but Dima was silent as cancer breeding in bones, as a thief-of-lives waiting for the target to arrive home, as a feral cat slinking through a waste-lot in search of some refuse to consume.

"Y'all can leave," Ranger said, quietly, the words falling into a flat silence as the iron-colored clouds thickened and a pale winter sun dimmed. "Or y'all can die. Your choice."

)(

There was no answer. For the scavengers had no mouths.

ENTIRELY DIFFERENT

The ride back to Ranger's was a bone-jarring gallop, the black horse slipping and sliding, melting into a motorcycle at odd moments, throwing itself across small streams once the desert faded and they were back in rolling prairie again. The sun was a low bloody coin disappearing behind the distant bruise-shadows of western mountains, and Nat was fully occupied clinging to reins or clutching handlebars, her shoulders aching every time the big beast veered. Sparks struck from its iron-clawed shoes sent up tiny acrid puffs—very possibly brimstone, though she'd never smelled it before—and she was sure it was doubling back once or twice, running alongside a deep swift cold stream chuckling with sharp menace.

Just waiting for her grip to loosen. Just waiting for her to fall.

Sheets of icy water thrown up on either side, her tailbone bruised as the beast landed stiff-legged, bolts of pain zipping up her back, her teeth clicking painfully together over and over again—even the worst bus ride was a cakewalk compared to this. No fluid union, no sense of connected togetherness, just an endless rattling, jarring, thumping as her head bobbled and she clamped her knees to elastic, heaving sides.

Finally, the song of hooves rang on concrete instead of dirt and rock; Nat was almost tossed from the saddle as the horse shook himself angrily, shrinking into a motorcycle again. His whinny became a scream of defiance, but Nat's fingers had cramp-tangled in the reins and her knees, while numb, still stuck like glue to his sides. He rattled over washboard road at a punishing pace, pavement breaking away on either side in great frost-heaved chunks; nobody had driven here for a very long time.

Icy wind roared, stinging her face, and instead of too hot and sweaty in a magical desert, she was now miserably cold. The horse howled, shaking his head again as his mane whipped, stinging her hands, but Nat held on.

There was no other choice.

Finally there was a long rubber-smoking howl as he swelled into horse-shape once more, a jolting as if the entire motorcycle would shake itself to pieces as it shifted back, and a billow of nasty black smoke. The world shuddered to a stop and Nat let out a surprised cry, saved from being a girlish scream only by the fact that there was no air left in her lungs to fuel it. Westering orange sunlight escaping under a long low band of snow-bearing clouds filled her eyes, and there was a shout.

"*Hi* there, you bastard!" It was Ranger in his fringed dun rancher's jacket; he darted close and grabbed at the horse's bridle. "Ain't no way to treat a lady, you just *mind* yourself now."

Oh, thank goodness. I'm back. Nat couldn't make her fingers unclench. The reins swelled and stiffened into handlebars once more; the engine's choppy growl smoothed out and died with a resentful rumble. Fitful warmth returned, her entire body ached, and she couldn't wait to have her boots on solid ground again.

But she was no thief, and had forced this thing—whatever it was—to bring her back. As bad as the ride had been, she suspected accepting its offer to show her "shortcuts" would be even worse.

"Get her off," Ranger snapped. "Oh, you sumbitch, thought you'd take the long way home, did you? None of that now."

Another tooth-snapping sound cut cold air; Nat flinched. Every girl loves horses, yes, but this thing was only horse-*like*. The shape didn't make it as advertised; whatever was trapped in its galloping, restless body wouldn't have hesitated to shake her free in the middle of a river, or while it galloped across the shimmering surface of a winter pond.

And then, those teeth—not the blunt herbivore-seeming ones, but the other set—would close around whatever mouthful it could grab. Or so her imagination informed her, and Nat Drozdova was very sure whatever she could imagine was far less awful than the truth.

For once.

Ranger made a swift movement, his brown fist pistoning out, a bright golden flashgleam lingering over knuckles. There was a crunch, and the horse's growl cut off cleanly. "I said *mind*," the cowboy continued, mildly enough, but his dove-gray hat was slightly awry, his hazel eyes blazed, and if he ever looked at her like that, Nat's heart might well stop. "And get her *off* there, horsethief!"

"Don't shout at me, *kovboyski*." Dmitri sounded just the same, and Nat's fingers finally creaked open enough to slide free of solid, chilly metal handlebars. The gangster's hair was a wild mess instead of slicked back, his black eyes burned with carnivorous glee, and even though he might very well murder her sometime in the very near future he was still familiar, and Nat was almost glad to see him. "Eh, *zaika moya*, have fun? Should've let me drive."

"Th-th-that w-w-wasn't . . ." Her teeth chattered, chopping every word into bits. *That wasn't part of the deal.*

"I know." He dragged her free of the motorcycle, his lean tanned hands strangely gentle; Ranger had the handlebars now and pulled the resisting hunk of glossy black metal, silver springs, wheels, and still-grumbling engine towards the barn. The porch light of Ranger's trim blue ranch-style house was on, a golden beacon, and more incandescent light spilled through the half-open barn doors. The cold was even worse now that they'd stopped, which shouldn't have been possible; the warmth in Nat's core fought a frigid blanket.

"Breathe." Dmitri held her up, coiled strength belied by his leanness; Nat's legs wouldn't quite work. "That's it, nice and easy. Take drink."

There was a chill metallic tap at her chin; the gangster tipped a mouthful from a dull silver hip flask past her lips. Nat spluttered; the liquid burned like vodka and most of it went straight down her throat without so much as a hello, a nova exploding inside her ribs. The heat was amazing, tropical, and very welcome; she decided she liked temperate zones better than desert or this winter-prairie bullshit. Going from winter to summer and back again couldn't be good for your immune system.

Did divinities get colds? Did they need flu shots? There were so many questions, and nobody she could trust to answer them.

Nat went limp, every bone inside her aching flesh quivering at a slightly different rate. Her forehead rested against Dima's shoulder; the flask vanished and he dug for something else in his pockets. His arm was a steel bar holding her upright, and that unhealthy, unsteady heat blazed from his jacket and jeans like a gasoline-greased pile of burning tires sending great gouts of black smoke heavenward.

"There," he crooned, with lunatic calm. "Hush now, little *zaika-zaya, krasotka moya*." He was stiff-tense as if ready for a punch or some other violence, but Nat was too tired—and too glad to be stationary—to care much. "Eh, Cowboy? They gathering again."

"I know." Ranger sounded grim. "Where the hell did you run to, horse?"

"*Silly girl,*" the horse replied, its voice full of shrapnel and burning oil. He made a low, shuddering, grinding moan, a motorcycle's various metal joints resisting. "*I offered her shortcuts. Stupid, silly girl.*"

"For the love of . . ." Ranger sighed. There was a creak, another sharp thump—sounded like he'd punched metal. "That girl ain't no horsethief. You and your mischief; I swear I'm half ready to remake you."

"*Go ahead.*" The beast was completely unrepentant. "*You'll never have a faster horse.*"

Ranger muttered a blistering obscenity, and for once didn't follow it up with a *pardon my French.* "Curses work both ways."

Whatever Dima had forced down her throat worked wonders, or maybe Nat was stronger than she thought. In any case, she found her legs would finally work again; pain receded like the tide going out on a pebbled beach, and she pushed ineffectually at the gangster's disconcertingly broad chest. "I'm all r-r-right." Even the teeth-chattering was going down.

A dark line showed high on Dmitri's left cheek. It looked like a knife-cut, but there was no blood, just flesh sealing itself back together. The sun's bleary red eye slipped behind distant, serrated mountains, and a crackling-cold wind brushed over Ranger's house. There was an uneasy mutter from the barn, animals moving; Nat shuddered.

What else did he have in there, next to the big black motorcycle-horse? She found she didn't want to know; there was a limit to even *her* curiosity. Go figure, adulthood was 40 percent figuring things out for yourself, with another 40 percent of avoiding knowledge that might drive you crazy.

Not that she had far to go to reach that state. The remaining 20 percent of being grown-up was probably taxes and approaching mortality, though the idea of Uncle Sam pursuing Dmitri Konets for not filing a return was bleakly hilarious.

Was there an Uncle Sam? She'd probably find out, if this kept up.

"You came back." Dmitri tucked his chin slightly, peering into her face. A flush of effort pinkened his cheeks, and his black suit was a bit rumpled. Had he and Ranger got into a fight?

I don't care. Nat supposed she looked a little worse for wear too. *I just want to go home.*

But that wasn't quite accurate, Nat discovered. The thought of going back to her mother's little yellow house on South Aurora was even more unappetizing than riding Ranger's predatory magical horse.

Nat's backpack, warm and heavy, finally settled against her shoulders like it was relieved to be off the carnival ride as well. It was the closest thing to "home" she had now, smaller and far more bedraggled than a snail's spiraling domicile.

"I don't w-want to be a h-h-horsethief," Nat managed. Her throat was so dry the words were husks of themselves, left propped and forgotten in a field while a faded scarecrow leered from a listing pole.

Dima's faint flush drained away, and his jaw hardened. "No other way to get what you want, Drozdova. Not when rich bastards sit on it."

Oh, so you're a real Robin Hood. Go figure, twenty seconds in his presence again and she was already irritated. The sharp unsteady feeling was a tonic, filling her with fresh strength, and her legs felt more like her own usual bodily possessions now instead of just insensate noodles. "I'm h-happy to s-see you too."

Ranger reappeared, swinging the barn door closed; Dmitri stepped away from Nat like she was carrying something fatally communicable. She swayed, but the steady fire in her chest poured strength through the rest of her. The sense of deep, inalienable energy filled her again, and she wondered if she looked burningly vital, impossibly *real*, like the two men.

The two divinities.

"Sorry about that." Ranger's iron-toed boots ground icy gravel as he hurried towards her; he could probably crack a boulder by kicking it. "You did right well, Nat. He just takes some gettin' used to, that beast."

So I gathered. And even if she liked the cowboy, even if he said he liked her more than her mother, he still hadn't warned her that the horse—or whatever it was, trapped in a shapeshifting body—was very strong, not to mention wholly murderous. "It's all right." There was nothing else to say.

Ranger's fringed jacket was torn too, and Nat was abruptly tired of men and their squabbles. Even if she didn't agree with Mom on everything, Maria Drozdova's frequent assertion that males were saved only from being more dangerous by their unending stupidity held a great deal of water.

"No, it ain't." Ranger glanced over her shoulder, his full, sculpted mouth tightening. "Y'all better go. I'll do what I can, horsethief."

"I could call you something worse," Dima muttered, and jabbed his left hand at the black car crouched leonine before the ranch house's stairs. His right, Nat saw with a sinking sensation, was full of that same dull-black gun he'd had before, except with no long silhouette of a silencer. "Come, *zaika*. Into car we go."

Wait a second. "What *happened*?" Nat shuddered; the bright white vapor of her breath shivered and plummeted, thin ice breaking on hard ground with a soft musical noise. "What the hell?"

"Oh, naw." Ranger shrugged, a loose easy motion, and stretched his neck, tilting his head from one side to the other. His lean, capable right hand rested on a revolver butt, slung hip-low on his broad leather belt; the matching gun on his other side gleamed secretively from its well-worn holster. "Hell's entirely different, ma'am, pardon my French. You go on now. Come back and visit anytime."

Yeah, not so sure I want to, now. Nat summoned a polite, weary shadow of a smile, and tacked unevenly for the black car. Dmitri walked backward, placing each foot with a cat's finicky delicacy, and Ranger's boots made soft stealthy sounds as he set off in a different direction.

Towards the road, not his house. Maybe they hadn't been fighting each other at all. The wind was knifelike, her breath froze as it left her mouth, and though Nat had quickly grown used to not feeling the weather, she shivered.

"*Potoropis'*." Dmitri peered past her, his black eyes narrowed and his lip lifting slightly. Strong white teeth gleamed, and though his snarl wasn't directed at her, it still sent a shudder down her back. "Quickly, *devotchka*. Not many of them left, but always more come."

Well, that's not terrifying or anything. Nat's boots were almost too heavy to lift; her backpack now weighed a ton. Even the stealthy, hidden glow of the Cup and the black-bladed Knife in its depths wasn't comforting. "More what?" *The starving things, of course. Great. Fantastic.*

"You didn't tell her?" Ranger laughed, every scrap of warmth gone and his voice cold as the gangster's. "Course not, why am I surprised? Get gone, I'll keep your trail clear as I can."

Dima swore, lifting the gun. Its muzzle pointed past Nat, carefully not *at* her, but she still hurried, not liking how big and bottomless the hole at the end seemed.

Like the Well, only without the quicksilver glitter in its throat.

She skirted the black car; its engine throbbed into life and she flinched, letting out a small hurt sound. Suddenly its interior seemed like an old friend she couldn't wait to meet again, but she paused at the open passenger door, the dome light sending a distorted golden rectangle onto the pavement, touching the edge of the porch's wooden stairs.

There was very little twilight on the prairie in winter; day ended like a descending guillotine blade out here. Glimmering stars, peeking through dusk's veil, were snuffed behind a lowering sky pregnant with fresh snow. Nat tasted the penny-metal of approaching precipitation, and a tiny, cold flake kissed her cheek.

Dark shapes, gleaming slightly, clustered a fair ways from Ranger; behind them, the driveway warped like the glimmer over hot pavement on a blinding summer day. Nat's breath froze again, whisper-thin ice falling down the front of her peacoat; she stared, almost unable to believe her own eyes for the hundredth—or thousandth—time since walking into the Morrer-Pessel Tower to negotiate for her mother's life.

She will eat you, Drozdova. After you bring her what she wants so she can bargain with Baba Yaga to allow the theft of a native-born child.

She wanted to call what the metal horse had said a lie. She wanted to call all of this a hallucination, a cruel practical joke, a forgiving insanity.

Anything other than truth.

TO BE CONTINUED

ACKNOWLEDGMENTS

Thanks are due first and foremost to Devi Pillai and Lucienne Diver, without whom these books would literally not be; much gratitude is likewise due to Claire Eddy and Sanaa Ali-Virani for their heroic patience and diligence through a worldwide pandemic and other assorted nonsense. Writing is a lonely job, but it's made easier when there are good people standing guard at the cave mouth.

A resounding thank you goes to my children, to my beloved Bailey, and to Mel Sanders and Skyla Dawn Cameron, fellow miners at the word-veins. A portion must also be measured out to Nikolai Petrovich, who always answers my disturbing, outlandish questions with calm good temper.

Last but never, ever least, I thank you, my dear Reader. Let me repay your kindness in the way we both like best, by telling you yet another story. . . .

ABOUT THE AUTHOR

LILITH SAINTCROW was born in New Mexico, fell in love with writing during second grade, and has continued obsessively ever since. She currently resides in the rainy Pacific Northwest with her children, dogs, cat, and a library for wayward texts.

lilithsaintcrow.com
Twitter: @lilithsaintcrow